Easy Reading

Easy Reading

Cristina Morales

Translated from the Spanish by Kevin Gerry Dunn

JONATHAN CAPE

LONDON

1 3 5 7 9 10 8 6 4 2

Jonathan Cape is part of the Penguin Random House group of companies
whose addresses can be found at global.penguinrandomhouse.com.

Penguin
Random House
UK

Originally published in Spain as *Lectura fácil* by Editorial Anagrama, Barcelona, in 2018.
Copyright © 2018 by Cristina Morales

First published in English by Jonathan Cape in 2022

penguin.co.uk/vintage

A CIP catalogue record for this book is available from the British Library

ISBN 9781787332676

Typeset in 11.5/14.75 pt Minion
by Integra Software Services Pvt. Ltd, Pondicherry

Printed and bound in Great Britain by Clays Ltd, Elcograf S.p.A.

The authorised representative in the EEA is Penguin Random House Ireland,
Morrison Chambers, 32 Nassau Street, Dublin D02 YH68

This publication was supported by a grant from Acción Cultural Española (AC/E)

AC/E
ACCIÓN CULTURAL
ESPAÑOLA

This book has been selected to receive financial assistance from English PEN's 'PEN
Translates!' programme, supported by Arts Council England. English PEN exists to
promote literature and our understanding of it, to uphold writers' freedoms around
the world, to campaign against the persecution and imprisonment of writers for
stating their views, and to promote the friendly co-operation of writers and the free
exchange of ideas. www.englishpen.org

Supported using public funding by
ARTS COUNCIL
ENGLAND

ENGLISH
PEN

Penguin Random House is committed to a sustainable future for
our business, our readers and our planet. This book is made from
Forest Stewardship Council® certified paper.

MIX
Paper from
responsible sources
FSC® C018179

To my aya Paca: a Bernarda Alba who, with a cackle or with white-gloved stealth, defied the authority of relatives, geriatricians, caregivers, nurses and caseworkers.

To the teenage breasts that Francisca Vázquez Ruiz still possessed at the age of eighty-two (Baza, 1936–Albolote, 2018).

We must not mistakenly believe that because people with problems are drawn to dance, dance itself causes problems.

Amador Cernudo Lago,
'The Psychopathology of Dance'

I affirm that my mother is the whore
and that my sister is the whore
and that I am the whore
and that all of my brothers are faggots.
It is not enough to merely state or scream our differences:
I am a woman,
I am a lesbian,
I am a mother,
I am a whore,
I am mad,
I am Indigenous,
I am old,
I am young,
I am disabled,
I am light-skinned,
I am dark-skinned,
I am poor.

María Galindo, *Feminismo urgente:
¡A despatriarcar!*

There are gates installed in my temples. They slide shut from each side, like the ticket gates at the metro, and seal off my face. Picture two hands playing peekaboo with a baby. Where's Mommy? Where is she? Heeeeere she is! And on the 'here' the hands part and the baby bursts out laughing. But the gates in my temples aren't made out of hands, they're made out of a smooth, clear, resistant material, with rubber strips lining the edges to cushion them when they close and ensure an airtight seal. Just like the gates at the metro. You can see everything happening on the other side, but they're too slippery to climb over and too low for you to crawl underneath. When my gates close, they cover my face with a hard, transparent mask that allows me to see and be seen, and even though it looks like there's nothing separating me from the outside world, the information has stopped flowing from one side to the other and only the basic stimuli necessary for survival make it through. To get into the metro, you have to climb over the ticket scanner that connects and divides every set of gates. That or pay for a ticket, obviously.

My gates aren't always a hard, transparent mask. Sometimes they're a shop window, and I'm looking through them at something I can't buy, or I'm being gazed at, desired by another window-shopper. When I talk about my gates like this, I'm not speaking figuratively. I'm trying as hard as I can to be literal and explain how this mechanism works. When I was little, I couldn't understand song lyrics because they were full of euphemisms, metaphors, innuendos and all those shitty little rhetorical tricks, shitty frameworks of predetermined meaning, like when Ana Torroja sings about 'a woman against a woman', but she doesn't mean two women fighting, she means two women fucking. What a twisted, subliminal, rancid way to write a song. You'd think she could at least say 'a woman with a woman', but no, whatever it takes to avoid acknowledging that two grown women are licking each other's cunts.

My gates aren't a metaphor, I'm not talking about some kind of psychological barrier that cuts me off from the world. My gates are visible. There's a retractable hinge in each of my temples, and my gates engage and withdraw along grooves that run from my temples to my jaw. When disengaged, they're stored behind my face, each occupying the reverse of one half: half a forehead, an eye, half a septum and one nostril, a cheek, half a mouth, half a chin.

The last time they activated was at my contemporary dance class, the day before yesterday. The instructor took six or seven brisk, gleeful seconds to dance on her own, then marked the choreography a little more slowly for us to memorise and copy. She hit play again and stood in front of the mirror so we could follow along, which is easy for me if she goes slow. I do the steps about a second after her, glancing at what she's doing and trying to remember what comes next, but I move decisively and confidently, which is gratifying and makes me feel like a good dancer. I am a good dancer. But that day the instructor felt more like dancing than like teaching us how to dance and I couldn't keep up. She counted five-six-seven-eight and off she went, hair blowing in the wind she herself had stirred up, calling out the steps over the music without slowing down. The retractable hinges activated and the polyurethane panels slid cleanly and silently across my face, where they sealed shut. Now I'm not dancing, I'm just grudgingly flailing around. I take a couple of half-assed steps, skip parts and copy the women who know what they're doing in an attempt to get back into it, but eventually I stop and lean against the wall to watch the others. It looks like I'm studying them to learn the routine, but it's just the opposite. I'm not trying to untangle the ball of yarn that is the dance to understand its movements. I'm not grabbing the loose end of the string so I don't get lost when they turn this way and that, finding their way through the labyrinth that is the dance. I'm just batting at the ball of yarn like a kitten, thinking about my classmates' bodies and outfits.

In among the seven or eight women in the class is one man. A man, yes, but first and foremost a male, his malehood on constant display within the group of women. He's ill-shaven and long-haired in washed-out clothes, and he's always blabbering on about community and culture and yadda yadda yadda. In other words, a fascist. Fascist and male are synonymous as far as I'm concerned. It's hard to watch him dance; the man is made of wood. I can't fault him for that, just like I shouldn't be faulted for my gates, which, by the way, all of the women in the class noticed, so they left me alone. The male, on the other hand, acted like he couldn't see them and, when the routine was done, he came over to enlighten me about where I'd gone wrong before offering some corrections. Turns out his brain is made of wood too, and that's something I can fault him for. Mmm, hmm, yeah, yeah, I answered, not moving from where I stood. Just let me know if you ever have any questions, he concluded with a smile. Jesus fucking Christ. Thankfully my gates were closed and the full force of his malehood was muffled by my total lack of interest in my surroundings. This is a great example of when the gates are a shop window and I'm on untouchable display.

And, for the record, it's not like I couldn't follow the chore-ography that day. I just didn't want to. I didn't feel like dancing in step with seven random women and one male prick, I didn't feel like jacking off the fantasies of the dancer who'd ended up as an instructor at a municipal civic centre and fancied herself a choreographer, I didn't feel like pretending to be part of a professional dance company when we're really just a bunch of girls in a daycare centre for grown-ups. But people never get it when not doing something is the thing you actually want to do.

I don't know if I was any better off under state totalitarianism, but seriously, fuck market totalitarianism, says my cousin, who broke down into sobs this afternoon when she went to a meeting at the Platform for Action on Housing (PAH), where she learned she'd have to earn at least 1,025 euros a month to get access to social housing.

Don't cry, Marga, I say, handing her a tissue. At least now the market has a woman's name: the totalitarianism of Mercadona, the supermarket chain where the security cameras are pointed at the cashiers instead of down the aisles, so we can swipe deodorant and pads and even remove condoms from their alarm-stripped boxes and carry them out the door in our pockets. I've told Margarita she should switch to a menstrual cup and quit stealing pads and tampons. That way she'll have room in her bag for other, more expensive shit, like honey or Nesquik.

She says menstrual cups cost like thirty euros and she doesn't have thirty euros, and they don't sell menstrual cups at the supermarket so you have to get one from the pharmacy, and it's basically impossible to shoplift at the pharmacy because there they do keep the cameras pointed at the customers plus they have those doors that beep when anyone goes in or out. She's got a point – one time I wanted to steal a menstrual cup for a friend for her birthday and I couldn't find anywhere to do it, not even at a department store, and a pharmacy felt too risky.

What about late at night, at a pharmacy with a really old pharmacist? I ask.

How about you quit stealing condoms and switch to the pill? she says to me. Unwrapping the forty layers of plastic around the box takes forever and it's super conspicuous.

Fuck that, I say, I'm not going to shoot my body full of hormones and be systematically medicated just so some male can experience the thrill of not pulling out. I don't get what's so fucking liberating about the pill. Dermatologists prescribe it to girls for their zits, because of course teenage acne is a medical condition, it's got nothing to do with looking hot, nothing at all to do with turning yourself into a semen receptacle. This is the health of our teenage girls we're talking about. Sure, whatever. But you can't sleep around without condoms, Marga, what about STDs?

Oh, so STDs are a real medical condition? she says.

Are they not? I ask.

But AIDS isn't even real, Nati, come on. Less than one per cent of the population. In Spain there are more suicides per year than AIDS diagnoses.

But I don't fuck Spanish dudes, Marga, because they're all fucking fascists.

Jesus, Nati, you're a bigger reactionary than the Pope.

And you're a dirty hippie, go cut your hair already.

At another contemporary dance class at Barceloneta Adult Daycare (BADDAY), a different instructor told us to take off our socks. We were practising pirouettes and she wanted to make sure we didn't slip. Everybody took off their socks except me because I had a blister on the big toe of my right foot. The instructor repeated her veiled command. It was veiled in two ways: first, she didn't say 'Take off your socks', she said 'And now we're going to take our socks off'. That is, she didn't give the command at all, she described its result, exempting herself from the unpopular task of using the imperative. And second, she didn't acknowledge the hierarchy that exists in all classes, from dance to constitutional law, between us, the students, and her, the instructor. She didn't say 'All right, class, take off your socks', she said 'And now we're going to take our socks off', including herself in our otherness and thereby making it invisible, creating a fallacious 'us' that doesn't distinguish between instructor and student.

She repeated the veiled command by re-veiling it. I was the only person in the studio wearing socks at this point, but even so, instead of saying 'Take off your socks, Nati', she just worded it a different way, still including herself: 'Now, let's get those socks off!' So in addition to repressing the imperative and concealing our otherness, now she was pretending like more than one of her pupils had disobeyed her. If a few had kept their socks on, she would have grasped that this minority, however small, had some reason for behaving differently, and she might have tolerated the difference. An insubordinate minority can achieve respectability. But a lone insubordinate? Forget it. Everybody looked at everybody else's naked feet. I'm nearsighted and I have to take off my glasses to dance, so I can't say with certainty whether the other students were staring at my still-clad feet or not. Fortunately, my gates are prescription-grade: -2.25 dioptres in the right panel and -3.10 in the left, so I get a crystal-clear view of the fascism around me even as my gates shield me from it.

After both of her veiled commands failed, the instructor – who is Swedish, her name is Tina Johanes – came to the conclusion that besides being nearsighted, I must also be either deaf or unable to speak Spanish. In the spirit of human compassion, she pressed play and, while the other students were practising pirouettes, she approached me, interrupting my awkward twirl, and spoke, finally, to me and me alone.

'Are you OK?'

'Me?'

'You understand Spanish?'

'Yeah yeah.'

'Oh, it's just that you haven't taken your socks off.'

'Oh, it's just that I have a blister on my foot.'

'Ah OKOKOK,' she said, taking a step back and showing me the palms of her hands in a sign of apology and conflict-avoidance, and to make it clear that she wasn't hiding any weapons in her leggings.

After that, no pirouettes, no nothing. Just the uninterrupted observation of my surroundings, of the others, of Tina Johanes, of myself. Fuck this whole pretence of learning to dance. Fuck the four euros an hour I still have to pay for classes after the unemployment discount. That's four euros I could spend on a train ticket to the rehearsal space at the university, where I can dance alone, naked, mamboing as terribly as I like. Four euros I could spend on four beers at the Chinese bazaar, four euros that could get a party started or have me out cold in bed not thinking about death. I am at the Barceloneta Adult Daycare (BADDAY). Everyone else here is either a left-of-centre moderate or a pro-Catalonia separatist. Tina Johanes is an authority figure. I'm a bastardist with a Bovaristic past, and thanks to that shit heritage I spend all my time thinking about death, so I might as well be dead already.

Can't you get to the university by jumping the gates at the train station? That's risky: it's a long ride and being on the lookout for the ticket inspector the whole time wreaks havoc on my nerves; my stomach goes haywire and I end up needing to shit, so I spend twelve long stops trying to quell the cramps. I start letting out silent farts, clenching my butt so they don't make a noise, balancing on my sit bones, embarrassed by the smell. A few times I've shit my pants by the time I get to the university. If you let yourself poo a little it's easier to make it the rest of the way, but then you have to go six more stops with a lick of shit on your ass. Aren't there toilets on the train? No, not on Catalan commuter rail. If you want to piss, shit or fuck you've gotta take care of it before boarding. There are toilets on the national rail lines run by RENFE and the Ministry of the Interior. If you want you can have sex on the train from Cádiz to Jerez, which are about as far apart as Barcelona and the university. Thus, we can conclude that the absence of toilets on the commuter rail is yet another form of oppression and that, insofar as toilets and trains are concerned, the Generalitat of Catalonia is more totalitarian than the Spanish state.

Spit it out, Angelita, I know what you're thinking and I want to hear you say it: Tina Johanes was asking you to take

9

off your socks for your own good (Angelita didn't say Tina Johanes, she said 'the teacher'). So you wouldn't slip. So you wouldn't fall and hurt yourself. So you could dance better. The same as the guy in the other class when you fell out of step with the choreography (she didn't say choreography, she said 'the dance'). You always jump to these crazy conclusions. You have zero empathy (she didn't say it like that, she said: 'You don't know how to put yourself in someone else's shoes and you're selfish'). You paid for dance classes, which means you paid to take orders (she didn't say it like that either, she said: 'You signed up for dance classes and what's the point of signing up for dance classes if you don't want to learn to dance?'). You can't have it both ways (that part she did say in those words). Not to mention, Nati, you're starting to sound like a Spanish nationalist. There it is, Angelita, that's what I was getting at! That's the dress I wanted to wear out tonight! Thank you, thank you, thank you! (And now she's all offended because I called her by her original Spanish name, Ángela, and not by her Catalan rechristening, Àngels, plus I tacked a condescending -ita on the end.) Nati, you know people only let you get away with being all reactionary like that because you're not bad-looking (she actually said: 'You act like a snotty little girl and no one ever says anything about it because you're cute'). If you were less attractive or downright ugly they'd see what a resentful little bitch you really are (that is: 'If you were ugly or old or fat, people might feel bad for you but they wouldn't listen to you'). You're wrong, I answered. You're very wrong. A girl who's half pretty – and don't even get me started if she's beautiful or hot – doesn't have the right to be radical. What's a pretty girl like that got to complain about? How could a pretty girl like that be unhappy? Where does a pretty girl like that get such a foul mouth? That's so unattractive in an otherwise

10

attractive girl. How dare she get all ugly with me when I cat-call and whistle at her! Can't the cunt see I'm trying to give her a compliment? The other form of censure heaped upon pretty radicals looks a lot like what you just said, Angelita: they can afford to be critical because they're attractive, they can afford to be outspoken because they're attractive, and they think that if they wrap their protestations up in the pretty little packages of their bodies, people might actually listen. But watch out, Angelita! Because – pass me the beer – that's a crock of shit. That's the kind of logic spouted by those twenty-somethings with flowers in their hair and bodies like *America's Next Top Model* who parade their tits in Parliament or at the Vatican, those hippies who call themselves Femen but ought to be called Semen, in honour of the nocturnal emissions they provoke in the very agents of the patriarchy they're targeting.

I love drinking with Ángela because, though you wouldn't know it from the outside, on the inside we're bouncing off the walls, we get crazy talkative and her stutter gets worse and worse and we end up alienating the handful of other people at the gathering, though usually it's just Ángela, Marga and me. Sometimes my half-sister Patricia joins us with one of her friends. The friends are always Semen girls, unless they're guy friends, in which case they may or may not be males – I can't say for sure, since they're not Spanish and I've never spoken to any of them for more than fifteen minutes because they're inevitably self-styled bohemian types and therefore even more insufferable than the Semen girls, their natural comrades-in-arms. But the only time my half-sister has ever shown her tiny boobs in public, nipples clinging to her smooth pectorals like egg yolks, was at the ticket counter to get into a porno-terrorist show, after the woman behind the counter said if she flashed she'd get in for free.

11

Marga reads literally nothing, not even magazines at the hair salon, not even magazines at the hair salon with nothing except pictures of different haircuts, so it was incredibly generous of her to bring me a zine from the anarchist social centre that the PAH referred her to. It's a reprint of the happy moment when Bolivian activist María Galindo coined the concept of bastardism, on pages 106 and 107 of her book *Feminismo urgente: ¡A despatriarcar!*, published in Buenos Aires in 2013:

Because desire did not and does not circulate freely in society, because desire has been regimented under a colonial code of domination, we cannot talk about the condition of assimilation and racial mixing known as *mestizaje*.

Given the colonial domestication of erotic desire, I prefer to talk about *bastardism*. There was mixing, yes, the mixing was so extensive that it encompassed all of society, yes, but the mixing was neither free nor horizontal; it was always forced, subjugated, violent or clandestine, and its legitimacy was conditioned on extortion, policing and humiliation.

The half-truth of mestizaje, behind its veil of shame and hypocrisy, is bastardism. The half-truth of mestizaje, beneath its make-up, its dissimulation and its disguises, is bastardism. It is a half-truth from a brutally troubled, heart-rendingly unresolved, ardently illegitimate, repeatedly forbidden social space. To call it by its rightful name – to say here there are no mestizas, only bastard daughters – is an act of liberation. The status of white women, like the status of Indigeneous women, is a kind of fictional shelter to conceal something far more distressing, the unresolved question of origin.

You could say that bastardism is my ideology, even though María Galindo despises the notion of ideology because it's authoritarian and academic and, therefore, embedded in the hierarchical structures of patriarchy. In fact, she never talks about bastardists at all, just bastards, plain and simple. I was the one who added the -*ist*, that classic signifier of ideological adherence.

I saw the author give a talk at the Barcelona Museum of Contemporary Art a few months ago, before her books, which are impossible to find in Spain, were zineified and distributed in anarchist spaces. She brought copies with her from Bolivia, and even though they were very cheap (ten euros for more than two hundred pages, with colour photos and even a DVD), I have no money, and I wasn't about to steal a copy from the woman whose talk had made me cry. At first I thought I was crying the way newborn babies do, from the passage from one life to another, the passage from darkness to light. But that implies pain, and Galindo's words hadn't hurt me at all, they'd caressed me, they'd held me, they'd made love to me like an understanding, experienced lover when her beloved says it's her first time. I was a virgin in bastard consciousness. Galindo doesn't believe that pain and trauma lead to liberation. I must have cried, then, from pleasure. In this particular case, from the pleasure of politicisation, of radicalisation, of emerging from the mire of a subjugated state. The pleasure of discovering your index finger, extending it and turning it towards your oppressor. The pleasure of passing from victim to subject. The politicisation happened quickly, in the brief fifty minutes she had to speak.

Some white lefto-feminist will say that Galindo is talking about Bolivia and I can't transfer the context of her experience to my own situation of oppression in Barcelona. We should reply to this Eurocentric femifascist as follows: Did you perchance live in England in 1848? And does that stop you from conjuring ol' Grandpa Marx every time you talk about social class? Did you experience the Gulag in the thirties? And does that prevent you from summoning the authoritarian spirit of trusty Uncle Trotsky? Do you not have a lay altar to our frivolous bourgeois aunties, Simone de Beauvoir and Simone Weil, even though you weren't born in peacetime Paris or Berlin? It seems like the only political theories our shitbag neoliberal sister-in-arms considers universal are the ones that come from the West; somehow those aren't susceptible to problems of context. It's important to remind her that even on the margins of development, people are still articulating, writing and applying critical thought, and if you're not a snot-nosed Occidentalist brat with a liberal arts degree, you'll learn to recognise the binding power that extends from those originating margins to our own. I speak not as a bastard but as a bastardist, and I do it to lend bastardism a theoretical scope that, as María Galindo proposes, transcends its context, to such an extent that it has resonated with me nine thousand kilometres from its origin.

When I was younger, I founded the Bovary Club, also known as the Boobery Club, depending on the degree of asinine gusto with which we carried out our amorous chores. There was no initiation ceremony. It was better that way. Of our four members, only one had read *Madame Bovary* and only I had seen the two films based on the book, which I,

14

with tremendous effort and an unwavering commitment to the history of literature, was unable to read past page 14. The films, on the other hand, are stimulating, edifying. Madame Bovary is blonde in one and brunette in the other. The two other members of the club represented greater and lesser degrees of Bovaristic malaise and they didn't know anything about *Madame Bovary* besides what the girl who had read the book and I told them. I think the transition from Bovarism to bastardism is normal and a sign of maturity. I think that not finishing *Madame Bovary* is also a sign of maturity and an early manifestation of bastardistic inclinations.

My Bovaristic phase coincided with my years at the dance conservatory. It peaked during my master's and came to a grinding halt when I joined a research group for my doctorate. Now, looking back on it, I see that the Jiminy Cricket of bastard consciousness was whispering in my ear from very early on. I remember how one afternoon I was studying for the third-year classical dance exam and I felt true alienation in my flesh for the first time. For the second time. The first time had been four years earlier, when I was sixteen, at a protest against the second invasion of Iraq. Just like when I was reading *Madame Bovary*, I had to quit after fifteen minutes. An unambiguously bastardist act.

Alienation can be one of two things: the original version as described by Grandfather Marx, or the version that's adapted to each individual's particular circumstances of oppression. Grandpa Karl said alienation is workers' estrangement from the product of their labour. I say alienation is the identification of our desires and interests with the desires and interests of power. That's not the heart of it, though; that's just a constant in democracy: we think voting benefits us, so we vote. We think our company's profits benefit us, so we work efficiently. We think recycling benefits us, so we keep four different bins in our thirty-square-metre apartments. We think pacifism is the answer to violence, so we march ten kilometres banging drums and blowing whistles. No, the core of our alienation isn't this ridiculous civic life, but its recognition: the instant someone realises she's doing as she's told from the moment she gets up in the morning to the moment she goes to bed, and even then, she sleeps in obedience, because she sleeps seven or eight hours on week nights and ten or twelve at the weekend, and she sleeps straight through the night, without allowing herself to get up, and she forces her body awake all day, without allowing herself naps, and if her sleep doesn't conform to the stipulated hours then something must be wrong with her: insomnia, narcolepsy, laziness, depression, stress. In the face of the omnipresent civic jubilation, three things can happen. First possibility: you don't realise how obedient you are, so you never feel alienated. You remain a good citizen with a wide range of electoral and sexual choices. You'll keep studying third-year classical dance because that's what you're expected to do. That's why they gave you a scholarship, after all. You'll keep going to protests and chanting no blood for oil, chanting patients over profits, chanting one-two-three-four-we-won't-take-it-any-more, because that's what freedom of speech is for, and this is what democracy looks like!

Second possibility: you realise how obedient you are, but it doesn't make a difference. You don't feel alienated because you rationalise due obedience. You say our system is flawed, but it's better than the alternatives. The lesser of two evils becomes your mantra and you readily apply it to politics. You champion all things public. You keep studying classical dance because it's your only viable option, because it beats waiting tables, because you're hoping to get a decent job. You keep going to protests and chanting Catalonia is not Spain, chanting housing not handcuffs, chanting five-six-seven-eight-stop-the-po-li-tics-of-hate. Because whose streets? Our streets!

Third possibility: you realise exactly how obedient you are and you can't fucking take it. Now this, this is alienation. Congratulations! You can no longer tolerate waiting in line for the privilege of tapping your credit card. Lining up to pay, instead of them lining up to take your money, is the pinnacle of alienation! You can't stomach Election Day: the well-dressed, clean-shaven electorate goes to their designated polling stations, where they run into their neighbours and make small-talk about how they're voting and why. They read the whole ballot, take a look at all of the candidates, and allow themselves the tiniest margin of doubt over their choice, but the decision they made at home always prevails in the end. They even bring the kids along! They scamper around and play tag with the other kids, and Mom or Dad lifts them up to the ballot box so they can insert the little envelope, or, if they're big boys and girls, they put it in themselves. Some people even take home a pamphlet from each party for their collection. And then everybody goes and gets a beer, some-place with an outdoor patio if the weather's nice. The festival of democracy! Win or lose, the real winner is always the democratic process! During the last EU election I went to the polling station to reaffirm my repugnance and everybody was staring at my tits. I was wearing no bra and a tight T-shirt. The joyful, civic-minded men and women blathered away, worms wriggling out of their mouths as they made animated Sunday-morning chit-chat and shifted their gaze from their neighbour to my nipples, from the registration table to my nipples, and they struck me as sanctimonious, stick-up-the-ass benefactors and benefactresses of prostitution, even if none of the men had ever gone whoring (despite frequently fucking girlfriends and wives who clearly had no interest) and none

17

of the women had ever technically charged for sex (despite frequently fucking their boyfriends and husbands when they didn't feel like it, impelled by the sex-love contract that binds them). The men, whoremongers. The women, setting the table for when their men got home. And to be clear, I wasn't the whore in this scenario, nor did I represent her, since the full extent of my insinuation was to exist. I was silent, I didn't harass anyone, and I left as soon as I felt my gates starting to activate. The whore, that is, the person over whom they were lording their authority, was nowhere to be found. Her presence at the polling place was unnecessary, because the political task of the voter – insofar as it's mystic, insofar as it's symbolic – doesn't need an object to subjugate. Unlike the tyrant or the rapist, whose political task requires an immanent object and experience of domination, the voter is happy with the mere illusion of possession, happy to hold someone's destiny in his little envelope. The festival of democracy is a Mass, the whole banquet reduced to one consecrate wafer per person. And inevitably the voters were left hungry for dominance, so they wolfed down my erect nipples with their eyes. With their eyes and, to be sure, nothing else, because I don't fuck Spaniards or anyone else who has voted in local, regional, national or European elections, primary elections, union elections, or referendums on declaring independence, signing a peace treaty, extending presidential term limits, amending the Constitution, rejecting the European bailout or withdrawing from the European Union. Civic imbeciles, every last one.

The male has a daughter, poor girl. He was walking hand in hand with her this afternoon near the Barceloneta Civic Centre. Who was picking up whom? It's like in those topsy-turvy fairy tales where the prince falls in love with the witch and you eat your soup with a fork: at BADDAY the kids pick up their parents, aunts, uncles and grandparents from daycare. This afternoon, the children were patiently bringing their adults to the daycare's final performance, which starred twelve adults ready to demonstrate all they'd learned in nine months of workshops on contemporary dance, dance theatre and gender mainstreaming for the performing arts. The performance would take place on the street and, while the adults and their Italian director, Eleonora Stumpo, waited the requisite fifteen minutes for any latecomers, the kids kept their parents entertained by allowing themselves to be lifted like planes, by dancing along with them to the bursts of music coming from the soundcheck, and even dancing to no music at all, pretending like it didn't hurt when they fell flat on their faces during those erratic boogies, holding back tears to the perennial adult entreaty of 'You're all right, bud, don't cry!' and not crying so they wouldn't embarrass their parents in front of the other grown-ups, who were trying to have their little adult party in peace.

Those delicious summer evenings in Barceloneta! It's five degrees cooler than every other neighbourhood in the city, the air tastes clean, and once you're a few blocks from the beach, the number of tourists per square metre drops to tolerable levels thanks to the first-generation Xarnegos and the Pakistani families who have seized the public squares, setting up tables, chairs, radios and televisions so they can play cards or dominoes while they watch football and game shows. The tourists can't bring themselves to transition from one kind of concrete to another, from the pavement to the occupied square, and so they content themselves with taking pictures from a distance. If I were one of those old ladies playing sevens, I'd chase down the tourist who'd just taken my picture without my consent and make him delete it in front of me, just like during riots, where there's always some journalist, insufferable hipster or eager-beaver tourist thrilled with the only dose of reality he'll take home from Barcelona, snapping close-ups of rioters in hoods and bandanas while they smash shop windows and ATMs. Then, without fail, a masked-up rioter who's taken it upon herself to lay into over-zealous citizen journalists emerges from the fray and breathes down the shitless photographer's neck, her stick at the ready, as he deletes all the photos. After his hood-and-bandana series comes the endless vintage-filter-selfie series, and, to show his good faith, the petrified journalist/hipster/tourist keeps swiping through his camera roll: a pair of dainty feet with toenails painted different colours, mirror flexing, driver and wingman clinking drinks in the car, kissy face and peace sign, bursting cleavage, plates of food, pints of beer, blown-out sunsets where everything just looks dark, flowers, cuddling pets, artsy shots of the Sagrada Familia, the statue of Columbus, Catalan sausage at the Boquería Market, Gaudí's lizard, and three hundred more, and even though the rioter is long gone and the protest has moved elsewhere, the shittourist/hair-gel hipster/journalist documenting his own existence is stuck to the asphalt, in hunched submission to his phone, swiping mechanically, blindly, for hours, not responding to texts, not answering the calls from friends he'd made plans with, not getting off the street when the police open it back up to traffic and the cars start honking, immune to drivers' insults as they manoeuvre around him, immune to the cop saying come with me, buddy, immune to the nurse putting an arm on his shoulder and saying come with me, buddy, nothing works, the journalist/shittourist/hair-gel hipster cannot be torn from his phone or from the street. He looks like a Butoh dancer, or like if you balanced a medicine ball on one of those round-bottomed roly-poly dolls' necks, there's no way to make him fall or walk or lift his head, not even when the most handsome nurse tenderly places a hand under his chin, the prelude to a cinematic kiss. His core is tight in dancerly or pugilistic tension, ready to leap five metres into his partner's arms or throw a knockout right jab. There's no choice but to subdue him; the needle seeks some exposed patch of skin and finds it on a hairy blond calf. The nurses tighten their circle around him and the first thing to go is his phone, which one of the nurses opportunely saves from impact and tucks away for safe keeping. The knees go next, and there's another nurse ready to grab him under the arms. His head was already bowed, so it stays put, though it bobbles as he's transferred to the stretcher.

At eight fifteen the adults emerged from the daycare centre and, in a very soldierly fashion, took their positions in Plaza Carmen Amaya. That's also where I live, so I watched through the tree branches from my second-floor balcony. Director Eleonora Stumpo approached the audience and, without a microphone because there weren't many people, explained that this street performance would take place in different parts of the neighbourhood and the audience should feel free to watch it from wherever they pleased. She would guide them to the first scene and, from there, the dancers would suggest the next stages. Stumpo, accustomed as she was to herding adults, couldn't stifle the kneejerk 'Any questions?' Oh, Eleonora, Eleonora, you're such an excellent dance instructor, and my gates so rarely sealed shut in your class. Why must you, too, succumb to didacticism? Why do you believe the audience must be taught how to watch? Do you, too, think that education is innocent? Do you too, Eleonora, believe, like every other schoolteacher marching against budget cuts, there is such a thing as literacy outside of emancipatory politicisation? Do you fake it, Eleonora, because that's what brings home the bacon? Is that why you keep letting yahoos like the ill-shaven masculofascist enrol in your classes? I stopped going because of him. So, Eleonora, you can draw your own conclusions about the real ideology of community centres, and about who has the power to expel whom.

One time the male even corrected Eleonora Stumpo's accent. She said 'pairforrrm' instead of 'perform' when she was saying 'to pairforrrm this movement'. We were all facing the studio mirror, in our positions, ready to start, when the male cut in:

'It's pronounced "perform", Ele, by the way.'

'I'm sorry, my accent is very bad, I know sometimes you don't understand me. We don't have the same sounds in Italian! Thank you for correcting me. To pairform this movement –' she repeated with effort, looking at the male in the mirror.

'No no. You're saying paiiiiiiiiirform, it makes you sound foreign! *Per*-form. Can you make the "er" sound? Per! Per!' he insisted teasingly, spittle flying from his lips.

'Ah, it's so hard!' Stumpo said, still smiling, her huge mouth invading her smooth olive cheeks. 'Per!' she gah-gahed back at the baby. All the other girls giggled like it was still the era of Isabella II, but I barely heard it because my gates were also making popping sounds as the gears moved into place. They needed oil after a period of happy disuse.

'You have it! Just like that! *PER*form.'

Safely enclosed like the front window of a riot van, I could clearly see that no one who hadn't beaten the shit out of a panhandler the night before should keep dancing, even though there was still half an hour of class left and all the females had played along with the phonetic joke, their six sweet cosmopolitan smiles blooming in the mirror. I released my head from the dancerly stillness to which the rest of my body remained bound so I could talk to Eleonora and not her reflection.

'We understand you perfectly and you speak very well. And in any case, pairform sounds very pretty.'

'Ah, thank you! I always appreciate when my students corrrrect me so I can improve. Let's continue?'

'Of course, that's why I corrected her in the first place, Nati, because that's how we learn to speak new languages properly, isn't it?'

'Eleonora, your accent is beautiful and only a fascist would try to make you change it.'

The word fascist transformed the male's scarecrow button eyes into real eyes, his stitched red mouth into a real drooler, and his broomstick arms into the open hands of non-violent protest.

'Whoa whoa whoa whoa whoa! I didn't say anything like that. Did you hear me insult anybody?' he said to my reflection, unwilling to relinquish his position in the choreography so he could look at me directly.

'Hey, guys, don't worrrry about it, it's not worth fighting over,' Eleonora implored as the smiles in the mirror began to wither. We were still maintaining the ethereal composure of the dance, our heads at the proper height, our shoulders down, our knees slightly flexed, our feet perfectly parallel, the volume of our buttocks sufficiently compressed, and from that position we watched our conflict unfold in the mirror. I was the first to break formation:

'And do you think speaking properly means talking like they do on TV? Why don't you correct my pronunciation too, since I say "*per*-form" instead of "per-*form*", because that's how they say it where I'm from? And while you're at it, why don't you correct your own Andalusian accent?'

'Look, I make mistakes too, I get it.' The male forced himself to calm down, still holding his position, which he understood to be standing to attention, and he didn't dare gesticulate for fear of losing the abandon and alertness, the resistance and relaxation required for the dancerly stillness he had worked so hard to achieve. 'But I can say per-form perfectly well. I say lots of things wrong, but not that word in particular. Per-form, per-form, per-form, see? Per-form, per-form ...'

I laughed so hard my gates started steaming up, and of course all the other girls followed suit, mistaking my yellow teeth for a white flag. Then, in a never-before-seen display of intelligence, the male grasped that I was laughing at him and that the hissing sound coming from the space between my incisors, muffled a little by my gates, was the guilty verdict being handed down on his idiocy. He subsequently mistook the other women's innocuous giggles as further ridicule and lost all control of his eyes, which bounced across the mirror like billiard balls after the first shot. He was the second to break formation:

'Can we take a step back for a sec? What the fuck makes me a fascist? Aren't you the fascist, putting labels on people you don't even fucking know? Can't I correct a friend's accent without some girl jumping down my throat?'

Eleonora Stumpo broke ranks and the rest of the tableau followed. She proffered a feeble 'Hey, please', or something like that, and a new tableau formed: the other dancers turned their backs to the mirror and formed a semicircle around the male and me. They were trying to de-escalate the situation, but the new spatial arrangement just goaded me on and prompted me to take a step closer to the male, bucking my gates like a horn:

'What? You can correct a woman's accent, but you can't deal with a woman correcting your own shitty behaviour? Here's a label for you: chauvinist fucking prick.'

And then the same thing as always happened: the male says you're just being hysterical and rude, he doesn't have a sexist bone in his body, and the females grab you lovingly by the shoulders and tell you not to get flustered. And you shake them off and respond that you're not flustered or hysterical or rude, what you are is sick of them laughing along with the male's macho humour without ever realising the joke is on them. They all silently accuse you of spoiling the class. They all silently sympathise with the male, who has had to endure your excesses. You hope for some expression of female solidarity, but everyone keeps their eyes down, including Eleonora Stumpo. When the tears start to well, they take it as remorse, or as the eruption of nerves frayed by God knows what personal troubles that they now have to deal with through no fault of their own. Not one of them takes it as rage or frustration or humiliation that's immediate and immanent to that morning, to that dance class, to them. They think you need consoling when what you need is for just one other person within those four fucking walls to understand the meaning of 'correct', 'speak properly', 'sound foreign', 'make mistakes', 'some girl'. The first one to console you is, who else, the ever-sensitive male. He apologises for whatever might have offended you, says you both got a little tense but hey, it's nothing, we're all human, it's over now, no big deal, and you fall quiet instead of headbutting him with your gates, which slowly retract as

25

if there weren't still a roomful of amiability to protect you from, leaving you vulnerable to further macho subjugation while you tie your shoes. For the umpteenth time you swallow the screams like a pellet of hashish, for the umpteenth time you spend a day carrying it in your stomach; the next day you shit it out and, as you smoke your afternoon spliff, you have to admit that the male was right, it's over now and it was, in fact, no big deal.

Gari Garay's Case for Okupation
Referred by the PAH
Acció Llibertària de Sants, 18 June 2018

My name is Gari Garay and I have a case to present to the Okupation Office for Squatter's Rights. Four cousins, all of them intellectually disabled, live in an apartment at 1 Plaza Carmen Amaya, second floor, unit 2, in the Barceloneta neighbourhood. The least disabled cousin watches the most TV, has the fanciest smartphone, and has been deemed 40 per cent disabled, which entitles her to a monthly benefit of 189 euros. She's the one in charge, but she's easily ignored by the other three cousins, who are arranged in a hierarchy that varies according to their stubbornness and psychomotor skills. The cousin with good posture who swings her arms when she walks (who's not the least disabled cousin because the least disabled cousin is obese so she waddles from side to side when she walks, with her arms flat against her body) has the authority to tell the other three to stop on the street if they have to cross to the other side or if she or one of the other cousins wants to look at something in a shop window. That doesn't mean the other cousins listen to her, it just means they let her give harmless orders and don't put up a fight, and no one protesting is enough to make the order-giver happy and feel like she's being obeyed.

The two cousins who're able to cut their own nails (the least disabled and the second-least disabled, you can tell them apart because the second-least disabled can smoke without coughing and she wears make-up) have the authority to decide when the others' nails need cutting, and by extension when and what colour they should paint them and how they should get their hair cut, but for the haircuts the least disabled cousin, the waddler, forces them, and this order they can't ignore, to go to the salon (she pays, since her participation in Mercadona's Integrated Workforce Pilot Programme as a restocking assistant legitimises her as household treasurer), even though the second-least disabled cousin, who has been deemed 52 per cent disabled and awarded 324 euros a month, wants to cut her family members' hair herself.

The third-least disabled cousin is the quietest, with the sweetest expression, and takes the most pills because the psychiatrist told her that besides being disabled she's also depressed about being disabled, because one day she, Margarita (66 per cent, 438 euros), the third-least disabled, came to the glaring realisation she was mentally retarded and the three women she lived with were too, and this discovery and subsequent depression, according to the psychologist, explained why Marga kept quietly masturbating in every corner of the flat like a domestic cat urinating and defecating in protest when you leave it alone for too long, or masturbating locked in her bedroom so she wouldn't get told off or spontaneously slapped by her cousin Patricia. Patricia is the second-least disabled cousin, the one who wears make-up.

With her lucidity clouded by the pills, Marga can once again exercise her authority over the thing she knows best: cleaning. But since, at the end of the day, Marga is almost the most disabled cousin in the house, her second cousin Patricia and her first cousin Àngels, the ex-Mercadona employee, don't listen to a single thing she says. The most disabled cousin, whose name is Nati, is the only person who sometimes helps depressed Marga out. The caseworker, Susana Gómez, and the psychologist, Laia Buedo, insist that poor Nati, because she has something called Gate Control syndrome (70 per cent, 1,118 euros), should be taken out more often to do some of the things she likes, but her half-sister Patricia and her second cousin Àngels don't like going out with her because they're afraid of recreating the attitudes of all the non-disabled guardians, disability aides, nurses, social workers and caseworkers they had to work so hard to emancipate themselves from. Just like the other three residents of this so-called supervised flat run by the Generalitat, Nati has a set of keys, and supposedly she can come and go as she pleases. I'm Margarita – Marga – but when we're talking about okupation, I'd rather you call me Gari, just to be safe.

When we heard the music, we all ran onto the balcony in our respective nightgowns, which are lilac, sky blue, pistachio green and lemon chiffon. The lemon chiffon is mine. They're all exactly the same except the colours and they make us look crazy or at least like old ladies because these days no woman who is thirty-two (Nati), thirty-three (Patricia), thirty-seven (me) or even forty-three (Àngels) wears a nightgown. They're from the Chinese bazaar downstairs, so they're synthetic and hot as hell, but I can't take it off without showing my tits, which would be fine with me because I'm a redhead so I have nice tits, but every time I show them Patri fights with me about it because relative to me she has 14 per cent less disability but 99 per cent less tits, and whenever I'm naked or even wearing a bra she just stares straight at them with her 52 percentage points of mental retardation and her lower lip, painted *rouge*, flopped open. So in order to avoid seeing my cousin's epithelium I leave the nightgown on but I do tuck it

29

into my panties (also sweltering synthetic material from the Chinese bazaar) so I can at least feel the breeze on my legs, my redhead legs with their cellulite dimples under the butt cheeks, voluptuousness guaranteed.

Nati, in her pistachio-green nightgown, said the dancers were from the municipal civic centre across the street and they were her ex-classmates from dance class. Àngels, in her bulging sky-blue nightgown, asked Nati why she wasn't in her class's final show, but she was looking at her phone and laughing when she asked, so it looked like she was laughing at the phone or something on the phone. Maybe that was why she was laughing and the question about why Nati wasn't dancing with her classmates was serious. In any case Nati, who either can't take jokes or doesn't get them because of her Gate Control syndrome, took it seriously just like she takes everything seriously, and answered the same way she always does: because they were all fucking fascists and because the municipal civic centre was a daycare centre for grown-ups and it was even worse than the Occupational Centre (the Occupational Centre doesn't have anything to do with okupation, by the way, it's just a place where intellectually disabled people go to do arts and crafts). It's true Nati is a bigger reactionary than the Pope, but it's also true Àngels is the least disabled and Nati is the most disabled so it's easy to laugh at her, even though she's the one who walks the straightest and she's more graceful than the rest of us, because she was a dancer I guess.

Patricia, in her lilac nightgown and with her lilac fingernails and toenails, told them to shut up because the performance was starting. A woman sitting on a bench in the square was playing a cello and two others were moving like cats on the bench in front of the Chinese bazaar, and the owner, Ting, had come out to watch. A third dancer twirled vaporously around the fountain dedicated to Carmen Amaya and skimmed the water with the tips of her fingers. A fourth dancer robotically climbed up and down the stairs that connect the square to the tourist superhighway on the waterfront promenade. A fifth, already on the promenade, was grabbing a railing with one, with two, or with no hands, and that was her whole dance. Each one was wearing a different colour, like us, except unlike us they were all wearing different clothes. Our nightgowns all match because Ting let Àngels have four for twelve euros, according to the receipt. To be allowed to live in a supervised flat like ours, we have to give a receipt to the Generalitat at the end of every month for everything we buy, and we have to follow the proper chain of command: Patri, Nati and I give our receipts to our cousin Àngels; Àngels gives them to Diana Ximenos, who is the director of our flat, which means she's the one who makes sure the four of us meet our integration, normalisation and independent-lifestyle targets; and the director gives them to the Generalitat. For Àngels' and Patri's receipts, that's where the chain of accountability ends, but for Nati and me, the Generalitat still has to give them to the person who declared us legally incompetent, i.e. the judge of first instance, who is responsible for safeguarding that our guardian, the Generalitat of Catalonia, safeguards the best interests of the incompetent individual, i.e. us, even though the judge is the Generalitat, Diana Ximenos is the Generalitat, our cousin Àngels is the Generalitat, and Patricia, Natividad and I are also the Generalitat, which means the whole chain of command thing is really just a bureaucratic delusion.

So Patricia tried to get Àngels and Nati to shut up with a shhh, but none of us has the authority to tell the others to shut up, not even by shushing. Not telling each other to shut up is actually the golden rule in our apartment, because we spent our whole lives in schools for mentally retarded children, in Rural Centres and Urban Centres for the Intellectually Disabled (RUCIDs and UCIDs, respectively), and in our Aunt Montserrat's house, being shushed for talking out of turn. Àngels and Nati heard Patricia's shhh but they acted like they didn't. I was quiet because I was watching the performance and trying to understand what the dancers were dancing, paying attention like Patri, who was pensively smoking, enjoying her role as an audience member. I was feeling good because by then the sun wasn't shining on the balcony and the breeze was cool, and because whenever I got tired of looking down I could look out and see the ocean, and when I got tired of looking at the ocean I could look down and see the urban nymphs, which I think is what they were trying to convey with their dance, that they were pixies scattering their magic dust across the overheated summer asphalt, pixies emerging from their hidey-holes to bring the beautiful nightfall and release the city from the monster of blistering daytime, encouraging the city dwellers, cooped up in their houses or at their jobs with their box fans and their air conditioners and their televisions, to finally throw open the windows, have a shower and take to the streets smelling like shampoo and coconut body milk, their wet hair drying in the breeze, wearing sandals with thin leather straps and cotton shorts or light summer dresses, the tennis balls ready to be tossed and the dogs ready to fetch, the babies barefoot in their buggies or slings.

Fuck your shitty fucking performance! yelled Nati. Most of the freshly showered audience stopped looking at the dancers and turned to look at our balcony, or stopped using their phones to film the dancers and turned to film our balcony, so Nati insisted: Fuck this shitty fucking excuse for a shitty fucking performance!

Now every single member of the audience was looking at us, and Nati was feeding off the attention and of course the three of us knew what would happen next: her gates activated. The transparent mask sealed shut over her face, dampening her voice and forcing her to yell twice as loud, so she had to press herself against the railing in her pistachio-green nightgown and hinge forward to make herself heard, totally berserk at the prospect of ten seconds of what she calls direct action and what Patricia calls direct abuse: What kind of choreofascist shitshow is this? Amélie in fucking tights? Raise your hand if you're an anally retentive ass-clencher or an Ada-Colau-voting, human-chain-for-Catalan-independence neoliberal or both! The cellist kept playing and the dancers kept dancing, but during those few seconds of direct action or direct abuse that coincided with the time it takes a non-retard to realise that we were four retards, the cellist and the dancers all slowed down and the freshly showered audience was unsure for a second if this was part of the performance or if they really were being accosted by some psycho bitch in a nightgown who couldn't keep her gates in check. One guy with dreadlocks was muttering to himself and, even though he eventually registered Nati's mental retardation, at first he was so indignant that he almost responded to her direct action/abuse (which was, of course, exactly what she wanted) as if she were a valid interlocutor and not someone to pity.

Patricia doubled down on the forbidden order of silence. Shut up already! I will not shut up! Nati pointed her threatening gates at her sister. But she did shut up, storming off the balcony and out of the apartment, slamming the door behind her. We saw her walk across the square with her graceful dancer's stride, ploughing straight through the urban nymphs' performance without looking at or sidestepping anyone, gates still firmly in place, like a riot cop in a pistachio-green nightgown.

That's the case I made two weeks ago at the Platform for Action on Housing (PAH from now on), who determined that

33

I am not in a critical housing situation but that I'm actually a lost cause. That's why they referred me to you, because, as they told me in the one brief moment they dropped their stuffy official parlance, their pahrlance, 'the anarchists in Sants are more direct'. At the PAH they just shook their heads and explained that I clearly wasn't the victim of a foreclosure or eviction and that I didn't have any dependants, so before starting an okupa and claiming squatter's rights I'd have to exhaust all the other legal avenues at my disposal, since that would make the okupa look more legit and it would take the owner longer to kick me out. At the PAH they don't understand that I'm my own dependant and that's already too much, and I don't have any money because my cousin Àngels keeps it all. And the other thing they don't get, even though I said it to them just as clearly as I'm saying it now, is I don't want anything to do with government services ever again because I've spent my whole fucking life locked up in institutions, and a judge has declared me legally incompetent, so if I go to a government employee complaining about the supervised flat, then the government employee is going to call social services and social services is going to send me straight back to the UCID/Occupational Centre (which, again, has nothing to do with okupation with a 'K', it has to do with 'having an occupation', with 'keeping yourself occupied', specifically keeping yourself occupied making cardboard bookmarks and wicker baskets, even though if I do succeed in okupying a space I'm going to call it my 'Okupational Centre' just for laughs), because the UCID is also a government service available to me and that's the whole problem. The pahrasites don't understand that the legal avenues at my disposal aren't going to be exhausted, they're going to multiply (when I said this, the pahchyderms got indignant and went quiet) because all the government wants to do is lock me back up so they can scold

34

me every time I show a boob. Or maybe the pahcifists under-stand perfectly and they just think I'm one of those uppity tards who complain about the State giving them room and board – for free! – even though all I want is to get out of that apartment with those three retards who I swear are making me even more retarded, because being depressed and seeing things for what they are (or seeing things for what they are and consequently being depressed) is the best thing that has happened to me in my entire life.

I want to thank Jaén for kindly and patiently putting my words in writing since I don't know how to write.

<u>Gari Garay</u>

35

Statement by Ms Patricia Lama Guirao, made before the Fourth Investigating Judge of the Court of Barcelona on 15 June 2018, as part of the court proceedings for authorisation of the sterilisation of an incompetent individual arising from the action brought by the Generalitat of Catalonia against Ms Margarita Guirao Guirao.

Investigating Judge: The Hon. Guadalupe Pinto García

Clerk: Mr Sergi Escudero Balcells

With the Hon. Judge having been informed prior to this hearing by Ms Laia Buedo Sánchez, resident of Barcelona, psychologist with licence number 58698, from the Urban Centre for the Intellectually Disabled of Barceloneta, where the Declarant engages in recreational and independent-living activities, that the Declarant suffers from a speech disorder (logorrhoea), the Hon. Judge concedes that it is preferable for the Declarant's statement to be recorded, rather than transcribed by the stenographer.

The Declarant and the stenographer, having been informed of this deviation from standard proceedings, both agree to the change.

Here follows the transcription of said recording, which the Declarant was given the opportunity to read at an extraordinary session held on the following day for her approval and signature, after which it was appended to this file.

Your Honour, I promise I'll tell you things exactly the way they are, the truth, the whole truth and nothing but the truth, just like they say in American movies.

Àngels did a good job from the start, but the start had to wait a few years because it took her a long while to figure out what a RUCID was, what a UCID was, what the LISMI was and what a PNC was. Before she could do anything else she had to figure out what all those acronyms meant, because the staff at the RUCID never got what she was saying, or if they got it they pretended not to. Àngels is a stutterer and she stutters more when she's nervous, and like 'stuttering Stanleys' all over she doesn't stutter when she sings, except Àngels doesn't sing so I guess it doesn't matter. She'd try and say 'What does UCID mean?' but she could never get it out. She'd see all four of the words clear as day in her head, but when she tried spitting it out she'd get caught on the 'D' in 'does' and it just sounded like she'd swallowed a fishbone. And she couldn't write for crap so she didn't even try.

It had been eight or nine months since her mom slash my Aunt Loli died – she'd had Àngels when she was forty-eight and that's why they say Àngels was born retarded [*sic*]. Now, Your Honour, I shouldn't say what I'm about to say because it could cause a hunk of trouble with Social Security, but I want you to see I'm not hiding anything and I want to do right by you: I don't think my cousin Àngels is really retarded [*sic*]. Me, I'm clearly retarded [*sic passim*] to the tune of 52 per cent and climbing because even though I'm pretty sexy thanks to a teenage eating disorder and I have a way with words thanks to my speech disorder, I have a splotch of tuberous sclerosis in my frontal lobe and another splotch in my eyes, that's why I have to wear these Coke-bottle glasses and sometimes it pisses me off when I'm looking at my phone and I can't read the letters so I hurl it against the ground. The phones didn't used to break because they used to be tough like those old Nokias and Motorolas, thick as a brick and all, but now they keep making them fragiler and fragiler [sic] and when I throw them the screen shatters into bazillions of pieces and now they won't buy me new ones any more.

They think Àngels is retarded just because she stutters and she's a hundred and twenty kilos and she never passed any of her classes in school, but that girl wasn't even always clinging to her mommy like you know retards usually do, she was independent as anything, Your Honour, always out alone or playing with the dogs or the other kids because my Aunt Loli, she was over fifty and spent her whole life sitting outside, she'd bring a fold-up chair and go and sit under a fig tree about halfway between the house and Los Maderos and just sit there all day long. For as long as I can remember Los Maderos has been what they used to call a 'house of ill repute', Your Honour, it was built in an old house that Àngels and I's other relatives sold to the pimps before we were even born.

What I think, Your Honour, and I'll tell it to you the same as I told it to Àngels, because I owe her a lot, is I think Aunt Loli was a 'prozzie' and Àngels is one of her customer's daughters, because Loli never got married and it'd been ages since she'd 'shacked up' with anyone. Àngels always objects and makes me doubt myself when I say this, which just goes to show as far as disabilities goes she doesn't even have the minimum 33 per cent you need to be allowed to sell lottery tickets, so she always objects, I mean, she says if her mother had set out to steal customers from the 'prozzies' right in front of the 'house of ill repute', the 'prozzies' or their pimps would've put a stop to it and teached [*sic*] her a lesson.

One day Marga roused herself from her depression to tell us we watch too many movies: 'Aunt Loli slept with her Portuguese cousin Henrique one night after a dance during the Easter break. You,' she said to Àngels, 'are retarded because you're a haemophiliac, just like the rest of us,' she concluded, and hearing this actually made Àngels and I super happy, Your Honour, because she was acknowledging she has a disability and that's progress. But of course a step forward in Marga's treatment is exactly the opposite for Nati, or I mean it's like it's a string she has to pull or a scab she has to pick or a hot ember she has to blow on, and we had another gate incident on our hands. She looked up from the bicycle wheel she was fiddling with on the balcony where she was dripping grease all over the place and lectured at us with her wrench:

'Moviegoers, haemophiliacs and male [*sic*] fascists to top it off –' that's what she calls us, Your Honour, your guess why is as good as mine – 'can't you get it in your heads that a forty-eight-year-old woman might just want a good [*expletive*]? A quick one-night stand and that's that, end of story?' It's not appropriate talk for a courtroom, Your Honour, I know, but that's how my sister Nati speaks. 'You can't get your heads around Aunt Loli having a little baby girl without loving and tending to her all the rest of her days. No, no, she has to be a –' I'm sorry, Your Honour, but this is the word she used – '[*expletive*]. She has to get paid to –' I'm sorry again, Your Honour, but I have to say it exactly how she said it – '[*expletive*]. There has to be a good reason she spends the whole day away from her daughter, the market must have some justification for this lack of maternal love.' She has the mental age of a teenager, Your Honour. 'Otherwise, you can't explain it. Can't she just have a [*expletive*] for the fun of it? And isn't it possible she might just not give a [*expletive*] about her daughter?' Nati is one of those people who goes around saying [*expletive*] this and [*expletive*] that all day, Your Honour. 'Does it not occur to you that maybe a mother might not want anything to do with her kid just like the –' and she doesn't know how to make a point except by calling people names – '[*expletive*] father nobody here is even talking about?'

It's true me and Àngels check lots of films out from the library then watch them later on the computer and I admit I got my theory about Àngels' mother from one where an old lady gets all dolled up and takes a chair out to a dirt road every afternoon and has sex all day until a man drives her home. But since my pain-in-the-[*expletive*] sister Nati's gates were acting up I quietened [*sic*] down because we have a rule where we don't tell each other to shut up even though in reality I'm shutting up all day every day as long as I don't have to fight with my superzealot sister who as retarded as she is is the [*expletive*] who's determined to win every fight by putting up her gates and then tearing apart any argument you make until you feel like an 'idiot consumer capitalist fascist' and you can try and scream back at her and really hit her where it hurts but it doesn't matter, Your Honour, her gates repel everything and it all just kind of bounces back at you if you know what I mean. But the day I'm talking about I lost it for real and I admit I told her to go shove it.

Our flat is right right right in front of the beach, and Your Honour, it's the envy of all the supervised flats in the entire Generalitat, five minutes from the metro and five seconds from the bus, four bedrooms, two bathrooms, a big living room with a big-screen plasma TV, a big kitchen with an electric stove, a laundry room, and, the crowning glory, a balcony wide enough for a table and chairs so you can sit outside and have a beer and some crisps and a cigarette, and that's exactly what I was doing that day, Your Honour, I was smoking away on the balcony, at peace with the world, [*expletive*], at peace with myself and the world after a lifetime of lights out at ten o'clock in the UCIDs and RUCIDs, at peace with myself and the world because Marga and me had finally got over our latest spat about keeping the flat clean, because a flat as good as ours ought to be clean and tidy, Your Honour, not to mention we've got the caseworker Miss Susana Gómez on our case, and the first thing she does whenever she shows up for her inspections is run her finger along the shelf because cleanliness is next to kindliness [*sic*] and it's the first item she puts in her report since cleanliness, self-care and personal hygiene are the categories they can use to justify kicking you out of the flat and revoking your 'retardation probation', which is what Marga's been calling it since she became aware of the fact that she does in fact have a disability, Your Honour, but so anyway here, since we're right right right by the beach, all this sand ends up in the flat and we have to sweep and dust and sweep and dust because social services could show up without warning at any moment, the same as the labour inspectors who show up at nightclubs at three in the morning, put a rum and Coke on the Generalitat's credit card, then demand everyone's papers. I know all about it because my friend waitresses at Mágic where they busted the boss for paying all the girls off the books.

So, the four of us were out on our big beautiful balcony enjoying the fresh air. I'd just pulled out some chairs and opened a bag of crisps and a litre of beer (the oriental man at the bazaar downstairs rings up beer as orange juice on the receipts we give the Generalitat: I want Your Grace to see you can trust my testimony so I'm even telling you secrets that can get me into trouble) and I offered the three of them tobacco (there's no getting the tobacco lady to ring up rolling tobacco as stamps or gum on the receipt so I pay a friend who doesn't live in a supervised flat and he gets tobacco for me and then later the two of us go and buy whatever he needs from Mercadona and we ask them to put the receipt in my name).

Nati was the only one who wanted to smoke and I had to roll her cigarette for her because even though with her disability she can dance *Swan Lake* the poor thing doesn't have the psychomotor skills to roll a cigarette, and the only one who wanted crisps was Àngels, who kept automatically grabbing handfuls full [*sic*] without taking her eyes off her phone. Marga runs hot and she had her nightgown rolled up and stuffed in her underwear but this time I didn't say anything because at least she wasn't hairy, I'd done her entire legs and her bikini line the day before. That's the compromise Marga and me agreed on: she can show her breasts whenever she wants wherever she wants, fine, but no hairs on her nipples, please. If she wants to go out on the terrace in her panties, fine, fine, fine, as long as panties is all people see and not thick curls poking out around the panties. Like I said Marga runs real hot so she at least was enjoying the cold beer I'd brought out, and it made me happy to see my cousin relaxed, watching the dance in the square below. Relaxed and not depressed.

Some women from the civic centre had started doing an old-timey, New Age dance to a nostalgic, daydreamy music track, and it was like watching an ad for a really fancy cologne, a Chanel or a Cacharel or a Lancôme, you know, one of those classy, elegant ads where you only see the model and never the man because he only exists in the way the model looks at him, and she flirts and teases the unseen man like she doesn't even really want him, like she keeps her desire under lock and key. I had just been picturing myself in that moment of passion that always feels like it's about to arrive but never quite gets there, but then Nati started screaming like a wild animal, shouting all her usual insults, the ones she calls 'direct action' even though what they really are is direct abuse plain and simple, Your Honour, crazy, hysterical abuse like you've never heard before. The dance and the music had been transporting me to that moment when you can just almost feel the love, not the moment when you kiss but the moment of tension just before the kiss that's always more interesting, even though you end up making out because at that point that's all there is left to do, your lips are a millimetre away so of course you kiss the guy, you can't just pull away and call it a wrap. But one thing you can do is shift to the side for a peck on the cheek and buy yourself time for more of the good stuff, not tonsil hockey but hide-and-seek, because in our little scene the night is still young and there's no bigger thrill than saying no to keep him on his leash. But then Nati had to go and [expletive] the whole thing up with her [expletive] syndrome, for [expletive]'s sake! The girls from the civic centre couldn't have been more inoffensive, Your Honour, but something set Nati off. She started screaming about how they were all 'filthy fascist anal retentives'. Does Nati get a pass or what? She just kept screaming all this political stuff about Mayor Colau and Catalan independence that had nothing to do with the dance. And something about the movie *Amélie*? Have you seen it? It's precious! What on earth did *Amélie* ever do to my sister? We all know what Nati's deal is and when her gates activate we know it's best to leave her be and not agree or disagree with anything she says, don't do anything, just sit quiet, because if you contradict her she won't stop until she proves her point and if you tell her she's right, even if she really is right, she gets this twinkle in her eye and she'll make you go with her to sabotage something or settle scores with someone, and she

43

won't leave you alone until you help her commit some atrocity or at least be her lookout.

But that day I couldn't take it any more because I felt like she'd blown up at the people in the square for absolutely no reason. She was being so intolerant and rude and even though we're intellectually disabled, Your Honour, even though the Ministry of Health and the Ministry of Education murdered us slowly with children's books and behavioural therapies and afterwards we rose from the dead and now we're intellectually disabled zombies, intellectually disabled brain-eaters, intellectually disabled experts in intellectual disability, even with all that, everyone still deserves our respect and good manners, even our worst enemies, because the director of the supervised flat, Ms Diana Ximenos, a great professional and an even better person, Your Honour, she doesn't just come to our house, she asks around the neighbourhood about us too. She asks the oriental man who runs the bazaar, she asks the neighbours, she asks at the civic centre, and there we're really [*expletive*] because the people at the Municipal Civic Centre of Barceloneta say they're extremely respectful of Nati's special situation and they let her take dance classes the same as everybody else, they all adapt to her needs and tolerate her more-than-occasional outbursts, but Nati, because of her severe intellectual disability, it's not her fault, she doesn't appreciate or notice the efforts her teachers and classmates make to include her, so whenever something she doesn't like happens she goes on the attack and disrupts the class, or else she isolates herself and puts everybody in an awkward situation, because on the one hand they don't want to get mad at her but on the other hand she doesn't let them dance in peace. Not to mention us being allowed to stay in the flat is riding on it, on our communication skills, our involvement in community life, our ability to adjust our expectations to our

44

real capacities, our willingness to tolerate frustration, and our ability to find healthy outlets for certain comments and forms of expression in order to foster proper self-knowledge, and I swear to [*expletive*] God, Your Honour, my sister is going to get the entire *Aberrant Behaviour Checklist Community Version Second Edition* into her head if I have to shove it under her gates with a battering ram.

Guadalupe Pinto
Judge

Patricia Lama
Declarant

Javier López Mansilla
Stenographer/Transcriber

NOVEL
TITLE: MEMOIRS OF MARÍA DELS ÀNGELS
GUIRAO HUERTAS
GENRE: EASY READ
AUTHOR: MARÍA DELS ÀNGELS GUIRAO HUERTAS
CHAPTER 1: INTRODUCTION

UCID means Urban Centre
for the Intellectually Disabled.
You don't say 'they put me in the UCID'
or 'they committed me to the UCID'.
You say 'I was institutionalised'
and then you don't have to say UCID at all.

I wasn't always institutionalised at a UCID.
First I was institutionalised at a RUCID.
RUCID means Rural Centre
for the Intellectually Disabled.
It was near Arcuelamora.
Arcuelamora is the village I'm from.

I was institutionalised there
because when my mother died
the bank took our house.
My mother had a lifetime usufruct on the house.

Lifetime usufruct means you and your kids
can live in a place until you die.
The same year the same bank
took the Los Maderos club.
The prostitutes didn't have a lifetime usufruct.

I went to live at Uncle Joaquín's house
and after three months a social worker showed up.
Her name was Mamen or Miss Mamen.
Social worker means lady who helps
people at risk of social exclusion.
Mamen is short for María del Carmen.
Social exclusion means
being a person who begs for money,
commits crimes, takes drugs
or doesn't have a house.

I'm a person at risk of social exclusion?
I asked Mamen.
She said unfortunately I was.
I asked her why.
She said because I had special needs
and at my uncle's house there wasn't even a bathroom.
I said shit, there wasn't a bathroom anywhere in Arcuelamora
except Los Maderos.
Were the hookers the only people in Arcuelamora
not at risk of social exclusion? I asked Mamen.
She said we were there to talk about me
and not about anyone else.
She also said we don't use words like shit and hooker
we say shoot and prostitute instead
because if we use impolite language

we put ourselves at even more risk of social exclusion.
That was when I learned the word prostitute.

Mamen came to do lots of interviews.
Interviews are like what they have in magazines and on TV
except at your house.
She came to my uncle's house a lot,
sometimes in the morning and sometimes in the afternoon,
in winter, in summer, in spring and in autumn.
But they were really boring interviews
because she always asked the same questions.

Once she gave me some pyjamas
and once a sweater too
but they got old and fell apart.

Then one day the interviews were over
and after that the two of us didn't take walks any more
like we used to
and she didn't come to the garden
when Uncle Joaquín and me
were picking fava beans or apples
or when we were using the plough,
or when we were feeding La Agustinilla.
La Agustinilla was my uncle's horse.

And she didn't stand outside the front door
to get some air with the neighbours any more either.

That day Mamen asked my uncle and me
to come inside the house
like we sometimes did in winter

even though it was summer
and she said to sit down
because she wanted to tell us something important
in private.
But it wasn't just one something,
it was four somethings:

1) The first something was she said the government
was going to give me a Social Security benefit.

The government is the politicians who talk on TV
or give speeches at village festivals.

A Social Security benefit means
they give you money every month
but to get it
you have to open an account at the bank.

Account at the bank means
the government gives money to the bank
and then the bank gives it to you.

We opened the account at the same bank
who took the house where I lived
and the house where the prostitutes lived
because it was the only bank in Arcuelamora.
The bank is called BANKOREA.

BANKOREA means Bank of the Region of Arcos.

Everyone knows what a bank is
and what the Region of Arcos is
so I don't have to explain it.

2) The second something she said
was I could go live at the RUCID in Somorrín.
Somorrín is a bigger town than mine
and it's close if you drive
and it's where the doctors and shops and school
and BANKOREA and town hall are.

Town hall is where the politicians are.

If you go on a bike or a horse and cart
Somorrín isn't very close
but they always took me in a car.

3) The third something she said
was I was giving the RUCID permission
to keep almost all my benefit every month
to pay for my room,
my clothes, my food,
my bathroom,
my weekend trips
and everything I needed to live.

You can do whatever you want with the rest of your money,
Mamen told me.
That's good, Miss Mamen, I said.
You can drop the Miss! she said.
We're friends by now
and anyway I'm only six years older than you!

I was 18,
so Mamen was 24.
Now I'm 43
and if she isn't dead, she is 49.

When I'm 49,
if she isn't dead, she will be 55,
and so on as long as neither of us dies.

That's when I started calling Miss Mamen
just Mamen.

My cousin Patricia didn't call her Mamen
she called her 'La Mamen'
just like she calls me 'La Àngels'
and her sister 'La Nati'
and her other cousin 'La Marga'
and the Chinese guy downstairs 'El Ting'
and she puts a 'La' or an 'El'
in front of everybody's name
like Catalan people do
when they speak Catalan
and also like they do sometimes when they speak Spanish
because they're used to it.

But my cousin Patricia
isn't Catalan and she doesn't speak Catalan.

I'm Catalan through my aunt
and my name is Ángela.

Ángela, in Catalan, is pronounced Àngels.
Now I live in Barcelona, which is in Catalonia,
and I have to integrate into Catalan society.
I have to respect their linguistic diversity
so the Catalonians respect
my neurodiversity.
That's why in Barcelona I go by Àngels.

It's not a lie.
It's just a translation.

In Catalan you can say 'La Àngels'
or 'La Marga' or 'La Nati'
but not in Spanish.
In Spanish it sounds bad
and it's rude.

Back when Patricia called her 'La Mamen'
she always used to tell the same joke
which was whenever anybody who lived in the RUCID
asked for something
or complained about something or needed something
Patricia said:

Jesus, Mary and Joseph Stalin,
suck my dick or ask La Mamen.

Because of the 'Jesus, Mary and Stalin' thing
lots of times they took away Patricia's TV privileges
and her allowance and her Sunday walks.
I told her maybe she should stop saying it
and she listened to me
and started using polite language.
Then she didn't say La Mamen
and she didn't say just Mamen either.
She said Miss Mamen.
That time Mamen didn't say you can drop the Miss.

Mamen was 34 then,
because I was 28,
and Patricia was 18.

Patricia had just been institutionalised
and didn't know the rules very well yet.

I think Mamen liked the Miss
because she wasn't Patricia's friend
and because by then
she was the director of the RUCID in Somorrín.
Director is the person who's in charge of a place
and has the biggest office.

Then one day a resident
said he couldn't find the orange crayon
and Patricia said:

Jesus, Mary and Mrs Stalin,
suck my dick or ask Miss Mamen.

I don't remember what that resident's name was now
but I remember he had Fragile X syndrome.
I know Fragile X syndrome is a hard thing
and I know most people don't know what it is
but I don't have time to explain it right now.

I only brought it up because that was when
they put Patricia on the pills
because they said she had
aberrant behaviour.

What I said about Patricia
and the boy with Fragile X syndrome
are digressions.

Digression means starting to tell a story
in the middle of another story.

When you write in Easy Read you have to avoid digressions
because they make the main story
harder to understand.
The main story in this text
is mine.

I still have to explain
the fourth something Mamen told
my uncle and me.
It was the most important one.

But when you write in Easy Read
you also have to explain
all the hard or not common words
for people who might not understand.
So now I'm supposed to explain
Fragile X syndrome
and aberrant behaviour
and Easy Read.

But that would be three more digressions.

I've found a problem
the 'Guidelines for Easy-to-Read Materials'
from the Section for Library Services
for People with Special Needs
can't solve.

So.

I'll tell my support person
at my Tuesday afternoon

self-advocacy group.
Until then I'll do my best.

I'm not going to explain
what Guidelines means
or what Section for Library Services
for People with Special Needs means
or what support person means.
OK?

I'm only going to explain
what self-advocacy group means
because it's something very important.
It's not the same something very important
as the fourth something
Mamen told my uncle and me
but it's also important.

Since I'm the one writing this story
I guess I get to decide what's important
and what's a digression.

On page 19
of 'Guidelines for Easy-to-Read Materials'
it says very clearly:

'Do not limit the author's freedom too much.'

And below that
something I don't totally understand
but I think means
more or less the same thing:

'Do not be dogmatic.
Let fiction be fiction.'

I think fiction
is like science fiction
like 'Avatar' and 'Star Wars'.
That sounds good to me
so I'll just keep going.

Self-advocacy group means
a group formed by adults
with intellectual disabilities
or neurodiversity
who meet once a week
to do six things:

1) Acquire communication skills.
2) Achieve greater personal and social autonomy.
3) Increase their chances of speaking
and making decisions for themselves.
4) Learn to make decisions in their daily lives.
5) Learn to participate in community life.
6) Discuss topics of interest to them.

For now I'm not going to explain
what intellectual disabilities means
or what neurodiversity means
or what community life means.
OK?

When you write in Easy Read
you have to use short sentences
or make your sentences into short lines

because that way you read faster
and you get less tired reading.
You get less tired writing too.

In Easy Read you don't indent the text
so the lines all have to start together
on the left side of the page.
That's what not indenting is.

And you don't justify the text either
which has nothing to do
with making justifications.
Since the lines all go towards the right side of the page
you have to let each one
go as far as it goes
even if some are longer and some are shorter
and the text isn't a perfect column.
That's what not justifying means.

One of the tests for making sure
a text is a good Easy Read text
is turning the page on its side.
When you do that it's supposed to look like
the sentences are blades of grass
or mountains
or buildings in a big city
like in films.

There are a lot more guidelines
in 'Guidelines for Easy-to-Read Materials'.
I'm trying to learn them
and I think I'm pretty good at it.
My support person

from my self-advocacy group
says if I keep it up
I can write a book about myself
and publish it with a publishing house.

Publish it means it's in bookshops
and they sell it so other people read it.
Then I would be a writer
and you would be my readers.
I think that's crazy.
It's the craziest shoot that's happened to me
in my whole life.

I haven't been able to think about anything else
ever since Laia said that to me.
I spend all day studying
'Guidelines for Easy-to-Read Materials'
from the Section for Library Services
for People with Special Needs.

This digression has been really long.
This material,
like the guidelines book says,
isn't publishable any more.
That makes me kind of mad
because I spent four days writing it.
But I also know in films
writers make lots of paper balls
with things they wrote that aren't publishable
and throw them into the wastebasket
like basketballs.

I can't wait to finish this sentence
so I can plug my phone into the computer,
and download all these
unpublishable digressions,
and print them out,
and make a paper ball
and throw it in the trash.

I was running hot enough to hop the turnstile at the metro and I rode to Plaça d'Espanya feeling like a bastardist guerrilla. Everyone on the train was staring at me because I was in a nightgown and my gates were sealed shut, though saying they were staring at me is generous because on the metro no one stares at anything except their phones. I'll say, then, that they kept glancing at me, so I crossed my legs and started jingling my keys, the only thing I had with me. They deserved to be upbraided with a what the fuck do you think you're looking at, put your head back in its yoke and get back to ploughing your smartphone screen, but when you hop the turnstile you have to keep a low profile because at any moment the rent-a-cop with the puppy could show up, and he might call the ticket inspector and the ticket inspector might call the real cop and the real cop can stick you with a hundred-euro fine, and if you refuse to show your ID they'll beat the shit out of you before the unwavering passivity of the screenploughers who will, at best, in a heroic show of citizen journalism, lift their phones and document the excessive use of force so they can post it online while you lie writhing on the ground.

I headed down Bordeta, which is the only single-lane street off Plaça d'Espanya, meaning it's the quietest, the dirtiest and the one with the fewest shops. I hate bars, but I hate shops more than anything. Clothes shops are the worst, followed by bookshops and supermarkets. On Bordeta there isn't a single bookshop and there's only one clothes shop. There are two Pakistani supermarkets, one appliance store, one sports shop, one bank, one old man selling odds and ends heaped against the shop window, one high school, one daycare centre, five or six hovels for the local drunks, the offices of the PAH-Barcelona where Marga went to ask for information and left with her tail between her legs, and the Bloc La Bordeta (mothership of the Sants Housing Group), which was originally okupied by the PAH but has since been expelled from that organisation because ever since the PAH-Barcelona's patron saint Ada Colau was elected mayor, they can't allow the Bloc to promote unlawful squatting so joyfully, spitefully and efficiently. The two organisations coexist on Bordeta, but since they have radically different political outlooks (PAH-Barcelona is conciliatory insofar as it's allied with social services, whereas the Bloc is confrontational insofar as it's an illegal squat), they don't so much as acknowledge each other's presence. That's why the PAH sent Marga ten blocks west, to the anarchist social centre, which the pahcolauists, being innocent bureaucrats, consider a place with no real political impact where all she'll do is smoke weed.

Even though hardly anyone was looking at me now – partly because my gates were starting to pull back but mainly because people walking around in their nightgowns is nothing unusual in Bordeta – I grabbed a pair of pants I found on top of a dumpster. They looked all right, not shit-stained or blood-stained, soft cotton, loose, cool and lightweight, no pockets or buttons, with just a few small bleach spots, which must've been why the owner decided they didn't want them anymore. This leaving of clothes, furniture, books and food in good condition on top of or beside dumpsters, rather than inside them, is a common practice that I haven't seen anywhere in the world like in Barcelona. It's really an act of generosity, an anonymous, unconditional, easy, silent generosity with no intermediaries or bureaucracy, characteristics that set it apart from charity, NGOism and state welfarism.

The evening air wasn't refreshing because Bordeta isn't Barceloneta, and where Barceloneta has the polluted Mediterranean, Bordeta has the exhaust from the city's busiest avenue a few streets away. I always wash clothes from the trash before wearing them, no matter how decent they seem, but I was so hot in my synthetic nightgown that I decided to keep rummaging through the scrunched-up bundle left by a generous stranger for something else to wear. I pulled out a T-shirt with a cracked screen-print of a tacky kitten, which must have been why they threw it out (the cracking, not the tackiness). The generous stranger was starting to get on my nerves, because the kitten T-shirt clearly wasn't in usable condition, yet he'd deemed it good enough for the kind of people who go through the garbage looking for things they can't or won't buy at the store. If he were truly generous, he would have tried to get what was left of the cutesy kitten off before offering it to the public. Or, if he didn't feel like doing that, he should've put his shitty T-shirt in the dumpster with all the other garbage, or kept it to use as a rag. But no, there was nothing generous about this stranger. He was not a participant in the citywide dumpstertop supply network. He had gone to take out his dutifully separated trash and recycling, including clothes, for which there is also a dedicated bin (the only one apart from the glass bin from which you can't extract the contents) and, when he saw there was no clothing bin in the vicinity, after going to the trouble of looking for one up and down the block, the faux altruist decided to empty the contents of his bag (which he has to take back home to reuse – after all he paid two euros for it) on top of a dumpster, as he's seen and silently censured as a blight on the urban landscape dozens of times before, so he doesn't have to put his separated recycling into the wrong receptacle.

Clearly he has never taken anything from the garbage himself – not clothes, not food, not books, not furniture – because, if he had, he'd know you only leave things on top of dumpsters when they are at least minimally decent, when all they need is to be touched up or have the worn-out parts removed, if only out of respect for the human beings who go from dumpster to dumpster looking for sustenance. These people deserve respect not because they're underprivileged (as a charity would tell you), or because they're victims of savage capitalism (as an NGO would tell you), or because they're citizens of the Spanish state with equal rights and responsibilities (as the Commission on Family and Social Welfare would tell you). No, the dumpster-diver, the shoplifter and the tab-skipper deserve our respect and admiration and ought to serve as role models because they aren't complicit in supporting the true blights on this city, the motherfucking shops and the motherfucking bars.

In short: I threw the garbage in the dumpster, put the pants on underneath my nightgown, and took the nightgown off so I was left wearing only my bra, as cool and as ogled as can be, then went to drop in on the anarchists, the ones the PAH had referred Marga to, to see if they were doing anything that might wash the bad taste of the Barceloneta dancers from my mouth, maybe a party or a talk or some other opportunity to exchange pure, simple truths rather than personal opinions.

Never in all of my time in academia going to conferences, seminars, roundtable discussions and masterclasses had I heard such clear-sighted talk as that first time Marga and I went to the anarchist social centre. Babbling talk peppered with genuine pauses for thought, pauses that lasted as long as the speaker needed without some eager replicant seizing the silence. There were no rehearsed speeches, just talk passed through the twenty filters of the body. Since you could see how some people spoke with their cunts, others with their cunts and their calves, another with his limping leg, another with their carotid and another with her clavicle and her coccyx, there was no need for the speaker to offer opinions on the matter. The speaker owned their topic and universalised it for the rest of the room. I remember someone describing how much difficulty he'd had trying to throw Molotov cocktails at the front of a certain police station during an action because of the distance between the barriers and the building, and it wasn't some kind of testimony or personal story; there was no bomb-throwing hand and therefore there was no anecdote. There was only meaning, only the unveiling of a formerly hidden reality that the speaker, with his words, gave freely to whoever cared to listen. Thanks to the speaker, the rest of us became more discerning throwers of Molotov cocktails with regard to the complicated facade of that police station. What a gift, what a difference there is between selling an idea and giving the gift of meaning. What foul rhetoric in the commerce of ideas, in persuasion and insinuation, and what a happy lack of seduction in the free exchange of meaning! That was true generosity like good food left on the lid of a dumpster!

When Marga and I first visited, they had been discussing the potential benefits of joining a strike called by the Workers' Commissions and the General Union of Workers, whom they despised, but whose action they wanted to exploit for their own ends. They sat in a circle with no system for taking stack because they didn't need one: such was their capacity for listening, so easily did they perceive one another's desire to talk, so well did they discern the appropriate moment to contribute without bulldozing over anyone else, and when someone did begin bulldozing, how swiftly did the bulldozed speaker denounce the infraction; instantly he was joined by others, who tried to make the bulldozer see the error of his ways and warned that this was no place for prophets. The bulldozer didn't back down, he just got defensive and haughty, so the group argued him into a corner and the bulldozer ended up shouting over everyone and hurling insults. He was then invited to leave the premises, an invitation which of course he declined with those magic words: you're all a bunch of fucking fascists. I lost it! It was happening there, too! It turns out that fascists all come from the same factory and every one of them is programmed to say the same thing whenever anyone challenges their authority. It's the masculinist maxim, the dickbag dictum: for fascists, tolerance means the other person coming to their side. Chauvinazis can't stomach alterity unless it's grovelling before them or, at the very least, complicit with them, or, barring that, silent when it's around them, and really it'd be much better for everyone if alterity just went and killed itself. Marga and I had gone to the anarchist social centre without knowing anything about its syndicalist roots, and I can't speak for Marga, but within half an hour of arriving, I, a perfect stranger, had already been given the gift of an entire strike, and my gates had activated against this ungrateful tightwad who couldn't play nice with the other kids. When the time came to physically and verbally force him out, they told him: 'This is a politicised space, not a safe space for you to force your fascist bullshit down our throats. Take it to a fucking bar, or a fucking civic centre,' then slammed the door in his face. Everybody returned to their seats to resume the meeting.

What a beautiful afternoon that had been! What a desire to mash meanings together in my mouth so they could kiss and nourish one another! A new city had formed before my eyes, as if in the course of two hours Barcelona had burned to the ground and a new civilisation had risen in its place. That day they had looked at Marga and me like we were undercover cops dressed as allies, which is how they look at all unfamiliar faces the first time they set foot in an okupied space, or when they shout particularly loudly at a protest, or when they strike up a conversation with a Black street vendor or a sex worker or a scavenger pushing his shopping cart full of scrap metal down the street. But when I showed up this time, they looked at me differently because no police informant, no matter how committed to her role, walks down the street in just a bra with hairs twisting from her armpits. When I arrived they were watching a misogynistic insult of a documentary about Syrian women warriors that didn't feature a single Syrian woman warrior and, to make matters worse, the two times over the course of an hour that a woman did appear on the screen, it was so she could talk about the male warriors or set the table. But since afterwards there was going to be a three-euro dinner and a conversation with the director and a real live Syrian woman warrior, I stayed to eat and chat. I said, first of all, the documentary was filmed from the viewpoint of a well-meaning misogynist, for which the director recused himself by saying that the Syrian women warriors were the ones who declined to speak or appear on camera. Then I told the woman warrior I didn't know how she was with an assault rifle, but I thought she was absolutely incredible at serving tea, at which point the woman warrior and all the other anarchists accused me of Eurocentrism. And finally, I said I didn't have any money for dinner, but at the anarchist social centre, if you're broke and you say so, you don't have to pay.

An improvised porté that goes well is almost like a surprise kiss. A wished-for surprise kiss. Instructors say porté, which is French, but I've also heard them call it a pickup: we're going to do pickups, what a solid pickup, be careful when coming down from those trickier pickups. The latter term strikes me as ideal because it's sometimes used in sexual scenarios, and portés are essentially kisses that vary in length and pleasure, with or without a collision of teeth. I like to think that dancers who call it doing pickups are hoping to inculcate lubricity in their students, but after more than twenty years dancing I know that's not the case; they only call them that because they associate portés with the rancid art of classical ballet. The world of dance, sadly, is a conservative one.

That was what I said when they asked me about portés at the self-advocacy meeting that Patricia and Ángela attend every Tuesday, and which they forced me to go to this week. I did it for Marga, because she's a masturbatory mastermind who has successfully dildofucked her way to freedom: she is no longer required to attend the self-advocacy shitshow because she has been declared officially depressed. After spending weeks wrangling the diagnosis from the psychiatrist she finally received it yesterday, bucking reports from our psychologist and our caseworker claiming she's just sensitive to the heat and this has been an especially stifling summer, which they argue has prompted the recent uptick in the exhibitionist episodes that cause strangers to laugh or panic or call the Guàrdia Urbana, and which, in a few rare instances, have culminated in a sexual encounter, Marga's ultimate goal, the non-attainment of which has her locked in her bedroom masturbating with anything she can get her hands on. Needless to say, our psychologist Laia Buedo and caseworker Susana Gómez found this behaviour unacceptable and proposed purging her cunt and mind through a regimen of more frequent attendance at social and recreational activities organised by the local and regional UCIDs, including the Tuesday self-advocacy meetings, as these include educational sessions on sexual and reproductive health, with the aim of facilitating Marga's interaction with people her own age and from her own community, thereby favouring the establishment of a healthy intimate relationship with a male or female partner.

To my cousin's relief, and in an assertion of medical fascism's dominance over psychotherapeutic fascism, Marga's psychiatrist suggested and ultimately imposed one tablet of Tripteridol every twelve hours for two months and said that, after the pharmaceutical has worked its taming effect, Marga should not be forced to do anything she doesn't want to. And seeing as the caseworker frowned disapprovingly the other day when I came home at ten in the morning, right in the middle of her lecture on how to spread butter on bread, and since Patricia and Ángela would eat dick in order to keep the supervised flat, they've resolved not to let me out of their sight and decided to quit hounding Marga, who in any case has been taking the Tripteridol whenever her body craves it, and in the three hours it takes us to get to the self-advocacy meeting, sit through the self-advocacy meeting, and come back home from the self-advocacy meeting, Marga can head down to the street, bring whoever she wants to the apartment, and fuck them in peace (all the more so if she's tripping on the teridol), and if there are no takers or she doesn't feel up to it, she can masturbate in front of the living-room mirror and wail like a hog brought to slaughter. My cousin will masturbate with whatever's within reach, but her clitoris is so sensitive and her technique so advanced that she can get off without her hands or any object. She just kneels on all fours and moves her pelvis so that it rubs against the seams of her clothes; she can even do it with no contact at all, stimulating her genitals with movement alone. I taught her that: it's a warm-up exercise we do in dance classes. It loosens up all the muscles and joints below the hips. What you don't want to do is stretch like a cat; then you'll lose focus on the pleasure and work up a sweat for nothing. What you want to do is mentally locate, even just approximately, your hips, your lower abdomen, your pubis, the outer lips of your vulva, your perineum, your coccyx, your sit bones and your anus. The next level is locating your inner lips, vagina and rectum. After mentally locating all that, you stabilise yourself on all fours. Stabilising yourself means making your limbs like the four legs of a table. For this exercise, think of the tabletop as starting where the elastic of a very high-waisted pair of underwear would sit and ending at the crown of your head, which means your neck should be aligned in such a way that your gaze falls exactly on the floor between your hands. The way you hold your neck is critical. If your gaze falls further back and you're looking at your legs, or if it falls too far forward and you're looking at the wall, the exercise ceases to be masturbation and becomes a simple stretch to prevent lower back pain.

Once you've become a table, you need to become a table with an engine, except the engine should move you internally rather than through space; or you need to become a table holding a crystal ball pulsating with the vectors of the future: your internal engine or your crystal ball is the masturbatory system you identified previously. Massage it in the air, knead it with the air and knead the air with it, guiding it back and forth, in circles or semicircles, bouncing a little or not at all, slower or faster; follow your body's lead and it won't let you down. It's a low-intensity stimulation but it's surprisingly consistent over time. Ten minutes of this is like a ten-minute caress down the middle of your cunt. I've never come this way, but by the end my clit is sharp and tingling like it's gone through a knife sharpener. I come out of tabletop position to masturbate in the classic fashion and I'm good to go in three seconds flat.

That's what I'd started to say at the self-advocacy meeting, because I was the guest dancer. They asked about my classes and I started at the beginning, with the warm-up exercise and the latest trends in contemporary dance, which include the activation of the genitals, but as soon as I said the word vagina, the fascistically inevitable occurred: Patricia interrupted and prodded me to change the topic. My gates went click and the red LED lights scrolling across the front spelled IF YOU DIDN'T WANT ME TO TALK WHY DID YOU BRING ME HERE, YOU SUCKER OF PRECARIOUS CIVIL SERVANTS' COCKS. But in addition to being a sometime fascist, my sister is half blind and can't even read a flashing neon sign. This whole bit about LEDs is figurative, my gates aren't fitted with lights. What I mean is that Patricia is short-sighted and she was sitting some distance from me, so she didn't realise my gates had clicked into place or that the figurative message spelled out in LEDs was about to become a literal message on my lips. It's not my fault she's blind as a baseball bat and it's not my fault she's got a fascist streak, and she deserved to be smacked with a why did you invite me to speak if you just wanted me to echo your ding-dong talking points that aren't even yours, but I refrained. I felt sad for Patricia making a

70

politically correct spectacle of herself in front of the meeting's clown with a frown, by which I mean the self-advocacy support person who is in charge of moderating, which is to say rechannelling, which is to say censoring the conversation if it goes in certain directions, but whose censorship proved unnecessary in this case because my sister had taken the role of late-afternoon-talk-show host for herself. I felt sad for Àngels reading the first paragraphs of her novel from the screen of her phone and being congratulated. I felt sad for all the others who, when the support person asked where they were going on vacation, said PortAventura World, and I felt especially sad for the other self-advocate who had gates like mine but was holding them back with an exercise headband. It hurts like hell when they take the headband off, because as soon as they do, your already-tripped gates slam into each other and might even crack.

'What you want to do is mentally locate, even just approximately, your hips, your lower abdomen, your pubis, the outer lips of your vulva, your perineum, your coccyx, your sit bones and your anus. The next level is locating your inner lips, vagina –'

'Wow, Nati, the warm-up really sounds interesting. But since we don't have much time, why don't you skip right to telling us about that wonderful thing you do when you dance with a partner?' prodded Patricia.

I retracted my gates so her command could penetrate rather than ricochet back like salvos of authority usually do, so they wouldn't strike her full-on in the face and shatter her inch-thick glasses. Long-term planning is capitulation. Medium-term planning is capitulation. Short-term planning is capitulation. Any future projection is an institutional, which is to say a militaristic, which is to say a capitalistic pipe dream with which we've been indoctrinated and which does nothing but inhibit our immediate reaction, thereby giving the advantage to the aggressor, in this case my sister. And yet there I was, thinking I'd pocket her salvo to cash it in for something later.

So I left my description of the masturbatory apparatus half finished and told them about a dance jam where a bearded stranger and I did an extremely fast porté that lasted no longer than three seconds, but which was so well executed, so clean and ethereal, that I could still taste it on my body. That was when they asked me what a porté was and I gave the explanation about pickups. They also asked me what a dance jam was. I answered that it was a kind of improvised performance among dancers who may or may not know each other beforehand. Then they asked me to explain portés again because they still didn't get it.

'Is it a sex thing?' a self-advocate named Ibrahim asked with his forced guttural language, his shrunken hands, his knock knees and his walker.

'Ibrahim, with your one-track mind!' my sister interrupted again, only to be interrupted in turn by the support person:

'Patricia, please, why don't we let Ibrahim and Natividad talk?'

'Sorry, Laia.'

Such good manners from the fascist Laia and such unwavering obedience from my fascist sister.

'Well, sometimes it's a sex thing and sometimes it isn't, Ibrahim. It's sexual if you're predisposed to pleasure at all times. That doesn't have to mean you want to fuck all the time, it just means you're a pleasure-seeker, sort of like a detectorist scouring the beach for coins. It's very unlikely that a porté will give sexual pleasure. You and your partner have to miraculously act as the metal detector, both of you attentive to both bodies, listening for the beep, which means that you've touched or been touched in such an exact, precise way that you jolt awake and suddenly life has meaning, and everything you're thinking and everything you're doing comes to a halt and you start digging for buried treasure, meaning you give yourself over to your partner's arms, legs, back, or wherever the porté is going to materialise, and your partner, in turn, becomes your saviour, becomes the only person in the world for you, the person who will not let you fall under any circumstances and will stay with you until the end of the flight. That union is a good improvised porté. Is it the penetration of one body by another? No. Is it solitary or reciprocal masturbation? No, it's not that either.'

'You mean it's a quickie?' gargled Ibrahim.

'I have never experienced it as a quickie. For me, it's like a kiss, a long, soft-tongued kiss, where your tongue melts like ice cream on contact with the other's. So, returning to your original question: do we understand that kiss – not any kiss, but the one I just described – as a source of sexual pleasure? My answer is a resounding yes. So, if a porté is equatable to that kiss, then is a porté a sex thing? I must conclude that it is.'

'Thank you for explaining, Natividad. I have a hard time understanding what you say, but some of it sticks.' I had an even harder time understanding such a long sentence from Ibrahim, who has to slurp saliva with every word, but I think that's what he said. A good-looking male dudebro sitting beside him hurried to translate for me. At the same time, my male sister Patricia started translating my description. How thoroughly they've been indoctrinated not to ask others if they need or want help. How readily they've internalised the assistentialist maxim that helping means acting on behalf of others, which is to say representing them, which is to say replacing them. Behold, a legion of unpaid social workers under the command of one paid social worker, who watches from a folding chair as her conscripts wage war on the dark modes of speech: non-normalised serfs doing battle against their own non-normalised tongue to ensure that the normalised tongue, the language of the norms, the language of Angelita's novel, emerges triumphant. Fascist upon fascist and male upon male, the dozen or so self-advocates seized on the break in the usual enforced silence and erupted into loud chatter, giving Ibrahim and me sufficient cover to finish our conversation.

'No, thank you for asking about dance, and I'm sorry, I don't know how to express myself another way.'

'No problem. Do you understand me when I speak?'

'I can catch almost everything, and I can figure the rest out from context.'

'Then I'm going to ask you another question.'

'Go for it.'

'Do you think I could do a porté with you or you could do one with me?'

**Anarchist Social Centre – Acció Llibertària de Sants
Okupation Working Group
Meeting Minutes, 25 June 2018**

From the inventory of potentially okupiable dwellings, Gari Garay has requested the working group's assistance in scoping out the flat on Carrer del Duero, number 25, the flat on Viladecavalls, and the house on Mossèn Torné. She says she only explicitly mentions the number of the flat on Carrer del Duero because the inventory lists more than one dwelling on that street, and she stresses that except for in this one instance, she always keeps the numbers secret in all her conversations.

Mallorca tells her that scoping out a flat and okupying it are virtually always the same thing, except when it's in such uninhabitable condition that it has to be abandoned. This is because, Mallorca continues, opening a flat can be very complicated and it requires a lot of time and planning and people, which makes scoping out several dwellings before choosing one impracticable.

Badajoz agrees and recommends that G.G. check out the building from the outside to get an idea of its condition, and that she try to go in through the front door like a resident or a leaflet distributor to see how the stairway looks, and the lift, if there is one. Badajoz offers to go with G.G. to inspect the outside of the building and adds, lastly, that while it's important to be discreet when talking about okupation, among ourselves – whether in a meeting or just chatting informally – it's fine to say the street number.

Murcia offers to go with them and adds that the Mossèn Torné house is falling apart, he doesn't know how it's ended up on the inventory when the roof is half caved-in.

Coruña responds that the inventory had to include all of the uninhabited dwellings in the area, to which Murcia responds that besides being uninhabited they should also be okupiable, to which Coruña responds that the Mossèn Torné house is perfectly okupiable, and in fact it would be easier to okupy than lots of others because it's abandoned and dilapidated, which means it would take longer for anyone to realise you're living there and evict you. Murcia says it's hard to believe Coruña has been a squatter half his life and still doesn't know that the celerity of the eviction has more to do with the offers the owner is hoping to get from developers than with the condition of the house itself. But besides that, Murcia continues, okupying isn't just breaking and entering, it's breaking, entering and living with dignity, which is what this working group is for; that's why we self-designate as a self-managed space and why we advocate for self-management of other spaces, such as okupied houses, to which Coruña responds that living with dignity could mean different things to different people and maybe dignity should also be self-managed, seeing as everyone has different needs which they satisfy in different ways, because a family of five, for example, would need a flat with at least two bedrooms to live with dignity, at a push, whereas just one person could make do with a loft or a studio.

Or maybe they couldn't, says Ceuta, maybe one person needs three bedrooms and a patio for their own special needs.

Or their own preferences, says Tarragona, since there's nothing wrong with having preferences and we're not here to judge anyone's needs or motivations or whims.

Murcia says actually we are here to judge people's needs, because if a neo-Nazi shows up and says they need help okupying a house to hold their neo-Nazi meetings, we'd bust their ass and kick them out, wouldn't we?

Coruña responds that the eventual hypothetical suicidal neo-Nazi who's brazen enough to set foot in an anarchist space would never say that, and he asks Murcia if he's going to ask everyone who comes through the door if they're a neo-Nazi and what they plan to do in the house we're going to help them okupy.

Oviedo intervenes to say that, by the same token, we'd have to ask all the men who come to the okupation office if they're planning to abuse their girlfriends in okupied spaces, and adds that this is a very interesting thought experiment but we're approaching it from a position of postmodern banality with all this relativising of people's needs and dignity, because even neo-Nazis and wife-beaters need a home where the roof isn't caving in to live with dignity, on that point we'd agree even with the neo-Nazis and the wife-beaters, for which reason Oviedo thinks that surely we can agree on it among ourselves.

Murcia says he still doesn't know whether Oviedo has a favourable or unfavourable opinion regarding the Mossèn

Torné house and whether it should be struck from the inventory of okupiable dwellings.

Favourable, of course, Oviedo responds, but Murcia remains unsure and asks Oviedo if she means she has a favourable opinion of the house or a favourable opinion of striking it from the inventory, a question that unleashes a flurry of simultaneous comments that have not been entered into these minutes.

Several seconds later, resuming the normal sequence of listening and responding, G.G. says she doesn't know if she understood right but she thought she heard earlier that this working group advocated for self-management, to which several of those present respond in the affirmative, G.G. did understand correctly, absolutely, we are a self-managed space that advocates for self-management. G.G. then asks if that means we're self-advocates, to which Coruña responds he's never heard anyone use that term but it seems logical to him that if we advocate for self-management then we're also self-advocates. Badajoz objects, saying that that word reminds her of political advocacy and lobbyist talk, and she doesn't consider herself a self-manager, self-advocate or self-organiser, just an anarchist, plain and simple, since by calling herself an anarchist she's already implying that she manages her own conflicts and advocates for her own desires without forming part of the institutional, economic, social and cultural neoliberal circuits that forcibly organise all of us for our entire lives.

Ceuta says he believes in self-management and advocates for everyone to self-manage, so, bearing in mind that for whatever reason G.G. was the first one to take an interest in the Mossèn

Torné house, he suggests that she should be the one to decide if it's worth going to the effort of opening that house instead of another house that seems nicer.

G.G. says that seems good to her and Ceuta says she doesn't need to decide right now or tomorrow or next week, she can take as long as she needs to scope out the different buildings, calmly think it over and come back to the working group whenever she wants to share her decision.

G.G. thanks Ceuta for all the help and advice but says the thing that seems good to her is okupying the Mossèn Torné house right away, because she doesn't have enough time to calmly think it over because her current housing situation is critical. G.G. goes on to say that she made the decision while the other members of the working group were talking and she definitely understands that starting an okupa is never easy but it seems like that house might be easier than most.

Several members of the group insist that the house is in very bad shape, but if that's what she wants, more power to her.

Others insist that the house is in such bad shape that if they move forward with the okupation, once G.G. has got inside and sees how horrible it is she'll regret making such a hurried decision.

Tangier says that earlier someone said okupying isn't just a matter of breaking and entering, but breaking, entering and living with dignity; he adds that okupying isn't just a matter of breaking, entering and living with dignity, but breaking, entering, living with dignity and making all the repairs the house might need since, Tangier continues, you can't live with much dignity sleeping curled up in the corner because of the wind and rain, or shitting in a bucket, or not being able to make yourself a cup of coffee for breakfast, and he asks G.G. if she's up to making, or, rather, self-managing, all of those repairs, especially seeing as she wants to live alone.

Palma says that until a century ago everybody shat in a bucket, in a chamber pot to be specific, and nobody saw it as a matter of any great dignity or indignity. He also doesn't see how having coffee for breakfast is any more dignified than having, say, a croissant and a glass of orange juice, which you can make without gas or electricity, if it was the lack of gas and electricity that Tangier was referring to in his discussion of the dignity of coffee.

That's assuming that you bought the croissant at a bakery or stole it or took it from a dumpster, responds Tangier.

Of course, responds Palma, because I'm taking for granted that we don't usually bake croissants at home, which would of course require gas or electricity.

Or maybe not, since there are also wood-fired ovens, counters Tangier, who asks the working group if there is any likelihood that the Mossèn Torné house has a wood-fired oven so G.G. can make croissants for breakfast.

Ceuta says that there could definitely be a fireplace because it's a very old house.

Tangier says all this about shitting in buckets and having coffee for breakfast has really livened up the discussion, and he thinks that's wonderful, but we still haven't said anything about sleeping in a corner because of the cold and the rain, which would certainly seem to pose an obstacle to living with dignity and which seems to be the real issue with the Mossèn Torné house, given the half-caved-in roof.

Oviedo says that she personally shits not in a bucket but on the notion dignity, or, if not on dignity, the definition of which isn't very clear to her, then on the way we're using the expression 'live with dignity', which strikes her as newspapery and institutional, which is to say profoundly capitalist, because it refers only to the material conditions of life, as it implies that sleeping snug and warm is more dignified than sleeping frozen stiff. By that logic, Oviedo continues, someone sleeping on a memory-foam mattress is living with greater dignity than someone on a box spring, and a seafood platter on the water-front is a more dignified lunch than chickpea stew on a folding table, or McDonald's, or no lunch at all!

Tangier responds that she's taking things to extremes and lumping bourgeois comfort together with basic needs, the undoubtedly material needs that human beings, who are also, in fact, made of material, must have met just to survive; to which Oviedo rebuts that yes, she deliberately made an apagogic argument because we should take our thinking to its absurd conclusions to test for fallibility, i.e. its burden of reason, i.e. its truth, and this rationale about the dignified life doesn't hold up. Oviedo goes on to say that she consciously employed the *reductio ad absurdum* but that Tangier had just inadvertently employed two *reductiones ad identitatem*, i.e. two cases of analogy, progenitor of propaganda, by identifying or conflating, first, the material needs of human beings with human beings themselves and, second, by identifying or con-flating the bourgeois materialism to which she had referred earlier with the flesh and blood and bones and nerves of which we're all made.

Mallorca asks Oviedo to please explain a little more, and, when several others in attendance join in this request, Oviedo responds that she would be, in her words, delighted to. Tangier's analogies are, she says, fallacious in the argumentative sense and tending towards capitalist apologetics in the ideological sense. This is because Tangier establishes a link between dignity and material possessions, thereby reproducing the assistentialist, paternalist State discourse that says dignity where it ought to say welfare or well-being. And what is welfare? Oviedo asks, or rather asks herself rhetorically, before going on to say that she's referring to the welfare of the Welfare State, because in point of fact she believes that the concept of welfare did not exist before it was invented by the Western powers emerging from World War II or, if it did exist, it certainly didn't have the connotations that the aforementioned powers gave it and implemented from that point on. Post-war state welfare was erected, then, as the mechanism necessary to revive the economy in a devastated Europe and propel the United States into capitalist superstardom. Unemployment benefits, health insurance, bonuses, paid holidays, incentives to boost the birth rate, subsidised industries, cheapening of former luxury goods, expansion of school and universities systems. Oviedo goes on to say that she's not exactly breaking new ground when she talks about Keynesian recovery and the birth of consumerism, so she poses the question, this time to everyone and not just rhetorically to herself, of whether we're interested in what she's saying or if it would be better to go back to talking about the roof of the Mossèn Torné house, because we might be putting the horse before the cart by talking about, and Oviedo asks us to forgive the pun, an old nag like Keynes when we should be asking who can get their hands on a cement mixer.

Coruña responds that all this is new ground for him and Ceuta says that as far as he's concerned there is no distinction between reflection and action, as action, in this case okupying a derelict house, must always derive from a cause, and our cause is the establishment of an anarchist society. If that weren't the case, it would be an apolitical action, or at least unpoliticised in the radical sense, and insofar as it was non-radical it would be rendered inoffensive, disarmed, and vulnerable to attacks by the oppressor, the oppressor(s) in this case being the property owners who would want to reclaim full domain over the house, the judge who would order the dispossession of its occupants and the Mossos d'Esquadra who would carry out the eviction. Ceuta concludes that if our action is not going to be reduced to mere activism, then he views it as not only good but essential for us to talk about okupation, cement mixers, the price of potatoes, John Maynard Keynes and Paulo Freire all at once, and he implores Oviedo to please continue, and Oviedo continues, but says that before continuing on the topic of dignity she wants, first, to thank Ceuta for his very emboldening reflection and, second, to have the meeting minutes reflect that the seemingly benevolent subsidies she mentioned earlier would not exist without the other hallmarks of the Welfare State, including the hardening of the criminal code, the expansion of prisons and mental hospitals in size and number, television and advertising, the psychiatric and pharmaceutical industrial complexes, the annihilation of rainforests and other natural spaces, and the periodic instigation of wars in countries on the margins of development for the exploitation of natural resources, to name just a few of the self-evident pillars of this Welfare or Well-being that has convinced us all, including many in attendance at this meeting, that living well means enjoying ease of consumption, elevating the consumer lifestyle to the category of living with dignity, thereby dispossessing dignity of its former moral weight, a moral weight that this working group ought to lay on the table, Oviedo argues, as we ask ourselves if, when it comes to helping G.G. start an okupa, we should prioritise strictly material considerations, such as the roof and the lack of running water, or considerations without objects as their ultimate goal, such as, for example, the need to escape from a critical family and personal situation, as G.G. herself wrote in her case for okupation and as she repeated here only a moment ago, which constitutes no less than a peremptory need for emancipation on which the cold, the rain and the chamber pot have little bearing.

Tangier replies that he doesn't think having a house with a roof and a toilet constitutes succumbing to consumerism and capitalism and, moreover, it seems to him that branding the desire for basic sanitary conditions as bourgeois is the kind of argument made not by the bourgeoisie, but by a far more vicious kind of oppressor, namely, the revolutionary leader who uses the rhetoric of emancipation to justify the misery of the pawns of the revolution. Following Tangier's comment and before the other attendees continue the debate, this notetaker reminds the working group that it's nearly midnight, that the primary interested party, G.G., left half an hour ago, and that we still haven't addressed any of the other items on the agenda.

Palma asks if we should continue the debate on living conditions and dignity, though it makes little sense since G.G. had to go, or if we should move on to the other agenda items, or if we should all go home and continue in an extraordinary session tomorrow or the day after, to which this notetaker is the first to respond, emphasising that he has to go right this very second because the metro closes in five minutes, getting up, gathering his things, finishing this sentence on his feet, asking everyone to let him know what they decide over Telegram and announcing that somebody else will have to take over the minutes.

NOVEL
TITLE: MEMOIRS OF MARÍA DELS ÀNGELS
GUIRAO HUERTAS
SUBTITLE: MEMORIES AND MUSINGS
OF A GIRL FROM ARCUELAMORA
(ARCOS DE PUERTOCAMPO, SPAIN)
GENRE: EASY READ
AUTHOR: MARÍA DELS ÀNGELS GUIRAO HUERTAS
CHAPTER 2: THE JOURNEY BEGINS

4) The fourth something Mamen
told my uncle and me
was actually the first thing,
but Mamen explained it last
because it was the most complicated.
It turns out the fourth something
was what made the other three possible.
If I wanted the Social Security benefit
and if I wanted to live in Somorrín
I had to go to the doctor
and the doctor had to see me
and I'd have to show Mamen
the papers he gave me.
The sooner I went to the doctor

and the sooner I had the papers
the sooner they would give me the money
and the sooner I would go live in Somorrín.

My uncle asked Mamen
if I was sick
since I had to go to the doctor.
Even though my uncle wasn't very smart
and didn't even know how to read
it was like he
was reading my mind.
Then Mamen said
I was healthy, thank God,
but healthier in my body than in my mind.
Then my uncle asked
if Mamen was a doctor
since she was so sure
about whether I was healthy or not.
And he asked if what she said
about my mind being less healthy than my body
meant I was crazy.
Then I got kind of scared
because I never heard Uncle Joaquín
talk so seriously
or lean so far forward in his chair.
He was almost touching Mamen
on the other side of the table.
Even at my mother's funeral
he didn't look so serious.
My mother was Uncle Joaquín's sister
and at her funeral
my uncle sang the song 'El Vito'.

The words are
Con el vito vito vito
con el vito vito va.
The words don't mean much
and it's not a sad song.

Mamen didn't get mad at my uncle
for being so serious.
She said she was sorry
because she wasn't doing a good job explaining it
and she asked me
to please leave the house for a minute.
The house only had one room
and we were already in it.
The only other room
was La Agustinilla's stable.

I want to make something clear:
in Spanish, when you say an animal's name
you can put an 'El' or a 'La'
in front of the name
even though you're not speaking Catalan.
That's why you can say
'La Agustinilla' or 'El Refugiat'.
But if La Agustinilla was a woman
and not a horse
and if El Refugiat was a man
and not a dog
you would have to say just
'Agustinilla' and 'Refugiat'.
El Refugiat is the last stray dog
in Barceloneta
and maybe in all of Barcelona.

I decided I might as well start
picking the biggest heads of lettuce
while Mamen and Uncle Joaquín were talking.
A neighbour came over
to ask what my uncle was doing
and I said he was with Mamen
talking about getting papers from the doctor.
The neighbour was Romualdo's mom, Eulalia.
She took care of Romualdo
and Romualdo took care of the rabbits.
Eulalia said the same thing happened to her
because they wanted to take Romualdo away
but she didn't let them
because if they took him to the house in Somorrín,
they would replace his child benefit
with the mental retardation benefit
and even though the mental retardation benefit
was more money
they would keep it all
and besides
if her son went away
Eulalia would be alone
without anyone to help her in the field.
Then she said she was going to take Romualdo
to the mental retardation doctor herself
and submit the papers herself
so she could keep the money
without anyone getting in the way.

That was the first time I heard
someone say mental retardation
and even though I didn't usually listen to Eulalia
because everyone knew

she was a drunk
and she used poor Romualdo
like a pack mule
I kept thinking about what she said
about the mental retardation
and how there was lots of money.

I wanted to ask Mamen about it
but when I went back she was gone.
You can say lots of things about Mamen
but you can't say
she didn't answer your questions.
Mamen had an answer for everything.

Since she wasn't there
I asked my uncle.
But he had already talked enough
for the day and for the whole week
and didn't answer.
He just said
if I wanted to go to Somorrín
I should go
and that was that.
I knew it would be dumb to insist,
so I washed the lettuce
and made dinner.

The next day
I went to talk to Romualdo
when he was alone
and working hard in the field
which was how he
spent most of his time.

He said he didn't want to go to Somorrín
even though it was true a lot of people
from Arcuelamora and other villages
had gone there.
He said it was OK for them
because they didn't have to work like him
and they didn't have
rabbits and hogs to feed.
Did you know the Gonzalos went? he said.
Old Gonzalo or young Gonzalo? I asked.
Both Gonzalos, he said.
Both Gonzalos? I asked
because I thought it sounded weird.
Both Gonzalos, he repeated.
I thought old Gonzalo had a girlfriend, I said.
I guess he doesn't any more.
You know Tomás's daughter Encarnita from Cuernatoro?
he said.
What about her? I said.
Her and her cousin
went too, he said.
Cuernatoro is a village
about as big as Arcuelamora.
They're famous for a procession with Jesus on the cross
that happens in October.
I remember the conversation about Encarnita
because she was the prettiest girl at my school
and the best singer
and I thought if she went to Somorrín
it couldn't be so bad.

I remember the conversation about the Gonzalos
because they were famous in Arcuelamora and other places

because when they were in the army
they beat up a sergeant
and then all the other sergeants
beat them up back.
They were beaten up so bad
young Gonzalo ended up with a limp
and old Gonzalo ended up with one eye
but they were also lucky
because they didn't get the death sentence.
The death sentence is when the government kills you
for doing something very bad.

Young Gonzalo was also famous
because back then people kept saying
he was the one who got Aunt Araceli pregnant
with my cousin Natividad,
who lives with me now,
who was four or five years old back then.
She has the same Gypsy nose as young Gonzalo
and the same front teeth.

I remember how when Romualdo
told me the Gonzalos
went to Somorrín too,
I couldn't imagine Encarnita
living in the same house as them.
But then I remembered Mamen saying
the house in Somorrín was big
and I thought maybe it was so big
they wouldn't bother each other.

Romualdo told me about lots of other things
but he didn't know anything

about the mental retardation.

I want to make sure something else is clear.
The conversations I write here
didn't go exactly like the way I write them.
I write them like I remember them
and I might forget things
or add things.
They always do that in books
so readers understand better
because if I had to write
all the things Romualdo said
about his rabbits and his hogs
I would never finish this book in my life
and my readers would get bored
and I would get bored too.

On page 72 of the book
'Easy Read: Methods for Composition and Evaluation'
by Óscar García Muñoz
from the Royal Board on Disability
at the Ministry of Health, Social Services and Equality,
it says to eliminate any kind of unnecessary
content, ideas, terms and sentences.
Content means what's in the book.
Terms means words.
Sentence means lines of words
and it has nothing to do with the death sentence.
Unnecessary means not necessary.
It also says on page 72
to only give the reader information he can use
and to leave out anything he doesn't need to know.
The reader of this book about my life

can be more than one person,
even though it says reader not readers,
and he can also be a woman,
even though it says he and not she.
He can even be more than one woman reader,
so he'd be women readers.
But whoever he is
he can't use information
about Romualdo's rabbits and hogs
but he does need to know
that I didn't know
how much money they give you for the mental retardation
or what the mental retardation doctor was going to do to me.
I only went to a doctor
two times before in my life.
I went the first time because I fell off a rock
and they gave me stitches in my head and a shot.
I went the second time
so they could give me the shot a second time.

A few days later Mamen came back
but she didn't go straight to my house
like she did the other times.
First she went to Josefa's house.

Josefa was my cousin.
She lived with her father,
who was my Uncle Jose,
and with her half sister Margarita,
who is one of the cousins I live with now
but back then she was 11 years old.
When my mom died

I wanted to live with Uncle Jose
because he was younger and talked more than Uncle Joaquín,
and because me and Josefa were friends,
but there was no space left in his house.

Mamen left Uncle Jose's house
holding Josefa's hand
and also holding a string of chorizo she got
as a gift from the last slaughter
of one of Romualdo's hogs.
She opened the door in the front of her car
on the side the driver doesn't sit in
and Josefa got in
and just sat there
with the door open
saying goodbye to half Arcuelamora.
My uncle was in the field with La Agustinilla,
and I was darning a shirt and sitting
on the tree stump we used to hull almonds.
I got up to go and say something to Josefa
because I figured
she must know more than me
about the doctor and the money
and she looked happy.
But then Mamen started walking towards my tree stump.
It was summer and people were staring at Mamen
because she was wearing really short shorts
and a strappy top.
Uncle Jose and other men
who were there to say goodbye to Josefa
called her pretty and said other things about her too.
About Mamen, not Josefa.

Mamen smiled
and kept walking straight to my stump.
She kissed me on both cheeks,
and looked at my shirt
and said I was very good with needles.
I was embarrassed by my shirt
because the strappy top Mamen was wearing
was so pretty.
So I told her a lie.
I said it was Uncle Joaquín's shirt
and not mine.
She asked if she could talk to him
and I said he wasn't there.
That wasn't a lie.
She asked if I'd thought about it.
Thought about what? I said.
About coming to Somorrín, she said.
It was my last chance
to ask her the important questions.
Mamen, what's the mental retardation?
I asked.
Then Mamen's eyes got really big
and she asked who said that to me.
I played dumb
because I felt like I said something bad
or told a secret.
I thought maybe Eulalia
taking Romualdo
to the mental retardation doctor
so she could keep the money
was a secret.
And since I didn't want

to get Romualdo in trouble
I played dumb
and let Mamen talk.
She grabbed both my hands.
I was still holding the torn shirt
and I got stuck by the needle
but I didn't say anything.
She said: Angelita,
you are not retarded.
The person who said that to you is retarded.
Eulalia, I thought,
but I didn't say it.
Then Mamen said:
You're a young woman
with your whole life ahead of you
and you have the right to do
all the things the other girls your age do:
get a job,
go out with your friends,
get dressed up for parties,
instead of being stuck
in a village in the middle of nowhere
mending an old man's clothes.
The next time someone calls you retarded,
you just tell them:
retard schmetard nipple twister
the retard here's your daddy's sister,
all right?
That's what Mamen told me.
I think she thought
Uncle Joaquín was the one
who said the thing to me

about the mental retardation,
because she didn't even wait
for him to get back from the field
to put my clothes in the trunk,
even though Mamen was usually so polite.

Statement by Ms Patricia Lama Guirao, made before the Fourth Investigating Judge of the Court of Barcelona on 01 July 2018, as part of the court proceedings for authorisation of the sterilisation of an incompetent individual arising from the action brought by the Generalitat of Catalonia against Ms Margarita Guirao Guirao.

Investigating Judge: The Hon. Guadalupe Pinto García

Clerk: Mr Sergi Escudero Balcells

I'll say it to Your Honour just like I said it at the self-advocacy group, and maybe you can explain to me some reason on earth why Nati and Marga think they've got to jump the gate at the metro even though the four of us already get Pink Cards for being disabled and that makes it three times cheaper than the normal ten-trip ticket. A T-10 costs €10.20, with the Pink Card it's only €4. That's forty cents a trip! What people wouldn't give to save that kind of money and not risk getting caught! I mean sure, Your Honour, there was a time I used to jump the gate too, back when Àngels, Nati, Marga and me first got to Barcelona. But that was just because back then we didn't have a pot to pee in or even enough cash for cigarettes because Aunt Montserrat was keeping all Nati and

Marga's money for herself until the Generalitat declared them legally incompetent.

Do you have any idea how many cigarettes I've had to bum off strangers? Hundreds! At least if you're a woman you can always get one off a guy as long as you 'skank it up' a little. No man's ever denied me a cigarette in my life, but I guess if you're young enough and hot enough you don't even really have to 'skank it up' at all but, well, you do anyway out of gratitude. So yes, at a time when I was so clearly at risk of social exclusion I did jump the gate and I get why other folks in that same situation do it too, I'd never dream of judging someone for it, not like those old farts who're always out there shaming people for jumping. Even though they get their own Pink Card for being seniors! It's easy to tell someone they ought to pay €10.20 for a T-10 when you've got a €4 Pink Card in your pocket! But that's the generation gap for you, Your Honour, the difference between old politics and new politics.

I'm saying all this because it has to do with the points in favour and against. See, I got my cousins and my sister together the day it was my turn to cook and I told them I wasn't gonna make lunch until they heard what I had to say, and believe it or not none of them put up a fight. Àngels was watching *The Simpsons* with a bag of Cheetos between her legs, she was eating with one hand and writing her novel on her phone with the other. Marga still hadn't showered and she was staring off into space on the balcony, out in the blazing sun at two in the afternoon, how she stands it I couldn't tell you, and Nati, she was in her room reading one of her little booklets with one leg up in the air.

We gathered in the living room and Àngels turned off the TV without being asked first, and I thought that was polite of her, though she only did it because she already knew what this was all about, since originally she was gonna be the one to break the news before we agreed I should do it, one because Àngels can never get past her stutter when she has to talk about serious things and two because we didn't want Nati and Marga thinking she was taking advantage of her position as the treasurer and the least disabled in our flat (God help us, Your Honour) to go lecturing at us. I will say, sometimes I have to remind them it was Àngels who got us out of the hellhole of Somorrín and sneaked [*sic*] across Spain with three cousins hiding beneath her skirts until we got to Aunt Montserrat's house in Barcelona, and then after that it was Àngels who fought to get us out of Aunt Montserrat's house and into the supervised flat, so what I'm saying is if Àngels wanted to, and if she could get a sentence out without stuttering, she might have a lecture or two we could stand to hear.

I was feeling anxious so I pulled off my glasses and pinched the top of my nose like anxious people always do in movies, and I stared at the floor with my forehead in one hand and my glasses in the other. I was wearing my dress with the parrots on it, it shows off my back really nicely, backless dresses changed my life, Your Honour, because my tits might be nothing to write home about but I have shoulder blades that jut out like knives and they're sexy as [*expletive*], it's like having tits on my back. Then I spat it out: Nobody panic or anything, but our caseworker and the director of the flat haven't been too happy with us lately.

Silence for several long seconds. I figured Àngels was keeping quiet so as not to influence the way our cousins responded one way or the other, and I thought Nati and Marga must be chewing on what I just said, or maybe as the most and second-most retarded [*sic passim*] in the flat they hadn't understood and I'd have to find another way to explain it. But then I put my glasses back on and what do I see? Àngels is still tapping away on her phone, Marga's still staring out onto the balcony, and Nati's still reading her little booklets. Apparently, I hadn't managed to convey with my words a serious but optimistic message that expressed the gravity of the situation and still allowed room for dialogue. So what the [*expletive*] had I conveyed? What part of 'the boss ladies aren't happy' was so hard to understand? Easy now, gorgeous, cool your jets, I told myself. Uncross a leg, cross the other, and tell them again, glasses on this time, use that expression of yours, halfway between sexy and alarmed, like a female superhero when the bad guy's got her chained up at the wrists and ankles, and see if you can't dig the other three pairs of eyes out of their flowerpots and onto yourself, like they're the Van Gogh sunflowers hanging on the wall in the laundry room and you're the mothertrucking [*sic*] sunshine. So I went at it again, a sentence for each of them: Guys, there is something important you have to know. Miss Diana and Miss Susana are not happy with us because of a handful of little incidents we've had recently. But don't worry, because the only thing in life that can't be solved is death.

Did I not say this with the best manners possible? Did anything in my tone suggest I was faking [*sic*] the piss? Didn't I deserve some kind of reasonable response, something other than Nati saying to me, 'Sorry, Patri, I'm so sorry, but you're wrong, death can, in fact, be solved'? I unrecrossed [*sic*] my legs again, dug in both my heels and resolutely told her I had no intention of getting into an argument with her over whether or not death can be solved, because with my half-sister you can't have a civilised argument about a single [*expletive*] topic because I swear to God if there's one thing that can't be solved it's her [*expletive*] attitude seeing as this whole time she'd just been flipping through her booklets even though someone was trying to talk to her and in these particular circumstances that someone happened to be me. And when she finally stops reading it's so she can correct me, she says they're not booklets, they're 'scenes' or 'seams', some word I didn't understand, and she asks why don't I say the same to Àngels? Isn't Àngels also being disrespectful by not putting down her [*expletive*] phone? She had a point, Your Excellency, I don't think it would've killed Àngels, as the least disabled, to set the tiniest snitch [*sic*] of an example by putting down her [*expletive*] phone for five [*expletive*] minutes, but anyway since Nati had used the word [*expletive*] instead of dealing with Àngels I went off on Nati for using such foul language with her own sister.

Now I was all worked up by this point and I knew it was coming across so I just let it all out: Miss Susana gave us an unfavourable report this month and Miss Diana confirmed it and she called Àngels a few days ago, Miss Diana did I mean, to say she was concerned about us. Isn't that right, Ángela? I asked my cousin. And, Your Honour, I was in such a rage at this point that by accident I called her 'Ángela' in Spanish instead of 'Àngels' in Catalan and, lo and behold, Àngels, who hadn't even looked up from her phone to watch *The Simpsons*, looks up at that exact moment so she can correct me too, saying her own name with as much Catalan in her accent as a rural Arcuelamoron [sic] stutterer can manage.

By this point my right heel was tapping away like a sewing machine needle and that was making my whole leg and the parrots on that side of my dress jiggle. Perfect, Your Honour, I am not. When, in this life, have I ever claimed to be perfect? I've got to be corrected and educated just like anyone else, because all anyone on this earth is born knowing how to do is eat and [*expletive*] and [*expletive*], and even then, we only know how to eat and [*expletive*] and [*expletive*] like animals, not like people, and that's what I've been trying to do for thirty-three years: learn, with the proper support structures, the aptitudes and social skills necessary to become a fully-fledged member of the community and an integrated citizen whose neurodiversity contributes to the plurality, welfare and abundance of democratic societies.

'Patri, you talk like a two-bit public servant impersonator. It's too bad. You used to be such a delinquent,' Nati says to me, and at that point I'd totally had it and I told them they could all [*expletive*] a duck and [*expletive*] it out their [*expletive*], and I stormed out of the living room to make lunch but when I hacked at the carton of tomato sauce with the scissors it splashed on my dress and glasses and I started crying, and they'd put *The Simpsons* back on so they couldn't hear me and obviously that just made me cry harder. I always watch myself in the mirror when I cry, I've done it since I was little. Psychologists from all the different schools of thought will tell you crying is healthy and restorative because it means you aren't holding back. But if crying is healthy, man oh man, watching yourself cry in the mirror is like being born again. Your sobs start stretching longer and longer and you cough and splutter and heave and kick and knock things over and fling tomato sauce and pull everything out of the cupboard and hurl it on the ground and pour out all the milk and olive oil and bite the scouring pads and flip the trash and soon, soon you're not crying about what made you cry, no, you're crying for the sheer joy of it. And after you run out of steam you get a sweet hit of lethargy and it's not from Valium or Xanax, oh no, it's from all the 'hysterapeutics' in the mirror. You've gotta make the most of the fits when they strike, so I grabbed an aluminium pot lid to watch myself in because we don't have any mirrors in the kitchen, just a tiny reflective magnet slash souvenir on the fridge. I would've relieved myself with my compact except it was in the other room and I couldn't leave the kitchen because I wanted them to hear me sobbing alone and feel bad, but none of those fatties was gonna hear a thing because they were too busy having the same fight as every other Monday, where Nati says it's her day to choose what they watch on TV and her choice is to watch nothing and keep the TV turned off, and Àngels says if Nati gives up her right to pick the show then it transfers to someone else because we fought too hard for our rights to waste them, and Marga says if the right to pick the show transfers to someone else why does it have to go to Àngels and not to her because she wants to watch a dirty movie and not *The Simpsons*. But thanks to her new-found depression Marga didn't have much fight in her so she moped her way into the kitchen and saw me and said: 'Patricia, you really are a hopeless retard.' As soon as she said that I grabbed the sharpest knife in the block because I swear to God she said 'retard' just to [*expletive*] with me, Your Honour, she's been such a [*expletive*] since she became aware of her disability. Me and her both went to the CEMICA school until we were seventeen but Marga doesn't call it 'the CEMICA school' any more (because God forbid anything anyone says in our flat should be [*expletive*] normal and undramatic), she spells it out and says 'the Centre for Mentally Impaired Children of Arcos'. Do you have any idea what kind of a look people give you when they hear that? So of course then my face contorts to look all impaired! She won't say FAMR any more either, she spells it out and says, 'The Federation of Advocates for the Mentally Retarded cordially invites us to a talk by Pablo Pineda, the first European man with Down's syndrome to get a university degree and win Best Actor at the San Sebastian International Film Festival.' But there I've got her because after fifty-one years, FAMR has finally changed its name and now they call it Inclusion Europe. How do you like that, Miss Margarita, huh? What do you have to say to that, huh? Huh? Huh?

Honestly I knew she'd have a comeback, but I also knew it'd take her a minute to think one up, and for that one glorious minute, Inclusion Europe and me were the winners.

Right, so basically she called me a hopeless retard and in legitimate self-defence, Your Honour, I made an exceptional, proportional and decisive response, as one must give in such situations, and said, 'Retard schmetard nipple twister, the retard here's your daddy's sister.' She smiled her depressed smile, gap teeth like the bars of a cage where something's trying to fly free behind the tartar build-up, some sparrow not used to being caged or a butterfly with its wings sticking to Marga's yellow saliva, and she goes and says back to me: 'Patri, you do know my daddy's sister is your mother, right?' Now I'm sorry, but that's not awareness of disability, that's just hurtful and rude. I was still holding the knife but I'm a pacifist so I just picked up the aluminium lid and went back to my hysterapeutics.

At this point Àngels comes in with her phone still in her hand and stares at the mess from the doorway and asks me if I'm trying to get us kicked out too, then Nati comes in asking what's all this about getting kicked out and telling me I'd thrown a pretty top-notch tantrum. As soon as she comes through the door she puts a hand between my shoulder blades and goes: 'Like back in Somorrín!' With all three of them in the room I eased up on the crying a little and started cleaning. At the RUCID we used to have this drama teacher who always said it's easier to talk truthfully and naturally when your hands are occupied and she was right, because as soon as I started sweeping I felt like talking again. I said they'll take away the flat if we keep this up, and Nati stepped out of the way of the broom and said if we keep what up, and Àngels started stuttering her way through the *Aberrant Behaviour Checklist Community Version Second Edition* saying if we keep up the problematic behaviour, disruptive actions and slash or behavioural disturbances. Then she glanced at her phone and typed something quickly. At this point I knew lunch wouldn't be ready until after four because Nati just couldn't help herself and said, 'Ángelita, have you ever considered shoving that phone up your [*expletive*] and leaving it there until it prompts you to enter your PIN like an ATM?' I know, I know, my sister Natividad's got quite a mouth on her, Your Honour, I'm sorry. By now I'm super sedated from all my crying, and I very politely and lovingly explain to Nati how that's exactly the kind of language they're gonna kick us out for, and Àngels butts in to say for our information she's on her phone so much because she's writing her memoirs. Truth be told, Your Honour, the phone is good for my cousin Àngels, if she can spend all day on her phone she doesn't need Valium or Tripteridol or hysterapeutics or anything, it makes her so tolerant and mild-mannered that a guy on the beach could come up to her and say he'd like to [*expletive*] all over those cow tits of hers and all she'd do is take a photo of her cleavage to see for herself. But Nati lost it, couldn't get it through her head that Àngels was writing a novel on WhatsApp and sending it to the whole self-advocacy group WhatsApp group chat. And it's not Nati's fault, the poor thing. Back in the day she went to the dance conservatory and university and got good grades and all the scholarships, but since the Gate Control syndrome got hold of her she hasn't been able to wrap her head around lots of advanced technologies like smartphones, so it makes sense she gets frustrated and upset, and it's understandable she can't find other outlets for her frustration, it's just like I always say, Your Honour, we've got to be humble, got to be inclusive, can't go treating each other like second-class citizens, because neurodiversity can strike at any point in life, without warning, when you least expect it, like it striked [*sic*] Nati two months before getting her PhD. But have no fear, her sister Patri is here to explain things to her, twenty times over if I've got to. I said: 'Nati, the book Àngels is writing is a point in favour of not kicking us out of the flat. On the other hand, you showing up at ten in the morning and swearing in front of everyone and not paying for the metro and encouraging Marga not to pay either are all points against us. A point in favour would be if you'd start going to the integrated dance classes Laia told you about at the self-advocacy meeting.' (Miss Laia Buedo, Your Honour, is the psychologist who acts as our self-advocacy group's support person.) I could hear Nati's gates shifting into place so I stopped listing the points in favour and against her and said, still very kindly, 'It's not all your fault though, OK? There's lots of points against Marga too,' and then I turned to my cousin and, again, with all the loving kindness in the world, I said, 'Look, Marga, a big point in our favour would be if you got a boyfriend, because the main point against you is you go out in the middle of the day the same as a "prozzie" and people in the neighbourhood end up calling the police for public indecency, and you go into strangers' houses the same as a "prostiputa" except you don't get paid.' 'Would it be a point in our favour if they paid her?' Nati asked with all the retard cheek God gave her. I said to myself, 'Don't pay her any attention, Patri, you gorgeous thing you, like water off a duck's beak [*sic*], don't let Nati bring you down to her level, today the kitchen is "Patrician" territory.'

I was trying to do what our old drama teacher said, about words coming out more authentic when your hands are occupied, but when you're a nearsighted sclerotic like me it's hard to talk and clean and be authentic all at once and I was just making things worse, sloshing around the concoction of olive oil, milk, tomato sauce and canned beans, and while I was busy explaining the points in favour and against, my cousin Marga, she started cleaning with this special touch she's got, she was born to clean. If she ever felt so inclined (and if she could get the stimming in her hips under control for a few hours at a time), she could make herself some good money working at Eulen or Castor Cleaning, I'm sure the Generalitat would give her permission, Your Honour, what with it being in the best interest of the incompetent individual and all, they'd probably even waive the companies' Social Security contributions to reward them for hiring someone legally incompetent. Oh, and it'd be a point in favour of letting us keep the flat! Since she'd be taking steps towards independent living and all. And if they won't give her the work authorisation or the companies don't want retards on the payroll, Marga could just put in hours off the books at somebody's house, because check this out, listen to what a gifted mop-jock my cousin is: first she picks up the forks and knives and the dishes that didn't break because they're metal or plastic or wood and puts them in the sink. Then she lays down paper towels to soak up most of the liquid and picks up the shattered glass and ceramic, and that all takes a while because the kitchen had really gone to [expletive]. Then she goes to the laundry room for the mop bucket and she rinses it out in the washbasin because there's always a little bit of grits [sic] left from the last time she used it. Then she goes to the laundry room barefooted because her flip-flops got mucky in the kitchen and she doesn't want to track muck all over, so she takes them off and leaves them oriental-style on the dirty fake parquet floor in the kitchen. She comes back leaning a little to one side from the weight of the bucket, holding it with her inner arm tense all down her hand where she's holding the bucket handle like she's making one of those solidarity fists except upside down, pointing towards the ground instead of towards the sky, and at that point she puts her flip-flops back on and does a first pass with the mop, without floor cleaner the first time so we don't slip but also so when she starts sweeping the broom doesn't get gunked. What more do you need to know to see the girl's got a gift? Me, I'm 14 points less disabled than her, and that kind of a cleaning tactic would never occur to me in a million years!

Meanwhile I was talking Nati's ear off and for her part Nati was glaring into the living room and talking Àngels' ear off because Àngels had just put *The Simpsons* back on, and Nati was all, do you think you own this flat or what, do you think just because you're ten years older than us and you've got your own bank account we all have to do whatever you say, do you think just because you got us out of Somorrín and brought us to Barcelona you get to lord it over us the rest of our lives, and the whole time Àngels is just quiet as a house [*sic*], typing a jillion words a minute on her phone while Nati keeps railing at her like, do you think not responding is some kind of sign of distinction or moral high standing because if you do you're dead [*expletive*] wrong because all it is is a sign of resignation, all it is is 'silence is consent', whatever that means, Your Honour, but Nati said it meant Àngels really did think she was the boss of the flat and more intelligent than the rest of us, but what Nati doesn't understand, Your Honour, is that that's partly true because Àngels is the least disabled of the four of us. But my sister Nati is severely disabled to the tune of 70 per cent and doesn't have awareness of her disability so she never understands nuanced things like that.

Then I felt a pang, but in my soul, because in the middle of this whole clusterfunk [*sic*] poor Margarita was still in the kitchen cleaning without a word. I told Miss Laia Buedo the psychologist about my pang and she says it's remorse, i.e. I felt bad watching my cousin silently cleaning, even though I didn't feel a pang when I saw Àngels sitting silently in the living room, but Nati says that's different because Àngels is silent the same way President Sánchez is silent when he doesn't take questions at a press conference or like the same silence as when guys on the street say baby you got such pretty eyes I wanna eat your whole [*expletive*] but when you stop and ask them to repeat what they just said they don't. So why was I 'panged' by Marga's silence but not Àngels'? Before I told Miss Laia about my pang I told Nati, and she said it was because Marga's silence was different and my pang wasn't remorse, it was recognition of an injustice, in this case the injustice of Marga having to clean up my mess without my help, all of her own volition, even while I was lecturing her about all the stuff she's always doing wrong. And she said since it wasn't remorse but a recognition of an injustice, the pang wouldn't go away if all I did was say sorry, it would only go away if I told Marga thank you and another day when it was Marga's turn to clean I grabbed another brush and joined in. 'How?' I asked my sister, taking off my glasses and wiping away my tears, which were, you could say, the defecation of the pang in my soul. 'How can I join in when my condition is degenerative and my eyesight gets worse by the hour and I can't even see where my own [*expletive*] starts and where it ends?' And she said, 'Whatever way you can. If all your myopia lets you do is dry teaspoons, then dry teaspoons.' I understood about the spoons: little acts that mean a lot, got it. But then Nati started talking in her ununderstandable [*sic*] gate language, and with the day I'd had and how sedate I was feeling from all the hysterapeutics in the mirror, I didn't feel up for trying to make sense of the crazy way she talks. She was saying something about how I shouldn't just run to Marga's room and start blubbering and 'appear' or 'repeal' or 'up-heel' to a 'federal love' or a 'frat-nurtle love' or a 'free-turtle love' I have with Marga because Nati says I know perfectly well there's no free turtle bond between Marga and I. And I'm just nodding along like I'm talking to a lunatic: yes, yes, oh yes, I know it perfectly well, I say. And then she says she's not trying to console me, she's just trying to explain something as clearly as she knows how. And I'm there thinking, oh yes, clear as day, but I don't say anything because I'm dozing off behind my Coke-bottle glasses anyway, they're so thick people can't usually tell when my eyelids are closing. But Nati's still going, she says I ought to be grateful for the pang in my soul, and I'm thinking, oh yes, over the moon, because she says what I'm feeling is much more than a pang, it's an 'epitome' or 'any piccany', I don't know exactly what she said, Your Honour, some ununderstandable [*sic*] Nati word, but according to her the pang meant I'd finally seen the 'damnation' or 'dummy nation' or 'dalmatian' I was exercising over Marga, and I was finally seeing just how truly bad and hurtful that dalmatian was. She said Marga's silence was (and this part I did understand, Your Honour) 'a form of some mission'. 'And what's that?' I asked, pretending to be interested. 'It's her tactic,' Nati said. Of course, her cleaning tactic, just like I said! If the words come out better when your hands are busy cleaning, then the cleaning must come out better when Marga concentrates and keeps her mouth shut.

Guadalupe Pinto
Judge

Patricia Lama
Declarant

Javier López Mansilla
Stenographer/Transcriber

'Do you remember the first time we went to the anarchist social centre?' Marga asked as soon as she saw me come out of class. They've put her in charge of dropping me off and picking me up from the new dance school. They say that by taking on small, everyday responsibilities, like dropping off and picking up her cousin on the other side of the city, Marga will feel useful, gain self-esteem, shed her depression little by little and, incidentally, be forced to shower. You'd have to be pretty clueless to not see that what they're actually doing is keeping her out of the flat during the hours when she'd otherwise be home alone, which is practically every afternoon, because Patri and Àngels, ever-fearful of being kicked out of our state-sponsored accommodations, have redoubled their efforts to fellate (it's fellatio, not cunnilingus) Overseer Susana Gómez from the slave labour camp (Urban Centre for the Intellectually Disabled), Kommandant Laia Buedo from the cameraless interrogation room (the Barceloneta Self-Advocacy Group) and grasping PhD student Diana Ximenos from the Central Laboratories for Improvement of the Race (Inclusion Europe, formerly known as the FAMR). That way they prevent Marga from bringing strange men, and occasionally strange women, up to the flat, or watching porn so loudly that pedestrians congregate under our balcony. And, as an added bonus, they put some distance between me and Barceloneta Adult Daycare (BADDAY), because apparently my presence

113

there is upsetting to the fascists and, as has been the way of the world since the beginning of time and since three years ago when Ángela got us out of the Somorrín Concentration and Extermination Camp (Rural Centre for the Intellectually Disabled), instead of keeping the fascists away from me, they force me to keep away from the fascists, this time by sending me to a dance school at the Les Corts stop on the green line, near Camp Nou Stadium, which is to say, in the east asshole of Barcelona.

'This is not a dance school,' explained the director of the dance school when I went with Patri and our caseworker to learn about their so-called integrated dance classes. 'This is a factory for the creation of movement.'

'This is a pile of horseshit,' I said, but I said it with a smile because I liked the place.

It's an old multiplex cinema that's been converted into expansive rehearsal spaces. The ceilings are high, the light is low, and the rooms are quiet because they're still soundproofed; anyone can use the kitchen and canteen, the Wi-Fi password is posted in plain sight, there are couches, the locker rooms are pristine, and the jet of hot water lasts long enough that you don't have to push the button to turn the tap back on twenty times during your shower. And most importantly: nobody says shit to you if you spend a whole afternoon wandering around looking at the ceiling and availing yourself of all these amenities.

'Of course I remember that first, wonderful time we went to the anarchist social centre,' I said to Marga, who's recently been going more regularly than me to talk about her okupa. She always comes back with anarchist zines, pamphlets and newspapers for me because she knows I like them. Marga reads literally nothing since she barely knows how to read, so she chooses the zines at random. Today she brought me a copy of *Aversion* from three months ago, with an article attacking International Women's Day. And she brought me a zine called *Burn Your Phone*, another called *Collective Sex: From Scarcity to Sexual Abundance* and a pamphlet about boycotting the Corte Inglés department store. I actually enjoy them more because she grabs them at random, the pleasure of non-premeditation. It produces an unexpected kind of politicisation, free from the bureaucracy of thought. A joy like when the clothes you find by the dumpster fit like a glove; a joy free from hassle and expenditure, and which imparts a sudden clear-sightedness, a dropping of the blindfold like one evening four years ago when, after the squatters in the Can Vies building were forced out and a bulldozer began its destructive task, a hundred anonymous individuals set fire to the machine. According to the woman at the anarchist social centre who described the blaze, letting us savour the gift of her story, for minutes and minutes and minutes, there wasn't a siren to be heard as they contemplated the flames. All around them was peace, the collective affirmation of a truth and spontaneous absence of conflict, not to be confused with pacification, which is the concealment of conflict by force, or, in other words, repression. Twenty minutes of blessed peace before the police, firemen or other violent forces of pacification arrived on the scene. That's why I like the zines I receive haphazardly but without fail from my cousin Marga.

The sun was setting over the presidential box at Camp Nou and Marga looked tired, but from boredom, not exhaustion. She would've been waiting for me since five, because it doesn't make sense for her to take the metro all the way back to Barceloneta just to come and pick me up again half an hour later. Other times she's more animated because the Cineplex is close enough for her to drop in on the anarchists in Sants if she walks fast, though whenever she does that she

115

screws up her legs and lower back because she tilts her trunk forward when she walks, like a hunchback except the hunch is in her kidneys. She gets tired when she does that, too, but from exhaustion, not boredom. I've learned to distinguish between those two kinds of fatigue in Marga, which are in turn different from the third kind, which occurs when she gets laid then forces herself to go out in the world even though she's warding off post-coital torpor.

'You know if you biked, Marga, you'd be there in five minutes, it's downhill the whole way. And it'd only take you ten to come back uphill and get me, and your calves and hips wouldn't hurt at all. Cycling is all in the thighs, and you have incredible quads! Let me teach you!'

'Nati, remember the guy that day who was talking about Molotov cocktails?' Marga doesn't know how to ride a bike and she doesn't want to learn and she doesn't want me to talk about it because she's scared.

'How could I forget! He wasn't just talking about Molotov cocktails, he was giving them away like a verbal gift. Remember how he explained everything so intelligently and humbly that by the end even you and I thought we could have a go at a few police stations?'

'Turns out he's an informant, Nati.'

'You're fucking with me.'

'They told me today at the social centre. They've barred him from there and from Can Vies and from everywhere else in Barcelona. They're gonna put up posters of his face on the doors of all the okupas.'

'You're sure it's the same guy?'

'Positive. That day they kept quiet and let him keep talking so he wouldn't implicate anyone but himself, but apparently it's been a decade since anybody's thrown a Molotov cocktail in Barcelona. Now they just throw eggs and balloons full of paint, like we used to at the festivals in Arcuelamora.'

'But wait wait wait. How do you know for sure he's an informant and not just some insurrectionist looking for accomplices?'

'They told me you would never talk about Molotov cocktails at an open meeting like that, with the door literally wide open, which was how you and me got in that time. You talk about stuff like that separately. And also the way he looks. His hair was too perfect, with his mohawk stiff and the rest of his head shiny. He'd have to shave it every single morning. That was the big giveaway I guess. Punks don't spend that much time on anything. Quechua-brand clothes, Marlboro rolling tobacco. And apparently he said weird things, like instead of okupa, he'd say occupied house. And in the martial arts training he'd talk about honour and fraternity and teaching respect to the Romanians and Gypsies on the street.'

'Jesus. I ate it up.'

'Well, so, I've been sleeping with him before or after the meetings and I just fucked him again right now.'

'Marga! You fucked a cop?'

'We'd been hooking up in Can Vies, in one of the storage rooms at the back. And today we fucked on the toilet at your dance school. We left the centre together, and I acted like I didn't know anything about the ban that's gonna go into effect tomorrow. I figured it was now or never, I'm not going to see him again either way, but also I figured they wouldn't let him into Can Vies, and the clock was ticking, since I had to be here to pick you up in forty minutes. So I told him to come with me because I was in a hurry, and we did it in the locker room at your school. They smell amazing!'

'So you're tired from fucking, not because you're bored?'

'I mean it wasn't the screw of the century, but it's always nice to come with a dick inside you, it gives you more of a jolt, and it's exciting to do it fully dressed and totally quiet so you don't get busted. And thinking it's your last time together is a turn-on, even if the other person doesn't know and thinks he's gonna fuck you again next Thursday so he holds off on the biting and sucking and whispering goodbyes in your ear. But really it was just your average quickie on a toilet seat, where if his cock isn't super big and he doesn't pull you down onto him particularly hard, then he doesn't get deep enough for you to feel much. So I'm half tired because I'm bored and half tired from fucking.'

'Fascists with tiny pricks, a psychoanalytic breakthrough.'

'He's the only one I've been able to fuck in the four weeks I've been going to the okupa meetings, Nati. I don't get it.'

'Sexually reactionary anarchists, another breakthrough for psychoanalysis. But you know what, Marga?'

'What?'

'Listening to you talk is turning me on.'

'I'll keep going then. Here, let me carry your backpack like a mom with her kids after school.'

'Hang on though, Marga.'

'Jesus, this is heavy. What?'

'Oh, my water bottle's weighing it down, here, let me take it out. Marga, did you know he was a cop when you started fucking him?'

'How was I supposed to know! I didn't know anything about mohawks and Molotov cocktail delusions until an hour ago. I thought an undercover cop was a guy in cargo shorts arresting Pakistanis for selling beer on the beach or a woman in a miniskirt fining club promoters at eleven at night, or a girl in a leather jacket and skinny jeans buying from a dealer in El Raval then pulling out a pair of handcuffs. Are you still turned on or is this bringing you down a little?'

'It comes and goes. But if you'd known, would you still have slept with him, even though you're trying to start an okupa?'

'I don't know, Nati. Probably, right?

'And he knows you're going to break into that house the day after tomorrow?'

'Shit, Nati, I don't know. I'm stupid!'

'Did you tell him you were going to?'

'No. Sorry: I might fuck till I'm blue in the face, but I can be discreet too, I'm very discreet.'

'Marga, I'm not sure discreet is the first word I'd use to describe you.'

'No no, I'm not saying I fuck discreetly. What would even be the point. I'm saying I don't talk with my pussy, and besides, I only ever told him my okupa name, Gari Garay.'

'God, you have the coolest name. I want one too, not an okupa name because I'm not starting an okupa, but a stage name, as a dancer. Sorry, I cut you off.'

'I'm saying that anyway he doesn't go to the meetings because you can only go if someone vouches for you, because the whole thing's so shady. I got in because the PAH told them I was coming. I saw him during open meetings, where they just talk about general stuff and don't say anything compromising: when to have a party, what to put on the posters, who should organise the next talk, who's in charge of the bar, how much to charge for beer ...'

I always want a beer after I dance and now my craving intensified. But the cheapest Chinese bar in Les Corts charges €1.80 for a beer. For the price of a small draught, you could get two tall cans and drink them on a park bench, and for thirty cents less, you could get a litre bottle of Xibeca. Plus there's the whole song and dance of getting the waiter to put it down as a Coke rather than a beer on the receipt. The rhetorical demands of dissimulation, the need to speak the language of the enemy, having to say they're travel expenses, we're on a per diem. Can't you see I'm a dancer? Isn't it clear from my accent that I'm not from Barcelona and I'm here with my colleague, rehearsing at the Centre for the Creation of Movement? Here, how about this, you don't even have to lie, just put down beverage. Not Coca-Cola, not beer, just put beverage €1.80 and that'll be perfect, if it's not too much trouble, thanks so much.

'I know what name I want, Marga. Nata Napalm. Do you like it?'

In the end, at my suggestion, we indulged in the lumpen luxury of a beer from the tap and the miserly justification of our expenditure, because as our geriactivist grandfather Karl Marx rightly noted, dance is a bourgeois art, and as they rightly say in my village, everything sticks but good looks and manners. After spending the afternoon dancing with technical and emotional precision, which is to say, after finding pleasure not in repetition and taking flight, which are the pleasures of ecstasy (so difficult to achieve by mechanical means), but rather having found pleasure in synchronisation and repetition, which are the pleasures of decorum (so easy to achieve by mechanical means), I was still dripping with decorum, still feeling the after-effects of being entranced by order, the same order that, as Grandpa Karl saw, provokes bourgeois tears during the opening scenes of a ballet, provokes bourgeois applause when a rhythmic gymnast sticks her landing without so much as a wobble, and provokes bourgeois euphoria when you find a cheap flight or a bargain in the clearance section; the rapture the petit bourgeois feels when he manages to eke out an orgasm at the same time as his partner, because the simultaneity ensures that the sex will not continue, that he can stop exerting himself because the pleasure, thank God, has arrived for everyone, and now we can all move on to other things. The same attraction to order that, when all was said and done, left me dissatisfied with the prospect of drinking a litre of cheap beer from the bottle with my cousin on a bench and made me yearn for the terrace of a restaurant, where I could order a personal, nontransferable beer that was perfectly bitter, perfectly aromatic and perfectly priced by the Estrella Damm corporation. After you learn new choreography, the allure of exactitude stays with you for a while, and it even had me convinced that by paying more I'd converse better with Marga, more volubly; I'd be more relaxed and have greater appreciation for my cousin, and make better use of the limited time we had together before Patri realised we were unaccounted for and went back to ruining our lives.

'You think he was fucking me to get information about the okupas?'

'Marga, honey, it's an open-and-shut case. He never asked you anything weird?'

'Nati, all he ever asked was if he should come inside me or on my face or in my mouth, and if I liked it slower or faster, and if I liked it more or less in the ass, and if I preferred spit or lube.'

'For fuck's sake, Marga, I'm joking! It just turns me on to hear you. What an obliging fascist you found for yourself! If he didn't ask you anything weird, he's not an informant. He's obviously a wingnut who thinks there's a revolution brewing at Can Vies, but he's no more of a wingnut than all the other paranoiacs at the anarchist social centre who see an informant lurking behind every corner, when all that's happening is a dude and a woman who barely know each other are fucking. And in anarchist spaces no less!'

'Wait, Nati, sorry, I don't get it. Do you think he's going to fuck up my okupa or not?'

'Marga, no! The only people jeopardising your okupa are the okupiers themselves!'

'Now you're the one saying weird things. Those people are helping me.'

'Those people are reactionaries, Marga. They've helped you and they'll keep helping you the same way the Little Sisters of the Poor help lepers, of course, but at what cost? You're fucking a guy that both you and all of the anarchist punks only recently met. Straight away, that makes them suspicious: who's this wing-nut blabbering about Molotov cocktails and sleeping with our sister-in-arms? What's he looking for? What's he here to do? To fuck our women? Follow their suspicion, Marga, it'll lead you to the heart of their bigotry: the anarchists suspected him but not you. They believed that he was the informant, and it never once crossed their minds that the police infiltrator could be you. He struck them as dangerous, you struck them as innocuous.'

'I was referred by the PAH, Nati, I already told you.'

'As if the PAH weren't Ada Colau, and as if Ada Colau weren't the mayor, and as if the mayor didn't leap to the cops' defence every time they beat the shit out of Black street vendors. And as if the cops didn't vote for Colau! Why would an anarchist have more reason to trust you, having come straight from the PAH, than they would someone who openly talks about committing violence against the police? The world turned upside down!' Marga was listening to me in that way of hers where she doesn't wait for the right moment to reply, that way of listening that doesn't scrutinise every word and every argument for something that can be refuted, her non-existent need to butt in or strike back, her non-existent interest in debating. She just treasures your message and judges you calmly and at length. Is it the Tripteridol, or does Marga sometimes not understand me? 'Do you understand what I'm saying, Marga?'

'More or less. But things aren't as clear-cut as you make them out to be, Nati.'

'What's not clear, Marga?'

'It doesn't matter.'

'It does matter. I'm the one who needs to make myself understood. You and this guy are fucking. Everyone knows it and you don't hide it, right? Or are you stealthy about it when you go into that room in Can Vies?'

'No.'

'Are you stealthy about it when you leave?'

'No.'

'Do you get touchy in public?'

'A little, but not really. Mostly we just look at each other.'

'Do you look at each other stealthily?'

'Jesus, I don't know, Nati, get to the point, it's seven thirty already.'

'The point is exactly what I'm getting at: after you've been openly fucking for two weeks, they banish this guy and not you. Why is that?'

'Because he's an informant.'

'He's not! But fine, let's say he's an informant. Shouldn't they also suspect the woman the informant is fucking, given the rapport between them?' When I said this, Marga's expression changed, and it seemed like her judgemental silence had become complicit silence, like I had finally spoken clearly and she had finally understood me. The words started flying from my mouth like hot bread from the oven: 'The answer is yes. Being consistent in their suspicions and their precautions, the anarchists should wallpaper the okupas with your face, too. An informant's presence contaminates his entire environment, and anarchists, specialists in systemic analysis, know that better than anyone. They wouldn't trust the dog the informant adopted to complete his crust-punk aesthetic. And they have

123

even more reason to suspect you: you're new, you don't know their codes, and you've never been to a protest in your life. Which is to say, you're not politicised. You're naive and in possession of valuable information, and thus a threat to the movement. Why, then, I have to ask again, haven't they kicked you out?' For me this question had a rhetorical function, but Marga thought it was aimed at her; she was about to answer, but instead gave the world's tiniest smile, the smile you give when you realise something obvious, took a long sip of beer, spilled a little on her chin and wiped it with the back of her hand. I continued: 'But they haven't kicked you out, Margarita, because in their heart of hearts they don't really think that boy's an informant. That was just their cover, an excuse that's powerful and incontrovertible in clandestine settings that I will now controvert. It's an excuse that exerts its power in two ways. First, it acts as a mental and intimate rationalisation for the anarchists on an individual level, because it allows them to refrain from considering their true motivation for black-listing the Molotov-cocktail-flinging wingnut, a motivation too shameful for them to even imagine, an unspeakable taboo among radicals that I will speak about shortly. And second, the excuse exerts its immense rationalising power not just men-tally and intimately, but also externally and collectively, seeing as, once the label of informant has been applied, none of the wingnut's anarchist compatriots will want to entertain other possible motivations for the ban that more closely resemble the true motivation, the unverbalised motivation which I will verbalise as soon as I finish exposing the mechanics of the excuse. Once the label of informant has been applied, no one will want to fraternise with the wingnut, given the risk it would entail: the risk that, if the wingnut were in fact an informant, he would inform on his former accomplices, leading to arrests and court proceedings. A risk, then, against which measures must be taken. These measures, which constitute the excuse the anarchists use to mask the motivation I'm about to unmask, are faultlessly outfitted in ideological, tactical and combative terms, as they are the central cohesive force of radical politicisation and, thus, of anarchist awareness. They generate satisfaction among the individual members of the group, satisfaction and a feeling of rightness, a feeling of victory, because banishing the informant means identifying the fascist and forcing him to dissociate from the objects of his abuse, which is the exact opposite of what we usually see in our fascistic day-to-day lives, like, for example, when someone can't take it any more at their job and they put in a request for leave on account of depression or anxiety or sexual harassment: the fascist bossman or bosslady gets to stay, and the fascist bossman or bosslady's fascist male and female asslickers get to stay, and the employee who refuses to play their fascist game leaves. It's the exact opposite, for example, of what happens when some dudebro harasses you on the street: you have to keep walking and the male gets to stay at the door of the bar, waiting for another target to walk past. The exact opposite, for example, of what Susana and Patricia did with me when they pulled me out of the BADDAY: they identified the target of the abuse, forced her to dissociate from her abusers, and left the fascist contemporary dancers in peace.'

I paused for longer than usual between sentences, and Marga capitalised on my brief silence to get up and go to the bar. She returned with a carbon-copy receipt for '2 beverages – €3.60'.

'Let's go, it's seven fifty.'

'We need the bar's tax ID,' I said. Marga snorted and I went to find someone who could give it to us. The owner didn't understand what I was asking for. A very young Chinese girl who spoke the same Spanish as all the teenagers from the south side of Barcelona, which is to say with a TV accent and no trace of Catalan, disinterred her head from her phone long enough to find a pen and write the tax number from memory with the same low, round handwriting as all teenage girls: numbers like coloured balloons scattered across the floor at an impeccably decorated birthday party.

Even though I hadn't finished talking, we walked to the pestilent metro together in silence. I don't infect my cousin with loquacity, she infects me with silence. Like so many times before, I felt myself pulled into the spiral of silence, which doesn't just mean not talking. It means falling quiet because you feel alone in your motives. You feel insecure about having talked too much even though you haven't, even though what really happened was no one reacted to what you were saying, not in support and not in opposition. And you weren't speaking alone, either: other people were there, listening to you and maybe even agreeing with you, but the only one speaking was you. They want you to swallow that mixed brew of religious notions according to which silence isn't capitulation and submission, it's elevation, distinction and respect, even though what your silence really says is that you're prettier when you keep your mouth shut. How painful to think that Marga, too, wanted to pull me down the drain into the spiral of silence!

'Marga,' I said as if I was asking her permission.

Les Corts is one of the new stations, so instead of turnstiles it has automatic gates that retract when you scan your ticket, which makes hopping them way more conspicuous, and even though I still jump over them if I'm riding high on indignant revulsion (though the only thing I was riding high on that day was bourgeois self-indulgence after the draught beer and it's possible I wouldn't have jumped even if I'd been alone), Marga's not so good at jumping and she'll only do it if she feels very secure and it's very late at night, so instead we coupled like railway cars and did a two-for-one. After riding out the usual dose of adrenaline – just enough to make you alert to security guards, ticket checkers and metro employees astray from their little booths – I kept talking:

'I still haven't told you what their unverbalised motivation for kicking out your fuckbuddy was. Do you want to hear it?'

She nodded silently, and squashed her wide hips onto the bench on the platform. Margarita was tired.

'The anarchists banished your fuckbuddy to protect you from sexual desire. The anarchists banished your fuckbuddy because they believe that the sexual initiative was entirely his. They think you, therefore, have been seduced. They assume that you are in a situation of weakness before the male, that he's taking advantage of you, because you're new, because you're not very punk, because you don't know how to say no consistently and systematically like the feminists at the anarchist social centre. What are their parties papered over with? With posters that say NO MEANS NO. What did the punks at Can Vies spray-paint at the last party they had at Plaça La Màlaga? DON'T LOOK AT ME, DON'T TOUCH ME, DON'T COME NEAR ME. Christ! And every letter half a metre high! You'd think at the very least they could graffiti YES MEANS YES next to it, in letters just as big, but no, of course they didn't, and an indiscriminate vow of chastity cast a pall over the entire party. The anarchists want to protect you because they don't understand that you want them to look at you, want them to touch you, want them to come near you, and you don't care if the person doing the looking, touching and coming is a complete stranger. These squatters criminalise having a sex drive just like the penal code criminalises them for not paying rent. They criminalise having a sex drive because in their view anyone who looks at you, touches you or comes near you is trying to take advantage of you. They want

127

to teach us women to get drunk and mosh and smoke weed and mask up just like dudes have always done. But there's something else dudes have always done that they don't want us to learn: to express and consummate sexual desire.'

The metro arrived and I paused for longer than usual between sentences, but this time Marga didn't capitalise on my silence as she had at the bar. She was looking me in the eyes and occasionally raising her eyebrows. I couldn't tell whether or not it was the spiral of silence. Was it possible that I was revealing something so significant to Marga that she didn't want to miss a single detail?

'For these anarchists of yours, a sex drive is dangerous. I agree: fucking is dangerous. Fucking is a wilful act, a political act, a place of weakness that encompasses everything from humiliation to death, by way of trance, ecstasy and obliteration. But the anarchists don't want to take that risk. They take lots of other kinds of risks, but not that one. Why don't today's anarchists take the risk of fucking, like their counterparts a century ago?' This was a rhetorical question, but again, Marga thought it was intended for her, an unequivocal indication that she was listening. She didn't know the answer so she shrugged. 'This shift in mentality merits careful consideration. Don't today's anarchists consider emancipation of sexual desire to be part of their struggle for emancipation from oppression of all kinds?' Marga shrugged again, and I answered my own question: 'It seems that they don't. Are they afraid of that struggle?' Again, Marga raised and dropped her shoulders like a schoolgirl being quizzed on a reading she hadn't done. I answered myself again: 'It seems that they are. Are they afraid of fucking? I think we've hit the nail on the head, hit the rioter in the head with the rubber bullet of sexual repression. They view sexual liberation as merely acknowledging and raising awareness about the non-heteronormative personhood of gays, lesbians, bisexuals and transpeople. They've coined this lovely concept of "sexual dissidence" to refer to the most superficial elements of sex: identity and appearance – precisely those things that ought to dissipate when fucking. Sexual dissidence is a woman growing a moustache. Sexual dissidence is a dude using they/them pronouns. Sexual dissidence is him taking oestrogen or her taking testosterone. They're all dissidents from the heteropatriarchy, fine. But what about a chick wearing an inch of make-up and dressed like Beyoncé, or a chick who gets lipo and fake tits, who wants people to look at her and touch her and come near her because that woman simply feels like fucking, not to earn money, not to sleep her way to the top, not to make someone jealous, but just because she loves it, it's the best thing in the world as far as she's concerned, because she doesn't idealise or categorise or classify the sexual act or the bodies that engage in it, because she doesn't think of fucking as a symbolic act, no, she thinks of it as something that more closely resembles fornication, which is to say, the act of putting all our powers in the service of pleasure – is she a sexual dissident?' No, Marga's silence wasn't the spiral of silence or the inattentive schoolgirl. We were sitting side by side and sometimes she would turn towards me not just with her head, but with her entire torso, in its natural forward position, like Sherlock Holmes or the Pink Panther following a trail of footprints to my lap, in such a way that her ear was at the height of my mouth and I could smell the hair she hadn't washed in days. 'For your anarchist group, that woman is not a sexual dissident. For your anarchist group, that woman is defective. That woman is putting herself in harm's way. That woman is being provocative, she's making it easy for the rapists, or at least for the fascist dudebros and the woke dudebros, who in the end are one and the same, and she's undermining the pillars of denial feminism, the feminism of refusal, the feminism of castration in which, paradoxically enough, the woman is once again submissive, because she can no longer attack from a truly offensive position, no, she can only defend herself, because she has yielded a phallic power to anyone who approaches her with sexual intent. The castration feminist assumes herself to be the object of domination for anyone who wants to fuck her, whom she assumes in all cases to be her oppressor. Like a good submissive, comfortable in a sadistic relationship which she not only doesn't resist but actively endorses, the self-castrated feminist finds pleasure in the denial her sadist inflicts on her. The denial feminist thinks she's the one denying the phallus, but she's fooling herself: what she wants is for the phallus to deny her. What she wants is to invert the classic roles of cock-tease and cock-teased. She no longer wants to be the seductress who won't so much as kiss the man who paid for her drinks. Instead of torpedoing those shitty roles, that shitty relationship where there's no flesh or truth but only rhetoric and seduction, the self-castrate wants to adopt the role of the teased and make the other her cunt-tease, the one who denies her body, the one to whom she invariably submits because she prefers to give up her sexual initiative, which comes with so much baggage in the form of creativity, responsibility and risk. So, in the act of denying, she avoids the unexpected consequences that can arise from the unpre-meditated fuck, the lack of premeditation being, who could doubt it, what distinguishes good sex from bad, not to mention what distances us from fetishism and brings us closer to true unbridled copulation, unbridled not in the sense of fast, but in the sense of unlimited, unconditional, lacking in formalities.' I was stroking Marga's hair. The fact that it was dirty, that it made my fingers glisten, that she smelled like sheets that hadn't been changed in many days made Marga the most intelligent presence on the metro, a natural, effortless spurner of this so-called form of public transport that, in reality, is a mass grave that Marga dared to defile with her smell of living person. Marga had grasped the alienating function that all subways play in any major population: to make us believe that uniting the four corners of a city also unites the city's residents, when really it liquefies them and makes them even stranger strangers to one another, forcing them to behave with what the Barcelona Metropolitan Transport Authority calls civility which is really none other than radical ignorance of your neighbour, radical non-involvement in the form of speaking, looking or smelling, and an extra incentive to never stop staring at your phone. 'But this feminism of denial preaches that saying no to sex is liberating because it views the sexual act as a historic tool by which the man dominates the woman. Woman: the less time and energy you dedicate to sex, that barbarian task, the more time you'll have to focus on yourself, to take up a new hobby, to practise self-care or even to fight for revolution. Show me a woman who doesn't fuck and I'll show you a free and independent woman, they say. Doesn't this sound like exactly what it sounds like: celibate mysticism? They call themselves anarchists then go legislating our cunts! Ironically, they advocate for shit sex, premeditated sex and, ultimately, bourgeois sex. Castration feminism finds pleasure in the conscious, calculated selection of sexual partners like consumers find pleasure in choosing a brand of mayonnaise at the supermarket, because these feminists think fucking is a matter of taste. Personal taste, nothing more!' It's no coincidence the metro riders who most gleefully commune with their phones are always the cleanest. It's no coincidence hygiene is the gateway drug to fascism. 'Taste and desire are very different things, just ask the woman who votes for Partido Popular and goes out dressed like Katy Perry on New Year's Eve. Taste, which is always moulded, if not entirely prefabricated, by power, is not that woman's

131

compass. No, her compass is the conviction that, in the state of sexual scarcity in which we live, any insinuation, any lascivious cadence of the eyelids, whether it's from a man, woman or child, comes from an accomplice and a comrade, and is the watchword of the insurgents against the regime.' I, however, had just showered at the school. Could that be why subversive, fragrant Marga was so hushed? Could her silence be a rebuke, resistance to me inhibiting her olfactory violence with my scent of economy-size body wash? 'Tasting, choosing, comes later, with the tongue already inside. That tongue might be no good. That finger might not hit home. That breath might not burn. But how can you know if you don't try? Taste is cautious, the risk is in the tasting, in drawing close to give and receive pleasure.' No, it wasn't rebuke or resistance either. Marga was drifting off in response to my caresses, little by little, until her head was resting on my chest. She lay like that for the nine stops until the transfer. I spoke more softly: 'Today's anarchists do hardly any tasting, so they fuck very little and, when they do, it's under the bourgeois banner of premeditation and personal taste. Do you know what they disparagingly call those of us who advocate for the opposite? Anarcho-individualists, which is one step shy of U.S. libertarians: capitalists non plus ultra, wild-eyed lovers of the liberty-and-merit amusement park that is the free market and bitter detractors of state intervention in the economy, though not detractors, oddly enough, of all the state intervention involved in establishing and defending a border, approving a criminal code, or forming a police force to protect property and all the misogynist, racist and, in short, fascist fuckery that property sustains.' I was cradling her with my words, and maybe her silence was the silence of a child being soothed by a constant maternal heart-beat, and, as our five senses were flooded with the dose of alienation that was our due as passengers on the metro, the feeling of Marga and me communicating in that way – though we weren't a mother and child and there was no lullaby between us – gave me an odd pleasure, odd in the sense of strange and odd in the sense of infrequent, a pleasure that filled the void in meaning of our neoliberal lives or at least of our metro ride, but no more, because it's a pleasure that's just right in degree and in justice, not ecstatic, not blinding, but lucid and conscious, a pleasure that the majority will never feel, because the majority is always tautologically democratic, and this is the pleasure of politicisation.

I was whispering in Marga's ear with a hand protecting my mouth from the noises of the metro:

'They brand us anarcho-individualists because, they say, we think there is nothing above the individual. They say we don't feel bound by what they decide in the anarchist assembly. They accuse us of not advocating for the collective and the community, they call us self-serving, they say that we're bound by a law too, the law of desire, a law that by all accounts is even more tyrannical than the social anarchists' laws because at least those have been adopted by the assembly, whereas we, in accordance with our law of selfishness, couldn't give less of a shit about their assembly. The irony, Marga! We're the ones calling for indiscriminate sex, the ones who want to preach promiscuity from door to door, the ones who want to do away with the notion of sexual partnership in favour of expansive, collective sex, and they call us individualists! Meanwhile they, the pleasure-denying premeditators, grown men and women with hair on their balls and cunts, look timidly at their feet when confronted with a sexual invitation, or even denounce the violation of their sovereign personal space, which is to say, the sovereign space of the status quo, the sovereign space that ensures you'll come back home as alone as when you stepped out, and, in short, the sovereign space of boredom, the very same people who, there's no getting round it, fuck one-on-one in bedrooms, behind closed doors, the very same people, that is, who choose to call themselves "social anarchists"! Have you heard their other slogan, IF YOU FUCK WITH ONE OF US, YOU FUCK WITH ALL OF US ... ? If only! If only that slogan weren't metaphorical, if only they were using "fuck with" literally and not as a euphemism for "assault". That would be true solidarity: IF YOU FUCK ONE OF US, YOU FUCK ALL OF US! But no such luck, Marga. These anarchists of yours do very little fucking, they can't understand why you fuck so much and they wish you wouldn't, so they've taken away your fuckbuddy under the guise of him being an informant. Fascist fucking anarchists, fuck.'

I was quiet for the remaining stops until the station where we changed trains. There, without any prompting from me, Marga stood up as straight as she ever does, with that slight tilt forward that makes her boobs swing when she walks. My cousin was calm and quiet, as if contemplating a job well done, and I was glad to have rid her of the fear that the wingnut would screw up her okupa. Either that or the Tripteridol cat has got her tongue, I thought. It was possible they'd done a test on Marga, found that there was no trace of the drug in her system, and taken her to task for it. We boarded the next train and sat back down, but this time Marga didn't snuggle up next to me because we were only going three stops. I missed her.

'Are you on Tripteridol, or are you not scared any more?' I asked gently.

'No, I'm good.'

I didn't understand her response.

'You don't need to be afraid, Marga.' I put a hand on her thigh and left it there until it was time to get up.

'Afraid of what?'

'Of that guy. He's not an informant, I promise.'

134

'He's an informant, Nati.'

'Marga, he's not. You're just too free for those repressed anarchists. But believe what you want. In any case, that house is going to be yours.'

She put her hand on my thigh and our arms crossed over one another. Marga's thigh is soft and mine is hard.

'He is, Nati, it has nothing to do with how much sex I have.'

'Obviously it does, Marga.'

'No, Nati, that's not what's obvious.'

Marga was also speaking to me gently, but her tenderness came from a place of condescension whereas mine came from a place of love. That lack of reciprocation shook me, but I don't think it showed.

'So what is obvious then?' I asked, pretending that my hand was still touching her thigh when in reality it had become a dead hand, paralysed by heartbreak, by the loss of my friend.

'I'm mentally retarded, Nati. It's obvious I'm retarded. And since that's obvious, I also obviously can't be a cop, so none of the punks in the okupation office suspect me or put up posters of my face. And the guy I was fucking is obviously not retarded, and that means he could be a cop, so they did put up posters of him. And since I'm obviously mentally retarded, and since it's obvious retards don't talk the same as non-retards, or about the same topics as non-retards, and don't care about the same things as non-retards, the punks think I might've said something to the informant between fucks or mid-fuck.'

'You're what, Marga? Retawhat? What about menthol? Sorry, I don't understand a word you just said.'

'Never mind, Nati, just me being me. Nata Napalm is a really cool name.' She smiled as she said this, now with an un-questionable tiredness around her eyes and mouth and, even so, she enlivened the hand on my thigh and gently massaged

135

my quadriceps for the remaining two stops until Barceloneta. I don't know if Marga knows about the pleasure dancers get from pressure any place on our bodies, but it was because of that, because of the free, wholly unexpected pleasure she was giving my leg that I didn't consider her own exhaustion, didn't stop her, didn't reciprocate by placing my hands on her shoulders and saying, Marga, the person who needs a massage today, to forget about all the shit with the informant, the okupa and the Tripteridol, is you. Turn around.

Statement by Ms Patricia Lama Guirao, made before the Fourth Investigating Judge of the Court of Barcelona on 12 July 2018, as part of the court proceedings for authorisation of the sterilisation of an incompetent individual arising from the action brought by the Generalitat of Catalonia against Ms Margarita Guirao Guirao.

Marga's so fond of it that if she walks past a table and the corner is at the same height as her [*expletive*], Marga will literally [*expletive*] herself with the corner of the table, Your Honour. Now don't get me wrong, she doesn't go out looking for a table to [*expletive*] like she goes out on the street looking for men, and I mean sometimes not only men. She'll just be clearing the dishes after lunch, for example, and I'll walk into the room and she'll be at the edge of the table, thrusting away, plates still in her hands, casual as a cucumber, looking kind of detached like she's on autopilot, the same way some women knit or iron clothes while they watch TV, or the way Àngels watches TV while she writes her novel on WhatsApp. What I'm getting at, Your Honour, is it's not like she has any kind of bad intention with the table, she doesn't even know what she's doing, she's just acting on instinct like an animal. Everybody's got instincts, Your Honour. Like me for example – when I see a homeless guy asking for money, I always check my purse to see if I've got anything for him. Even if it means I can't afford bread or the metro or cigarettes, my instinct drives me to give to people begging on the street.

But even animals can be trained, can't they? And just like you can teach a dog to not piss in the house or rummage through the trash or bite strangers, if I open my purse and I don't have any spare change, it doesn't matter what my instinct is telling me, I'm not giving a beggar a twenty or a ten or a five, no ma'am. Shouldn't we do the same with Marga? I don't think I'm saying anything so crazy. Take me for example. Right after they institutionalised me at the RUCID in Somorrín, I used to swear all the time and get mouthy with the staff and the other residents, and even the director! And what did they do? They punished me and said no going outside. Negative reinforcement. And what else did they do? They let me pick the Friday-night movie if I asked politely. Positive reinforcement. And if the reinforcement didn't work? They'd make me pop a Tripteridol and I'd be right as rain, Your Honour. Behavioural therapy in conjunction with pharmacological therapy. And did it work? You tell me: now I live in my own flat, with my own bedroom all to myself, and I get to decide what I do with my time. If I want to go out, I go out, and if I want to stay in and watch TV, then I'll darn well stay in. If I want to eat fried eggs instead of macaroni, then I fry them myself. If I want to smoke a cigarette, I smoke one. If I want to wear a miniskirt, I wear one, and if I want to wear a burka, I'm free to wear one of those too! If I want to bring a boy upstairs, I'll invite him up! And if I want to be alone with the boy in my bedroom with the door closed, well, that's just what I'll do, though I have good sense and decency enough to make sure no one can hear us. So you tell me, have the reinforcements worked or haven't they? Even though, truth be told, Your Honour, I'm a very private person and if I have a special friend I'd rather go to his place, even though I have to be back at the flat in time for dinner because sometimes Miss Susana Gómez, the caseworker, she can show up at any moment like those labour inspectors at a nightclub I was telling you about, so I have to be sure I'm home by eight forty-five at the very latest, not like Nati, God help her, with those gates of hers she doesn't have special friends or really any friends at all, the poor thing. That's why I keep wondering what she could've been doing that night she showed up at ten in the morning, right smack in the middle of Miss Susana's visit. The expression on Miss Susana's face when she left was something awful.

When, heaven help me, when, in those twelve years we spent at the RUCID, could we have dreamed of the freedom we have now? Do you think anyone has ever told Marga she can't have special friends? Of course not! All we want is for her to get a boyfriend and let us meet him so she can bring him upstairs without sneaking around all the time! I mean the RUCID was like a convent, Your Honour, I'll give you that, it was run by a bunch of old farts who infantilised us like you wouldn't believe. You couldn't even kiss a boy on the mouth without some caregiver pulling you off him and laughing in your face! You couldn't even do any 'self-care' without the on-call aide yanking your hand out of your panties! And you definitely couldn't maintain safe and healthy sexual slash affective relationships. If you and a boy locked yourselves in the bathroom together, they'd knock the door down and then, again, negative reinforcement. And if you tried to sneak into the boys' room at night, the aide on call would intercept you and then, what else, negative reinforcement. Can you think how bad Marga had it there? They had to tie her to the bed! We should've reported the Somorrín RUCID to the ombudsman, who I think actually is an ombudslady. And this is 2007 we're talking about, not the age of Methuselah like in that Almodóvar film about the boarding school!

But the professionals here are very different from the professionals there, Your Excellency, very very different. The times have changed. It's the old politics versus the new. Things are better when a city is led by a progressive activist like Ada Colau. In her party, one of the most important politicians has spinal muscular atrophy and one of the most important female politicians can pull out a breast in the middle of Congress to feed her baby. Now that's something! I wonder if that's why the cops in Barcelona are so respectful when they reprimand Marga for flashing her boobs in the middle of the street, not like the cops in Somorrín, who would throw a blanket over her like she was a refugee climbing out of a migrant dinghy.

Ada Colau is an advocate for people with disabilities, even though she isn't disabled at all herself. I mean, she's a little well upholstered, sure, but I mean even there she's championing women and challenging sexist standards of beauty by saying all kinds of differently upholstered women can still be strong and beautiful. So in a city like Barcelona, with a progressive mayor from the new politics, people with functional, intellectual and slash or developmental diversity have the right to a full, healthy and satisfying affective and sexual life, and it is the responsibility of public and private institutions within the sector to dispel myths about our sexuality, offer guidance to our self-advocacy group support persons and promote awareness of our sexual and reproductive rights. What I'm trying to say is none of us have ever told Marga there's anything wrong with a little hanky-spanky [sic]. No one here is sexually repressing Margarita Guirao Guirao, Your Honour. All any of us has ever done, self-advocacy meeting after self-advocacy meeting, psychological evaluation after psychological evaluation, is give Marga an affective slash sexual education that would help her

140

distinguish between appropriate and inappropriate displays of attraction, right? Between sexual slash affective expression that's suitable for public spaces and expression that should be limited to private and slash or intimate settings; favouring, *favour*-ing the creation of her intimate space, which, like the word says, means doing her a favour, right? The favour of giving Marga her own private space.

So that's what we were trying to do, and Marga's entire family unit was involved. I would leave home an hour before the self-advocacy meeting – a whole hour, even though the UCID is only three blocks from our flat! Good old Patricia would start getting ready at four in the afternoon, right in the middle of her afternoon snack, so we could leave by five and get to the self-advocacy meeting at six on the dot, because you know Marga, she's a poky puppy like no other, what with locomotor ataxia being part of her disability. And, miracle of miracles, for Marga's sake, Àngels learned to be more generous with the TV and started letting Marga watch a dirty movie every now and again. With the volume turned down low, obviously, nice and low so the rest of us don't get worked up. After that first serious meeting we had with the flat director, Àngels told Marga (or I mean at least she tried to tell her but you know how hard it is for her to tell anyone anything with that mashed-potato mouth of hers): 'Marga. We're all adults. There are no little girls here. This is your home as much as it is ours. You like "getting off", right?' That was how she said it, Your Honour, she was speaking the kind of language Marga understands. 'Well, here's a flash drive with thirty porn films I downloaded for you off the internet. You said the other day you wanted to watch porn, right?'

Honestly, when I see Àngels acting like that, it's so obvious to me how she's the least disabled of the four of us: she must have remembered that day when they were fighting over the

TV and Marga kept pestering her about watching a dirty movie. Marga's like a drug addict, she's spent so much of her life getting [*expletive*] that porn doesn't cut it any more, it doesn't turn her on or anything. All it does is relax her a little, take the edge off. But you can tell, you can absolutely tell that Àngels is the least disabled of the four of us, because she figured out that that was exactly what we needed: we needed Marga to relax. She had to watch some porn, do a little 'self-care' and chill the [*expletive*] out so it wouldn't be such a pressing matter next time she set the table.

Even my sister Natividad did her part, listen to this! Even Nati did her part to save the flat, and to help Marga! Marga kept bringing her these crumply black-and-white photocopies of construction-paper booklets like we used to make during occupational therapy at the RUCID in Somorrín, since Marga's disability also means she's like a puppy who brings things she thinks are interesting home for you. I don't know what the heck she thought Nati would want with those crappy home-made booklets since Nati's already up to her eyeballs in university books the size of bricks, but what I'm saying is she has an acquired disability, Nati does I mean, so even though she has a hard time reading a regular book for five minutes without throwing it against the wall, she wasn't born with her disability and, well, you can take the grad student out of the university but you can't take the university out of the grad student, Your Honour. If you give Nati just like a regular magazine, like *Pronto* or *Saber Vivir* or *Muy Interesante*, with glossy colour pages and the words all in regular, straight lines, two seconds later she'll throw it straight in the trash. I know because she threw mine in the trash once and me and her ended up in a shouting match and now I have to hide my magazines so she can't destroy them. If someone can read that well, and has read up on all kinds of specialist topics not just anybody could understand, and you give that person a little OT booklet that looks like it was made by a six-year-old, what do you expect her to get from it? Zilch, zip-a-dee-do-dah, that's what. But listen to this: Nati didn't want to disappoint her cousin because she knows she's depressed, so Nati, former doctoral student, sat down and read the booklets with Marga. She didn't throw them in the trash like she did with my magazines. She read every word! And that's not all, Your Eminence: after that, she went through them page by page with Marga, because Marga's illiterate, and she explained them in her ununderstandable [sic] gates language, but she did it as good as she could and with all the best intentions. I swear I almost cried the first time I saw the two of them there, on the sofa, so engrossed in what they were doing they ignored the TV and didn't even care that Àngels was watching *The Simpsons* or *Wheel of Fortune* or whatever.

Does Your Excellency see what my sister Natividad is capable of when she puts her mind to it? Do you see that we can all live in harmony if Nati wants to? In the two weeks when Marga pulled her vanishing act, Nati, to avoid throwing more fuel on the fire, started coming to the self-advocacy meetings, even though she used to hate hate hate them! She even took those crappy booklets Marga brought her and handed them out to everyone and helped the self-advocates who can't read to read them! She even started teaching them how to read using the booklets, for God's sake, and Nati's always been so smarmy and selfish, I couldn't believe my eyes! She even went to the occupational-therapy room and started making her own booklets. The occupational-therapy room, Your Grace, where they send the most severely disabled self-advocates to play with playdough! And that wasn't the end of it, she worked on her booklets at home, too. She went down to the oriental bazaar and bought safety scissors, a glue stick, a

143

pad of paper and some pens, and she came to me and very politely asked me for some old magazines I was done with so she could cut them up and make collages, and she started going to the municipal library to use the internet and write on their computers and print things out. For a whole month the only receipts she submitted were from the print shop, she didn't spend a cent of her allowance on anything else. I was so happy to see her quiet and concentrated at the living-room table like a schoolgirl doing homework.

So that, in short, Your Honour, is what we were trying to do. That's what Marga's entire family unit, namely myself, Àngels and Nati, were doing, and so were all of the professional support structures in place to safeguard Marga's best interests, namely Miss Diana Ximenos, director of the supervised flat, Miss Laia Buedo, psychologist from the UCID of Barceloneta, and Miss Susana Gómez, our caseworker who's also from the UCID. We were working on favouring, fostering and safeguarding Marga's well-being and human dignity. But Marga was the victim of institutional failure, Your Honour, the institutions and public agencies operating within the sector failed to safeguard Marga's right to the opportunity to learn to form healthy affective relationships. How did they fail her, you ask? Well, one day, the psychiatrist from the Hospital del Mar, whose name, to be honest, I don't know, since, let the record show, I haven't had to see a single psychiatrist since I got to Barcelona. But she showed up and said Marga was depressed, told the sexual education to shove it and prescribed 500 milligrams of Tripteridol. I don't know what's so [*expletive*] great about Tripteridol that psychiatrists prescribe it for everything. Aberrant behaviour? Tripteridol. Schizophrenia? Tripteridol. Depression? Tripteridol! What do a depressive, a schizo and an aberrant behaver have in common? It's like the beginning of a joke! Do they give psychiatrists kickbacks for prescribing it? They do, of course they do, I saw a report on La Sexta about how pharmaceutical companies give the doctors luxury vacations. Understand, Your Excellency, I'm not trying to discredit this lady psychiatrist or anybody else. Did I go to medical school? No. Am I trying to tell this psychiatrist how to do her job? No, of course not, in this life we must be, first and foremost, humble. I may not agree with the psychiatrist's decisions, but I respect her authority to make them. I respect her choices so much that I gave Marga her first dose of Tripteridol myself, I watched while she took it then said 'open your mouth' to make sure she had really swallowed it.

It seems to me like the person showing a lack of humility was the psychiatrist herself. You want to prescribe Tripteridol, fine, but why throw away all that progress on sexual education and person-centred care, the centred person in this case being my cousin Marga? Was nothing Miss Laia and Miss Susana did worth a crap? I wouldn't want to go casting aversions [*sic*], Your Honour, but it seems to me this psychiatrist, and, like I said, I don't know her and I don't have anything against her personally, but it seems to me she's one of those people who think psychiatric professionals, with their university degrees and their books and their conferences and their jobs, are better, more intelligent, more educated and more useful than disability-support professionals, even though disability-support professionals also have their own university degrees and conferences and talks they attend all around the world! Even in our rinky-dink self-advocacy group in Barceloneta, we're reading a book about disability by a man with Down's syndrome who's so smart that they put him in a very sweet film about living with Down's syndrome, and he's coming in September to talk to us at the UCID. He's the first person with Down's syndrome in the world to get a degree, and his book has sold thousands of copies and been translated into German, and the film has won all kinds of awards and everything! And he's been to Colombia, Argentina and Switzerland talking to people about intellectual disability, and he's been on TV and in newspapers and everything. Can't the world see that people with intellectual disabilities make incredible contributions to society every single day?

If you ask me, this psychiatrist seems like she's from the old politics, like she cares more about safeguarding her cushy position in the establishment than she cares about safeguarding the interests of the people. In this case, the establishment would be the psychiatry staff at Hospital del Mar and the people would be Marga. And the enemies of the people, in this case, would be the people behind the crisis of Marga's disappearance, when she was torn from her family unit and living in some abandoned house with no roof or running water. Just like the hovel she used to live in in Arcuelamora with her lardy father Jose and her half-sister Josefa! And now Miss Diana Ximenos says Marga did all that because life in our supervised flat doesn't adapt to her special needs? Because our family unit isn't equipped to give Marga adequate love, understanding and empathy? I may be 52 per cent disabled and climbing, Your Excellency, but I'm not stupid, I can tell Miss Diana is trying to cover her own [*expletive*] and pass the buck, because she was the one who failed to consider the educational, psychological and social-support measures, like the self-advocacy meetings for example, that should have been in place from the get-go to encourage Marga's affective slash sexual integration. And on top of that, Miss Diana didn't even think to get a second opinion, because, as any professional in the world of disability can plainly see, Marga's vanishing act had nothing to do with us or the flat. The only reason a person would drop off the griddle [*sic*] like that is if besides having an intellectual disability to the tune of 66 per cent they also have mental health problems. Or, more precisely, and as any professional in the world of disability could tell you, Marga is a clear case of a person with disabilities exhibiting behavioural disorder, disturbed behaviour, aberrant behaviour or problematic behaviour. So why do you think this psychiatrist from Hospital del Mar said Marga was an open-and-shut case of depression, no different from a non-disabled person who gets laid off and can't make the rent, or a non-disabled schoolteacher whose students walk all over him, or a non-disabled mother with empty-nest syndrome because her kids have all left home? I'll tell you why: because this psychiatrist views people with disabilities as second-class citizens, Your Honour. Because she doesn't see that we all have our own unique medical, social, psychological, biological, emotional and communicative traits. I'm aware you can't expect everyone to know everything and I'm aware doctors all specialise in different specialisations. Even those of us who're 52 per cent disabled can grasp that, with the proper support. But shouldn't a good professional ask questions when there's something she doesn't know? Can you tell me why, when this lady psychiatrist saw Marga's disability staring her in the face, she didn't stand up from her chair, leave her little office and walk down the hallway of the Hospital del Mar psych ward to find some colleague who specialised in aberrant behaviour in people with disabilities? It's like a riddle, Your Honour, if you've listened closely, I've already told you the answer: because she discharges patients with about as much care and attention as a churro-maker cutting churro dough into hot oil. And look, if Social Security is in shambles from all the austerity measures and this lady psychiatrist can't make ends meet, she should take to the streets and join the movement to stop cuts to health care, she should try to actually improve the system from the inside instead of flopping back uselessly in her ergonomic chair, lest some younger psychiatrist with a better work ethic who cares more about his patients sneaks up and pulls that chair right out from under her. Or, if she's not interested in democratic renewal, which we can't force on her, then at the very least she ought to have the humility to say, 'I'm not going to treat this girl, because even though I'm a licensed psychiatrist with 35,000 diplomas hanging on the wall, I'm not qualified to treat this girl with locolethargic [*sic*] ataxia and chafed knees from so much panty-dropping.'

But no such luck, Your Honour. Once again, the representatives of the old politics have abandoned a vulnerable member of society and been derelict in their duty, their duty in this case being to safeguard the best interests of the incompetent individual, because when Your Honourability declared Marga legally incompetent almost as soon as we arrived in Barcelona, it was in the interest of safeguarding Marga's best interests and not your own, because it seems to me Your Excellence is a judge from the new politics, if you don't mind me saying so. Your Excellence isn't a member of the establishment who only cares about the best interests of the establishment. Does Your Grace think I don't know you are going out of your way to have more hearings than are required by law to authorise a tubal litigation [*sic*]? I'm very up to date on the world of disability, that's what being a self-advocate is all about. I know perfectly well the law only requires the judge to read two doctors' reports plus the report from the public prosecutor's office, and you have to have a hearing with the incompetent party, who in this case is Marga. But Marga won't talk, so what does Your Honour do? Instead of saying 'great, one less thing for me to do', you go to the extra trouble of calling in Marga's cousin Patricia Lama Guirao and hearing what she has to say, because Your Honour is a professional who believes in the new politics, a progressive who doesn't treat people like numbers, which is all the more important when dealing with vulnerable populations such as minors and people with disabilities.

I trust Your Honour because you've proven we can trust you. Do you think I read all those papers where they copy all the things I say here? Never! I sign them immediately because I trust everything that comes from Your Honour, and anyway with the migraines I get and these Coke-bottle glasses, I don't see how you could possibly expect me to read all those pieces of paper with all that tiny little writing.

So if you look favourably on the statement from Marga's guardian, who you yourself appointed after hearing from the public prosecutor and the presumptively incompetent individual and the presumptively incompetent individual's family unit, which presumably means you made the appointment with every possible assurance it was a good fit, which, how could you doubt it, seeing as the guardian you appointed was none other than the Generalitat of Catalonia itself, which if you ask me is better than some family member or a foundation trying to hoover up the peanuts Marga gets from Social Security, even though unfortunately that's par for the course for legally incompetent individuals since not everyone is lucky enough to have the Generalitat of Catalonia for a guardian. I mean how could you compare having a RUCID in the middle of nowheresville for your guardian with having the Generalitat, with all its means and all its resources and all its civil servants safeguarding you? Let me tell you, if the Generalitat tells Your Honour that Margarita Guirao Guirao should have that operation and Your Honour thinks it's in her best interest, well, what can I say, have at her. Nobody knows why Marga spends so much time trying to get people to [*expletive*] her, and maybe it's because what she really wants is to get pregnant. Can you imagine how horrible that would be for everyone, starting with Marga and the child with neuro and slash or functional diversity? It takes a village, Your Honour, but what does it take for the village idiot? With my cousin [*expletive*] around so much, it's a wonder she hasn't got pregnant already. Maybe the sexual education didn't go completely to waste and she learned about condoms or the pill. Or maybe she was born that way, unable to have children, like a mule. Because if you cross a male donkey and a female horse you either get a molly mule that can't get pregnant or a jack mule that shoots banks [*sic*], so maybe when you cross my almost completely blind Aunt Emilia with her fat cousin Jose you get a Marga who can't get pregnant, because what kind of not-blind woman would get into bed with a tub of lard like Jose Guirao? No kind of woman I know. Maybe that's why one day Emilia realised she belonged to the species of sensorially impaired human beings and the father of her daughter belonged to the species of the morbidly obese tubs of lard and she and her blindness up and left the village. Everyone said Marga's father was a good person despite being a tub of lard because even though he had another daughter in the house, Josefa, whose mother nobody ever knew anything about, he also kept Marga, who at that point would have been eight years old and I'm sure by that age, even though she wouldn't have been evaluated by the multidisciplinary team at the Disability Assessment Clinic yet, was already clearly 66 per cent intellectually diverse. She was lucky to not come out retinally diverse like her mother, because even though she's not a tub of lard like her father, she is plump, chesty, cellulitic, but that doesn't count as functional diversity. And maybe, like I was telling Your Honour, apart from being born 66 per cent intellectually diverse, Marga was also born reproductively diverse. Maybe they don't need to operate on her [*expletive*] after all, maybe the multidisciplinary professionals at the clinic that assessed the severity of Marga's handicap twenty years ago overlooked her reproductive diversity. Maybe, Your Honour, they accidentally or deliberately failed to adequately fulfil their obligation to evaluate and determine the full scope of her presumptive handicap, and that distorted their assessment of the nature and degree of her disability as it pertains, Your Honour, to the calculation of the benefits, economic rights and services she is entitled to by law, and in doing so, Your Honour, failed to safeguard the best interests of the presumed person with presumptive disabilities. Maybe these multidisciplinary professionals are also part of the establishment, and they gave Marga a lower percentage than she deserved because they don't care about the common good, which in practice means a smaller Social Security benefit and misdirected therapeutic counselling, and that wouldn't favour her socio-sexual integration like those of us in her family unit and all the new-politics professionals I was telling you about are trying to do. Do you know what that would favour? That would favour her marginalisation, which is the opposite of inclusion, the opposite of well-being and the opposite of democracy.

Do I have a problem with my cousin Marga actually being more disabled than she is? I don't see why I should. Do I have a problem, or does Àngels have a problem, or does Nati, as best as she can, have a problem, with giving Marga more care and doing more to support her autonomy? The answer is no, Your Gracefulness. The four of us are the only family unit we've got. We have demonstrated that we can take care of each other and, to be honest with you, Your Honour, I think we're a model case of how living together in a shared flat like all girls our age do is the best path towards the beginning of our normalisation and complete integration as persons with intellectual and slash or functional diversity. If it turns out Marga is 20 per cent more handicapped than we thought because she can't get pregnant? Then we'll care for her that much more! If because of her higher degree of disability she has greater limitations and we need to get a lady to come and take care of the things Marga can't do? Then we'll get one, because if now she's 86 per cent diverse, she'll have a larger Social Security benefit and we'll be able to afford a caregiver! And if they give her another disability evaluation and it turns out the multidisciplinary team wasn't actually part of the establishment after all? If it turns out Marga doesn't actually have reproductive diversity and we have to disable or diversify her fallopian tubes? Then disable away, diversify away, and send the extra two hundred euros a month straight to her flat!

Guadalupe Pinto
Judge

Patricia Lama
Declarant

Javier López Mansilla
Stenographer/Transcriber

Bow-legged Ibrahim thought I'd forgotten his question about whether we could give each other portés, but a bastardist with a Bovaristic past never dodges a question, not even a so-called rhetorical question. Just like there's no such thing as a general idea for Julio Cortázar in *Hopscotch*, for a bastardist with a Bovaristic past, which is to say a bastardist whose entire childhood, adolescence and early adulthood were dedicated to the great and wretched pleasures of negotiating, signing and rescinding that particular kind of purchase agreement that is the sex-love contract, who since nursery school has been a legal expert in the rights and obligations of desire, a prostitute, therefore, since her tender infancy; for her, a bastardist with so much Bovaristic baggage, there's no such thing as a rhetorical question: all questions, even those that are seemingly irresolvable, unanswerable or stupid, require a response, response in the sense of answer and in the sense of confrontation. Sometimes questions must be confronted, rather than answered, meaning we have to reconsider the premise of the question, its formulation and the motivation behind it, like when a left-wing, pro-Catalonia separatist asks an anarchist: Catalan independence, yes or no? The anarchist responds that that's a bourgeois dilemma and like all bourgeois dilemmas, like whether to buy a handbag from Dolce & Gabbana or Victorio & Lucchino, for example, or whether to buy a chalet on the Costa del Sol or a country

153

home in Béjar, it doesn't concern her, because the only initiative she supports with regard to any state or territorial subdivision thereof, including the Autonomous Community of Catalonia, is its destruction. But the Catalan separatist insists, she beautifies the question: What about an independent, feminist, environmentalist, pro-worker Catalonia? Isn't that better than a Spanish-ruled, chauvinist, bull-fighting, conservative Catalonia? The anarchist responds that she doesn't share those frameworks of meaning with respect to the state, since the state, which from its inception in the eighteenth century to the present day has been the model for controlling territories and populations, can never be feminist (it can, at best, be egalitarian) or environmentalist (it can, at best, subsidise environmental NGOs) or pro-worker (it can, at best, be communist), and what she, the anarchist, wants, is independence from both Spain and Catalonia, at which point she braces herself for the lefto-separatist's time-tested retort of 'what a coincidence that the anarchists and the Spanish nationalists end up taking the exact same position', to which the anarchist responds what a coincidence that in Parliament the lefto-separatists and the Spanish nationalists end up earning the exact same salary. 'But unlike other representatives, who are slaves to their donors, separatists give up to two-thirds of their €5,800 per month to the party to self-finance the movement, keeping them free from meddling by the financial sector and other lobby groups.' At this point the anarchist smiles: 'I also don't share your benevolent vision of political parties who claim they can't be bought, nor do I see any difference between the private-financial sector and the public-political sector; if you ask me, all political parties, including yours and Ada Colau's and Pedro Sánchez's, are for-profit enterprises in the business of cranking out public representatives.' And they go on like that all afternoon, the Catalan separatist asking questions, the anarchist confronting those questions until she is branded a reactionary and a fascist, the insults that reactionaries and fascists lavish on anyone who doesn't think like them. This is what happened to me with Ibrahim's disability aide/government-assigned minder/cop on the day of the portés debate. The first debate gave way to the second because it turns out that portés, Bovarism and anti-capitalist Catalan separatism are all sustained by the same ideology: the ideology of rhetoric, of domination through discourse.

Bastardists, by contrast, argue that all questions deserve a response, especially those that are usually deemed stupid, irresolvable and unrespondable, because as bastardists, cultivators of heaven in our homes, we believe in reformulating the criteria by which we judge a question's possibility, resolution and response. We are fiercely anti-rhetoric because we know rhetoric is the language used by power to distinguish between the possible and the impossible, to create what the powerful call reality and impose it on us. We seize and shatter their rhetorical devices, not by calling bread bread and wine wine (another rhetorical device), but by endeavouring to document how every day, without fail, a train of camels passes through the eye of a needle; by going to the forest with each new season to gather the green €100 notes that fall from the deciduous trees in springtime, the purple €500 notes in summer, the yellow €200 notes in autumn, and the grey €5 notes in winter; and by always carrying cotton and ointment, because we know there are kisses that sting and touches that burn. Bastardists are artists, creatures akin to pre-Socratic gods who whispered prophecies to the drugged priestesses in their unknown tongue, or perhaps we're akin to, or are, the entranced priestesses themselves, scorners of philosophy, which is writing, which is death (the very opposite of a Bovary, lover above all of seduction, and fearful beyond all of death).

155

Is it possible, then, for a dancer with more than twenty years of experience to perform a porté with Ibrahim, who needs a walker to move, and who has a twisted spinal column, uneven hips and legs of different lengths? Is it possible for him to perform one with her?

I raised that question at my integrated dance class at the converted multiplex cinema when, in a partner exercise, I was paired with Ibrahim. It was his first class, and he had arrived well dressed and clean-shaven, with a button-down shirt and gel in his hair, like he was going to a job interview instead of a dance class. He was accompanied by the Catalan lefto-separatist with whom I would later argue about independence and the state. I'd never met her, but even from a distance you could tell she was an aide/minder/cop from the centre where Ibrahim lived, a suspicion I later confirmed. You could tell because, first of all, she had that leftist-chic look, the uniform of all Barcelona residents born after 1980 who hold at least one advanced degree in social work (Quechua-brand hiking shoes, harem pants, bumbag, four or five piercings and a single ornamental dreadlock). Second, you could tell she was an aide/minder/cop because instead of letting Ibrahim introduce himself to the instructor, she made the introduction herself, with one hand on Ibrahim's shoulder and a big old smile on her face, one of those extreme, unjustified smiles that aren't a reaction to something funny or enjoyable or touching, but that burst forth from the smiler's conviction that her smile is doing good and transforming everything it touches into goodness and light. And third, you could tell she was an aide/minder/cop because she sat at the edge of the linoleum with her fellow aide/minder/cops to watch the dancers and specifically her charge, at first with great interest because it was the first time in her life she'd seen a woman whose body ends at the waist using her hyperdeveloped arms to drag her torso across the floor like an orangutan, or a paralytic skidding in his wheelchair, or a girl whose entire vocabulary consists of three words singing and doing laps around the rehearsal space. All that novelty astounded her for the first twelve minutes, after which she, like all the other cops, pressed the off button on the back of her neck and the unlock button on her phone, and spent the remaining one hundred and eight minutes of the class in that state, reanimating briefly at minute forty-two when she showed signs of boredom and rolled a cigarette with organic, unbleached papers and biodegradable filters.

'Oh, hey, Ibra, what are you doing here?'

'I asked about you last week at the self-advocacy meeting and they said you might not come any more because you're a really good dancer and you really love dancing.'

Ibrahim doesn't close his lips when he talks, and, since I hadn't seen him for two weeks, I was having a hard time understanding his guttural, wet speech. It's like listening to a foreign language you studied and know but haven't heard in a long time: you can identify the language and tell it apart from others, but you can only pick a few words out from the sounds flying past.

'Sorry, Ibra, did you say last week they told you I wasn't coming any more?'

'Yeah, Laia told me.'

'*Aya*? Your grandmother?'

'No, Laia, the support person.'

'Aaah, Laia Buedo, the psychologist! She told you I've been coming to these classes?'

'Yeah, she told me I could come and try a class if I wanted.'

'Try the class, you said?'

'Yeah.'

'Of course. And the first class is free anyway. Are you still going to the Tuesday meetings?'

'Yeah, Laia says it's very good to combine an associative activity like the self-advocacy meetings with a creative activity like dancing, and she says if I also join the new Easy Read Club, I'll have a good chance at getting a supervised flat like yours.'

'Jesus, Laia sure has a knack for making suggestions,' I said, and Ibrahim started making a croaking sound, which I immediately recognised as laughter, and I started laughing myself. My own laugh is closer to wheezing.

'And she says you're a very good dancer,' is what I think he said, although the croaking made it even harder to understand him.

'You said I'm a good dancer?'

'Very good!'

'I don't know about very good, but honestly, I'd rather dance like a drunk duck than go to another one of Laia's interrogation-coaching sessions.'

'I don't know what that is, but I –' Ibrahim started croaking again, and the croak spread all the way down to his shoulders, which gyrated slowly – 'I definitely dance like a drunk duck!'

'You don't know what a coaching session is, you mean? It's a fascist ploy based on the spirit of achievement and personal growth.'

'Fascist?'

'Yeah, you know, fascist.'

'Like the Nazis and Franco?'

'Exactly. And like Ada Colau and Pedro Sánchez and Laia Buedo.'

'The mayor?'

'The one and only.'

'Got it.'

'Anyway, welcome. You'll like it here. Spending the after-noon dancing like a drunk duck helps shake off the crap feeling that comes with being the subject of an educational and pharmacological market research study.'

'I don't understand what you're saying, Nati.'

'I'm saying dancing is a little less oppressive than playing guinea pig for the disability-industrial complex.'

'The what complex?'

'The assistentialist businesses and public institutions whose mission is to discipline us with medication and lecture us on the virtues of democracy and equality, including the lectures we get at those coaching sessions.'

'Discipline like soldiers in the army?'

'Exactly.'

'Got it.'

The instructor saw us laughing together and suggested we pair up for the first exercise, which involved balance and counterbalance. To balance I support myself against Ibrahim or Ibrahim supports himself against me, and to counter-balance we simultaneously support one another, finding an equilibrium between tension and release. The instructor demonstrated with a student who used a joystick to manoeuvre her whopping electric wheelchair. She barely has enough feeling in her arms and hands to control the chair, so she and the instructor, a dancer whose extremities are all functionally active, had to support each other in unconventional places. He grabbed a handle on the back of her wheelchair with one hand, and she put her chair in neutral. The instructor kept his feet together, very close to the wheel on the same side as the handle he was grabbing, and let his weight fall laterally. He stretched out his free arm with an open hand, forming a triangle with his body. The student was supporting the instructor: balance. Next, counterbalance: facing one another, about a metre apart, they leaned forward until their foreheads were touching. There, where their heads met, was where the force resolved itself, the point of tension and salvation: if either of them let up, both would lose their equilibrium, unequivocal proof that they had achieved counterbalance. Their bodies formed another triangle.

Ibrahim had got out of his slender wheelchair, which looked more like a supersonic bar stool, parked it near his aide/minder/cop and switched to his walker: the cheap kind Social Security gives you if you really grovel.

The walker squeaked as it moved and creaked whenever Ibrahim or I grabbed it anywhere besides the handlebars or tried to support our weight anywhere besides the built-in seat, and it whined like a sick dog if we both tried to sit at the same time. As music, this struck me as artistically interesting, and I was enjoying the exercise. I had the sensation I sometimes get where I feel like I'm a good dancer, like I'm an explorer discovering the possibilities of action. It's an odd sensation. But Ibrahim was apprehensive and scared and a little embarrassed, and it didn't seem like my feeling of safety and confidence was rubbing off on him. He couldn't bring himself to touch me, or he'd only touch me limply, with the excess of caution typical of people who have danced very little or not at all, not even at village festivals or in nightclubs. If, when trying to touch me, he had a spasm and failed to make contact, or if the spasm caused him to smack me, Ibrahim would apologise. That's another thing non-dancers will do: apologise whenever they fall over, crash into you, step on your foot, pull your hair, or stick a finger in your eye, or whenever they inadvertently touch a woman's breasts or anyone's genitals or butt. And they try to make eye contact when they apologise, which interrupts or slows down the whole dance and, apology accepted, it takes them a second to get back into it. They might not regain their former speed or intensity, so the dance becomes no more than a tedious caress. Those of us who dance regularly only apologise for significant accidents, and we only stop the dance (we never slow it down) if the affected party wants to stop; if you're the affected party, you only stop the dance (you never slow it down) if you're seriously hurt, the dreaded injury. Non-dancers will also apologise when they feel they've been ungraceful, and when they do something they perceive as an interruption in the quality of the movement, even if you're the one who caused the accident: I tore the seam of Ibrahim's shirt when I pulled his arm, and even then he said he was sorry. Sorry for what? For being dressed? They must be apologising to themselves for having the gall to dance, for the forbidden action of moving without capitalist purpose or utility. That's what I was thinking, but I didn't say it because I figured it was probably Ibrahim's first time at a dance class, and maybe even the first time, in his twenty-eight years, that he'd ever danced.

I kept responding to Ibrahim's apologies with a 'it's totally fine', or a 'it's no big deal', until they came in such quick succession that I just said 'no worries', and eventually I stopped responding altogether, incorporating his litany of apologies into the music coming from the speakers (which was more like background music, we didn't necessarily have to follow the rhythm), the music coming from his walker, and that other kind of music made by our breathing. The fourth or fifth time I didn't respond to his apology, Ibrahim stopped saying he was sorry and started to concentrate. I made a mental note of this anti-apology stratagem.

The exercise lasted fifteen minutes, during which we succeeded in getting him to encircle my waist with his arms from the seat of the walker, allowing me to fall forward: balance. And we managed to link elbows like two old ladies out for a stroll, both standing, facing the walker, each grabbing one handle. That wasn't balance or counterbalance, it was just a symmetrical figure. Then I suggested that Ibrahim let himself fall to one side without letting go of my elbow or the handle. He didn't understand. I explained again and he still didn't understand. Then I guided his body with mine to try to place it in the right position, but my touch made him nervous and he started falling. I grabbed him under the shoulders so he wouldn't fall on the floor: balance again, albeit unexpectedly.

'Sorry, Nati.'

'No, I'm sorry, Ibra. I shouldn't have manoeuvred your body without your consent and without telling you what I was going to do. I'm really sorry, it won't happen again. Are you hurt?'

'No, no, don't worry.'

'I'm so sorry, I behaved like a domineering fascist. If we can't balance then we can't balance, it's no big deal. Success shouldn't come at the expense of one of us dominating the other's body. That was a really shit thing to do, Ibra, I'm sorry.'

'It's no big deal, Nati. I like dancing with you.'

'You're really nice. Thank you.' I couldn't exactly say it back – that I liked dancing with Ibrahim – but then again, I'm not totally sure I know what liking something means, and I'm also not sure dancing should be a question of what we do and don't like.

Then came the porté exercise that prompted the debate. According to Lluís Cazorla, the instructor, a porté or pickup (he mostly used the latter term because porté reminded him of ballet, which contemporary dancers usually abhor on stylistic and ideological grounds) is the bliss of balance in motion. Lluís had it exactly right, I liked his definition: it was brief, simple, clear, effective and we all understood it. Ibrahim reminded me I'd talked about portés two weeks earlier at the self-advocacy meeting. Was that what the instructor was talking about? I said yes and his eyes lit up.

162

'Sex portés?' he asked, and then my eyes lit up too. It's so nice when you find someone who remembers the important things.

'They could become sexual, but they aren't always. To be honest, Ibra, getting sexual pleasure from a porté is highly unlikely. The porté I was talking about that afternoon was one in a thousand.'

'Got it, got it.'

We'd already spent several classes doing portés, Cazorla had a thing for elaborate staging I guess. It can be beautiful when a person with one or no legs forgoes her wheelchair or artificial leg to perform a porté. For example, María, who's an amputee from her thighs down, can place one of her strong arms between my legs and bend her elbow over my perineum so her open, firm hand rests on my abdomen. Then she fits her shoulder under my butt cheek and lifts me a few centimetres, guiding me on long, tiptoed strides and the occasional leap. She regulates my speed and elevation with her elbow and uses her other super-arm to support herself as she moves through space, bringing me with her. It's a really cool move we worked out with Lluís Cazorla's help, a low-flying porté that requires precise execution.

I'd wanted to be paired with María, because when all is said and done you go to dance classes to fly, solo or with a partner, but in any case, to fly. Or I could've been paired with Juli, who can launch himself and others into psychedelic flight because his blindness gives him a unique awareness of height and space; or with the gorgeous Rita, whose wheelchair is as light as she is nimble and strong, and who spins us both at ludicrous speeds before ejecting me in a wild leap. These portés aren't sexual because they aren't the product of improvisation (we have to make lots of adjustments and try over and over until both my partner and I are satisfied), so they can't be likened to stolen kisses. But they're festive portés all the same, brief banquets.

My partner that day, however, was Ibrahim. Since these are open-level classes, all the students are given the same exercise and everyone does their best and gets as far as they get. That means when the exercise involves jumping, for example, everyone jumps as well as they can, including, perhaps, someone without legs. Someone without arms might be asked to embrace their partner. A deaf person might be instructed to follow the rhythm of the music and a blind person might be instructed to mimic someone's movements. Someone with the memory of a goldfish, who can't remember his last step, might be told to develop a choreography, and someone who can't sit still for five seconds might be told to move only her diaphragm as she gently breathes in and out. Ibrahim and I were expected, then, to perform the best portés we could, regardless of how they'd turn out, according to our own understanding of 'the bliss of balance in motion'.

'The kiss of balance in motion, Nati, just like you said!' said Ibra, but I wasn't sure if he said 'kiss' or 'bliss'. I asked:

'Did you say bliss or kiss?'

'Bliss.' That time I'd swear he said 'bliss' and not 'kiss'.

'Bliss?'

'Yes.' I got the feeling he was messing with me.

'Right. Well, let's get going on that bliss or kiss or yes in motion,' I said, irked by his teasing but encouraged by his determination. I grabbed his hands (pulling them from the handles of the walker, which he was clutching for dear life), moved into the small space between him and the walker, and placed his hands back on the handles, closing myself in. His forehead was at the height of my neck and his neck was at the height of my breasts. We stood like that for a few seconds, silent but conversing with our breath (Ibrahim mostly breathing through his mouth as usual, restrained, me breathing slowly from the diaphragm). All around us, pairs were trying out different positions and grips, tripping, knocking over wheelchairs and walkers, falling off crutches, getting back up. My erstwhile partner María was trying to perform our porté with a short, cross-eyed kid whose name I can't remember, who had a fit of laughter every time María put her arm over his perineum; it just wasn't going to work. The kid's genitals must have rested on María's wrist like a bird's nest on a tree branch. Lluís Cazorla went from couple to couple, observing, suggesting adjustments or highlighting successes, sometimes helping the dancers work out their positions by putting himself in one of their places so they could see the possibilities and limitations of a given movement from the outside. I saw Ibrahim's aide/minder/cop had buried her eyes in her phone. Cazorla had put a sexy-blues Leonard Cohen song on in the background.

When he got to Ibrahim and me, he stood and watched our stillness, silent like us. If Ibrahim could barely stand my silence (and I wasn't even looking at him, not even at his hair, which was the only part of him in my field of vision), then Lluís's scrutinising silence, scrutinising and lustful, the silence of a spectator waiting for the performers to amaze him, must have been unbearable. He rushed to proffer twenty thousand nasal I'm sorries and released one of the handles in a clear invitation for me to leave through the opening, to get away.

'No apology necessary! What was your name again?' Lluís asked.

'Ibrahim.'

'It's totally fine, Ibrahim. The position you two chose makes it a little hard to start a pickup.'

'Does it?' I asked.

'I think so, Nati. Whatever you do, Ibrahim is going to have to support himself on his walker. You could grab him like a sack of potatoes, but not much else. And Ibrahim,' he said, turning, 'you don't really have the manoeuverability to pick up Nati. All she could do is hook around your waist or neck and let you drag her.'

'And that wouldn't be balance in motion?' I asked.

'Technically, yes, but you'd look less like you were doing pickups and more like you're halfway through your shift hauling boxes at the warehouse!' This comment made Ibrahim laugh, though I certainly didn't see anything funny about it. So what if we look like we're working at a warehouse? Is there something funny about working at a warehouse? Are we assuming that warehouse workers don't know how to do portés? Why is it considered choreographically pointless to imitate a warehouse worker but choreographically meaningful to imitate a swan? 'But go ahead and try, try it your way. The starting position with the two of you facing each other was perfectly nice, with you between Ibrahim and the walker. Try to think of ways to make it evolve into an easier position for a pickup.'

'It's so hard!' said Ibrahim, relaxed and smiling for the first time all afternoon, which I took as an indication of male-on-male solidarity.

'Nah, you got this!' Lluís replied, clapping him on the back, unmistakable confirmation of macho solidarity. Hadn't I been touching Ibrahim all afternoon, touching him so he'd look me straight in the eyes, like he was looking at Lluís now? 'Be patient and see where you get. Small movements and small balances are OK. One of you grabbing the other's finger and exerting force through that finger to move through space – that's already a porté.'

When Cazorla, with his comment about the displaced finger, concluded his observation and started moving towards the next couple, I raised the question about portés:

166

'Sorry, Lluís, sorry, could you come back here a second?'

'Sure, what's up?' he said, returning to me and Ibrahim.

'I think my friend is right, this porté business is pretty hard.'

'Don't worry about trying anything complex. Your bodies possess many possibilities for action, it's just a matter of discovering them. The simplest of movements can sometimes be the most effective.'

'That's not it, Lluís. The issue is with the underlying premise of the exercise.'

'The underlying premise? I don't follow, Nati.'

'The problem is the way portés and their feasibility are conceived relative to one another.'

'Mm, tell me more,' he said, stepping closer.

'Consider the seemingly simple question Ibrahim asked me three weeks ago. He asked, "Nati, do you think I could do a porté with you or you could do one with me?" What would you say to that, Lluís?'

'Of course he can. That's what this class is for.'

'Right, what else would an integrated dance instructor say? But I think the answer is no, of course we can't.' Cazorla's expression changed. He looked around, assessing how many couples he still had to observe and internally debating whether to carry on talking to me or carry on doing his job. 'Let's complicate this seemingly simple question that you just answered without hesitating. Can Ibrahim, with his twisted spinal column, his uneven hips and his walker, do a porté with me, a dancer with more than twenty years of experience? Can I, a dancer with more than twenty years of experience, do a porté with Ibrahim?'

This set off every ideological alarm in the building. The standard allotted time for this kind of exercise had passed and the students, impatient for a new activity from the instructor, started approaching Ibrahim, Lluís and me. One student had heard me and muttered 'snobby' or 'snotty', but I didn't respond because I was watching Cazorla's face, where I could tell he was crunching numbers: students pay thirty-five euros per month to attend his classes or, alternatively, ten euros per class. His students are platonic, Cartesian liberals, and they draw a clear distinction between mind and body, between action and thought and, therefore, between dancing and talking about dancing; they consider discussion of dance inappropriate for a dance class, where people go to move their bodies, which they view as different from their minds. Now, Cazorla is clever, and he might know better, but he also knows that attending to the discursive, non-dancerly needs of one student means neglecting the dancerly needs of the rest of the class. Is ensuring one student's loyalty worth jeopardising the loyalty of the remaining fifteen? The mathematical answer is obvious but, as I said, Cazorla is clever and he was trying to think beyond the obvious; I could see that on his face, too. Should he entertain this debate about dance and make his own views clear, thereby asserting his authority before the fifteen non-critical students, albeit at the expense of delaying the class in the platonic, Cartesian, liberal sense of the word? According to a rhetorical conception of language, which is to say a competition- and persuasion-oriented conception of language, Cazorla was assessing his odds of emerging stronger from the debate, and my odds, therefore, of emerging weaker, meek as a lamb and less keen on busting his balls. But could Lluís Cazorla be sure the other fifteen students would share his point of view? How could he make sure there were no dissenting voices among the Cartesian ranks, dissenting voices that may not want to come back to his classes? Isn't it wiser to not take sides, not put up a fight? Isn't it better to remain in blithe, big-tent ambiguity, the big tent of non-confrontation where there's room for all his students and their thirty-five euros a month? As Cazorla silently performed the calculation in his head, I answered my own unanswered question:

'A Bovary would say that yes, both Ibrahim and the experienced dancer can perform portés with one another, since willingness creates aptitude, and aptitude is only a step or two away from beauty, and beauty is the undisputed, reactionary objective of Bovarism. A bastardist, on the other hand, would say –'

'Sorry, Nati,' Lluís interrupted, 'but I don't know if you said Bovary, or what that is, or if I misheard you or what, but in any case, I'd like to know what that is so I can understand you. And I don't know if you said bastardist or if I heard you right about that, either, but, same thing, I'd love to know what that is too so I can understand you,' he said, getting flustered because teachers are supposed to exude self-confidence at all times. That's what happens when you think of dialogue as a tool for subjugation rather than a means of reaching the truth, you have to spend the whole conversation devising discursive strategies to defeat your verbal opponent and, naturally enough, you get nervous.

'You'll understand in no time, Lluís, let me finish and I'll get to it,' I answered sympathetically, appreciating his effort to step out of combat and join me in true conversation.

'All right,' he said, lifting the palms of his hands like Tina Johanes when I told her I wasn't taking off my socks because I had a blister.

'Bastardism would be like bastard, right? And Bovarism would be like being a cow, like bovine?' asked Andrea, a tiny woman with a melon-shaped head who's extremely good at detaching and reattaching the wheel of her wheelchair while she dances.

'Exactly!' I said, delighted. I knew the class couldn't be entirely composed of rancid eruditicians. 'And Bovary also comes from a famous story that was published as a series in a French magazine a hundred and fifty years ago then strung together and sold as a novel called *Madame Bovary*, about a woman who spent so much time with males she got malaise.'

'A series like on TV?' asked Ibrahim.

'No, a series like a book published in parts. The same as on TV except in a book, though there's also the film version.'

At this point the class had come to a complete halt, and most of the students were listening in. Others, the minority, had seen what was going on, decided they weren't interested, and gone about their business, talking about their lives or looking at their phones. The student who, in my opinion, is the best dancer in the class – the silent, slender Bruno – had continued dancing. He dances to music only he can hear. No matter what exercise Lluís assigns or what music he puts on, Bruno matches his movements to his own exclusive dance, spinning on one foot, then the other, with the unhurried cadence of a roly-poly doll, his arms lifted in a gentle cross, not tensed, but outstretched like wings, not to propel his twirls, but to soften them, to stop himself from getting dizzy. From time to time, he touches his face in a gesture of self-enquiry, with an expression of profound concentration, though it never interferes with his dance; sometimes he smiles only for himself, stretching his neck skyward and moving his lips but saying nothing, or nothing audible; other times, perhaps because he's finally become dizzy, he slows to a halt, letting his torso fall forward with his legs fully outstretched, or lowering himself into a perfect split, stretching deeply for variable lengths of time, for as long as he's getting pleasure from the stretch, before bursting back into a vertical rapture of twirling and self-enquiry. That's what makes Bruno the best dancer in the class: because he dances for pleasure alone, and watching that continuous pleasure from the outside is thrilling, dazzling.

Bruno kept his distance, availing himself of the space's two hundred square metres to dance for himself without anyone trying to teach him about balance, counterbalance or portés, without even having to worry about someone else's music interfering with his own internal soundtrack because, by this point in the debate, Cazorla had turned the stereo off. He had run the numbers and determined it served his interests as a freelance professional to stop the dancing and debate me.

'As I was saying, Lluís, a Bovary would say yes but a bastardist would say no, Ibrahim cannot do portés in either position. He can't pick up his partner, move her through space or return her to the ground safely or relatively safely, nor can he be picked up, moved through space, or returned to the ground safely or relatively safely, and he certainly can't do any of this with grace and fluidity, which is to say he is unable to do it with a minimal expenditure of effort. But effortlessness is the heart of pleasure and, ultimately, the heart of beauty, since, for bastardists, beauty is nothing more than politicised pleasure, pleasure imbued with emancipatory meaning. Unlike Bovaries, for whom the heart of pleasure is submission to the desires of another: that's why they love to play dominatrices, that paradox of sadomasochism, in which the slave is actually the master, because according to the terms of that particular sex-love contract, the false master modulates the degree of her violence (as well as the height of her heels, the lace of her lingerie, and the quality of her leathers) according to the petitions from her false slave and true master.' Many of my bipedal classmates had taken a seat on the floor, and the non-bipeds who had been dancing on their feet had returned to their wheelchairs and crutches. Ibrahim sat on the seat of his walker. Out of deference, I didn't sit down until Lluís did. He sat sprawled comfortably, but I used the opportunity to cross one foot in front of the other and tilt my trunk forward. This ischiotibial stretch is my favourite, it gives me a pleasurable gnawing sensation all along my hamstrings. I kept talking, lifting my neck like a turtle:

'In integrated dance classes, instructors talk about ambulatory and non-ambulatory dancers. I'm ambulatory and Ibrahim isn't, since he needs a walker or a wheelchair to move through space in a socially acceptable way, which is to say, in a way that approximates upright walking as closely as possible. In integrated dance, bipedalism is about the functionality of the legs, not just their existence. Even though Ibrahim has two legs, if he didn't use a walker or a wheelchair, he would have to crawl to move through space, so portés are clearly out of the question for him.' The barrage of Ibrahim's name in his aide/minder/cop's ear must have struck the on button at the top of her spine, because she looked up from her phone. 'He's also incapable of moving within the parameters of fluidity and safety of Western bipedal dance or achieving emancipatory bastardistic beauty, and he will only ever achieve reactionary Bovaristic beauty with great difficulty. What is a rhetorical Bovaristic spirit (which is to say, a democratic spirit, which is to say, a fascist spirit) trying to say when it claims that Ibrahim can do portés?' The corporate-organic intelligence of the Police Aide Corps prompted the other aide/minder/cops to look up from their respective smartphones and even look at one another. 'It's saying that Ibrahim can learn to mimic bipedal portés. That Ibrahim can put his twisted body at the service of the limpid movements of bipedal dance, proving that dance isn't just for canonical bodies, asserting that where there is a will to imitate, beauty will find a way to shine through even a contorted body like his. The democratic spirit is commending him, then, to another spirit: the spirit of achievement, that timeless fascist axiom that says overcoming what you are means having the strength to forget who you are and become someone

172

else.' What's going on? What do we do? the aide/minder/cops asked one another with a look, blinking and squinting as they adapted to the room's white light after so much time in a pixelated penumbra. 'Becoming someone else is desirable because someone else is better than you. This spirit of achievement, the can-do spirit, is present wherever there are models to follow, which means wherever there is hierarchy, which means wherever there is a thirst for subjugation. The spirit of achievement, the will to succeed and the drive to overcome adversity are a ploy cooked up by the marketing department at social Darwinism HQ to make us believe that we can achieve happiness if we just try hard enough and, in this particular case, to make Ibrahim believe that if he strives to perform a Western bipedal porté, even if he never achieves it, it will have been a worthwhile endeavour simply because he gave it his all.' In response to this interruption in the usual order of the class, the aide/minder/cops, from their seats, considered intervening and potentially re-establishing choreographic order, an option they weighed against the dictates from their higher-ups, whose instructions clearly stated that they should allow their wards, many of whom were self-advocates, to independently address the many unforeseen circumstances that arise during life in society except when such a circumstance becomes ostensibly unmanageable, thereby encouraging their wards to collectively exercise their individual autonomy and incidentally preventing themselves, the aide/minder/cops, from falling into paternalistic attitudes. 'Believing in self-improvement means believing in achievement, which means believing in accumulation, which means believing in capital, which means believing in progress, which means believing that something achieved with little to no effort is less valuable, or even worthless. This scale of values is the bedrock of the aforementioned hierarchy and the justification for the aforementioned subjugation. Which is more

173

valuable: a hard-won kiss after three weeks of courtship or a quick fuck with a stranger? They claim the value added from all that effort makes the kiss of courtly love more worthy. They even want us to believe it tastes better than a kiss that smacks of booze and cigarettes! Tell me, who's worth more: the lottery winner or the worker who gets up at six every morning? What about the worker who gets up at six every morning or the welfare queen and the dumpster diver? The girl who barely scrapes a pass on the test after cramming the night before or the girl who aces it after studying for two weeks? What's worth more, Ibrahim dragging himself onto the stage or Ibrahim being placed on the proscenium, releasing his walker and attempting to balance by extending his arms as far as possible, which isn't very far and makes him look like a crab brandishing its pincers? Ibrahim dragging himself across the stage or Ibrahim sitting comfortably in his wheelchair and bobbing his head to the music?' Ibrahim's aide noticed her ward was coming up an awful lot without him collectively exercising his individual autonomy in response. In fact, Ibrahim was right beside me, listening closely but not saying a word. His aide abandoned her post at the edge of the room and crossed the white linoleum floor in her Sunday-morning hiking shoes, coolly gauging the danger like a gunslinger, her phone locked at the hip, ready to draw in an instant, knowing her posse of aide/minder/cops had her back, as they had wordlessly indicated their support in the event that reinforcements proved necessary. 'Since I not only do not believe in progress and effort, but actively resist them day and night, and since I believe in listening closely to our appetites and their alliance with the appetites of others as the driving forces of life, I will not be complicit in this act of fascist self-improvement by attempting to twirl Ibrahim in the air when, at best, I can rock him in my arms, nor will I let Ibrahim hold me by the waist as I exaggerate my motions, feigning that he's the one moving me. So long as I am Ibrahim's partner, I will renounce portés and all other classic and contemporary dance figures that require bipedal skill or speed because, from a bastardistic perspective, which is to say, in the interest of true emancipation, Ibrahim should not be forced to adapt to any pre-established model of movement, nor should he be guided by some reactionary ideal of fluidity, safety or beauty. As Ibrahim's partner, I refuse to adhere to these dictates of Western dance, which would require subsuming his possibilities of movement within those available to bipeds, the privileged social class to which I belong.' Ibrahim's aide had joined the circle of listeners, albeit at the outermost edge. I saw her when I turned to speak to that part of the circle, and as soon as I noticed her demeanour – strictly silent, but also strictly threatening and strictly judgemental – I shifted to fully face her, interrupted my ischiotibial stretches on the floor and stood so our eyes were at the same height, a move that roused my gates and put them on alert: still out of sight in their retracted position but ready. 'I renounce all of my bipedal privileges insofar as they pertain to dancing with Ibrahim. I want no part in the stylisation of my friend's move-ment. I won't watch Ibrahim try to regularise the intensity of his convulsions in the interest of fluidity, I won't act as a crutch for his precarious upright posture in the interest of safety, and I won't develop a harmonious choreography of movements and pauses between Ibrahim and myself that would require repressing his spasms in the interest of beauty. Because after five classes, I'm starting to realise that's what integrated dance is all about: getting non-normalised bodies and minds to integrate into the governing system of norm-following bodies and minds.' Lluís Cazorla was also silent, but it wasn't the silence of a hunter waiting for his moment to fire; it was more like the silence of an audience watching a show, attentive and predisposed to surprise. And my classmates' silence? It wasn't total silence, because some of them were sighing or whispering, so they clearly wanted to speak, in dissent or in support or to add nuance, but they didn't, which meant their speech had been repressed; they weren't silent, but silenced. 'That's what stylisation sets out to do: to normalise. That's what the choreographic trident of fluidity, safety and beauty is all about: normalisation. That's the whole point of over-coming adversity: to become normal. Another citizen, another equal. Words are devious things: the spirit of achievement is none other than the spirit of normalisation. Stop being who you are so you can be mediocre like everyone else. The spirit of achievement is nothing more than the spirit of mediocrity. And what is mediocrity? Mediocrity isn't a runner coming in twenty-eighth place. That's just a bad runner. Mediocrity is winning the race, taking to the podium, and thanking the bank or oil company that sponsored you. Mediocrity is the inoffensive. Mediocrity is pop superstar Rihanna being repeat-edly abused by her boyfriend. Sensational is the housewife serving her husband his dinner then smashing his head in with her cast-iron frying pan. Mediocrity is non-politicisation, mediocrity is integration, and mediocrity, therefore, is inte-grated dance.' I paused here, waiting for a response, but everyone avoided eye contact, including Cazorla and Ibrahim. Blind Juli had been resting his ears for a while now, pointing them away from the torrent of my voice; eventually he got up, felt along the wall for his cane, and left. As the dancers broke away from the group, the Police Aide Corps mobilised to help their wards get dressed. I'm fully aware that silence is just a postmodern maxim for conflict neutralisation; I know this is further proof of the spiral of silence theory; I know that when others fall silent, they want me to follow suit so that all of us can trudge through life without fussing; and I know the hegemonic discourse is most forceful when it won't dignify you with a response; but even so, this silence from my classmates, in whose broken dances I had found so much brilliance, and especially from María, who took my pause as an opportunity to get up and go home, left me utterly deflated; Ibrahim's aide/minder/cop was the only person with something to say:

'You make a very good point. What did you say your name was?'

Everyone turned to her with renewed attention. The sound of someone else's voice after such a lengthy monologue was so dramatic and striking that it halted the spiral of silence's circular advance. It created a frontality, a dialectic.

'I didn't.'

'Oh, no? I thought you did.'

'No.' Gate mechanism activating, toothed gears beginning to turn.

'Right, excuse me. I must have heard the instructor call you by your name, then. What was it?'

'Natividad.'

'Nice to meet you, Natividad. I'm Rosa. Like I said, you make a very good point. It's important to always express our likes and dislikes with each other.' Gates emerging, initiating their facial transition. 'A question occurred to me while I was listening to you. Do you mind?' The extreme, unnecessary, infantilising amiability typical of power. Gates sealing shut.

'I don't mind in the least, please, go ahead.'

'I was just wondering if all your criticism might simply be because, the thing about you is, you just don't want to dance with Ibrahim.'

'That's your question? If all this is just an excuse to not dance with Ibrahim?'

'That's what I'm asking, yes.'

177

'Well, no, it's not, and it's astonishing to me that your question has nothing to do with anything I said.' Lluís Cazorla made a subtle pacifying gesture with his hand, which I neutralised by making an equally subtle gesture with my own. 'Your question is based on a suspicion that everything I've been saying for the past hour has been sheer pretence. That I'm playing. You're accusing me of rhetoric, when the very first thing I said was that I'm fiercely anti-rhetoric. Though, of course, how could you have heard me when you've been sitting over there on your phone since five o'clock.'

All the dancers, including Cazorla, smiled and turned to the aide, waiting for her to retrieve the ball and kick it back to centre field. Except Ibrahim, who hesitated. He had the same look of compunction on his face as when he kept apologising during the exercise, as if he felt guilty or embarrassed about his name being at the centre of the debate.

'You're right, I didn't hear everything you said, and I'm sorry about that. But please don't put words in my mouth, I didn't accuse you of pretending anything. If you don't want to dance with Ibrahim, why don't you just say so? Clearly you have no problem speaking openly.' Lluís Cazorla gave her a disapproving look (another attempt at pacification), which she repelled by lifting her hand.

'At least you acknowledge you didn't hear three-quarters of what I said. And I say everything openly, absolutely everything, it's part of the bastardist-emancipatory process, the bit you missed because you were playing with your phone.'

'I was on my phone, you're right, taking care of some work.' I was cracking up laughing on the inside, but I didn't show it. If you laugh at an aide/minder/cop then that's it, game over; laughter gets them triggered as hell, it's a more forceful repudiation than any insult. You can call them torturers or Nazis, but if you laugh at them, they stop listening and straight-up get you arrested, and I wanted this fascist to keep listening to me.

'Well, now that you're done working, let's talk. So far, I've offered a critique of the issue's underlying premise, but now comes the propositional part, where I suggest an alternative to the squalid state of affairs I just described, after which I'm sure you'll have no doubt that I do want to dance with Ibrahim.'

I moved closer to Ibrahim and he, without quite moving away, shifted as if he were uncomfortable with my proximity, the same way caged canaries flutter when you stick a finger through the bars. Was he afraid his aide/minder/cop would take this out on him, like parents beat their kids after a bad day at work? Especially since this was his first dance class, which he'd been so insistent on attending? Would she retaliate by not letting him come back and returning him to the self-advocacy meetings? The thought made me resume my exposition even more vehemently, eager to make myself worthy of Ibrahim's trust:

'Given this situation, and this place, my partner and I have to make a choice. Either we can stop attending these dance classes, which, after being kicked out of the BADDAY, would be my second choreofascistic defeat in under a year, or we can resist the fascism of integrated dance through the performance of disintegrated dance. I hope Ibrahim chooses the latter, because it is one of the paths that lead to freedom. Rather than stylisation, I propose degradation. Rather than self-improvement, I propose abjection; and rather than the spirit of achievement, I propose the spirit of fornication. I spent years mastering fluidity in dance, but I will forsake that fluidity in favour of Ibrahim's flustering convulsions. I can keep Ibrahim and myself safe as we dance thanks to my physical strength and self-possession, but I will forsake that safety so I can risk falling and injuring myself as I move with

Ibrahim's muscular atony and lack of bodily awareness. I can achieve beauty by moving in certain ways, or by standing in a certain position or in certain clothing, or even naked, but I will forsake that beauty because I want drool to drip off my chin like it drips off Ibrahim's, I want to piss myself like Ibrahim and smell like piss like Ibrahim, I want a twisted mouth, warped knees, tensed wrists and fingers like Ibrahim's, I want to repel the normalised demofascists all around me as Ibrahim repels them. I am asking him to cultivate the repellence that has always followed him wherever he goes, which has always made him suffer; and I am asking him to teach me that repellence. Rather than yielding to power in despondence and defeat, we can radicalise against it. We can become so thoroughly repellent that they wouldn't dare tell us to overcome our adversity, so repellent that instead of condescension, the only feelings we arouse in the normalised masses are insurmountable fear, dread and disgust.'

I finished speaking and Lluís Cazorla waited a few seconds for a response. It was only after no one said anything that he told us to gather our things, we'd gone over by twenty minutes and another group needed the space. Ibrahim, relieved, hobbled his walker over to his wheelchair, clinging to his aide/minder/cop's skirts. That made me suffer as I put on my shoes. With Ibrahim at her tail, the minder – livid but exuberant because she must have interpreted her ward's physical closeness as some kind of victory – came over and told me I should be ashamed of myself for saying all those horrible things about Ibrahim, I wasn't pulling the wool over her eyes, she knew it was just a ruse to not dance with him, I was just a brat who wanted attention, I hadn't seen the last of her. I finished lacing up my shoes, stood up and, without failing to comply with Cazorla's request for us to leave, told her to take her threats to Parliament or the board of trustees at some state-owned enterprise (since that's where separatists like her hang out), and when she takes the floor, she can threaten her fellow representatives and trustees with waging the Catalan revolution all she wants, but her threats weren't going to work on me because I didn't give a shit about her aide/minder/cop licence, and if I did have a shit to give, I would smear it into a map of the Països Catalans on the pro-independence flag that she no doubt had hanging from her balcony.

That was when she came up so close I could smell the sickly-sweet aroma of her Fructis shampoo, looked at me with the hatred authoritarians reserve not for their political enemies but for the lumpenproletariat and, switching from Spanish to Catalan, as if by doing so she were summoning the world's two million Catalan speakers to form the most powerful army on earth against which I wouldn't stand a chance, she said I wasn't just a liar and a bad person, I was something much worse: a Spanish nationalist. I love it when separatists do that, it's the last refuge of a rhetorical scoundrel, the only thing they have left to hurl at you after they've exhausted all their other bourgeois baloney. I had to go without my precious shower in the locker rooms and leave the school covered in dried sweat, carrying my towel, change of clothes and soap for nothing, so we could litigate the false dilemma of Catalan independence all the way to the metro. A false dilemma about which Ibrahim, apparently, couldn't care less; he lagged a few steps behind me and his aide/minder/cop and made small talk with Marga, who had come to pick me up as usual and for whom Catalan independence is about as interesting as a turd drying and crusting over in the Mediterranean sun.

Anarchist Social Centrr of Sants Barcelona
Okupation Working Group
Meeting Minutes, 2 July 2018

Tarragona:	Whose taking the minutes today?
Ceuta:	Looks like you are if your asking.
Tarragona:	I'm asking because Jaén took the minutes the last few times and I think its a task we should share among all of us just like cleaning and postering.
Jaén:	I can do it today its no problem. I actually like taking them.
Oviedo:	And you write the best to. When Palma takes the minutes they're total gibberish.
Palma:	Wow thanks Oviedo
Badajoz:	Its true dude hahaha
Coruña:	Hahaha Palma the notes you took that one time holy hell.
Palma:	Honestly half the time even I can't read them myself afterwards.
Tangier:	But anything can be taught. I agree we should rotate.
Mallorca:	Tangier is right otherwise we fall into roles and specialisations, professionalising our tasks. Just like we've subverted the notion that women are always supposed to be the ones who cook and

	clean we should subvert the notion that the writer should always be the one who writes.
Tarragona:	I think so to. Everybody writes differently but over time the people who don't write so well will improve. Its not a problem.
Oviedo:	I mean its a problem if the minutes are so bad we can't understand them.
Coruña:	Right but we can do it like we do everything, the folx who do it best can teach everyone else right? That way we pool our knowledge and our skills. Like when Gari dictated her case for okupation to Jaén. For me that's libertarian communism.
Murcia:	Why don't we start with an update on Gari's okupa? We can talk about it now instead of at the end since she always has to leave early.
Gari Garay:	I don't have to leave early any more since I don't have to go back to Barceloneta.
Murcia:	You got in to the house on Mossen Torne?
Gari:	Yeah
Murcia:	Ah I didn't know! Congratulations!
Tangier:	Me neither congrats
Gari:	Thank you
Nata Napalm:	But I still have to leave early because I still have to go back to Barceloneta and I'm interested in the agenda item regarding Gari. I only came to hear about that, I'm not even remotely interested in the other things this working group is going to talk about.
Murcia:	Don't feel like you have to be tactful please tell us how you really feel.
Various members:	hahahahahahaha … …

Gari:	This is my cousin
Murcia:	Ah this is your cousin
Ceuta:	Let's talk about the okupa first then.
Mayorca:	Right but first we have to figure out whose taking the minutes.
Palma:	I can do it
Oviedo:	But you can't write for shit!!!!
Various members:	Hahahahahaha …
Palma:	Yeah yeah but when folx started making fun of my minutes I turned the voice recorder on my phone on so I can record everything that way.
Tangier:	Palma, dude! Without telling us?
Badajos:	Informant alert! Haha
Nata:	Informant how?
Badajos:	Like by recording us, like an informant
Nata:	You people are obsessed with informants
Badajos:	Rightly so hey Nata? You know the Mossos desquadra came and raided us two months ago.
Nata:	We can talk about your informant fetish later tonight I'm in a hurry.
Badajso:	Add it to the minutes Palma we'll put it on the agenda for the next meeting.
Nata:	Long live bureaucracy and the politburo.
Various members:	Hahahahahaha …
Palma:	Yeah yeah later I'll type it all up verbatim in word so I don't have to worry about all of you saying how well or bad I write any more.
Jaén:	Fine but just swap our names out for the cities like always
Palma:	Of course

Oviedo:	And then destroy the recording after like Inspector Gadget when he gets a letter
Palma:	Hahahaha you got it
Tangier:	OK so this agenda item isn't resolved but let's move on to Gari's okupa so Nata can leave early and then we'll continue.
Nata:	Thank you
GG:	Well yeah Badajoz Mallorca Coruña Oviedo and Nata Napalm came and helped me. I got in three days ago. I left the okupa for the first time today because of what you told me about staying inside for 72 hours.
Murcia:	Has there been any weird activity? Cops, neighbours, someone ringing the doorbell?
Gari:	There isn't a doorbell
Mallorca:	Wait lets go in order. First let us tell you how we got in.
Oviedo:	Yeah so Palma doesn't get mixed up and botch the transcription
Palma:	Jesus enough already
Jaén:	Go easy Oviedo
Tarragona:	Yeah Oviedo if Palma's initiative strikes you as so terrible you can take the minutes yourself. Your attitude is very toxic and immature and its not like your proposing any alternatives.
Oviedo:	Sorry sorry your right your right. Sorry Palma. Its my fault, I'm a little stoned.
Coruña:	Well maybe you ought to step outside for a minute and let the buzz wear off. You keep interrupting and our friend here wants to talk about Gari's okupa.

185

Mallorca: Wow we can get side tracked. Can we try and focus a little folx? Back to the beginning, getting in. It was easy right?

Badajoz: Totally. Our first idea was to do it before sunrise around 4, but since Gari had problems getting to the neighbourhood at night we did it during the day. We put on a little skit.

Gari Garay: Yeah I couldn't get there at night because there's no metro plus during the day it was easier to leave the supervised flat without saying where I was going.

Badajoz: We met up at 5 in the afternoon because there's a school nearby and that's when the kids get out so there's lots of foot traffic, the shops are open, there's construction nearby …

Mallorca: I dressed up like a lock smith in a blue jump suit and carried a tool box and Oviedo dressed like a real estate agent in a skirt and heels with a brief case and everything. When she comes back if she wants she can talk about the misogynist abuse she had to deal with on her way to the house.

Tangier: Shit

Mallorca: Yeah some fucking dudebro gave her shit. And well I guess this could be another topic to discuss because Oviedo didn't react because we were playing it cool for the sake of the okupa but things went South anyway.

Badajoz: Nata tore him a new one

Nata: I did

Badajoz: Honestly it was super powerful and everything she said was right but seeing as our goal was to go unnoticed and brake into the house, I think Nata's reaction made us run an unnecessary risk.

Nata: I agree we ran a risk but I don't agree that it was unnecessary.

Badajoz: Call it what you like. But it was an excessive risk.

Nata: I'm not calling it what I like Badajoz. I'm calling it by its name and its name is necessary risk A risk that had to be taken to prevent this okupa, which ought to be a tool for emancipation, from becoming just the opposite, which is to say an act of oppression against our friend. Remaining silent in the face of that abuse would make us complicit. It would turn us into abusers ourselves. And it would corrupt the okupa which is supposed to be a tool for emancipation. And look how things turned out. Oviedo feels like shit, which is a euphemistic way of saying she feels oppressed, feels abused, feels like her co conspirators made no attempt at solidarity in the face of this abuse, even as she was standing in solidarity with Gari Garay by helping establish her okupa. When you say we had to act natural because our goal was to brake into the house your clearly arguing that the end justifies the means, that machievelian tenet of realpolitic that renowned anarchist murderer Leon Trotsky so wisely debunked when he told us that if the end is revolution the means can only be revolutionary or else the revolution will never come.

Jaén: What they said to Oviedo was that serious?

Nata: For me it was incredibly serious, but I don't think its our place to go assessing a situation's gravity or triviality before intervening. If there is abuse, we intervene, don't we? Aren't anarchist spaces always plastered over with posters that say SILENCE IS VIOLENCE? Look, I can see 2 from here. And in any case the fascist didn't say anything, he hissed it.

Palmas: I don't think the degree of the abuse is a minor point. I think the victim of the harassment should be allowed to asses just how harassed she feels and we should let her determine the response. And then of course after that she should be confident in our support and solidarity.

Murcia: Look I wasn't there when Oviedo got harassed but I agree with Palma. If we don't let the victim asses the severity of the abuse and choose whether or not to defend herself then we're just indulging a saviour complex, especially if we're men. That's just us doing what we've seen our whole lives, where some dude says something to a woman and her boyfriend or guyfriend or brother comes to the rescue and it devolves into a cock fight.

Nata: Just reminding you that I was the one who intervened and I am a woman.

Murcia: I was speaking in general terms.

Nata: If you have a modicum of respect for the person your talking to I suggest you avoid speaking in general terms.

Murcia: Fine fine. I just wanted to open the conversation up a little like when you were talking about Machieveli and Bismark and Trotsky. I didn't mean to offend.

Nata:	Machieveli Bismark and Trotsky are relevant because their political thinking influenced our own political thoughts and attitudes that afternoon. Meanwhile you're talking about cock fights even though not a single penis rose to Oviedo's defence.
Murcia:	Right sorry your right
Nata:	OK
Majorca:	I still say since this involved Oviedo Gari Badajoz and me and Oviedo was the victim and she's outside we should get back to talking about the okupa. What do you think Gari?
Gari:	Yeah OK
Nata	Sorry sorry but it's not really true to say Oviedo was the only victim. We were all harassed. Aren't your walls covered in posters that say IF YOU FUCK WITH ONE OF US, YOU FUCK WITH ALL OF US? Doesn't that mean that when they harass one of our friends all the rest of us have also been harassed?
Mallorca:	Yes of course but we also shouldn't put words in anyone's mouth or speak on their behalf.
Nata	I agree, and correct me if I'm wrong but I don't think I put a word in Oviedo's mouth at any point in this conversation. Haven't I been speaking this whole time about what I think, what I perceive and what I read on your posters and in your zines? Thankfully Palmas recording the conversation so we can go back and listen to how many times I claim to speak for someone else!
Palma:	Hey at least someone appreciates my way of doing things

Nata:	Of course Palma its fab your recording. We'll have a laugh later listening to all the stupid shit we say.
Badajoz:	I don't think we can move forward if we're going to be this prissy about every single word we say.
Nata:	If WE'RE this prissy? Dishonest plural, pacifying plural! Don't you mean if YOU'RE this prissy, in reference to me?
Badajoz:	And didn't you mean to say hearing all the stupid shit YOU say since apparently the only one speaking properly here is you?
Nata:	That could be. I didn't realize it but I can't say your wrong. We're a couple of shitbags, Badajoz, using that dishonest pacifying plural. Lets have the decency to get to the heart of our conflict like the anarchists we are.
Taragoan:	Folx I haven't been able to follow this conversation for a while now
Mallorca:	Let's get ooooon with iiiiiiit
Badajoz:	Alright Nata our dispute remains open. But seeing as we all have an interest in this working group's activities I suggest continuing at another time so we don't monopolise the meeting.
Gari:	Yeah Nati if you get back to the flat late they'll get suspicious and start asking questions.
Nata:	This thing you call our dispute doesn't just involve you and me, I'm sorry. It speaks to the entire group, to an issue and an attitude that affects everyone. Viewing it as a personal disagreement between you and me is little better than relegating it to what the bourgeoisie call the

private sphere, curtailing its political potential and thwarting the collectivisation of all spheres of life, which means thwarting libertarian communism, as Coruña put it so beautifully and succinctly just a second ago.

Badajoz: Whatever you say. Personally I could debate with you all night but there are a few other Libertarian Communists here and they might not want to talk about this, they might want to talk about something else because remember that this is the Okupation Working Group and that means all of us here are devoting our time and energy to okupation. Your trying to impose a topic for debate and force your interest in that topic to take precidence over the interests of 9 other people

Ceuta: So I'm not trying to pacify or ref the two of you but I do want to keep talking about how Gari's okupation went.

Tangier: I agree with Ceuta

Majorca: I do to

Murcia: Me too

Various members: Me too me too me too … …

Gari: C'mon Nata

Nata: You want me submissive before the power of the Assembly then?

Badajoz: That's completely twisted! What are you talking about!?!?!

Tangier: Its not like that at all Nata. We're talking about organisation. Assembly organisation is also a very important part of Anarchism. Its what

191

	ensures everyone's voice is heard and no one imposes their views on the rest.
Tarragona:	And it ensures circulation and collectivisation of expertise.
Nata:	Ensures is a bit much don't you think?
Tarragona:	Well it tries
Murcia:	One second one second. Didn't you say you wanted to hear about your cousins okupa and that was why we moved it up on the agenda?
Nata:	Yes
Murcia:	Well then? Can't you see the rest of us have adapted to your needs and preferences? Don't you think you should reciprocate the accommodation we made for you by not bringing up new points for consideration, which by the way a lot of us would like to prepare for and think about before hand? Reciprocating the generosity that has been extended to you is also in my view part of Anarchism. We recognise were among equals and value each other's wants and needs. If that recognition is one sided or if one party under values forgets or disparages everyone else's wants and needs then our horizontal organisation collapses and gives way to either leadership or condescension, which is one step shy of Assistentialist charity, the great launderer of capitalist monies and consiences. And forgive me for splitting hairs since I know plenty of hair has been split already tonight but I just wanted to say it seems like we're using Libertarian Communism and Anarchism interchangeably and I don't think they're synonyms.

Nata:	What you say is true. Murcia, right? What you say is true Murcia. I'm not saying you've convinced me or that your right. But what you say is true. I was engrossed in a rancid individualism that was closer to Liberalism than Libertarian Communism and didn't see it. I was lost in the lie of capital and you showed me the truth of Anarchist society. My gates had been sliding shut but when you spoke those truths they started retracting.
Murcia:	I noticed
Various memers:	Yeah we saw ...
Nata:	Happy to hear it
Ceuta:	Happy to have you here friend
Tarragona:	I'd like to talk a little more about what Tangier said because it seems like Nata views the collective structure of this group as authoritarian. It seems like for her the way this working group is organised with its minutes and items and its agenda is authoritarian and restricts free speech and spontaneous discussion. So I'm asking, is that what you think?
Nata:	That's what I think except what you said about free speech. Freedom of speech is a legal term from the realm of law and rights. The right to free speech. As if the law whose nature scope and limits are always established by power preceded our speech. As if a person could only express herself because power via law allowed her to do so. So yes. I think this working group is bureaucratic which is to say authoritarian, but

rather than limiting free speech I think it simply doesn't want to make space for dissenting voices. By that I don't mean voices that question how much to charge for beers or what film to play at the cineforum but people who challenge the very foundations and existence of the anarchist Assembly.

Tarragona: I think that's a very naive way of thinking. I'll explain. In my experience and from the very little I've read in this life I think that groups tend to consciously or unconsciously form structures. Attempting to not have one means over looking the question of how the group functions internally. Essentially not thinking about it. Unstructured and spontaneous meetings where everyone says whatever they want aren't blissfully free from power structures. We come to meetings and assemblies pumped full of all the hierarchical capitalist baggage from our families, school, TV all that. When we place our faith in spontaneous expression and relationships we just end up mimicking the power dynamics we've been infected with and exactly the kind of domination we're trying to escape. And now I'll shut up so we can finally talk about Gari's okupation.

Nata: I can respond to you first right? You were talking about rights before and I think the right of rebuttal is something they have even in the Congress of deputies.

Various
members: Holy hell madre mia hahahahaha …

Nata:	Your name was Tarragona? Well look Tarragona I think that you've said quite a few emancipatory truths to, like how we've all been drinking the Kool Aid most of our lives and that's something we have to acknowledge if we're going to combat it. But you've also said quite a few domineering lies including the flagrant whopping over sim-plification that conflates spontaneity with authoritarianism and pits it against organisation and anti authoritarianism. But like you I'll shut up now so we can talk about Gari's okupa.
Various members:	Yes please yes I also agree please lets move on …
Mallorca:	Where did we leave off? Oh right the disguises. We wore disguises. Gari and Coruña wore normal clothes but cleaned it up a little and looked like two relatives who called a lock smith to open the door to their house because someone squirted super glue into the key hole or something.
Gari:	I took a shower and washed my hair
Coruña:	And I shaved and wore a polo shirt and pleated slacks
Tarragona:	God what I'd pay to see that
Coruña:	I didn't look half bad! I wore my funeral shoes and everything
Jaén:	Jeez
Mallorca:	So we looked like a window display at Zara. And Badajoz and Nata kept watch on opposite ends of the street.
Ceuta:	Did they wear disguises too?
Badajoz:	Not really. I just cleaned up a little. Gathered my dreads in a pony tail and put on some skinny

195

jeans and a kinda bougie shirt with a picture of birds on it.

Nata: I wore dance tights and sneakers and a backpack.

Badajoz: Then we started the skit. Do you want to tell it Gari?

Gari: Right so we got to the door and everything was normal. It looked the same as the day before. We checked just in case.

Coruña: It was an old lock and the door was just normal wood. It wasn't reenforced or anything. It was actually rotting away in places. But we were worried it'd be latched on the other side and our whole lock smith routine would be pointless.

Mallorca: Because we saw the house had a back door the owners could've left through after securing the front entrance.

Coruña: We couldn't get in through the back door because it opens to a shared courtyard with other neighbours and we would've been really exposed We realised there was a back door when we were scoping the house out from the roof of a friends building nearby. Getting in that way wasn't really feasible.

Gari: Right

Mallorca: Do you want to tell us what it was like for you Gari when I started drilling?

Gari: Well yeah Mallorca took out his drill and put it in the key hole. It made a lot of noise. He crouched in front of the door, Oviedo and Coruña and me stood there and watched. I kept wanting to look around to see if anyone was watching us but we'd agreed not to look around because it would've made it look like we were nervous. I had to force myself to just look at Mallorca. We'd already said Nata and Badajoz would watch for police or whatever.

Jaén:	Was this before or after the street harassment?
Various members:	after after after … …
Jaén:	Wait I thought it was when you were braking in.
Various members:	no no no …
Coruna:	The harassment happened between here and the house on Carrer dolzinelles. Near the Herbalists.
Badajoz:	Honestly nobody was watching. The families with kids from the school just kept walking past like normal. At one point a Guardia Urbana car drove past me at the end of the street and we all lost our shit a little. I called Oviedo and hung up after one ring which was our signal and the 4 of them calmly moved away from the door acting like they'd forgotten something, walking down the street with their backs to the cop car. But it just drove past at a normal speed without stopping at the door or anything and then it turned towards Plaça d'espanya like no big deal.
Taragona:	Fucking nerve wracking though I bet
Badajoz:	Oh for sure
Nata:	But after it turned the corner at my end of the street Gari Oviedo Mallorca and Coruña walked back to the door. Casual like before.

Mallroca:	The lock was easy. We had it in 10 minutes. I used a 2 millimetre bit and got through all the pin tumblers on the first try
Nata:	What are pin tumblers?
Mallorca:	They're little cylinders inside the lock in a line so that the key fits perfectly underneath them. When you insert the key the teeth make all the pins a line so you can turn the handle and open the door. Its a lot easier to explain if you can see it. If you want I can show you how with some locks I have at home for practice.
Nata:	Thanks
Mayorca:	Once you have a feel for how most locks work even picking them isn't hard. It was only because Gari's housing situation was so critical I didn't have time to teach her so I opened it myself.
Jaén:	I don't think it's that easy. It takes a lot of practice
Mallorca:	Of course just like learning to read and write takes a lot of practice. I just mean its not open heart surgery. Its not like you need to take a lock smith training course or any thing like that if you get me. And a drill makes it so much easier. You just need to have a steady hand so the bit doesn't go all over the place.
Coruna:	And we were lucky the door wasn't latched or anything from the other side.
Taragona:	All this is sounding like Ableist Assistentialist charity to me. The whole time you were all acting like a proper lock smith company and mean while Gari was standing around doing nothing.
Mallorca:	I mean is it Assistentialism or is it just being nice?

Gari:	I can't tell you guys how grateful I am really.
Taragona:	See??????
Badajoz:	Christ Tarragona is it reactionary to say thank you now?
Jaén:	Its not true Gari didn't do anything Taragona. Just because she can't drill a lock and didn't have time to learn doesn't mean that she wasn't involved in the okupation. She checked out the houses, checked out the area several days before hand to see what time of day there were more people so we could go unnoticed ... ... To say okupying is just about busting open a door strikes me as pretty macho actually. Its like saying the only thing that really matters is the application of brute force.
Tangier:	But I think we can all agree busting open the door is the riskiest and most delicate part of the process. Its the most dangerous. Its the part that can get you charged with burglary or braking and entering.
Gari:	If I can say something I just want to say I knew you guys were taking lots of risks to help me out and I'm double and triple grateful for that.
Nata:	What a high price you Anarchists put on solidarity!
Badajoz:	OK this time I have to admit that Nata's right. Why the fuck do we keep talking about okupation like the person who opens the door has to be the person who squats. Occupying with a C might be an individual liberal endeavour but okupying with a K is a collective act where everyone contributes and takes risks according

to their own fucking ability and their own fucking needs. I can't with you folx right now honestly.

Nata: Many reactionary thanks Badajoz

various members: Hahahaha ... ...

Murica: Of course Badajoz but everyone's ability and needs if they aren't politicised in the Anarchist sense can transform into what we were just talking about. Roles and professionalisation and all that.

Nata: In the interest of the Anarchist truth you just shared about organisation I'd like to finish hearing about the door because like I said I need to leave early.

Palma: Don't worry in the minutes I'll put that this isn't settled. Its still wide open.

Murcia: I agree with Napalm

PAUSE FOR LAUGHTER VARIOUS COMMENTS

Coruña: Right so after drilling thru and making the key hole a little bigger all Mallorca had to do was insert the end of a flat head screw driver and give it a turn and voila.

Obiedo: It was so cool when the door opened

Mallorca: I've drilled through a bunch of locks but still every time a door gives way to the touch of your hand and you see that black strip of darkness inside widening and widening until the whole door frame is a black rectangle and your hit with that closed in smell thats all cold from construction inside its such a fucking high.

Jaén: When we opened the door to my place it smelled like paint hahahahaha It was a super modern

	building they'd just finished putting up when the recession hit and they never sold more than 4 or 5 flats.
Ceuta:	Hahahahaha brilliant
Gari:	So then I went in. I went in with Oviedo and we took a quick look at the house and everything looked good.
Obiedo:	I wouldn't have said it looked good. The floor is really uneven and like we said the roof has a hole the size of a table in it. But its like we talked about at the meeting 2 or 3 weeks ago about how a house can be good for some and not for others and Gari judged this house to be good for her and still thinks so so thats that.
Mallorca:	I went in for a minute to put on the new lock and its true the ceiling has caved in but its nothing a few day's work wouldn't fix.
Murcia:	There's still the risk of administrative eviction if they want to kick you out by having the building condemned.
Palma:	But in that case they'd be evicting you for your own safety hahahaha … …
Various members:	Hahahahaha … …
Gari:	I understood that about administrative eviction. But so far nothings happened. I'm really happy about that.
Jaén:	Finish telling us how it was once you were in and all that
Gari:	So I stayed there and everybody else left. I locked the new lock from the inside.
Ceuta:	And you said there haven't been any neighbours or cops or anything?

Gari:	Nothing. I've been completely alone the last 3 days except that first night when we did the thing with the pizza to get a receipt with the date. Since I don't have a phone Badajoz made the call. I paid for the pizza.
Nata:	What's the thing with the pizza Gari?
Gari:	The first or second day your squatting your supposed to order a pizza because whenever you order food for delivery the delivery guy gives you a receipt with your address and the date. That's proof so you can say you've been living there since that day. Because if you've been living in a house for more than 3 days they can't evict you as fast, right?
Various members:	Right right right …
Tarragona:	Right. If you can show you've been there for over 72 hours then they can't evict you right away because they can't claim they caught you in flagrantay.
Gari:	You can also order something besides pizza as long as they give you a receipt.
Nata:	Got it got it
Gari:	And that's it, since I didn't have any more money because I gave it all to the delivery guy Nata brought me food and water the next day and the day after and today I was able to leave and we went shopping for food and cleaning things together.
Coruna:	Are you able to cook?
Gari:	I have a gas burner but no gas.
Coruna:	Since its just you I suggest we give Gari the half used tank we have here. It'll be easy to carry

over since its mostly empty and doesn't way to much.

Tangier: I don't agree because of what we were saying before about Assistentialism. I think we should address that agenda item before we start giving things away.

Coruna: Alright fine I'll give you a half full tank I have at home Gari.

Tangier: I think that's a perfect solution

Coruña: You shouldn't think its perfect or imperfect or anything because its my damn tank of butane and I'll do what I want with it.

Various members: Hahahahaha ...

Oviedo: Were you guys talking about Assitnetialism when I was outside? I must've missed it.

Taragona: Yeah but I mean it was just the same debate as always.

Oviedo: Ah got it

Badajoz: Its 11:30 folx and we've still got to talk about the other okupation under way and the agenda item about how we take minutes.

Mallorca: One or the other because we don't have time to talk about both those things in depth. I say we talk about the minutes because the other okupation is mine and its on stand by because the buddy I was gonna squat with had to leave town for a family thing and we won't be able to pick things back up for a week or so.

Tangier: Right then since your the primary interested party ... ... before moving on to the minutes does anyone want to say anything more about Gari's okupa?

Gari:	I just want to thank you guys again and say your all welcome to come by whenever you want.
Various members:	No need for thanks your welcome that's what we do thank you for the invitation …
Palma:	I assume you don't have any electricity or water?
Gari:	No
Palma:	Well when you want to fix that just say so and well come and help. Right now you've got a hole in the roof in summer but think about what it'll be like in november.
NAta:	Many reactionary thanks Palma I was going to help Gari with that but I have no idea how to make cement
Palma:	No worries no worries. Er, I should be clear. Those of us who want to help will help and those of us who don't well I mean they won't. I was speaking only for myself this time.
Tarragona:	for fucks sake Palma just because Tangier and me wanted to have a stupid fucking conversation about Ableist Assistentialism doesn't mean we never want to help anyone with anything.
Palma:	Did I say that? If you feel called out thats on you
Murcia:	Your sarcasm is coming through loud and clear Palma. Can we keep the fecitiousness to a minimum?
Palma:	I swear on my dead relatives that wasn't sarcasm!!!! I meant it because I didn't want to speak for everyone since I know we don't all agree on this. Apparently I touched a nerve …
Ceuta:	Well look I think Palma will be a very good transcriber or transcriptionist or minutes

taker or whatever you call it because he won't include the fecit ... sarcasm or whatever. He won't interpret what we say hell just write exactly what we say and it'll all be super authentic

Muria: To be honest I don't think the minutes are really that important anyway. Its not like anybody reads them or I mean at least I don't.

Jaén: Oh great I guess I took them all those last times for nothing then

Oviedo: hey no Murcia I read them

Various members: Me too me to me too ...

Ceuta: You read Jaén's minutes a month after the meeting and you get a flash back like your there again.

Oviedo: No, you read Jaéns minutes and its like reading an article about Anarchism, an article from Aversion or Subversion or Cul de Sac – their really well edited and everything.

Ceuta: Jaén's minutes are better than the Assemblies.

Jaén: Thank you thank you.

Ceuta: We speak better in the minutes then we do in real life hahahaha!

Palma: They're right dude you make everything super organised and clear. I read them and say, shit did I really speak that well at the meeting when I came straight from working my ass off at work all day? when I was totally beat from working my ass off all day?

Jaén: Its because I don't do a literal transcription because as I understand it minutes aren't supposed to be a literal transcription. I get rid of

	the repetitions I get rid of all the things people say more than once when someone hesitates or stutters,,,, But without changing the content or the intent obviously.
Mallorca:	Sometimes I read things in Jaéns minutes and I'm like, but wait, it says here I reference a writer like a theorist or some other kind of author who writes about her experience— and I've never even heard of her! But I think its fucking awesome Jaén that's not a criticism. Really what your doing is adding references to clarify right? Like the whole point is to help us understand what we were talking about
Jaén:	That's how I think of it yeah
Tarragona:	I'm not so sure that should be the point. Clarifying would make sense if we were writing an article or a zine like Oviedo was talking about or if we were writing something for the public or a press conference, something that would be distributed outside of the working group. But minutes are an internal document and it should be faithful to what we say.
Nata:	I don't know what you mean by authentic and faithful
Ceuta:	You don't know what authentic and faithful mean?
Nata:	I don't know what those words mean as they relate to writing
Tarragona:	I think its pretty obvious
Jaén:	Sorry folx but like always its 11:50 and I have to go because the metros gonna close. I'm really interested in this topic–I propose we make it a priority at the next meeting.

Palma:	I'll put that in the minutes
Various members:	Hahahahaha …
Coruna:	Jaén get a bike already
Jaén:	Working on it
Murcia:	Me too I have to get to Sant Andreu and if I don't haul ass I'll have to take the night bus that goes around the whole fucking city
Nata:	To bad, this conversation about the minutes is so interesting and all of your perspectives are so valuable
Jaén:	Right right we'll continue next time. Later
Various members:	Later later later ……
Murcia:	Later
Various members:	Later later later …
Nata:	But the rest of us can continue off the record can't we? I mean I know bureaucratic proceedings are a major concern around here
Cueta:	Palma note the sarcastic tone in the minutes!!
Various members:	Hahahahahaha …
Coruna:	It'd be better to wait until the others can join us since their also interested in the topic. especially Jaén. Don't you think?
Tangeir:	Plus its late and we've got to close up
Nata:	Right but can't those of us who feel like it just go to a bar and keep talking or grab a few beers and sit on a park bench?
Badajoz:	Didn't you say you had to leave early?

Nata:	Yes but this topic is the most interesting thing anyone's talked about all night and now I don't want to go. Can't you see I'm a firm believer in spontaniety and freedom of speech?
Cueta:	Sarcasm Palma take note
Nata:	Shit you guys are lame. Do you people not even drink? Not even you Badajoz? Tarragona? Even though I know you don't like me?
Palma:	Alright noted and closed and finished and well talk about getting beers off the record or else I'll end up having to type 20 pages

NOVEL
TITLE: MEMOIRS OF MARÍA DELS ÀNGELS
GUIRAO HUERTAS
SUBTITLE: MEMORIES AND MUSINGS
OF A GIRL FROM ARCUELAMORA
(ARCOS DE PUERTOCAMPO, SPAIN)
GENRE: EASY READ
AUTHOR: MARÍA DELS ÀNGELS GUIRAO HUERTAS
CHAPTER 3: THE OLD RUCID AND A CREATIVE CRISIS

The old RUCID in Somorrín
was a big pretty house
in the town square.

I'm calling it the old RUCID
because after a few years
we moved to the new RUCID
the one they use in Somorrín today.
In this chapter I'm just going to talk about the old RUCID
but I'm not going to say old every time.
I'll make sure I tell you
when I start talking about the new RUCID.
It says on page 73
of 'Easy Read: Methods for Composition and Evaluation':
'Leave no room for confusion.'

The old RUCID had three floors
and every floor had three bedrooms.
Two or three people slept in each room
except the social worker
who got to sleep in a room by herself.
A different social worker slept there every night.

In the other rooms
there could be two or three boys
or two or three girls
but never boys and girls together.
My room was on the first floor
and it had two beds.
I was lucky because I got to sleep with Encarnita
who was very pretty and very good.

I'd never seen bathtubs so big
and that always had hot water
before I went to the RUCID in Somorrín.
I'm a little embarrassed to say this
but I'm going to say it anyway so you believe
everything I say is true.
I never used a toilet or a bidet
before I went to the RUCID in Somorrín.
At first I thought they were gross
because they were so white
and you could see everything you did
not like when you go outside
where your stuff mixes with the dirt
and you can't see anything.
But after a while I got used to it
because Mamen taught me how to use them
and how to use toilet paper.

Now I never do my stuff outside
except if I'm hiking or something.

It was like a house for rich people
except it was for us.
The rich people who owned the house
sold it to Mamen
and to the four other social workers
who worked at the RUCID.

The house's old owners
must not have been very rich for rich people
because they sold it cheap.
They sold it so cheap that Mamen
and the other social workers
could get a government subsidy to buy it.

Government subsidy means
the government gives you money
so you can do something
the government thinks is good.
But for them to give it to you
you have to follow the same rules
as you do to get your Social Security benefit.
So the RUCID had to open an account at BANKOREA
the same as a person has to.
Then the government gave the money to BANKOREA
and BANKOREA gave it to the RUCID.

The RUCID obviously wasn't a person,
it was a house.
So the social workers,
who were obviously people,

had to fill out all the paperwork
and go to BANKOREA themselves
to get the money.
But they couldn't keep the money
because it was for the RUCID.

I know this for sure
because another thing about government subsidies
is after you get the money
you have to send the government a letter
justifying how you spent it
on what you said you were going to spend it on
and not on something else.
If you don't justify it
you have to give back the money
and they don't give you any more.

Justify means
showing someone signed papers
to prove you really did something.
Justify is a word with two different meanings,
since like I said in Chapter 1
justify can also mean
making every line you write
into a perfect column
even though some of them are shorter
and others are longer.

That means the word justify
is a polyseme.

On page 71 of 'Easy Read:
Methods for Composition and Evaluation'

it says polysemes are a semantic accident
and should be avoided.
Polysemes are words with more than one meaning.
They don't have anything to do with polyester,
which is what clothes are made of,
or with seams,
which is where you sew pieces of polyester together,
or with the police,
which are like the Guardia Civil
or the Guardia Urbana
or the Mossos d'Esquadra.

Semantic is what words mean.
Accident is like a car or motorcycle or aeroplane accident
or like a workplace accident like my cousin Natividad had
when she was at university,
which is how she ended up severely intellectually disabled
with her Gate Control syndrome.

I know Gate Control syndrome
is a hard thing and most people haven't heard of it
but in Easy Read you're only supposed to say things
the reader needs to know.
And since this is my life story
the reader doesn't need to know
about my cousin's disorders.
I only said it to give an example of an accident.

I had never heard of polysemes
or semantic accidents.
I looked them up on my phone but I still didn't get it
so I asked my support person
and she looked it up on her phone

and she explained it better
and now I can explain it to my readers
because on page 73 of the 'Methods'
it says 'don't presume the reader
has prior knowledge'.
Presume is assume.
Prior is before.
Knowledge is what you know.
Since I can't assume
my readers have read
the 'Guidelines for Easy-to-Read Materials' or
'Easy Read: Methods for Composition and Evaluation',
I guess I have to explain everything
because you're not born knowing anything.

Accidents are tragic.
That's why the 'Methods' says
to avoid semantic accidents.
At first I felt guilty
about accidentally using the word justify.
I thought no one would understand me
even if I explained it a million times.
I thought if there was a semantic accident
in this book about my life
everything would be ruined
like when you're in an accident
and you don't die but you get paralysed.

But then I read page 72 of the 'Methods'
where it says 'Use language that is coherent with
the recipient's age and level of education.
If they are adults,
the language should be appropriate and respectful

for that age.
Avoid infantilising language.'
Coherent means consistent.
Recipient means reader.
Level of education means
if you went to high school or university
or if you didn't go anywhere.
Adult is you're older than 18.
Appropriate is polite.
Infantilising is they treat you like a little kid.
Then I thought the word justify
was a word for adults
because only adults can get subsidies from the government.

We had everything we needed at the RUCID
so even though the social workers left BANKOREA
with stacks of money like bricks
I'm sure they didn't keep any of it for themselves
except for their salaries and for the gas for their cars.
But even their cars were half for them
and half so they could drive us
wherever we had to go.

That meant everything was justified
and the government liked what we were doing
so it kept giving us subsidies.
So whenever the social workers went to a shop they always asked
for a signed receipt for all the things they bought:
for food and soap and shampoo
and clothes and medicine
and cleaning supplies
and materials for arts and crafts,
and tools, and screws, and paint ...

They even had to ask them for a signed receipt
for food for our parakeet and fish.
They even had to ask them for a signed receipt
for the nativity set and candy at Christmas
and for Three Kings Bread on Three Kings Day.
In the summer, they got receipts for our swimsuits and floaties
and armbands and rafts and ice cream cones.
During Carnaval, they got receipts for our costumes.
During Holy Week, they got receipts for our Easter pastries.
On Holy Thursday
and Good Friday
and the Feast of Our Lord of Knots
and the Feast of Our Lady of Puertocampo
and the Feast of Saint James
they got receipts for all the candles.
On Castile and León Day
they got receipts for the Castilian and Leonese flags
and we hung them from our balconies.
On Spanish Constitution Day
and on the National Day of Spain
and on days Spain played in the World Cup,
they got receipts for the Spanish flags
and we hung those from our balconies too.
On days Barça played
they got receipts for the Barça flags they bought for the Barça fans
and on days Madrid played
they got receipts for the Madrid flags
they bought for the Madrid fans,
but they didn't let us hang those from the balconies.

Even though it cost less than one peseta,
they got a receipt when they bought a box of white ribbons

at the store on International Peace Day,
and a receipt for purple ribbons on International Women's Day,
and for red ones on World AIDS Day,
and green ones on World Cancer Day,
and red ones again on Red Cross Day,
and pink ones on World Breast Cancer Day,
and black ones on days Basque separatists
blew something up or killed somebody.

On World No Tobacco Day they bought chewing gum
at the tobacco stand instead of tobacco.
So they got a receipt for their gum
and none of the social workers smoked all day
and the residents who were allowed to smoke
every once in a while
weren't allowed to that day.
When they saw my cousin Patricia smoking
they took the cigarette from her mouth
and snapped it in front of her face
and threw it on the ground
and stomped on it
and gave her a piece of gum
and watched to make sure she really chewed it,
but by then we were at the new RUCID.

They got a receipt for all the red roses on Valentine's Day,
and a receipt for all the flowers
for the cemetery on All Souls' Day,
and a receipt for all the books on World Book Day,
even though lots of residents couldn't read.
I knew how to read
but I have to be honest

and admit I was a very bad reader back then
because even though I knew how to read
I didn't understand what I was reading.
But on my first World Book Day at the RUCID
and on all the World Book Days after that
they took us on a trip to the library
and I liked it so much
and it smelled so good
and there were so many young people there studying
that it made me want to learn to read better.

So they took me to the adult learning centre
but I didn't like it there at all
because instead of boys and girls like me
there were just old men and old women.
I was the youngest one there.
But then something changed
thanks to my cousin Natividad.

I'm going to talk about Natividad now
but only because it has to do with the story of my life.

Before my cousin Nati got her
Gate Control syndrome
she read lots of books
because she really liked studying.
She went to school
and the dance conservatory at the same time.
Then she went to high school
and the dance conservatory at the same time.
And then she went to university
and still kept going to the dance conservatory

and took English classes too.
Dance conservatory is where people go to learn to dance.

When Nati was on break
or if it was the weekend, or sometimes during the week,
she used to come back to Somorrín
to go out with her friends from school.
While she was home she'd visit me at the RUCID.
First she visited me at the old RUCID
and then later she visited me at the new RUCID,
when Patricia and Marga were there too.

On her visits Natividad would read with me
and it was way better than at the adult learning centre
where we just read books full of infantilising language
or did workbooks for kids
even though it was called the adult learning centre.

But Nati and me would read books that were actually good
because they were about stuff that actually happened to people
and not infantilising stories for kids
that adults would never believe.

The 'Methods' says:
'Use politeness markers,
like please and thank you.'
Politeness means being polite.
Marker means a word or thing that makes a mark
like markers you use to colour with.
It doesn't have anything to do with trademarks
for clothes or cars or food or phones
like the logo for Zara or Volvo

or the colour red for Coke
or the name Samsung Galaxy 5G for my phone.
Just so you know, I'm not trying to advertise
any of those things.
I'm just giving examples of what a trademark is.

Marker also doesn't have anything to do
with bookmarks
or birthmarks
or people named Mark.

In this case the mark in marker means
writing a word that means something.
In this case it means politeness.
Be careful with the word mark
because it's an even worse polyseme
than the word justify.

I want to say thank you to Natividad Lama Huertas
for teaching me to be a good reader and writer
and finding books that were actually good in the library.
Thanks to her I started liking writers
and I started liking writing
and now I'm even trying to become a writer.

I feel sorry for Nati.
She can't read this politeness marker
because of her severe intellectual disability.

After she had her accident
and had to be institutionalised at the new RUCID,
every time they gave us books to read on World Book Day
she would start reading them,

but ten seconds later her gates would slam shut
and she would smash her new books on the floor,
or kick them,
or throw them at whoever gave them to her,
and scream at them,
or tear out the pages, or burn them, or bite them,
or get them wet,
and yell at us
not to read those books.
She even yelled it at the residents who couldn't read.

Even though that wasn't an appropriate way
to say something, I understand why she did it.
She did it because those books used infantilising language
because they were for kids.
But there are also some books for kids
that are really good
like 'Harry Potter' and 'The Lord of the Rings'
and 'Twilight'.

I'm not going to show Nati my novel on WhatsApp
in case she does the same thing with my phone.

But when my book is published
I'm going to sit down with her
just like she sat down with me,
and we'll read it together
and I'll help her like reading again.

Luckily these days we have Easy Read.

On page 21 of the 'Methods' it says:
'Easy Read has emerged as a tool

to foster reading comprehension and encourage literacy
among people who are not in the habit of reading,
or who have been deprived of it.'

That's just like with my cousin Natividad.

Then it says:
'This tool aims
to facilitate access to information,
culture and literature,
as such access is a fundamental human right
to which all people,
as equals in rights and dignity,
are entitled, regardless of their ability or disability.
The right to information is also critical
to the exercise of several other rights,
including individuals' right to participate in civic life,
to have a voice in important decisions that affect them,
and to chart their own development
at a time when humanity is producing more writing,
in both print and digital formats,
than at any other moment in history.
Information accessibility encompasses access
not just to literature,
newspapers, encyclopedias and textbooks,
but also to legislation,
government documents, medical reports,
contracts and the myriad other texts
that are part of everyday life.
Reading comprehension is a skill
that not all human beings possess,
unfortunately.'

I copied this very long section of the 'Methods'
because I think it's very important.
But I didn't copy it exactly.
The words are all the same but the shape is different
because in this book about Easy Read
the lines are almost all the same length
and they all go from one side of the page to the other
from the beginning to the end
almost without leaving any spaces.
That means these lines are justified and indented.

Now I'm realising this is a little weird.
The writer of this book says in Easy Read
you don't justify or indent the text,
but then he justifies and indents the text.

There's also another weird thing.
In those lines there are lots of hard words
like emerged, foster, comprehension,
facilitate, disability, participate,
civic life, chart their own development, formats,
content, accessibility, access
legislation, myriad, skill.
The writer doesn't explain any of these hard words
like I always do.
I explain almost all the difficult words
and when I don't it's just to avoid digressions
and because it's good for readers
to learn to use the dictionary.

But this writer doesn't explain any of the words.
That's a contradiction,
because on page 70 he says:

'Explain uncommon or complex words
with contextualisation and visual aids,
or by simply explaining the meaning.'
But he didn't say it the way I copied it.
I wrote it now without justifying or indenting,
but he justified and indented it again
and didn't explain what contextualisation and visual aids mean.

I'm scrolling through the pages of the 'Methods' PDF
and I'm realising the whole book is justified and indented
and almost none of the hard words are explained.
PDF is the way books come
when you download them off the internet.

And it gets worse.
In the part of the 'Methods' I copied
there's a semantic accident with a polyseme
because the writer uses the word tool.
There are lots of different kinds of tools
and he doesn't explain any of them.

If this writer writes a book
about how to write in Easy Read,
he's supposed to know lots about what Easy Read is.
Right?
So why is he so bad at it?
Or does this mean I'm bad at it?
It's really odd,
because my support person
who immediately reads all my WhatsApps
in the María dels Àngels's Novel WhatsApp group chat
always sends me lots of happy emojis.
Emojis are the little pictures in WhatsApp.

She always sends me the smiling emojis,
and the fingers going OK, and the clapping hands,
and the yellow surprised faces, and the yellow kissy faces,
and the yellow faces in party hats.
Other friends in the group also send me emojis
because even though they're not Easy Read writers
or experts in Easy Read,
they're people who are not in the habit of reading,
or who have been deprived of it.
Deprived means they took something that's yours
but not like when someone steals your phone or your money
or when BANKOREA took my mom's house.
Deprived means they took something away
even though you never had it in the first place.

I got kind of bored writing that explanation of deprived.
I wonder if I'm going through a creative crisis
like all writers go through
at some point in their career.
Creative crisis means you have no inspiration.
It doesn't have anything to do with the economic crisis,
or the unemployment crisis, or the banking crisis,
or the debt crisis.
Creative means you come up with stuff for art and culture.
Inspiration means art, imagination
and feeling like coming up with stuff.
Career is your job.

I'm realising this chapter of my novel
is twice as long as the other chapters.
Maybe I'm spending too much time working
and need to disconnect a little.
This weekend I'll get away to somewhere quiet

and go for a walk, and get a coffee,
see old friends and read some books that are actually good
to see if I can get some inspiration.
I'll ask my cousin Natividad
like in the old days
because even though she's severely intellectually disabled now
for days she's been using workbooks
to teach my cousin Margarita
and other members of the self-advocacy group
how to read.

I'm sure they're not infantilising workbooks
like we had at the adult learning centre
because she can read them
without her gates closing.

This isn't a goodbye,
readers in the María dels Àngels's Novel
WhatsApp group chat.
It's just a see you later.

See you later.

#ME TOO:

Why would you want to be normal?

HOLA sUEÑAS and PACO ALAMEDA in a film by TACOS AL PASTOR and ANTONIO CATARRO

LET ME BE A MALE LIKE YOU

Learn how you, too, can become a male, a fascist and a neoliberal by attending a heteropatriarchal pep talk by this film's leading man, Paco Alameda, at the Urban Centre for the Intellectually Disabled (UCID) of Barceloneta, next Tuesday, 5 September 2018, at 6 p.m.

Dispatch to the weekly hostages of the Barceloneta

Companions in captivity,

As if locking us in this sterile white room with fluorescent lighting

every Tuesday afternoon weren't bad enough,

now they've invited a fascist to come and talk us to death.

He's a male chauvinist prick

from the fustiest corners of the religious right

who starred in a film

and wrote a book.

His name is **Patxi Pereda.**

He was the main character in the film

that our jailer **Laia Buedo** forced us to watch two weeks ago

called *Me Too: Let Me Be a Male Like You*.

Since our expressions of boredom or indignation or astonishment

as we watched the film

weren't enough to sate her sadism

(typical of someone who's paid to exercise capitalist/institutional violence),

the following week she forced us to take turns reading aloud

from the masculinist screed entitled

Raising Boys with Sexist Needs (Handbook for Fathers).

As you can see from the titles alone,

this authoritarian neoliberal's work

revolves around maleness and its many benefits.

In preparation for the imminent arrival of this fascist neoliberal male, **Pepo Pallás,**

who will be escorted in by **Jailer Buedo** and **Warden Gómez**

Self-Advocacy Group and Easy Read Club

on **5 September 2018 at 6 p.m.**,

this zine will raise a series of questions

and propose a series of answers.

Its goal is to start a true discussion,

not to be confused with those things **Laia Buedo** calls discussions,

which are really interrogation sessions

in which we are forced to debate our opinions

after reading *Goldilocks and the Three Shitfucking Bears*

or some shitfucker news story

about political corruption or the shitfucking election,

as if we gave half a shit about the elites and their scheming.

We inmates are interested in discussing two things and two things only:

1. The conditions that make it possible for our oppressors to control
   every facet of our lives.

2. The means by which we can overpower, eliminate or evade such domination
   that is, the means by which we can emancipate ourselves from the yoke of
   manifold oppressors who police our daily lives: cops, wardens, ideologues, boss
   overseers, scabs, doctors, teachers, madams, whoremongers, stylists a
   authoritarian relatives.

We are through with them deciding everything, including what we talk about

in our Tuesday-afternoon self-advocacy group.

Today we're the ones asking the questions.

But our questions aren't directed at them.

We've already heard their money-grubbing lies.

Today we will ask the questions and we will provide the answers,

with no need for a moderator, whose purpose, as the name suggests,

is to moderate, pacify and therefore censure the way we express our concerns.

1) What makes Pepo Pallás a male/fascist/neoliberal?

2) Why are our jailers so excited about Pepo Pallás coming to speak
   to us in person?

3) Can and/or should the inmates at the UCID of Barceloneta do something
   about his impending visit?

CONCIENCIANDO SOBRE LOS SINDROME DE DOWN PARTE 2

https://youtu.be/U_0s7oD5rOw

"Master, you've been reading too much lately. Try watching more TV."

...of the Roma Project, pioneer, and Don Quixote of sorts in the fight to 'normalise' this syndrome. He's just published his second book, entitled Raising Boys with Sexist Needs (Hércules Ediciones), a guidebook for fathers.

5:37 / 13:36

Pepo Pallás: Families have this huge responsibility to their kids and family members with Down's syndrome, and they see me as a role model. And so, well, I have to keep being a role model. I can't lose heart. I can't... I can't lose heart.

Interviewer: You can't get discouraged.

Pepo Pallás: I can't get discouraged. I have to keep being a Don Quixote of Down's syndrome for families with Down's syndrome. Because raising a kid with Down's syndrome, believing in him ... it's hard. It's very difficult. And, of course, there has to be someone setting an example, a role model to help them keep the faith while they're raising their kid.

BRIEF INTRODUCTION TO THE TRAPS OF IDEOLOGY

1. DENIAL OF THE UNITY AMONG ALL OPPRESSORS

For strictly pedagogical purposes,

this zine will differentiate

between the three categories of

male, fascist and neoliberal.

This neat, analytical distinction

will makes these terms more accessible to those inmates

that have been deprived of the pleasure of politicisation,

who, because we live in a capitalist society, are the majority.

(Politicisation is the process by which we rid ourselves of ideology

and embrace reality. We will explain ideology and reality shortly.)

However, the attributes of male, fascist and neoliberal

are inextricable from one another in our everyday reality,

which is the only reality that exists

because it is the only one that can destroy us

and the only one that can be modified by us.

Reality has shown that all males are fascists

and all fascists are neoliberals

and all neoliberals are males.

Any identity relation established between these three concepts

is valid, logically sound and true.

Outside of our everyday reality there is only virtuality,

or ideology, which is another word that means the same thing.

Ideology is a set of ploys

that fascist neoliberal males and their accomplices use

to convince the rest of us

that the control they wield over us is a good thing,

even though reality has demonstrated that

for us, it is bad, because it causes us to suffer.

Control is only good for the controllers.

Where we find pleasure in politicisation,

they find pleasure in the accumulation of material and symbolic power

at our expense (exploitation), at their own expense (self-exploitation),

or at the expense of both kinds of exploitation at the same time.

(This is an adapted summary of something mouthbreather Karl Marx

and neckbeard Friedrich Engels said in 1845.)

That, fellow captives, is the ideology of control.

You can just say ideology without saying 'of control'

just like you can skip 'our everyday' and just say 'reality'.

That way, you save yourself two words.

Ideology says that males, fascists and neoliberals
are three entirely different categories in both theory and practice
and there's no reason to assume all males are necessarily
fascists and/or neoliberals, or vice versa or vice versa or vice versa.
So let's take a cursory look at the ideological distinctions they use
to disrupt the true unity between males, fascists and money-grubbers.
That disruption is part of the strategy of ideology:
they want us to believe that within so-called democratic societies
there is no all-controlling leviathan.
They want us to believe that
there are only individuals, businesses, collectives and political parties,
all of which have their own personal and political preferences, and
we have to respect those preferences as long as they,
in turn, respect the institutional order.
This is what ideology calls 'democratic pluralism' or 'freedom of thought'.

Thus, ideology calls on us to treat fascist neoliberal dudebros with respect,
but because we challenge the institutional order, the agents of ideology call us
disrespectful, hysterical, crazy, hateful feminazis.
According to ideology, we, the prisoners, are the fascists.

A recurring and widespread argument within ideology
is that there are many different ideologies,
the two most important and influential of which are
the ideology of the left and the ideology of the right.

he apotheosis of left-wing ideology would be communism,

nd the apotheosis of right-wing ideology would be fascism.

 between is so-called representative democracy.

owever, reality has clearly shown us

hat at both extremes and everywhere in between there are only fascists,

who are all identical except in their rhetorical use of discourse.

herefore, it makes perfect sense

o talk about left-wing fascists and right-wing fascists.

here's a reason they're always talking about

unity among all democracy-loving people'.

According to ideology, rhetoric is the institutional politician's dazzling oratory.

According to reality, rhetoric is the communication strategy the oppressor uses

to further his oppression and disseminate the lies of capital.)

According to ideology, fascism is only one ideology out of many

and it has existed at only two moments in history:

between the world wars and during World War II.

But reality has shown that fascism goes far beyond that.

Fascism is a technique used to control territories and populations.

Every state and empire in the world has applied this technique,

from the creation of the first bourgeois political parties in the mid-19th century

through to the present day.

On the topic of capital, we'll add that, according to ideology,
neoliberalism is the economic platform of the imperialist right wing.
Reality has repeatedly demonstrated, however, that neoliberalism
is the true economic platform of all present-day oppressors.
Left-wing fascists call it collectivism or state capitalism
and right-wing fascists call it the free market or laissez-faire capitalism.

Finally, according to ideology, 'male' is not a political category,
but a biological term that denotes a reproductive role within a species.
Ideology is concerned not with men but with misogynists.
A misogynist could be anyone who hates, disregards or objectifies women
and, in keeping with the fallacious distinction between modes of oppression,
there are supposedly more right-wing misogynists than left-wing misogynists.
But in reality, the woman-hater doesn't just hate women,
he hates anyone who doesn't fuck the way he fucks,
anyone who doesn't want to fuck when he wants to fuck,
and anyone who doesn't fuck whoever he thinks they should fuck.
Clearly the oppression enacted by the political male
has everything to do with the reproductive role
whose relevance ideology denies,
and in whose name he shames, rapes and kills.

Misogynist is the word that ideology uses
to encourage women's assimilation within neoliberalism,
which ideology calls 'universal suffrage', 'entering the workforce',
'striking a work-life balance', 'leaning in', 'equal opportunity',
'breaking through the glass ceiling', 'bridging the leadership gap'
or 'having it all'.

2. A SHAM COMMUNITY OF SHARED INTERESTS

We have already seen how ideology

denies that its desire for control is singular, indivisible,

and ubiquitous among all its agents.

We have also seen how it denies the necessary concurrence

of male, fascist and neoliberal attributes

in order to exert, replicate and perpetuate its control.

Even as ideology touts its supposed plurality

and denies its own unity or hegemony (as some left-wing fascists call it,

including, early on, Axelrod, Lenin and Gramsci),

it claims that the oppressors and the oppressed

all belong to the same community.

Within that community, all of us, oppressed and oppressors alike,

supposedly share the same needs and desires.

We prisoners can see how this is clearly false, virtual and ideological,

since, as we just saw,

the oppressors take pleasure in wielding control

whereas the oppressed and incarcerated find pleasure in politicisation.

The interests of the oppressors and the interests of the oppressed

are not only different, they are contradictory.

They want us to be subjugated

and we want to put an end to our subjugation.

They want to commit violence against us

and we want to emancipate ourselves from their violence.

Thus, this community of shared interests

that the oppressors have invented

is clearly a sham.

These communities are easy to spot,

because the names that the oppressors

give them and their members are always devoid of any trace of oppression.

Today, the ideology that sustains the male/fascist/neoliberal regime

calls the phoney community of shared interests the 'democratic state'

and calls its members (prisoners and jailers alike) 'voters'.

At other times and in other parts of the world, the ideology of control

has called the faux community of shared interests 'the people'

and called its members 'workers', 'regular folks'

or 'right-thinking men and women'.

It's also often called the 'nation',

and its members are called 'citizens' if it's a nation with a state

or 'freedom fighters' if it's a nation without a state.

Perhaps the largest false community of all

is 'humanity',

which is made up of 'human beings'.

There are also smaller communities of shared interests.

One of the most famous is the 'business' whose members are a 'team'.

Or the 'political party',

which is made up of 'democrats', 'proletarians' or 'patriots',

depending on whether they're left- or right-wing fascists.

Another very popular one is the 'family', whose members are 'relatives'.

In our own circumstances as prisoners within a community of shared interests,

our jailers call the UCID of Barceloneta an 'integrated community'

and say that both they and we are 'all members of one big family'.

The false community of shared interests, like the disruption of ideological unity,

is part of ideology's strategy.

It exists to make us think there are only small differences

between the oppressors and the oppressed,

i.e. between the jailers and the inmates.

Today, in our geographic area,

those differences are supposedly the product of the pluralism discussed above,

i.e. false differences that can be resolved through sham democratic processes,

i.e. through board games devised by the oppressors

to keep the oppressed entertained.

There's a reason they call the written and unwritten rules of these processes

'democracy at play'.

3. THREE EXAMPLES OF IDEOLOGY

Example no. 1

La Vanguardia, 11 May 2017]

and author of *The Web Is On Fire*,

What does post-censorship mean?
It means postmodern censorship, it means cancel culture. Censorship that's horizontal, rather than vertical.

Horizontal?
It doesn't come from above, it doesn't require an authoritarian state: you're censored by society, your peers, all kinds of different groups.

What groups?
Belligerent groups of animal-rights people, feminists, Catholics, left-wingers, right-wingers, Catalan separatists, Basque separatists, taxi drivers, Spanish nationalists … Try saying something they think is wrong: they'll get triggered and lynch you.

Cyber-lynching?
Every day we cancel someone for saying something insensitive, collect signatures to get them fired, boycott their show, get their books pulled from libraries …

Have you ever been part of a digital lynch mob?
No, because I'm not afraid of people freely expressing their opinions, even if they're Nazis or misogynists. Obviously I hate what they're saying, but I'd rather let them say it than have them silenced, otherwise they'll just turn into some kind of martyr or the next Trump.

And what if they decide to come for you next?
They already have, but I refuse to be a turncoat. They can make me the target of their digital lynch mob, but they can't force me to join it.

Can you give me some examples of what you're talking about?
The comedian Jorge Cremades was cancelled, Casandra Vera and Justine Sacco were cyber-lynched for things they said on Twitter, children's book writer María Frisa was blacklisted, the chef Jordi Cruz…

Their crime was…?
Saying something. Something someone found offensive. Casandra, because she made a joke about the Carrero-Blanco assassination. Justine, because she made a joke about blacks. The Woke Police think that what someone says – a joke, an opinion – creates reality. And that by changing representation, they're changing the world. This is obviously a dangerous way of thinking, because by that logic, censorship can be constructive.

And we'd be censoring half of the world's art and literature.
Ninety per cent! And the censors think they're striking a blow for social justice. They have no idea that they're censors, just like we had under Franco.

Do sexist jokes make people sexist?
If you cancel all the sexist jokes, you'll still have sexism … and you'll throw free speech out with the bathwater.

They'll call you sexist for saying that.
They've already called me 'sexist', 'racist', 'radical centrist' 'fascist', 'spineless', 'short-sighted'… Labels are a key part of post-censorship: 'Hey, you can't read that because he's a [label].' There's no way to defend yourself against that.

And we're more vulnerable now than ever?
Yes, thanks to the filters on our virtual bubbles.

What's a virtual bubble?
The algorithms on social media that show you content from like-minded people, so you get used to a one-sided discourse, and you miss out on pluralism … it's like living in a virtual small town …

Does post-censorship silence us?
Free speech generates a lot of loud noise, but people constantly getting triggered generates a lot of loud silence. We're turning into cowards … Better not say anything, just in case! Post-censorship hurts pluralism, it hurts you, it hurts me … it hurts us all! (…)

We should all try to get offended a little less often, then?
Getting offended is fine, just don't be masturbatory about your indignation. We don't need any more self-righteous jack-offs. (…)

What do you do to avoid becoming complicit in post-censorship?
I try to be like Louis C.K., the American comedian. I laugh at everything, especially the things that are most sacred to me! If you let comedy die, freedom will soon follow.

https://www.lavanguardia.com/lacontra/20170511/422479014955/la-poscensura-amenaza-con-enmudecernos-a-todos.html

According to Juan Soto-Ivars, the political opinions of nazis,

jokes about the assassination of Luis Carrero-Blanco,

jokes about black people

and jokes about women

are all part of what he calls pluralism, democracy or *free speech*.

Notice how he thinks

jokes about killing Carrero-Blanco

(a specific, individual person)

and the opinions of nazis

(who subscribe to a specific, well-known vein of right-wing fascism)

should be crammed under the same free, democratic, pluralistic umbrella

as attacks against two broad groups

that he calls 'blacks' and 'women'.

So according to ideology, a nazi insulting a black person

is doing exactly the same thing as a black person insulting a nazi:

exercising *free speech*.

Reality, however, has conclusively shown

that when nazis insult black people,

they're supported by their position of power within ideology,

which, because there's only one ideology, protects and benefits them.

Here's a simple example:

Think back to the most recent time the Guàrdia Urbana of Barcelona
beat the shit out of some black street vendors while screaming racial slurs.
They received support from their boss, Mayor Ada Colau,
and were never held accountable.

But if a black person bad-mouths a nazi on the street,
ideology represses and condemns her,
because this is a free country
and the nazi is allowed to believe whatever he wants
without being harassed or abused.

Now think back to when those same black street vendors defended themselves
against those same cops,
and how the City Council of Barcelona, led by Ada Colau,
took it upon itself to prosecute those vendors
to the full extent of the law
and promised the public that in addition to beating the shit
out of the black street vendors,
it would also make sure
that they were imprisoned or deported.

The pluralism praised by Juan Soto-Ivars also includes
the mere existence of *belligerent groups of animal-rights people, feminists,*

Catholics, left-wingers, right-wingers, Catalan separatists, Basque separatists, taxi drivers, Spanish nationalists … and he leaves the list open for more.

(Notice how Soto-Ivars glibly lists taxi drivers
as representatives of an ideology,
implying, first, that there are many more ideologies
than those on his list,
and second, that all taxi drivers think the same
and are somehow especially 'belligerent'.)

For Soto-Ivars, every one of those individuals or groups
has their own way of viewing the world, and that view must be respected.
*I'm not afraid of people freely expressing their opinions,
even if they're Nazis or misogynists. Obviously I hate what they're saying,
but I'd rather let them say it than have them silenced.*
Here again Soto-Ivars corroborates what we said in the introduction
about having due respect for males/fascists/neoliberals.

If we fail to respect them,
we put institutional pluralism/democracy/free speech in jeopardy,
and any threat to those institutions *hurts you, it hurts me… it hurts all of us!*
That is, it hurts the community to which the interviewer (*you*),
the interviewee (*me*), and any number of other people (*all of us!*) belong.

Example no. 2

Hate is fuzzy. It is difficult to hate with precision. Precision would bring delicate nuance, attentive looking and listening; precision would bring that discernment that perceives individual persons, with all their diverse, contradictory qualities and propensities, as human beings. But once the sharp edges have been ground down, once individuals have been blotted out as individuals, then all that is left are indistinct groups to serve as targets of hatred; then they can hate to their hearts' content, and defame and disparage, rave and rage: *the* Jews, *the* women, *the* unbelievers, *the* Blacks, *the* lesbians, *the* refugees, *the* Muslims, or perhaps *the* United States, *the* politicians, *the* West, *the* police, *the* media, *the* intellectuals.[1] Hatred distorts the object of hatred to suit itself. It forms its object to fit.

Hatred is aimed upwards or downwards, but always along a vertical axis: against those 'at the top' or the 'lowest of the low'. It is always the categorically 'other' who is oppressing or threatening the hater's 'self'; the 'other' is fantasized as a supposedly dangerous force or a supposedly inferior pest

Emcke, C., *Against Hate*, Polity Press, Cambridge, 2019, pp. xii.

First published in German as *Gegen den Hass* © S. Fischer Verlag GmbH, Frankfurt am Main, 2016

This English edition © Polity Press, 2019

The author of these words is Carolin Emcke,

a journalist and writer like Juan Soto-Ivars.

Carolin Emcke is a prominent journalist, academic and author. Her contribution to public life has been recognized with many awards, including the Otto Brenner Prize for Critical Journalism and the Peace Prize of the German Publishers' Association, Germany's most prestigious literary award.

In an article published twenty days after the interview, copied here,

Soto-Ivars cited her as one of his role models:

Carolin Emcke reminds us in *Against Hate* (Polity Press) that the only way to
achieve equality, or to come close, is to get to know one another better. To stop
seeing each other as opposing groups – white, black, Arab, woman – and see
each other as individuals. ″

Emcke is an even more sophisticated fascist neoliberal female male teacher

than her fascist neoliberal male male pupil.

Soto-Ivars acknowledges the existence of groups so he can criticise them,

but Emcke denies their existence entirely.

She thinks that all those human groups she lists

are nothing but quantities of individuals, people or human beings

with *diverse, contradictory qualities and propensities*.

Emcke, like Soto-Ivars, lumps together *lesbians* and *the police*,

politicians and *women*, *the United States* and *the Blacks*.

Notice how she uses a more devious approach than Soto-Ivars

to make us swallow this fictitious disruption to ideological unity.

Carolin Emcke wants us to believe that when they 'defame and disparage'

and 'rave and rage' against lesbians,

black people, jews or muslims,

it's no different from when they rave and rage against the police, the West,

the media, the politicians or the United States.

For Emcke, insulting a cop for being a cop

is just as wrong as insulting a muslim for being a muslim.

In doing so, she makes a specious comparison
between someone defined by their job and someone defined by their religion,
and she fails to mention the one consideration
that humanists always fail to mention:
the difference in the position of power (rather than personal characteristics).
The cop is an agent of authority and is therefore in a position to oppress
the muslim, because he practises a demonised religion,
and to oppress the woman, because she's not a man,
and to oppress the lesbian, because she's not a man and she fucks other women.

According to Emcke, we have only *fantasised*
the *dangerous force* that threatens us.
However, anyone who lives in the world of reality and not ideology
knows that all of those human groups possess or lack power in varying degrees
and that is what distinguishes them from one another.

Here we see the disruption of ideological unity in all its splendour:
we can't talk about 'the United States' as a whole
because, as Emcke would have us believe,
there are good United States and bad United States.

Notice how the ideologue Emcke puts her rhetorical engineering
in the service of capital:
she takes the official name of a state
(she could just as well have chosen Spain or Iran)
and, even though any state

is a singular self-proclaimed territorial and administrative unit

that declares itself the sole sovereign

and legitimate possessor of certain unalienable rights

(among these the use of violence and the issuance of legal tender),

she wants us to believe that 'United States' is some kind of plural body

rather than a singular controlling entity, as its own Constitution states.

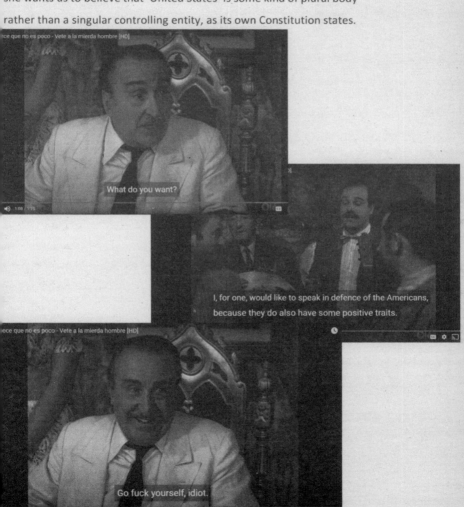

Consider, too, the ideological way

Emcke uses the word hate

to justify the phoney community of shared interests.

Ibid., pp.

110   *Against Hate*

Only when the patterns of hatred are replaced,
only 'when we discover similarities where we only saw
differences before'[2] – only then can empathy arise.

Where Soto-Ivars talks about belligerence and cancel culture

caused by the pluralist lie of differing opinions,

his teacher talks about hate by choice.

Carolin Emcke wants to depoliticise

our attacks against our captors

and deideologise our captors' attacks against us.

Thanks to hate, Emcke can sentimentalise and universalise all violence,

implying that, regardless of who is behind it,

it was caused by a defect in our shared humanity,

which commands us to love one another as the mere human beings we are.

If I attack a cop, it's out of hate,

and not because the cop is oppressing me.

If the cop attacks me, it's also out of hate;

and not because that's what he's paid to do.

Against Hate

We must resist fanaticism and racism not only in substance, but also in form. That means *not* becoming radicalized ourselves. That means *not* nurturing the fantasy of a civil war or an apocalypse by practising hatred and violence. What is needed instead is economic and social intervention in the places and in the structures in which the dissatisfaction that is being diverted into hatred and violence first arises. A person who wants to take preventive action against fanaticism cannot avoid asking what social and economic insecurities are being masked behind the false certainties of pseudo-religious or nationalistic dogmas. A person who wants to take preventive action against fanaticism must ask why so many people value their lives so little that they are willing to give them up for an ideology.

It's no coincidence that the release

of her screed *Against Hate*

coincided with the Ministry of the Interior's

Stop Radicalism campaign.

   stop-radicalismos.ses.mir.es

 GOBIERNO DE ESPAÑA MINISTERIO DEL INTERIOR

The fight against **radicalisation** and **violent extremism** is everyone's responsibility. If you see something, say something. **STRONGER TOGETHER.**

STOP RADICALISM

إن مكافحة عمليات التحول إلى الراديكالية والراديكالية نفسها مهمة الجميع
مساعدتك ضرورية أشد الضرورة لأننا أقوى معا

Your collaboration is important for all of us. Make a safe, confidential report today.

Did you know that citizen reporting is one of our most effective tools for detecting and preventing radicalisation?

هل تعرف أن المعلومات التي يوفرها المواطنون هي إحدى المصادر الأكثر فعالية للكشف عن عمليات التحول إلى الراديكالية وتحديها؟

إن تعاونك مهم جدًا للجميع
اتصل بنا
بطريقة أمنة وسرية

SOMETIMES, ANY DETAIL – NO MATTER HOW SMALL IT SEEMS CAN BE CRUCIAL TO SOLVING A LARGER PROBLEM.

إن معلومة صغيرة، وإن كانت بسيطة جدا، قد تكون مفتاحية لحل مشكلة أكبر

 BETTER PROTECTION THAN ALWAYS!

 ALERTCOPS! Extra Strength

 Download on the App Store   GET IT ON Google Play

What is Carolin Emcke, winner of the
Peace Prize of the German Publishers'

Association, Germany's most prestigious literary award

really saying when she praises freedom of speech and thought?
She's saying we can question absolutely everything
except the neoliberal masculofascist structure that upholds her ideal state.

That is, she's saying we can challenge absolutely nothing
except *anomalous ideas and practices*
of the good life, love or happiness,
which she reduces to *cultural diversity, individual life plans*
and *all kinds of rituals and festivals, practices and habits*
as she literally says on page 113.

On the very next line of her award-winning manifesto,
the great pacifier Carolin Emcke goes on to list a series of festivals in Germany
that she may or may not attend, but which, regardless, are living proof
that we can all live in harmony
in an open, liberal, secular society
where cultural, sexual and religious diversity reign supreme.

Against Hate

For my part, I find cultural or religious or sexual differences in a secular legal system *reassuring*. As long as I see these differences in the public space, I know that free spaces are granted in which I too am protected as an individual with all my distinctive characteristics, my longings, my possibly diverging beliefs or practices. I feel less vulnerable when I notice that the society I live in permits and bears with different life plans, different religious or political beliefs. For that reason, I am also reassured by those ways of living or forms of expression that are far removed from my own. They do not annoy me. They do not scare me. On the contrary: I am glad of all kinds of rituals and festivals, practices and habits. Whether people get their enjoyment in marching bands or at the Wagner festival in Bayreuth, in the F.C. Union stadium in old East Berlin or at the 'Pansy Presents Drag Race' in the West; (...) The affective bond

is precisely to this: living in a society that defends and protects my individual characteristics, even if they will never appeal to the majority, even if they are old-fashioned, new-fashioned, quirky or tasteless.

(...)

Really existing in the plural means mutually respecting everyone's individuality and uniqueness.

This banalisation of dissent, wherein its possibilities

are reduced to 'individual characteristics' and different forms of celebration,

is an excellent example of how ideology

constructs a masculofascist conception of the world

based on the capitalist logic of accumulation and consumption:

the more sexual options, the better;

the more religious options, the better;

the more individuals and the more life plans, the better;

in other words, think and talk about the world

like it's one giant supermarket.

Picozsa, Pablo, *Raising boys with Sexist Needs (Handbook for fathers)*, Hércules Ediciones, A Coruña, 2015, pp. 52–3.

EXAMPLE No. 3

Forms of Autonomy and Their Advantage

WHAT MAKES PÍO PALOMEQUE A MALE?

CHAPTER 2

The fact that he presumes to lecture women about how to be good mothers.

Because his notion of a good mother relegates women to the traditional, subordinate role of caring for their families, silently suffering and rearing children with whom they can only develop a meaningful relationship if it's built on dependency.

Mom: Cornerstone of the Family

SO YOU JUST HAD A BABY

The mother is the beating heart of the family; she created it, sees it through its problems and heartaches and selflessly bears the responsibility to make sure it keeps moving forward.

Mothers, you spend your days raising and nurturing your children, and you spend more time with them than anyone else. That's why you're so important to them: because in the beginning, they depend on you. But they may become vital to you some day, too, because you may end up depending on them.

When kids are small, you play a crucial role, rearing and educating them.

But when a child reaches adolescence and young adulthood, continuing to teach him discipline and good values will require special patience. And when he's finally fully grown, you might say to yourself, 'Now my task as a mother is finally over.' But that's a big mistake: once you're a mother, you're a mother for life, no matter how old your kids are.

(...)

Unlike mothers, fathers tend to focus more on their children's cultural and academic development; for that reason, they are usually the ones who realise that this 'disabled' child isn't actually disabled at all and, therefore, must be stimulated, the sooner the better.

Ibid p.26

But that's not the only reason Pío Palomeque is our masculofascist enemy.

Let's take a look at what his alter ego Daniel does

in the film *Me Too: Let Me Be a Male Like You*

when, after a night of sexual tension,

a co-worker he likes ultimately declines to sleep with him:

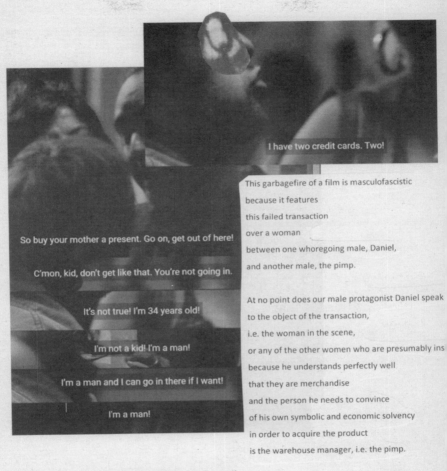

I have two credit cards. Two!

So buy your mother a present. Go on, get out of here!

C'mon, kid, don't get like that. You're not going in.

It's not true! I'm 34 years old!

I'm not a kid! I'm a man!

I'm a man and I can go in there if I want!

I'm a man!

This garbagefire of a film is masculofascistic

because it features

this failed transaction

over a woman

between one whoregoing male, Daniel,

and another male, the pimp.

At no point does our male protagonist Daniel speak

to the object of the transaction,

i.e. the woman in the scene,

or any of the other women who are presumably ins

because he understands perfectly well

that they are merchandise

and the person he needs to convince

of his own symbolic and economic solvency

in order to acquire the product

is the warehouse manager, i.e. the pimp.

The woman, too, understands perfectly well

that she must not negotiate directly with the customer.

Both times she speaks,

she addresses the middleman (the pimp)

in a half-hearted attempt to get him to close the deal with the customer.

Naturally, her opinion is ignored.

The take-home message from this

vilely masculine scene of prostitution

is that the would-be customer

is the person being treated unjustly

because he's barred access to the sexual product of his choosing.

The scene suggests that this is wrong

because Daniel is over 18 and has enough money to afford this product.

According to the film's male/fascist/capitalist morality,

this is a gross infringement of Daniel's rights

as a consumer and as a man.

Being the dudebroistic money-grubbers they are,

it never once occurred to the male directors or male screenwriters,

or to the male lead actor in his subsequent praise for the film,

to convey a message based on reality,

rather than ideology.

When we inmates at the Barceloneta UCID were forced to watch this film, we quickly bristled at the fact

that the victim of this masculocapitalist injustice

was the whoremonger and not the whore.

The reality is that the women present or implied in this scene

are the people being treated like objects by two exploitative males

and the women, therefore, are the ones who deserve our solidarity.

But ideology wants us to empathise with the man who loses the cockfight,

because he is unable to satisfy his sexual desire or assert himself as a man;

the women, on the other hand, do not express their sexual desire

or the price they would eventually like to charge for their services.

The cherry on top of this ideological concubinage

is that they go so far as to make the prostitute sympathise

with the aggrieved customer's sexual frustration.

In doing so, the film is trying to disguise the true masculinist injustice against her

and sell us on the ideological fantasy

of the acquiescent whore who is treated well by whoremonger and pimp alike.

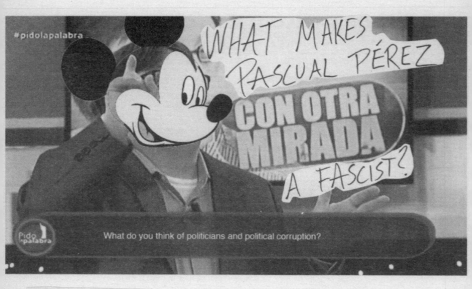

WHAT MAKES PASCUAL PÉREZ CON OTRA MIRADA A FASCIST?

What do you think of politicians and political corruption?

Pido la palabra

Pascual Pérez: Me, I wouldn't get rid of anyone, honestly, because everyone has a role to play, don't you think? Now more than ever. All hands on deck ... Yes, there are politicians who are out to get rich. They've even said so publicly. They're out there. Of course they're out there. But you have to be careful, because there are also honest politicians.

Member of the audience: Lots of them.

Pascual Pérez: And they're good, sincere, committed people. So, I don't think it's good to generalise about any demographic, including politicians.

Pascual Pérez is a fascist because he believes that the oppressors,

and therefore our oppression, 'have a role to play'.

But since he's an ideologue, rather than a realist like us,

that's not how he phrases it. He conceals it with the rhetoric of ideology.

He sets the first ideological trap that we saw in the introduction,

so perfectly illustrated by Juan Soto-Ivars and Carolin Emcke:

the trap of thinking in terms of good cops and bad apples,

denying the unity among oppressors and denying, therefore, oppression itself.

This denial is the product of Pascual Pérez's belief

that the only thing a politician can do wrong

is get rich by illegitimately cashing in on his office.

In other words, professional authoritarians have nothing to be ashamed of

when they commit legitimate, state-sanctioned violence against us

in every sphere of our lives until we're battered and bleeding

from the endless series of abuse and subjugation and trauma and compromise

that has become such a fixed feature of our daily lives

that we don't even notice it any more.

This is actually a good thing, Pérez says,

so long as when the oppressors batter and abuse us,

they do it with 'honesty, sincerity and commitment'.

The fascist Pascual Pérez even denies the existence of our oppressors,

whom he considers to form their own *demographic*

(in doing so, of course, he also denies the existence of us, the oppressed).

Notice how he uses the demofascist rhetorical technique of atomising society

into distinct groups according to superficial characteristics

rather than according to the degree of power they possess

and therefore the greater or lesser degree of control they can exert over us.

(We will politicise this concept in the following pages

when we look at the fascist Pascual Pérez's comments about 'minorities'.)

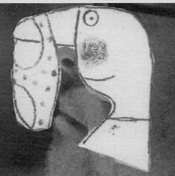

Societies that divide and marginalise minorities

are mutilated societies.

arte
InésAVARICIO

They're not united. Their members are like desert islands.

That's not our aim.

We want the opposite, our aim is to unite.

Remember that cramming all of us under the same democratic umbrella
is a strategy that ideology uses to neutralise conflicts of all kinds
by creating a sham community of shared interests,
in this case, *people*.

'We're all people' is another catchphrase
Pascual Pérez loves to share wherever he goes.
He wants to make us think that if we join him, together
we can be part of the same egalitarian collective: people.

Let's look at the extent to which Pascual Pérez denies
the existence of real-world differences between *people*:

Here, we're all just people.

In these stills from *Me Too: Let Me Be a Male Like You*,

we can see what Pascual Pérez means when he talks about minorities:

women in the minority,

black people in the minority,

and gay people in the minority.

Notice how his concept of the minorities

that must be protected, tolerated and integrated

mirrors his concept of the majority

that must be protective, tolerant and welcoming.

If the minorities are gay, black and female,

then the majority must be straight white men.

For the straight white man Pascual Pérez,

anyone who is not a straight white man

(the active, value-setting class)

is a passive recipient of straight white male values.

It's only when straight white males fail to set those values,

Pascual Pérez regrets to inform us,

that we become 'mutilated societies' that 'divide and marginalise minorities'.

WHAT MAKES PLINIO PACHECO A NEOLIBERAL?

When it comes to talking about Pacheco's neoliberalism,

it's hard to untangle

his love of capital

from his love of the vein of fascism known as democracy.

Take a look at these stills from the film,

which come right after his comments about minorities.

Notice how Pascual Pérez sees a connection

between having a job and 'having a voice in society'.

He believes that only those who generate economic value

can generate moral value,

and thus only they deserve to be heard.

He also suggests that we must fulfil our capitalist duty to work

not only so we can be effective members

of the phoney community of shared interests known as 'democratic society',

but even just to 'feel like' a part of it,

and that feeling of belonging is supposed to be enough to create community.

Work helps us to feel like we're part of this society.

Because we are, and we always have been.

And we want to have a voice in this society.

In fact, the false community of shared interests

requires not just active, dues-paying members,

but active, dues-paying members who, for no more than a sense of community

acquired through submission to work,

obey and legitimise those members

who are motivated not by feelings but by power.

Plinio Pacheco's eagerness to legitimise the rulers and the oppressors
is yet another reason he is a fascist.

Plinio Pacheco believes his legitimation of democratic power is justified
because capitalist economy needs to exploit us
as a means of production so that others can get rich.

That is yet another reason he is a neoliberal.

por

ÓMEZ CARDEÑA

After all, there's a reason it's called 'democratic'.

Thank you.

WHY ARE OUR JAILERS SO EXCITED ABOUT PORFIRIO PÁEZ
COMING TO SPEAK TO US IN PERSON?

Now that we've got a clear understanding of

the male who wrote the book they forced us to read

and who inspired and starred in the film they forced us to watch,

let's think about why our jailers are so excited about bringing him

to the self-advocacy group to give a talk

to the inmates at the Barceloneta UCID.

Our jailers think Porfirio Páez is a role model

and that if we see him in the flesh, we will want to follow in his footsteps.

They believe Porfirio Páez is an exemplary specimen

because he is perfectly integrated in society.

All of our jailers were taught,

whether at university, vocational training or their

rent-a-cop training course at the National Employment Institute,

that the ultimate goal of their profession

is the social integration of the inmates in their care.

Our jailers can point to Porfirio Páez

as living proof that their repressive methods work:

he's an inmate who, thanks to our institutions' efforts at integration,

has been redeemed and become an all-star jailer,

like those serial killers who become preachers when they get out of prison.

And what do their efforts at integration consist of?

How did they achieve such positive results with Porfirio Páez?

And how do they hope to do the same to those of us who remain unredeemed?

As you may have already guessed, their efforts at integration involve

turning us into fascists,

turning us into neoliberals,

and turning us into males.

Whenever our jailers and their showmen like Porfirio Páez

talk about integration,

the next word on their lips is normalisation.

Inmates can only achieve integration through normalisation.

As the name suggests, normalisation means becoming normal.

Normal like Porfirio Páez is normal?

Right again!

Because normal means fascist,

normal means neoliberal

and normal means male.

Only if we possess these attributes and use them to oppress others

can inmates like us tolerate this shitridden tourist theme park known as Barcelona

without opening fire on every fascist

and every neoliberal

and every male we encounter.

WHAT CAN/SHOULD THE INMATES AT THE
BARCELONETA UCID DO FOR THIS GREAT DAY?

The jailers and Porfirio Páez

want to restrain our unrestrainable desire for conflict,

which is our last and only hope

against the systemic subjugation we are suffering at the hands of our jailers.

But how is creating conflict

going to save us from our oppressors?

Isn't it true that, if we don't cause trouble,

we won't face retaliation from our oppressors?

Yes, we have many good reasons

to remain submissive and depoliticised.

One of these good reasons

is a fear that they'll make our lives even more unliveable.

That's what our oppressors do when we defy them.

We've seen it many times before, like when

a fellow inmate who liked to fuck around,

(thus violating the prohibitions of the male/fascist/capitalist code,

which says a woman cannot possess sexual agency

unless she is a prostitute)

was stuffed full of pills and had that agency brainwashed right out of her.

Or like our fellow inmate who refused to go back to work,

where she spent thirty hours a week packing catered meals

for just 150 euros per month:

now they keep her locked in the arts-and-crafts room

and pay her zero euros per month

to make decorations with cardboard and bread clay,

which they use to decorate the UCID like the Teletubbies' golf course.

Or like our comrade-in-arms who refused to join the aforementioned inmate

in arts-and-crafts captivity,

so they stuck him in front of the TV

and made him watch whatever the jailer wanted to watch,

and wouldn't let him choose the programme, or hold the remote,

or even leave the TV room.

If you refuse to take their pills,

three of them pin you down,

hold your nose,

and force you to swallow.

If you refuse to put on a clean shirt in the morning,

they make fun of your stench and the stains on your clothes, and don't let you leave the building.

If we're walking on the beach and you're lagging a few metres behind the group,
they tell you to keep up.
If we're walking on the beach and you're walking a few metres ahead of the group,
they tell you to slow down;
and if you don't speed up or don't slow down,
the jailers grab you by the hand and impose their own pace.

So how can conflict save us?
Creating conflict won't save us, it will only make our punishment more severe!

That is true according to the logic of colloquial or established language.
But speaking with colloquial or established language
means accepting the logic of the oppressors.
It means speaking with an acritical understanding of certain words
that our oppressors have loaded with meaning for us.

Our jailers conceal their abuse with administrative language,
like when they call their penal system 'social services'
or when they call themselves 'professionals'.
But we know they are not professionals
at anything but abduction and incarceration.
In the very act of calling our jailers jailers
and calling ourselves inmates,

we have already begun to expose the abusive relationship
between us and them.

Our first act as inmates
was to stop calling things by the names assigned by ideology
and start calling them by their true names.

Thus, where established language proclaims
'If you don't obey us, we will punish you',
we have started to hear something different:
'If you refuse to accept our way of seeing the world,
and continue to refuse no matter what we do,
you'll undermine our control over you.'

But established language still tries to salvage what it can
and warns us:
'If you misbehave for one afternoon,
you may be punished for days or weeks, or even permanently.'

Don't let yourselves be hoodwinked!
When our oppressors use established language to make spine-chilling threats,
it doesn't mean they are powerful.
It means they are afraid
and that we are the cause of their fear.

In other words: we inmates are ever closer to emancipation
and ever further from fascist/neoliberal/male oppression.

In other words: every act of disobedience towards our jailers
opens the door to more and greater acts of disobedience.

We will not be rid of punishment,
but our punishments will be relativised and stripped of the absolute power
with which our jailers justify all their acts of oppression.

The question isn't whether a day of defiance, conflict and emancipation
is 'worth it' for the punishment.
'Worth it' is just two more words of established language
that suggest:
'What's the point of resisting my oppressors
if they're just going to punish me for it?'

But we unmask the language of power and say
that punishment is never worth it
because 'it' has no worth.
Suffering has no positive value.

We are not martyrs.
We don't defy our captors and start a conflict
so we can be punished and suffer for the cause.

We defy them despite that suffering

and do everything we can to evade retribution.

We don't speak the established language of the honourable hero

who says only cowards 'throw the rock and hide the hand'.

We know that hiding the hand is the only way to keep them from cutting it off

and ensure we'll be able to throw another rock tomorrow.

We don't perform acts of heroism; we lie in ambush.

We don't want to raise awareness about the cause of our oppression, no,

we do everything we can to go undetected

so our oppressors can't pick us out of a line-up.

Question: You've never fallen for a girl with DS [Down's syndrome]?

Answer: Good question. It's one of the worst things about being a pioneer: I've never bonded with people with DS, and to be honest, that's not good: I feel like I've missed out on something. Sometimes I catch myself falling into the same prejudices I'm trying to combat. I walk down the street and I see them clinging to their mom or dad's hand, and I feel like there's this huge gap between us. They've been raised in this segregated, predetermined way, so they haven't evolved or learned. And then, when I spend time with normal people in my usual circles, I just feel so comfortable.

This is exactly what our jailers want to do to us.

They want us to feel comfortable with them

and disgusted with one another.

It's a classic tactic

that oppressive regimes from every era and every part of the world,

have used to prevent the oppressed from uniting

and to encourage them to identify with their oppressors.

Pita, Elena, 'A Day with Pablo Pineda', 15 September 2015

http://fueradeserie.expansion.com/2015/09/14/personajes/1442225139.html

We suspect this is what they did to Poncio Pilatos when he was an inmate

and the tactic clearly worked like a charm:

now he's a perfectly integrated, normalised citizen, happily serving their interests.

But the particular circumstances that prompted this particular man

to become yet another jailer

do not interest us.

We are here to hack the chains off our own wrists,

not the wrists of the profiteers cashing in on our oppression.

You see yourself as a pioneer in disseminating masculofascist capitalist doctrine

in UCIDS and RUCIDS all around the world?

You think we haven't 'evolved or learned'

according to the precepts of neoliberalism?

You feel a 'huge gap' between you and us?

You're comfortable around normal people but not around us?

The answers are yes, yes, yes and yes, asshat.

And your discomfort is only just beginning.

You were wrong about us.

They call us 'Don't-Won'ts'

because we don't study and we won't work.

And they're right, we'll never study and we'll never work.

We shit in the niche of your cathedral

to education and industry,

then close the glass panel,

eaving our venerable turd on display
beside this poem by a former fellow inmate
who was murdered by the police.
Her name was Patricia Heras.

Overqualified young Don't-Won't
Don't turn like a cog
or hook for the State
Won't be bought like an envoy for
the fucking Inquisition.

Young Don't-Won't overqualified
pisses on your street corners
too sick to stomach any more.

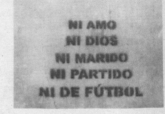

When they applaud Poncio Pilatos for talking about universal access
and eliminating the barriers to every facet of democratic life,
we know that they are applauding universal access to submission
and the erection of newer, more sophisticated barriers to real life.
The only universal access we want
is universal access to pleasure, politicisation
and a life that yearns to be lived, rather than mediated by our oppressors.

We are young Don't-Won'ts, overqualified
to strip the will to live from anyone who tries to bury us alive
and plant, in the newly dug and still-fresh soil of our common grave,
trees that flower with hundred-euro notes.

What do you think of the proposed abortion law reform?
It's an important, sensitive topic. We're talking about the future of this society. I don't want to come off as preachy. I don't like judging women because every woman is a world unto herself. I don't want to judge them, and I shouldn't judge them. Every woman has her own unique circumstances. But what I will say is that when they think about getting an abortion, they should think about the experiences they may be depriving themselves if that child isn't born. **If you kill your child, you're robbing yourself of a life with him**, all the joy he could bring you. I know I've brought my mother joy, lots of joy.

The Minister of Justice, Alberto Ruiz-Gallardón, said the psychological trauma that a foetal malformation could cause a woman may 'justify termination of the pregnancy'. Do you think this could amount to a de facto legalisation of abortion due to foetal impairment?
It's very sensitive subject. It's like in the song 'La donna è mobile', you never know how a woman's going to react, especially if her judgement is clouded, if she's been raped, if she's had a traumatic experience. But it's also true that 'every law has its loophole', and they can use this as an excuse, just like they use abuse as an excuse, but I also think you can't create a trauma out of nothing.

Getting raped makes us morons

What do you think about prenatal testing for trisomy 21?
Amniocentesis is the root of abortion. I **don't like** *à la carte* babies. Your child is your child. No matter his condition. The mother, if she's a good mother, should accept the child as is, so I don't see the point in testing. It's crazy to me. You're limiting your baby yourself. What do you care how the baby comes out? If your baby has Down's syndrome, what are you going to do, kill it? Let it live. There's nothing more tender than a baby. I stand on the side of life and healthy living. I believe in the value of life. It's a beautiful thing.

I'm a man, and I can go in there if I want.

I'm a man!

I'm a man!

Death to males!
Death to fascists!
Death to neoliberals!

See you 5 September !

2009	SPAIN	103 minutes	Color	1.85:1 Aspect Ratio

In Spanish with English Subtitles

don't want your society
won't wear your muzzle!

DVD VIDEO
OliveFilms

8 87090 02760 1

The exercise went through three phases that took place in silence, with imperceptible transitions and no break in the dancing. In the first I was perfectly still, and in the second they tossed me around some, but in the third my feet didn't even touch the ground, or they touched down for only the briefest instant so I could regain momentum or change from a difficult position before taking flight again. There were thirteen dancers with me and against me, half of the participants at the Cineplex's fifteen-day intensive. In an effort to transform choreographic creation and instruction into still more touristbait, they call this programme 'Summer Stage', or SS, an abbreviation that I think really hits the nail on the head, because for that fortnight in July, the Cineplex is positively hopping with dance tourists and dance fascists, which are one and the same. This year, the SS dedicated half its classes to 'Inclusive Dance', which is trying to sound woke and social justicey but it's really just the same garden-variety integrated dance by another name. Students from the conservatory and professional dancers have come to join us Thursday-afternoon regulars at the Cineplex, and some of them have travelled far for the opportunity. Apparently the instructors giving the classes are quite renowned fascists and at the end of the programme they're going to put on a show.

The first phase consisted of straightforward manipulation: standing motionless, I let myself be touched by the others.

With all those hands touching you at once, you lose your head a little, you're headless, despite the fact that it's being touched by at least four or five hands. The type of touch was not limited to stroking or massaging. It might be a brush, a quick sweep across your clothes or your skin, or it might be a smooth journey of the fingernails, or fingers pressing a bone or some fleshy spot; it might just be still hands warming your body. You feel like your body doesn't belong to you at all and also like it's yours more than ever. Your heel connects to your nipple, your jawbone to your butt crack, the nape of your neck to your ankle, your nose to your wrist, and hundreds of other simultaneous combinations. You don't just inhabit your entire body, you extend outward like you're tripping on peyote, and for as long as the touching lasts, you occupy a body with twenty-three additional hands (one dancer had only one hand and two others had no feeling on the right side of their bodies). If any of the twenty-three hands stops touching you, it's like it's been amputated; you miss it.

Anticipating just such a problem, the director ordered the touchers to crowd together, arrange themselves in tiers, negotiate physically and keep grasping and grabbing so that all hands were on you, the manipulee, at all times, except for any brief moments, as necessary, for the touchers to change positions so the touching could continue. From the outside (I know because when it was my turn as a toucher I stepped back to take a look), the others look like predators devouring the prey on which they've just pounced, although you are upright as they devour you. Another order issued: touchers were to make no abrupt movements that could cause you to fall, and you were to remain rooted to the ground, only taking steps when it was absolutely essential in order to keep your footing.

And then your jaw goes slack, your knees go weak, your eyes close, and you start to sigh. Sometimes as you oscillate, you have to shift all your weight onto one leg because there's more hand activity down one side than the other and you begin to lose your balance. Sometimes you lose your balance completely and when that happens you do, in fact, have to take one or two small steps to remain vertical.

You've been given a gift, twenty-three hands bringing you full awareness of your own body. The director explained it all at the start so that during the exercise, instead of communicating in the devious, stilted language of words, our bodies could speak in the non-rhetorical, loquacious language of inhalation, exhalation and movement. Another order he gave the thirteen manipulators before this first phase of the exercise: investigate the manipulee's body, be curious, probe it like medical examiners. Find out which parts are hard, which are soft, where there's tension, looseness, smoothness, dryness, and to what degree. Be gentle, don't hurt her. The order he gave me was: if something they do hurts you, speak up.

As I've said before, the world of contemporary dance is a conservative one. I'd done this exercise many times, but with fewer and less intelligent manipulators than the classmates I had the good fortune of dancing with that day. When I'd done the exercise in the past, regardless of whether you were a manipulator or a manipulee, the genitals, breasts, anus and sometimes even the glutes were strictly off limits. This also applies to contact-improvisation jams: the contact has to occur under the proper circumstances, and the improvisation is only permitted when it meets certain criteria. We can press up against our partner's entire body, but the second we feel the gelatinousness of a testicle, a breast or a droopy penis, or the tenderness of a vulva, the prohibited-contact alarm starts blaring and we yank our hand the hell out of there.

Once at a contact-improvisation class when I was still at the BADDAY, the male instructor divided us by sex to do the trust-fall exercise, in which everyone stands shoulder to shoulder in a tight circle with one person in the middle. From those positions, they start pushing and catching the person in the middle, causing her to sway continually, without falling over and, if possible, without even moving her feet.

I questioned the BADDAY instructor about the sexual segregation and he said all right, OK, organise yourselves however you want, by height, by the colour of your clothes, whatever, otherwise you'll call me a sexist. He's a well-respected and good-looking sexist, so all the male students and especially all the female students found this comment hilarious. After we formed our mixed-gender groups, he told the women to cross their hands over their chests as they swayed. The woman in the centre of the other circle immediately closed her eyes and went full-on Tutankhamun. She's a sweet person and we get along really well; whenever we're paired up to improvise together we go on some wild rides because she knows how to improvise for real. It hurt me to see her tutankhamunised.

'Why, Antón? Does that help our technique?' I asked, my gates still dormant.

'In case anyone's sensitive to pain in their breasts and someone pushes off their chest.' The classic smokescreen of health to justify sexual repression: masturbate too much and you'll go blind; keep sleeping around and you'll catch all kinds of horrible STDs.

'And men can't be sensitive to pain in their breasts?'

He pffted and smiled and didn't answer, like a Don Juan caught slipping out of one maiden's chamber and into another. My gates, still disengaged, prepared for their eventual closure.

'How could someone possibly hurt their chest doing something as gentle as the trust-fall exercise? And in any case, shouldn't people be allowed to decide what is and isn't painful to them?'

'Yes, fine, go, do it however you want.' The Don Juan had no choice but to acknowledge where he'd been and where he was going, and his male and female students, themselves aspiring Don Wannabes and fair young maidens waiting their turn to be taken, laughed along knowingly, complicit with his manly mischief.

'I have no problem with you touching my breasts,' I said that day. My circle of classmates, of course, avoided touching them with millimetric repression.

'I have no problem with you touching my breasts, my genitals, my perineum, my butt or my anus,' I found myself forced to repeat to the director and students at the SS after receiving the order to speak up if they hurt me, which, like most orders, was entirely unnecessary. 'In fact, I want you to touch me everywhere because I know it will help us dance better.'

There were enough arched eyebrows to build the cloister of a convent, plus wisecracks and giggles from one repressed female fascist and two repressed male fascists.

'If you like it too much, speak up.'

'Typical Nati.'

'Happy to!' one abuser said as he rubbed his hands together.

'The three of you aren't gonna touch me at all,' I responded calmly, surrounded by them and the other dancers.

The males who had just spoken up were a biped who dances like she's jumping over puddles and playing Ring-a-Ring o' Roses alone, and two men who use wheelchairs, one electric and one not. The man with the non-electric wheelchair was the abuser who rubbed his hands together. He dances well because he gets out of the chair and moves by dragging himself along, which is to say, he takes a risk in pursuit of pleasure. The guy with the electric wheelchair, on the other hand, dances poorly because his movements consist of making the wheels on his chair go round and round, round and round, round and round, the wheels on his chair go round and round, all through the Cineplex with bipedal females perched on his lap or on the armrest or motor of his chair, or sometimes straddling him or lying perpendicular across the chair like pin-up stick figures in a martini glass, bicycling their legs with pointed toes. He limits himself to using the control of his chair to parade the elevated bipedlettes and himself around the rehearsal space like a float in a Playboy cavalcade. His usual partners include the woman who does the solo Ring-a-Round o' Roses.

'What, you don't like us?'

'Oh, suddenly she's suuuuch a princess.'

'Come on, babe, you know you're gonna love it.'

'I won't do the exercise with the three of you because you're mocking my request to be touched everywhere.' I was calm; I felt shielded by the thirteen dancers who were unaffected by my comment, or who were affected in a positive way, looking at me, winking at me and nodding along.

'Nati, it's just a joke.'

'We're only messing around.'

'Don't take it personally, honey, we didn't mean to offend you.'

'As I understand it, you're laughing because you conceive of dance as a social service administered by public and private economic agents rather than an opportunity to shatter our patterns of movement and acquire new patterns that offer greater pleasure. Which is to say that for you three, a dance class might as well be a bag of crisps, just another product in the long chain of consumer acts that make up your lives.'

The students who didn't know me listened attentively and stared at the three fascists, who were shaking their heads, muttering and pffting. All this pffting and unwillingness to speak up roused my gates out of standby mode, though they

284

remained in repose, out of sight. My usual classmates looked like they were tired of listening to me, they wanted to start the exercise, they wanted to make the most of the 260 euros they had paid for the official purpose of attending an intensive dance course and for the private purpose of making a good impression at this covert casting call in the hopes that the director would give them a lead role in the show at the end of these two weeks. They looked at the director with the entitled expression of underlings waiting for authority to step up and restore order, which is to say waiting for him to tell me to shut up, since by dint of their 260 euros a month they had delegated to him not only the task of imposing limits on how to dance, but also of resolving any conflicts that should arise.

This director, however, appeared to be that rare dance professional who doesn't mind dance talk in a dance class, and so he listened to what I had to say. None of the dancers who hoped for a starring role dared break the three-tiered huddle surrounding me, because the authority they had conceded to the instructor meant that if he was listening, they should all follow suit; they did spread out a little though. Only the slender, circumspect Bruno, the best dancer in the group because he listens to nothing but the demands of his own body, left the formation and began performing solitary whirling dervishes. His silent departure prompted the director to give the same idiotic response authority figures always give when they've been put on the spot.

'You're saying you don't want to do the exercise with these three?'

'You heard me. That is exactly what I said.'

'Could you tell us why?' He spoke slowly and with exaggerated interest, placing himself in the first tier of the manipulator huddle. He's tall, skinny and nearly bald, with small eyes, short eyelashes and a hooked nose. He rehearses in clothes that could pass for pyjamas: a long-sleeved shirt full of holes and polka-dot pants with fraying cuffs. He has the deep tan typical of a very white man who spends time outside, with darker splotches betraying a sixty-year-old body that could otherwise pass for thirty-five.

Being questioned by power in such close proximity would put any non-fascist on edge. My gates sealed shut and from within I answered:

'I've already explained why. And it's clear the rest of the class is waiting for you to give the OK on my refusal to dance with those three. Or for you to give the not-OK and exclude me from the exercise since I'm the one who refuses to dance with them. Because you're the director and without your seal of approval we can't do a damn thing around here, even though you're the one who ought to be taking orders from us since we're the ones shelling out for this class.'

There was some stifled, incredulous laughter, stifled because no one who hoped for a decent role was going to start needling the director. Just like when they kicked me out of the BADDAY, I braced for the inevitable: the fascists would side with the fascists and together they would unburden themselves of the victim. But this time, miraculously, the inevitable didn't happen. An anti-fascist victory, but a bitter victory nevertheless because it was the authority figure rather than the dancers-turned-underlings who drove away the fascists. Which is to say, no fucking victory at all. Just the relief of having some distance between them and me for a few minutes.

'Why don't you three sit this one out?' the director ordered. And the three fascist lovers of authority – upstanding citizens who honour the democratic process and respect judicial decisions even if they disagree with them, dutiful consumers who had paid 260 euros just for the chance to prove how obedient they can be – left the huddle like good-natured martyrs whose only crime was to offer an opinion, though under their breath they cursed the Cineplex for marketing itself as a centre for the creation of movement while censoring the free speech to which every fascist, every male and every neoliberal has the God-given right.

The assistant director came out to intercept the aggrieved parties. The director joined them and said something the rest of us couldn't hear, his knees making a resonant crack as he squatted down to the same level as the two in wheelchairs. He was consoling them, clearly. Consoling the males who had ridiculed and objectified me. Explaining all the reasons they shouldn't go to the Cineplex's management and demand their money back, imploring them not to drop out of the SS or challenge the two core principles of integrated dance, which state that everyone has to dance goddammit, and goddammit everyone has to dance with everyone else. Whatever he told them, it worked, because they sat down at the edge of the linoleum among the backpacks, clothes, shoes, water bottles and aide/minder/cops (there to chaperone students like Ibrahim who weren't allowed out of their UCIDs without a minder) and watched as I surrendered myself to the manipulation for a full twenty-five minutes.

The director lets you know how long the manipulation has lasted once it's over, because no one, neither the manipulators nor the manipulee, is able to check the time. Worth noting, given our current moment in history: here is a pleasure you cannot experience while looking at your phone.

After an initial ten minutes as predators and prey, and following a signal that most likely came from the director's active intervention on my body, the touching gave way to manipulation in the full sense of the word. All thirteen dancers began to touch me more forcefully, mobilising the jointed parts of my body. Those were their orders: to bend everything bendable, from my highest vertebra to the last phalanx of my toes; to do so with any part of their bodies, no longer with just their hands, and to experiment with speed and intensity. They could bring my arm as far back as my shoulder joint would allow then forcefully launch it forward, for example, or they could bend me at the waist so my hair brushed against the floor then slowly pull me back up, one vertebra at a time. They could bend my knees and ankles and make me walk, or lay me out on the floor and make me roll; no longer required to stay rooted, the manipulee was now allowed to move in space, but no further than she was led.

At this point it was no longer possible for all thirteen bodies to act on me simultaneously, as they had initially done with their hands. Instead they took turns, and in those brief moments of separation from the manipulee, they now had to remain visually connected to her and to the other handlers, alert to the best moment to intervene. The best moment to intervene occurs when one manipulator identifies another manipulator's intention and helps bring it to fruition, or, if they cannot identify that intention, they imagine possible ways to advance a movement already under way. For example: if a manipulator nestles his butt into the manipulee's pubic bone, grabs her wrists, and presses her chest into his back with the intention of lifting her up, another observant manipulator might stand behind the manipulee and press into her back, creating a slight concave arch in the first manipulator's back and thereby pulling the manipulee's feet off the floor: a porté.

If the second manipulator continues pressing, the first will end up bending low so that the manipulee's hands, lifeless, touch the floor. The second manipulator, seeing that the first manipulator and the manipulee are now close to the ground, could straddle the manipulee's lower back without quite sitting on it, then lift her torso by pulling up on both shoulders, creating a new arch, convex this time, in her spine. The first manipulator, who had borne the manipulee on his back, can now pull away. End of porté.

A third manipulator would have already secured the manipulee's legs by pinning her knees to the floor, and a fourth, seeing how the manipulee was restrained – with her cobra arms hanging lifeless, her chest unobstructed and her head pulled backwards so her mouth and throat are open like a gutter – would notice the manipulee's sacrificial position and see an opportunity to break it, to save the manipulee, who is on the verge of coughing. The second manipulator, who had been straddling the manipulee, would step away, and the manipulee's cobra pose would loosen as the second manipulator releases her shoulders. The saviour, aware that he must still manipulate the manipulee's joints even as he's saving her, would stand shoulder to shoulder with the manipulee, grab her under the waist with one hand, and lift her opposite arm with the other hand, heaving the manipulee onto the side of the saviour's body. María did this last move on me, and since she has no legs and she's so much shorter than I am, even when I'm kneeling, she didn't just lift me onto one of her sides, she lifted me onto both, which is to say she lifted me onto her entire back, draping me over herself like a stole. Another porté. The top of my head touched the ground, I supported myself on my palms, and another manipulator came and pulled my hips upwards, off María's back, so that I was standing on my head; then she carefully rotated my hips between her hands while the other manipulators helped keep me balanced. The manipulation continued like this for the remaining fifteen minutes of the second phase, which, from the outside, looked less like a pack of wolves feasting on a deer and more like a game of giant chess in which each player is waiting for their turn to make a move.

I had to let go and let it happen, just like before. Now I was going to be a puppet, but a puppet with a survival neuron that would prevent me from crashing into the floor if no one held me up, and which would enable me to put up a resistance or speak up if something hurt. Once again, the absurd order to say something if I was in pain. The pyjamaed director's dance students bombard him with so many demonstrations of just how goddamn eager they are to follow his orders, they even need his permission to complain.

But it only hurts if you don't know how to let go, if you don't trust the strangers touching you. If your muscles and joints are tense, any contact will hurt, because no matter how gently the other body manipulates you, it will encounter resistance, leading to collisions rather than communication. With your muscles and joints relaxed, another body enters yours like ice cream, lick by lick, and it no longer makes sense to describe the exercise as manipulation because, as a very wise contact instructor I once had put it, the word manipulation implies one person being active and the other being passive, but in this exercise, if you're able to take pleasure in the feeling of vertigo, those roles cease to exist, and dance is what emerges in their place. Thanks to that pleasure, the manipulee's response to being touched conditions the manipulator's movements, to the point that the so-called manipulee is the one who, through the mere reactions of her body, guides the so-called manipulator's actions.

'You mean like when you get raped, Nati?' a woman at the self-advocacy group asked when I told them all this. It was my turn to share at Interrogation Tuesday.

'Gosh, dance is just fascinating, isn't it? Go on, Nati, tell us how you stand on your head!' That was my sister Patricia, tapping her heel like a flamenco dancer preparing for lift-off.

'Patricia, please, it's Remedios's turn to speak,' replied Psykommandant Buedo, playing good cop, taking notes and leaning forward to convey that we had her full attention.

'Well, Reme, I've never been raped, I don't think, though I wouldn't stake my life on it because plenty of times women fuck men when they don't want to, and we think it's the most normal thing in the world so we don't call it rape. I can re-member that happening plenty of times, fucking some dude despite losing interest mid-fuck, or before we'd even started. Sometimes I'd never wanted to fuck him in the first place! But still, forcing myself to fuck him or keep fucking him against my own wishes, for the sake of pleasing the male and not being a prude or a cock-tease.'

'It's so wonderful when you wish for something and it comes true! Don't you think, Laia?' Patricia interrupted with a raised hand, so on edge she couldn't make her arm stop trembling.

'The other day I wished it wasn't eleven at night so I wouldn't have to go back to the UCID and I looked at my phone and it came true,' said one self-advocate.

'Well, the other day I wished the heat would ease off and that didn't come true.' Another self-advocate.

'I wished I'd get to dance with Nati one day and it came true.' Ibrahim.

'It's not the heat that makes it so hot. It's the humidity.' A third self-advocate.

The self-advocates all launched into their own conversa-tions and I did the same with Reme. The psykommandant had to make proportional use of violence to restore order, as authorities such as herself are expected to.

'We can talk about all our wishes later, that's certainly another very interesting topic, but first let's allow our friends Remedios and Natividad to finish!' she shouted over the commotion. She uses our full names whenever she's being explicitly authoritarian. When she's being implicitly authoritarian, which is all day every day, she uses our nicknames. 'Natividad, please finish answering Remedios's question,' she commanded after all the self-advocates had been silenced.

'I finished.'

'And do you, Remedios, have any other questions for Natividad?' She sounded like a goddamn priest marrying us.

'I asked her already,' Reme said. Psykommandant Buedo was fucking livid that we didn't thank her for restoring silence and that we wouldn't give her another pound of flesh to scribble about in her notebook.

'I would like to ask her if a cock-tease means she teases your cock with her hands or with another part of her body,' said the group's resident dudebro egomaniac, giggling his dick off, and the self-advocates resumed their unregimented cacophony without waiting their turn to speak.

'Sorry, Laia, but I raised my hand first and Antonio didn't even raise his,' my sister fussed as Buedo glared at her with implicit authoritarianism.

'Here's what it means, Antonio: a cock-tease is a woman who chops the cock off a male like you then drops it in a boiling pot of tea.'

'No shit I'm a male, bitch!' he spat back, and Laia Buedo had to stand up and clap her hands to stop the self-advocates from feasting on this smorgasbord of swear words. The only person not talking was my cousin Angelita, who saw this breakdown of self-advocatory law and order as an opportunity to flaunt the prohibition on phones and get back to fingering hers like the integrated citizen she's become.

'And then your gates closed and all the usual stuff happened,' Marga says, impatient, slouching in a red plastic Estrella Damm chair, one of the few pieces of furniture that was in the okupa when she broke in. She's in panties and a bra and her butt is sticking to the seat. I know because when she gets up, the chair rises a few centimetres with her, and when she crosses her legs, her skin peeling off the plastic makes a sound. She procured two more chairs yesterday from the Monday furniture collection. It's hard to believe she's already been here a week.

'They did close, yeah, and they didn't open until the meeting was over and I had five minutes to talk to Reme alone before they loaded her back into the aide/minder/cop prison van, the only unsupervised time inmates are allowed before being taken back to their UCIDetention facilities.'

I'm sitting on the exposed floor, having left rehearsal at the SS without stretching so I'd have time to come and see Marga. While we talk, I work the stiffness out of my quads and roll my lower back on the floor, which is covered in broken tiles that make geometric shapes on the rough concrete. Tiny slivers of grime collect in the cracks, and Marga keeps herself busy scraping them out with the tip of a knife. When I showed up she was on all fours, scraping away under a bare light bulb, and at first I thought she was doing the hands-free masturbation exercise I'd shown her. I came from the SS to bring her clothes and food; I always carry a backpack to class, so I was able to take stuff from the flat without Angelita and Patri catching on. I bought the beer from a Pakistani shop on the way. Cold beer and crisps go down so easy after rehearsal.

'Don't you have to be back at the flat for dinner?' Marga asks after taking a swig from the litre bottle of Xibeca, flashing her brown armpit hair in the process. Then I look at her crotch, which I see is also in flower, with a few stiff hairs poking through the fabric of her panties. From my vantage point on the floor, I can see a recent spot of discharge, still damp, when she spreads her legs.

'Not since they cast me in the SS show, because rehearsals end at ten,' I say, turning away from her cunt, lying face up and grabbing my feet with my hands like a baby. On the next exhalation I pull my legs further apart and keep talking. 'Supposedly I have to be at the flat by eleven, but nothing'll happen if I turn up later. The overseer came last night to make her inspection, and I was right on time yesterday, so she won't be stopping by for another two weeks at least, not like that time she caught me sneaking in at 10 a.m. then "dropped in on us" the next twenty mornings in a row.'

Marga stands up. The chair rises with her until her skin and the plastic finally pull away from their tender kiss. She goes into the kitchen and switches on another bare bulb, illuminating the extremely clean, extremely white, extremely broken tiles, and returns with a clay bowl full of fruit. She puts it on the living-room table – also taken from the Monday furniture collection – obliging me to stand to have a look. I get on all fours, lift my knees and finally raise my torso, not stretching it but rolling it up like a set of blinds. I straighten my head, drop my shoulders back and step towards my destination, acknowledging the act of walking for the privilege it is.

'Thanks for bringing food and clothes, Nati, but you don't have to. I get groceries from a food distro run by a couple of the anarchists and clothes from the free shop at Can Vies,' she says, taking a bite from an apple and washing it down with beer.

'Fucking amazing, Marga!' I say. Today I decline the apples and peaches because what I'm really craving is a baguette, a ham baguette if at all possible. I pull the bag of crisps wide open and dump the remains directly into my mouth. 'You mean distro like distribution?'

'I guess, that's just what they call it.'

'How does it work?'

'The biggest distro is the one at Entrebancs. Fifteen of us bring shopping carts to ten or twelve supermarkets and dumpsters just when they're closing and take everything out: meat, fruit, bread, pastries … even pizzas! Enough bread and pastries to fill two whole shopping carts. There's always tons left over after we split it up between us, so we just leave the rest on a park bench for whoever.'

All this food talk makes me hungrier. I go into the broken white kitchen and poke around. I find bags full of bread and pastries. The baguettes are hard, but the round loaves and multigrain breads last longer and they're still soft. I grab a wholewheat loaf, small but dense and heavy like a paving stone, and packed with sunflower seeds, sesame seeds, walnuts. The kind that'd cost you four euros at a bakery. And Marga gets it free.

'Do you actually go in the dumpster?' I ask, looking for a knife to slice the bread. The scant kitchen utensils lie clean and neatly arranged on a chipped countertop so worn down that the marble is starting to look like ivory. I pick up a knife with a rounded tip and a few measly teeth. Marga notices and, from her red Estrella Damm throne, holds out the sharp one she's been using to clean the floors.

'Not the small ones with the individual store names on the side. We just pull out the bags and open them. You have to go in the big ones, though, where lots of different places put their trash, since some stores don't have their own dumpsters. I go in just like everyone else.'

'Is it gross?' I ask, offering her a slice of the bread. She scrutinises it carefully; it must be the first time her haul has included the paving-stone bread.

'No grosser than waiting in line at the supermarket checkout.' The immediacy and brilliance of her answer leaves me stupefied mid-chew. Marga thinks it's because I don't like the bread and says, 'Don't eat it if you don't want to, try a different one. There's lots.' I swallow and tear off another piece. It's really good bread.

'The bread's great, Marga. It's what you just said about grossness and the supermarket. That was a punch in my bourgeois teeth and I ought to give you a kiss on the lips with my bloodied mouth. That was a politicised reply that politicised me in turn, and I'll leave your house different from how I came in,' I say, my mind still reeling. There are gradual politicisations, like the ones I experienced (and I'm sure Marga experienced) after several visits to the anarchist social centre, talking to the punks and reading their zines. Then there are drastic politicisations like this, where one person asks a question motivated by capital and the other responds with an anarchist truth. Only a male/fascist/neoliberal would emerge unscathed from having such a truth revealed to them, and only a male/fascist/neoliberal would refuse to concede the point to someone with reality, rather than ideology, so clearly on her side.

'The dumpster smells like shit, but the food is almost good as new in the bag, and you can tell which bags are from the supermarkets. The big black ones without drawstrings. If you're looking for meat that expired that day or yogurts or grab-and-go meals or those fresh juices they keep refrigerated, it helps to wear a flashlight on your forehead like a miner.'

'All that time waiting in interminable checkout lines, even when there's no security guard and nothing you're buying has an alarm strip, and still you suck it up and wait and pay for your groceries out of fear, delusional fucking fear of the imaginary retaliation you'll face if you get ratted on by some good Samaritan customer who's pissy because he doesn't have the cunt to leave without paying and you do! Fear the cashiers will catch you, even though you know damn well they'll never see a thing because they're the ones being watched, because they've got cameras pointing down their necks to make sure they bleep a hundred bar codes a minute! Lining up to pay instead of them lining up to take your money is the fucking bedrock of this oppressive regime we live in, Marga!'

Whenever I get worked up like this, my cousin checks out. She doesn't consider herself politicised. She thinks she's just doing whatever the fuck she wants, which makes her an even more elusive dissident, even harder to detect, even more lumpen and even more powerful. Like La Banda Trapera del Río or Los Saicos, who were doing punk a decade before the industry gave it a name; who dressed like misfits in their Sunday best, in buttoned shirts and pressed trousers, and who would later repudiate the punk rockers who tried to claim them.

Marga goes into the kitchen and comes back with another clay bowl with the same design as the fruit bowl, a set that someone had diligently left at the foot of a dumpster for Marga to take home. It's full of something resembling pipirrana salad. She cuts a few more slices of wholewheat bread and heaps a spoonful of pipirrana onto each. I'm drooling.

'Peppers, tomatoes, cucumbers and onions from the distro. Oil, vinegar and salt borrowed from the social centre.'

'What a feast.' I scarf my slice in two bites and grab another. Now we're both sitting at the table. She has pulled her throne over and I'm in a chair with a tall back and velvet upholstery, the uncomfortable kind families sit on at Christmas dinner.

'I'm gonna see if I can get a hotplate or one of those portable stoves so I can make a vegetable stew sometimes.'

'I can get you one at the bazaar by the flat. I'll ask them to ring it up as markers and poster board. I've been doing a lot of colouring lately.'

'Great, thanks.'

'How much are those? Twenty euros?' I say with my mouth full of joy, the joy of smothering your hunger.

'Something like that.'

'OK, I'll ask them to put glue, scissors and some rulers on the receipt too.'

'Thanks a lot, Nati.'

'No need. Hey, where's that famous hole in the roof?' I ask, passing the litre of Xibeca.

'It's in the bedroom,' she says, finishing off the beer and flashing her incredible armpit again. 'Let's finish eating and I'll show you.'

I didn't get them to touch me everywhere during the exercise, but in the third phase, I did succeed in getting most of the manipulators to leave their hands wherever they'd ended up in the heat of such a large-scale improvisation. If someone happened to touch my chest, instead of yanking their hand away, they would continue the movement from that position, pressing into my breast with their palm, which is to say, squashing it and causing that side of my body to twist. There was one bold manipulator who, when he inadvertently made contact with one of my breasts, sought symmetry by reaching for the other. Every time someone squashed my chest with their hands, it either sank in or, just the opposite, stretched open like the hood of a cobra, depending on whether they squashed me skyward, pushing my boobs up like I was wearing a corset, or downward, like a nursing baby was tugging on my nipples. One exceptional manipulator found himself holding my two breasts in his two hands and, instead of pressing into them, squeezed.

For this third phase of the exercise, the pyjamaman director had ordered both me and the manipulators to move freely. Unlike in the first two phases, I had the option of resisting their movements, going along with their movements, evading their movements, or playing dead. I was to do those four things as much as I liked, to the degree that I liked, involving or dissociating whatever body parts I liked.

The manipulators could also move me and touch me as the body commanded, which might involve caressing me and massaging me as they had done in the first phase, or bending me as they had in the second, but now they could also move and touch me while I was in motion, a motion that, according to our orders, ought to involve displacement through space, a displacement that either they or I could cause to start, stop or change course. The other thirteen dancers' distribution throughout the rehearsal space would facilitate their bodies' involvement with mine, since any of them could approach me and I could approach any of them. As in the first and second phases, the tacit in-situ negotiations between manipulators regarding how, when, in what order and in which alliances they would manipulate my movement and trajectory came with the stipulation that they mustn't hurt me, but in this third phase, there was an additional stipulation: they were to lead the manipulee places she could not go by herself, and the manipulee had to be willing to go to those places. That is, I could dance however I desired so long as I made use of the other dancers, and the other dancers were to expand my dance in accordance with my desires.

The pyjamaman didn't say that last part, I'm adding it now; the director is very careful not to use the word dance when explaining the exercise. This discretion is an oft-visited place in the geography of contemporary dance, which eschews the notion of dance and its formal, academic and elitist connotations, and replaces them with the notion of movement, which the world of contemporary dance considers pure, scientific and even democratic. Pure, because according to the denizens in the vast region of the contemporary, mere movement is a natural thing. Scientific because, according to those same denizens, movement is an artistic category that accommodates a multitude of actions, including both conventionally choreographic actions, which is to say actions that, when performed, we all agree constitute the act of dancing, as well as any number of other actions we wouldn't call dance steps, e.g. digging wax out of your ear or cooking an omelette. And democratic, because this region we're talking about isn't simply a physical demarcation of the terrain of the contemporary, but an entire nation; its denizens are not simply residents of the material and symbolic territory over which any nation exercises its sovereignty, but citizens with rights and obligations. The nation of movement is democratic because it believes any citizen is capable of movement and every citizen has access to movement: you need only lift your wrist to check the time. In stark contrast with this positive appraisal of movement, in which all citizens are united, there is the rank, elitist notion of dance, according to which not all citizens have access to conservatories and not all citizens are dancers, because not all citizens are capable of Flying-Low technique or being hoisted in a grand-porté. That's why the Cineplex isn't called a dance school but the Movement Creation Factory, which sounds like a branch of Bauhaus or the Spanish Falange.

'Bauhaus like the home-improvement stores?' asked a self-advocate whose body is shaped like a pear, with tight shoulders and wide hips.

'Pretty much, Vicente. A hundred years ago there was another Bauhaus, a school for lefto-fascists who built posh furniture and posh houses and said they were doing it for the good of humanity. They named the home-improvement chain after the posh lefto-fascists.'

'The Bauhaus by the Burger King in Zona Franca actually is kind of posh, now that you mention it.'

'Well, there you go,' I said.

'It's just posh if you're looking for posh things, because they sell nicer products and stuff that's maybe a little more expensive, but they've got more affordable things too. I know because I live next door so I go there a lot just to get tools and things for my drill and screws and stuff. You can get good-quality products made in Germany there and not just stuff from China, so even though that's why those things are maybe a little more expensive, the stuff you get lasts longer too, though. It's important to know how to shop smart,' pontificated the self-advocacy group's resident good-looking dudebro all-star, so pleased with himself, pleased as peaches. The more self-satisfied he becomes, proud of his ability to parrot TV talk, taking care to enunciate and to keep his camel-eyelashed squinting to a minimum, the harder I laugh. His vanity is so over the top that he doesn't realise people are laughing at his ridiculousness. If someone starts laughing during a self-advocacy meeting, it inevitably becomes infectious, though the person who catches it might not be laughing at the same thing, they might just be laughing for the pleasure it brings. Psykommandant Laia Buedo quickly challenged all this unjustified merriment, but she did it quietly, the way dignitaries speak when they believe they oughtn't to be forced to raise their voice to make themselves heard; the result being, of course, that nobody heard what she was saying.

'We're laughing at you, Antonio! Your masculomania has got so bad you can't even hear yourself, you sound like an anthropomorphised radio ad!' I said without my gates activating, shooting off my clacking machine-gun laughter, firing round after round into the male and inciting the other self-advocates to help me gun him down. But of course, like all fascists, the dudebro acted like none of this had any effect on him, firm in his conviction that anyone who criticises him must be a moron. He turned to his superior, Buedo, and made the gesture where you bend your elbows, point the palms of your hands at the ceiling, shrug your shoulders and turn your lips inward until there's only a line where the mouth used to be. And then my prick of a sister Patricia did the same, even though she hadn't made a peep in minutes! What a fine pair of two-bit neoliberal money-grubblettes they made: eager to interrupt me or call me a bitch, but even more eager to sit down and shut up the instant Buedo scolds them.

'Be nice, Nati, they're just trying to earn brownie points, the same as you going every Tuesday now. It's not like people go to the meetings because they think they're fun,' wise Marga says, illuminated by the street lights shining through the hole in the roof.

'I don't go to the meetings to earn brownie points, Marga. I go with a politicising purpose.'

'Well, I think there's a reason Laia's letting you talk so much.'

'Of course there is, Marga: she wants me to tell them where you're hiding.'

I say this and the orange light sweetly washing over Marga's hair and shoulders transforms into an overhead spotlight that blasts the shadows off her face and shines down on the white cups of her bra, producing two half-moons that envelop her belly in darkness.

'Natividad.' Full name deployed by the psykommandant. 'Would you like to finish telling us about that integrated dance class of yours? I thought that was a very interesting topic.' I'm so disgusted to hear her even speaking to me, Marga, seriously, especially when I was having such a lovely time laughing at the dudebro. I dried my tears, took a breath and responded from within my gates, reminding myself that I was voluntarily attending this weekly abduction for a just cause.

'Integrated dance is a village in the nation of movement, even though, paradoxically, it's called integrated dance and not integrated movement. The people whose money or prestige is riding on it don't see this as a problem. They see it as a benefit, actually, because that's exactly what the people being integrated want, to be included in normalised dance circuits: in theatres, classes, universities, prizes. Even though the Democratic Republic of Movement has colonised and annexed the village of integrated dance, the integrates' objective is not to move, as they are instructed from the metropolis, but to dance, with all the formal, academic, elitist connotations from which the metropolitans of movement have distanced themselves, plus one more association from which contemporary dance has been trying to distance itself for five decades: to dance beautifully. The integrates want to be beautiful at all costs. Under no circumstances can they allow themselves to look bad or ugly. The integrates would murder for the chance to set foot in a dance studio or on a stage, to prove they are just as handsome, just as refined as Pina Bausch and Vaslav Nijinsky.'

I stop my self-advocate story because I get weary remembering how weary I got telling it to the psykommandant. Marga flops back on the bed and I do the same. It's a double mattress on the floor draped in oversized sheets. I feel a spring every once in a while, but it's a firm mattress with no dips in it.

'So they're looking for me,' she says.

'Of course they are, Marga. But don't worry, your secret is safe with me,' I say, rolling onto my side and trying to make eye contact.

'How do you know they're looking for me, Nati?' she asks, turning only her head.

'They're off their shit looking for you, Marga. First Patri and Angelita, then Diana and Susana, then a pair of Mossas d'Esquadra. Patri and Angelita couldn't sleep a wink the first night you didn't come back, they were up all night grilling me, and predictably, Patricia started throwing plates and even tried to smack me! I had to dodge out of her way, and then she had the nerve to go and start crying.'

'What'd you tell them?'

'I didn't tell them anything, Marga. Nothing at all. Zippo, nada.'

'But did you just not answer their questions or did you lie?'

'I stuck to one script: that afternoon you'd come with me on the metro to the Cineplex just like you do every Tuesday, and the whole yellow line was crammed full of fucking British and Yankee imperialist tourists just like it is every summer, and then poof, you were gone. And I still went to my super-duper integrated dance class, and I was super-duper happy to be at the SS, and wow isn't Barcelona just the most wonderful land of opportunity.'

'I mean, Nati, you must be a little happy, right? Didn't you say you were picked for the show?'

'They didn't pick me, Marga. Everyone who pays gets to be in the show, the only difference is they're giving some of us more prominent roles. But yeah, they're making me the manipulee in a large-scale manipulation scene, which is lovely, but no, it doesn't make me happy. It provokes me, it challenges me, it makes me fly a while, but it doesn't make me happy. Happy is what I'd be if the dancers weren't chomping at the bit to follow the orders of the director and his assistant, and if it were the norm rather than the exception to dance from your tits and genitals.' Marga crosses her hands behind her head so her bushy armpit is millimetres from my nose. It smells like good sweat, sweat that hasn't been filtered through synthetic clothing. It smells like spending the whole day naked. 'Want to finish hearing what it was like when the SSes danced with my tits and cunt?'

'Sure,' she says smiling, thrusting her chin forward. It's the first time all night she's open-mouth smiled at me and that's something else that makes me happy, so happy.

'You smiling makes me happy though, Marga,' I say, and when I say it she smiles even more! Through what I assume is the hole in the roof we hear the bang of garbage trucks as loud as if they were in the house. Marga covers her ears and contorts her entire face, but her smile doesn't fade. I wait for the noise to finish and keep talking. 'I told you there were a couple of manipulators who, when their hands landed on my boobs, would press into them with their open palms, like this.' I recreate the action for Marga, but since I'm lying down without a bra, my boobs just flop to the sides. I have to gather them up, bring them to the middle and exaggerate the pressure. 'That was how one of the new dancers did it. It's such a joy to dance with strangers who come with no prior sympathy or antipathy towards you, where communication comes only from the pulsing of our bodies. And later another dancer ended up touching my boobs the same way the first one had, by accident, but he squeezed them instead of squashing them into my chest.' Again, I gather them up from either side and squeeze with both hands.

'He groped them,' Marga specifies.

'Right! Something never seen before in a dance class! And he didn't just grope them, Marga, he used them to set the direction. He pulled on them, like this –' I pull my tits upward like I'm trying to make them stand upright. 'The manipulator wanted to dance with my boobs. He adjusted the way he was grabbing them a little because he realised pulling them from that clutch-grope position wasn't easy, they kept slipping away from him. So he tried a prehensile grip: each thumb under a boob, nestled into my ribs, and his fingers at the top of my sternum, digging into my chest and overcoming the rigid structure of my sports bra. It was like he wanted to pull my boobs off my chest. In each hand, a ball of breast.' I try to manoeuvre myself into the same position, but doing it to yourself is impossible. I sit up from my side and do it to Marga.

'Ay!' she whines, and I let go automatically.

'Sorry. Your boobs are bigger so I had to clutch harder to keep them from getting away.'

'Do it softer.'

'Your underwire must've dug in when I tried to grab you with my thumb, I didn't mean to hurt you, I'm sorry,' I say, gently stroking the cups of her bra like an itsy-bitsy spider, so gently I'm only grazing the fabric. Marga lifts her torso a little, supporting herself on her elbows, brings her hands to her back, unhooks the bra, takes it off and lies back down.

'Try now.'

'You have such nice boobs,' I say, resuming the gentle stroking but now only on her nipples.

'You too,' she says, sticking a hand under my T-shirt and moving it from one breast to another. I caress her nipples faster, and with more of my hand. They're long and pointed like a nursing mother's; I spike them into my palms and make circles. Marga quickens her caress of my tits, too; she grabs one, draws me towards her, and speaks into my mouth. 'Do that squeezing thing to me.' Her breath smells like onion from the pipirrana, with a hint of beer, which must be what I smell like to her, too. We lick each other's tongues. She speaks to me from within the kiss: 'Do it, Nati.'

Marga's orders don't sound like orders but like supplications; she doesn't call for obedience but for compassion towards her pleasure, solidarity with her desire. I sit up again. I have to grab her tits hard because they're so big, plus she's lying down and they fall to the side like mine did earlier. I pull them to the middle and from there I grab and pull. This time Marga doesn't whine; she moans. At first her moan confuses me, I'm not sure if it's a whimper, but she clarifies, tells me not to stop. The flesh that doesn't fit in my hands peaks through my fingers, smooth and hard from the pressure. I pull my fingers apart a little so her nipples press between them like prisoners clutching at bars, so I can lick them. All of one pokes through; I suck and bite. Marga moans and puts her hands back under my shirt. She massages my nipples with the very end of her fingers, pinching every time she feels the tip. I groan with her nipple in my mouth. I move to lick the other one, but I don't release the first captive; I tighten my grip and pull upwards again. Marga's moan gets hoarser. I let up a little and bend down to kiss her by way of apology and consolation for any undue pain caused. The kiss is drier this time, more hurried because pleasure breeds urgency.

'Did I hurt you, Marga?' I breathe.

'No, keep going,' she breathes back, and her call to solidarity makes me shoot straight back up, taking her whole torso with me, and her stifled cry ends up in my ear. Now we're both sitting. I can't take off my shirt because I'm clutching her breasts, so Marga rolls it up to my neck. She gazes at them and caresses them with her mouth half open and her nostrils flaring. Finally she bends towards me and licks my tits with her whole tongue like a mammal grooming her newborn. She tenses her tongue at the bottom of my breast, then releases, making it jiggle. The sight of my tits glistening with her saliva makes my cunt salivate. The more she licks me, the more I pull on her breasts, and the more I pull on her, the less Marga licks my breasts and the more she starts sucking them, biting them, and finally tugging at them. We're pulling at each other and our moans are sharp or hoarse according to the traction, our backs arc or curve, our elbows extend when the other's breasts pull away or bend inward when they return, our kisses and bites land on the mouth or the neck. I shift from sitting beside Marga to straddling her. Now our grasping hands are prisoners to our grasped breasts. Each of us releases the other's tits and our four breasts kiss with the saliva Marga has left on mine.

She puts her hand in my underwear. She goes straight for the vagina and finds it on the first try. She doesn't penetrate me all the way even though she could; instead she bends her finger, her index finger I think, and pulses the opening with her knuckle. I start moving my hips forward and back, I ask her to put it all the way in. She shows solidarity, I release our embrace so she can move, I pull my panties and shorts below my ass, they're both elastic so I can still wrap my legs around her. I draw back my shoulders and lean on my arms stretched out behind me. Marga hooks one of her arms around my waist and gets a firm grip on my hip bone. She uses that hand to regulate my lunges so they aid in her penetration. With the palm of her other hand turned upward, she slides her middle finger into me. I moan loudly when I first feel her all the way inside, a moan that's a thank you or a welcome or an exclamation of surprise. Though she's not being penetrated, Marga also moans and gyrates her hips, which only makes me moan and gyrate more intensely. My moans are more like sighs, my tone low. Marga's moans are an infinite, spasmodic 'ahh', exactly like her speaking voice in tone and timbre. She emits her ahhs with a grimace like the Dolorosa Madonna. My own expression is more spaced out, my head is bobbling. But Marga's gyrations, because she's moved into a curved posture for improved manoeuvrability in my cunt, aren't what they look like. From the outside it would seem as if she's rubbing her butt crack on the bed, when in fact – and this time I know I'm right – she's practising the hands-free masturbation I taught her, the activation of her central masturbatory apparatus without even having to kneel on all fours: precise, constant thrusts that start in the marrow of her pelvis and end at the tip of the last hair on her cunt.

Pausing for only a second or two at most, Marga releases all her grips on me to remove my panties and shorts (which are starting to annoy us both), repositions me on top of her, and returns us to our configuration. She clutches harder with her arm and takes my tits in her mouth whenever she can because she's out of hands to grab them with. Her own tits drop to the top of my open thighs, brushing against me intermittently.

Marga adds fingers in successive penetration until three, I think, are inside me, all the while encouraging my hips to swing more and more until my vagina is thwacking at her hand, a hand that's now not only penetrating me but quivering from side to side. It's the quivering that pushes me to the point of no return, that point where you know if you lose focus you won't come no matter what they do, you'll just be struck with that staggering sadness. Her fingers make squelching noises inside me. I lean all my weight on one arm and use my free hand to set my clit to a thousand revolutions per minute.

'I'm gonna come, Marga,' I exhale with my frenetic mastur-bation, and Marga releases her hold on my hip, sucks on two of her fingers, places her wet hand on her cunt and touches herself while still penetrating me. She never took off her panties and her hand looks like a trapped animal fighting to break free. And I come, I come, I come, I come and I come, fuck, with electric-chair convulsions. I relax the arm that had supported my weight and my movements during the last five minutes of the fuck. There's almost no time to get a finger inside Marga, or maybe the brief penetration with my finger is precisely what precipitates her orgasm and the convergence of her moaning ahhs into one single suffocated cry. Her curved vagina swallows my index finger, I pull it out dripping, and by the time I enter her again Marga has already come. She grips my wrist to keep my finger inside her.

'I want another one,' she says. She lies face down and I take off her panties. I get on all fours and lick the inside of her thighs with my finger still inside her, then start eating her pussy. I'm surprised how compact, symmetrical and neat it is, what with her being so shag-happy, and her labia are hairless, too, even though Patricia isn't here to make her shave.

First I lap my whole tongue up and down her pussy. It smells like dick, dick that smells like barbecue. I knew it – Marga has spent the day fucking.

My fingers fall into a natural rhythm with my tongue, with the progressive insertion of the two, three, even four fingers she asks for. I make sure to lick them first, and I lift her butt cheeks, spit a fat gob on her vagina, and put her back down on the bed. With my free hand I squeeze her thighs or reach my arm out to grab her tits, but I find Marga's hands already there, kneading them, sucking on them.

She's more focused now, her face even more like the Dolorosa Madonna; her moans have relaxed into slack ahhs and her gyrations have become millimetric, working with extreme efficacy in collaboration with my tongue. A choreography develops between the subtle motions of Marga's hips and the subtle motions of my masturbatory apparatus, which, since I'm on all fours, is rotating away in absolute, serene freedom.

I transition from whole-tongue licking to a targeted frenzy on her clit, unhooded like a minuscule glans, and in an instant I find Marga's two fingers joining in the stimulation. We cohabitate for a while, but she reaches such speed (the speed of solo masturbation) that her fingers smack against my face and evict my tongue.

'Are you gonna come?' I ask, and she nods without lifting her head from the pillow, her face still the portrait of infinite suffering. I let go of her tits and bring that hand to my clit, keeping the four fingers of my other hand inside her, and the rhythm with which I'm penetrating my cousin automatically keeps pace with my own masturbation. Now my hips gyrate

311

and thrust in the air along with my finger, which has found my clitoris eager and on the brink. I draw a single circle and I can already feel the teardrop of the orgasm sliding down the chute of my vagina. Marga and I join each other in a shared cry that prolongs our climaxes, mine less intense than my first, hers I couldn't say.

We lie facing each other for several seconds, resting, making a rhombus with our open legs, listening to the neighbourhood's nocturnal sounds coming through the ear that is the hole in the ceiling. Eggs being beaten, a TV blaring, silverware clacking against dishes, a motorcycle exhaust pipe modified to sound like a hydraulic hammer, a distant conversation, a nearby conversation, a doorbell, a robotic voice through an intercom, an electric charge opening a door. A cold draught, too.

'Marga, where do I pee?' I ask, getting up. She's flipped from her side to her back, with her head on the pillow.

'The bathroom's to the right, but there's no water. You have to pour some from one of the bottles by the toilet,' she responds, half asleep.

'Got it.'

'And bring me back one of the emptier ones to drink from?'

'Got it.'

'There's no light, you have to turn on the one in the living room to see.'

'Perfect.'

'The switch is near the front door, where you left your bike.'

I walk over naked. The hole in the roof casts enough light from the street lamps for me to walk without crashing into the house's sparse furniture. The patterns and lacquered coolness of the old floor make it pleasant to walk barefoot. Marga must have been cleaning it on all fours, scrubbing away with her masturbatory apparatus activated like a horny Cinderella.

With the light from the bare bulb in the living room I can see the wide tiled bathtub; the sink, square like a pedestal and also wide; the mirror, wide enough to be a window; the bidet, wide enough and deep enough to wash a baby; and the toilet so wide you could fall in and so comfy you could fall asleep taking a piss. Battered five-litre jerrycans line the perimeter of the wall. There's a faint smell of pipes but my bare feet still aren't picking up much grime. I lounge back on the toilet, fart a little and pee; I look for the toilet paper and find it thoughtfully placed on top of the tank: bar napkins, the stiff kind. I wipe my cunt, throw the napkins in the bowl, stand up, grab the closest bottle and pour out a healthy measure. I grab another napkin and wipe off the drops that splashed on the seat. It'll be easy for me and Marga to drink straight from the bottle since there's less than a litre left, so I bring it back to the room.

'Get the light, Nati?' she says, leaning against the wall. I put down the bottle, go back to the living room, and turn off the light. 'To be safe,' she explains. I walk back, grab the bottle, go to her side and pass it to her. 'I'm a pain in the ass, sorry. Thanks.'

'No, don't worry, I get it. Your bathroom is super nice,' I say, lying down next to her.

Marga lifts the bottle with both hands above her head, her breasts rising like inverted hot-air balloons and her long nipples pointing horizontally, parallel to the floor. I lick the water dripping down her throat and she coughs, almost chokes, and some water gets on me too.

'Sorry, sorry, sorry!' I cry, hugging her arm. 'God, what's wrong with me!'

Marga peels away from the wall and smiles as she coughs. I thwack her on the back until the cough subsides.

'You mean you want more?'

313

'I mean, a screw in the hand is worth two in the bush, Marga, the more you get the more you want,' I say, drying her breasts with my palms, then drying my palms on my breasts.

'You were fucking someone already today, that's why you want more,' she says.

'You mean other than you?' A sigh slips into my voice, what with Marga so close and talking about fucking, about having already fucked and continuing to fuck.

'Yeah.'

'How do you know?'

'Because you smell like it.'

'But, Marga, it was just a rushed, furtive fuck with no rubbing and barely any penetration. There's no way the smell stuck to me like it did to you. Your pussy smells like barbecue.' I say this and Marga sniffs the fingers she masturbated with then makes a face like she doesn't smell anything.

'Who was it with?' she asks.

'Someone from rehearsal. And the barbecue guy? Your pseudo-informant?'

'They drove him out of the neighbourhood, remember? It was someone from the social centre.'

'One of the punks? You're a legend, Marga.'

'Talk to me about your furtive fuck, Nati, maybe it'll work me up for more.'

Statement by Ms Margarita Guirao Guirao, made before the Fourth Investigating Judge of the Court of Barcelona on 15 July 2018, as part of the court proceedings for authorisation of the sterilisation of an incompetent individual arising from the action brought by the Generalitat of Catalonia against the Declarant.

Investigating Judge: The Hon. Guadalupe Pinto García

Clerk: Mr Sergi Escudero Balcells

Pursuant to Additional Provision 1 of Organic Law 1/2015 on Reforms to the Criminal Code, the court hereby conducts its examination of Ms Margarita Guirao Guirao, declared incompetent by this same court's Judicial Ruling No. 377/2016 of 19 March 2016, the sterilisation of which individual is sought in Proceeding 12/2018.

As the Declarant suffers from an intellectual disability affecting her volitional capacity, Ms Diana Ximenos Montes is present for the examination on behalf of the Generalitat of Catalonia, of which the Declarant is a ward. Ms Susana Gómez Almirall, a caseworker sharing the residence in which the Declarant resides in a flat supervised by the Generalitat, is also present.

The Declarant declines to make any statement or answer any question posed by the Hon. Judge, the representative of the Generalitat or the caseworker. Despite exhortations by Ms Susana Gómez that the Declarant answer only those questions she deems opportune, the Declarant continues to refuse, prompting the Hon. Judge to suspend the examination.

Guadalupe Pinto
Judge

Declarant

Javier López Mansilla
Stenographer

Statement by Ms María de los Ángeles Guirao Huertas, made before the Fourth Investigating Judge of the Court of Barcelona on 25 July 2018, as part of the court proceedings for authorisation of the sterilisation of an incompetent individual arising from the action brought by the Generalitat of Catalonia against Ms Margarita Guirao Guirao.

Investigating Judge: The Hon. Guadalupe Pinto García

Clerk: Mr Sergi Escudero Balcells

Before answering the questions posed by the Hon. Judge, the Declarant asks if everything she says is going to be written down. The Hon. Judge responds that it is.

The Declarant then asks if it will be written both 'in normal' and 'in Easy Read'. The Hon. Judge tells the Declarant that everything will be very easy, that the Declarant should take as long as she needs to answer, and that if there's anything she doesn't understand, she only needs to ask and the Hon. Judge will explain everything the Declarant needs to know, so there is no reason for the Declarant to get flustered because all of us are here to help.

The Declarant responds that she just has a stutter, she's always had one, and maybe that's why the Hon. Judge thinks she's getting flustered, but the Declarant states that she is not nervous because in fact she is a very calm person.

The Hon. Judge responds that if the Declarant is calm, all the better, that way they can begin. The Hon. Judge asks the Declarant how she gets along with her cousin Margarita Guirao, to which the Declarant responds that the Hon. Judge still has not answered her question.

The Hon. Judge asks, What question was that, María de los Ángeles?

The Declarant responds, I asked if everything we say is going to be written 'in normal' and 'in Easy Read'.

The Hon. Judge asks what 'Easy Read' is. The Declarant responds that how can the Hon. Judge not know what 'Easy Read' is if it's part of the Accessibility Act passed by the Parliament of Catalonia in 2014 and she's a judge and she's supposed to know all the laws.

The Hon. Judge responds that it is impossible to know everything in this life, but asks the Declarant to please tell her what it is because it sounds very interesting.

The Declarant states that Easy Read is books, documents, websites, etc. written following the international guidelines from Inclusion Europe and the IFLA. IFLA is the acronym for the International Federation of Library Associations and Institutions;

Guidelines means rules, international means from lots of different countries. Acronyms means putting the first letters of lots of words together to make them shorter;

A federation is when lots of associations work together and an association is when lots of people get together because they like the same things, in this case libraries and institutions;

Inclusion Europe is the same thing as the FAMR but for all of Europe. FAMR is another acronym, it means the Federation

318

of Advocates for the Mentally Retarded, but they don't call it that anymore.

The Hon. Judge states that the Declarant has explained many interesting things but has yet to tell her how those documents are Easy Read.

The Declarant responds that she was just getting to exactly that and tells the Hon. Judge that Easy Read is a way of writing for people with temporary or permanent reading difficulties, like immigrants, people who have had deficient schooling, adult late readers, people with learning disabilities or neuro-diversity, or senile people;

Reading difficulties means you know how to read but it's a lot of work. Temporary means it doesn't last your whole life and permanent means it does last your whole life. Immigrants are people who come from another country;

Deficient schooling is when you went to school but you got bad grades and had to repeat lots of years;

Late means not on time and readers means people who read, so adult late readers is adults who never had time to read;

Learning disabilities means you're sick in a way where you can't learn the things they tell you in school;

Neurodiversity is what the Declarant states that she has, it's a degree of intellectual disability. And senile means old people who are starting to lose it.

The Hon. Judge asks if that means Easy Read is a writing method that makes it easier for those people to read.

The Declarant responds that it is, but besides making it easier for them to read, it also ensures all people's access to culture, information and communication, like it says in the Universal Declaration of Human Rights. The Declarant asks the Hon. Judge if she knows about the Universal Declaration of Human Rights or if she wants her to explain that too. The Hon. Judge responds that she is familiar with that one.

The Declarant states that we also have Easy Read because there's lots of texts that contain excessive technical terms, complex syntax and unclear presentation;

Excessive is too much. Technical terms are difficult words and only a few people who have studied a lot can understand them. Syntax doesn't have anything to do with sins or taxes, it means sentences. Complex means difficult;

That's why it's important, so things people write can be in Easy Read and fulfil the Universal Declaration of Human Rights and the Catalonia Accessibility Act, and also the Convention on the Rights of Persons with Disabilities, which the Declarant forgot to mention earlier, but anyway, that's why it's important to use simple words and explain complex terms so everybody can understand.

The Declarant states there are lots of rules about how to write in Easy Read, so the Declarant will not explain them all to the Hon. Judge, just the most important ones:

You have to avoid using compound tenses. Compound tenses are when you say 'I have done' or 'you have eaten' or they can be even more complicated.

You have to avoid the passive voice and use the active voice instead. 'I eat bread' is the active voice and 'the bread is eaten by me' is the passive voice. The Declarant states that this one is a little tricky, that she had a hard time understanding it, and that she is going to try to explain it to the Hon. Judge the way she understands it: the active voice is you're active because you're eating the bread, because you're doing something, you're eating the bread. Passive voice is the bread not doing anything, because it's bread and not a person. The bread can't eat you but you can eat the bread, and the sentence has to show that, it has to be an active sentence, where you, clearly, eat the bread.

The Hon. Judge tells the Declarant that she understands and asks if now they can begin talking about Miss Margarita. The

Declarant responds that she was just wrapping up. The Hon. Judge responds that in that case please continue.

You can't use auxiliary verb constructions, the Declarant continues. Auxiliary verb constructions are when you say things like 'I must eat bread' or 'I ought to eat bread'. All you have to do is look at the name to know auxiliary verb constructions are very difficult.

Another very important rule of Easy Read is sentences have to be short, just subject, verb, predicate and that's it; every sentence should only have one message and not a bunch of messages stuck to each other. You can't combine 'I eat bread' with something that doesn't have anything to do with bread, like for example, 'I live in Barcelona.' You can't combine them and say 'I eat bread and I live in Barcelona', because those are two very different messages, because bread and Barcelona are totally different things.

The Hon. Judge thanks the Declarant for her wonderful explanation because now she understands what Easy Read is, but the Declarant insists on telling the Hon. Judge about another rule that is very, very important, maybe the most important one of all, about not justifying or indenting:

In Easy Read you don't indent the text, so the lines all have to start together on the left side of the page. That's what not indenting is;

And you don't justify the text either, which has nothing to do with making justifications. Since the lines all go towards the right side of the page, you have to let each one go as far as it goes, even if some are longer and some are shorter and the text isn't a perfect column. That's what not justifying means;

It's like writing WhatsApps. [*The Declarant pulls her mobile phone from her pocket and shows it to the Hon. Judge.*]

The Hon. Judge thanks the Declarant for her explanation and the Declarant responds that the Hon. Judge is welcome.

The Hon. Judge then asks about the health of Margarita Guirao Guirao and how she has seemed lately. The Declarant responds that earlier she asked a question and the Hon. Judge still has not answered it.

The Hon. Judge asks, What have I not answered, María de los Ángeles?

The Declarant responds, My question about if everything we say is going to be written 'in normal' and 'in Easy Read', since that's what I just explained all about Easy Read for.

The Hon. Judge responds that everything is going to be written exactly as it comes out of our mouths, that's what the person sitting beside her, called the stenographer, is typing non-stop on his computer for. The Hon. Judge explains that what he writes is going to be an exact copy of what we say, so the Declarant has no reason to worry because that way nobody can claim anyone said anything they didn't say. In fact, as soon as the Declarant finishes her statement, the stenographer is going to print it out on that printer on the table and the Declarant can read it, and if there's anything that she doesn't think is right, the stenographer can fix it right up as many times as the Declarant wants.

The Declarant responds that that all seems very good but that that wasn't her question. She asked if her statement was going to be written 'in normal' and 'in Easy Read', by which the Declarant means following the guidelines for writing she just explained. Did the Hon. Judge not understand the Declarant's question?

Yes, the Hon. Judge understood it. The Declarant asks the Hon. Judge, Well? The Hon. Judge responds, Well, the stenographer is going to write it the same way he always does, which he happens to do very well.

And not in Easy Read? the Declarant asks. Ask him yourself, the Hon. Judge responds, and the Declarant asks this

322

stenographer if he is going to write the text 'in normal' and 'in Easy Read', to which this stenographer responds that he will only write it in the normal way.

The Declarant offers to translate the normal text into Easy Read when this stenographer is finished, explaining all the hard words and getting rid of the indents and justifications, because the Declarant claims to be an Easy Read writer who writes novels.

The Hon. Judge responds that that is not going to be possible and that this is not a novel, this is reality, and that in order to faithfully represent reality we have to literally copy everything that's said in the courtroom. Not to mention that statements from proceedings regarding incompetent individuals such as Miss Margarita are confidential and cannot be distributed.

You mean you're not in favour of neurodiverse persons receiving accessible information about what happens in their communities? Don't you believe that without accessible information we'll be deprived of our right to self-determination and others will make our decisions and choices for us? It's all right if you don't know how to do it because writing in Easy Read is very difficult, but why don't you accept help from the Declarant, who's spent a long time studying the guidelines? the Declarant asks the Hon. Judge and this stenographer.

The Hon. Judge tells the Declarant that there's no reason to get flustered, that we can talk about that later, that the important thing right now is to talk about her first cousin Margarita Guirao Guirao, who went through some very tough times recently and who is still going through some very tough times and who needs the Declarant to help her by telling the truth.

The Declarant responds that she is not flustered, that she just has a stutter and that she is aware it makes her talk more slowly. The Declarant asks the Hon. Judge if the Hon. Judge is the one getting flustered by the way the Declarant talks.

The Hon. Judge responds that she is certainly not 'getting flustered' and that she is merely doing her job the same way she has been doing it every day for the past ten years.

The Hon. Judge asks, María de los Ángeles, can you tell me if Miss Margarita has ever had a boyfriend or girlfriend?

We can talk about that later, the Declarant responds. But if the Hon. Judge cannot assure the Declarant that her statement is going to be written in Easy Read, the Declarant does not intend to make a statement, the Declarant states.

The Hon. Judge responds that it will not be written in Easy Read and the Declarant responds that in that case she will not make a statement and that goodbye.

Guadalupe Pinto
Judge

María dels Àngels Guirao
Declarant

Javier López Mansilla
Stenographer

Statement by Ms Natividad Lama Huertas, made at the Urban Centre for the Intellectually Disabled of La Floresta, Province of Barcelona, on 15 July 2018, as the delicate condition of the Declarant's health prevents her from travelling to make her statement before the Fourth Investigating Judge of the Court of Barcelona, according to a report by Dr Neus Fernández Prim, psychiatrist at the Vall d'Hebron University Hospital (licence number 14233); the foregoing as part of the court proceedings for authorisation of the sterilisation of an incompetent individual arising from the action brought by the Generalitat of Catalonia against Ms Margarita Guirao Guirao.

As the Declarant suffers from a severe intellectual disability affecting her volitional capacity and was declared incompetent by this same court's Judicial Ruling No. 378/2016, Ms Diana Ximenos Montes is present for the statement on behalf of the Generalitat of Catalonia, of which the Declarant is a ward, and in her capacity as director of the supervised flat in which the Declarant has resided for the past year.

Investigating Judge: The Hon. Guadalupe Pinto García

Clerk: Mr Sergi Escudero Balcells

You can go flick your [*expletive*] and wipe your [*expletive*] with the same rolled-up €100 bill you use to snort the coke you seize from the dealers in El Raval, you pathetic [*expletive*] male [*sic*] femi-fascist [*sic*] neoliberal [*expletive*]. The kamikaze who ploughed his van into the pedestrians in La Rambla last summer is a lily-white soul compared to terrorists like you, you and your court, bent on extinguishing even the faintest sign of life in dissidents like my cousin Marga. The only signs you give a [*expletive*] about are the ones being waved at the festive, peaceful, Sunday-morning protests against cuts to public services so you can retain your privileges as Cerberus of state and capital. I hope you get death threats from the women or UCID inmates whose abuse allegations you dismissed, I hope the threats come thick and fast and you can't take a piss without looking over your shoulder, and I hope one day they make good on their promise and finally pull the trigger on you. As if you weren't already the walking, talking dead. As if coke could get the blood pumping back through your veins. If your heart beats at all it beats to the rhythm of the silent march against victims of domestic violence, violence you yourself instigated, murderer, murderer, murderer.

As far as you're concerned, kidnapping my cousin, having her prodded by doctors, interrogated by shrinks and judges and etherised on the operating table for her compulsory sterilisation is just one more item you can cross off your long list of terrorist acts against the dissident population. That thing your emetic hypocrisy calls 'protecting the incompetent individual from the consequences of a potential unwanted pregnancy' is just state-sponsored genetic cleansing that you, you, you enforce. Eugenicists like you don't want women capable of radical freedom like Marga to reproduce, and even if you end up sticking it to your bestie the Generalitat and decide not to authorise the tubal ligation, even if you swallow the same rhetorical brew of fundamental rights that you and your constitutionalist hacks force us to glug down, even if you deem Marga 'capable of sexual self-determination', this Via Crucis from condemnation to crucifixion you've put her through, having her evicted, separated from her lovers, drugged, isolated, interrogated and subjected to psychiatric and gynaecological probing, has nothing to do with that other ingredient in your concoction you call 'rule of law' and everything to do with your need to suppress and wear down the emancipatory fervour of a woman who spits that concoction back in your face.

They ought to forcibly tie the tubes on you, you and all your fellow female system-breeders who spread your legs wide to rapists and signatories of the sex-love contract, that particular form of purchase agreement that you, their mates, gladly countersign so you can retain your male [*sic*] privileges.

I like that you're afraid of me and I like that you're cowering by the door, cowering even though your macho stewards have strapped this headband around my gates and tied me to this bed.

Guadalupe Pinto
Judge

Declarant

Javier López Mansilla
Stenographer

Statement by Ms Patricia Lama Guirao, made before the Fourth Investigating Judge of the Court of Barcelona on 25 July 2018, as part of the court proceedings for authorisation of the sterilisation of an incompetent individual.

Don't worry, Your Honour, I'll tell you anything Your Honour asks me and anything you don't ask me, too, just like I've done since the very first day you summoned me to come and make a statement, a month ago now, because I know not long ago you summoned my cousins and my half-sister to come and make statements and none of them told you a [*expletive*] thing, I know because the director of the supervised flat, Miss Diana, told me so. When, Your Grace, have I ever failed to appear in your chambers? Never, that's when.

Now, before I continue, and with all due respect, I want to make sure it's clear to Your Honour that just like you wouldn't compare apples and oranges, we can't mix up Nati's booklets and the operation on Marga's [*expletive*]. First off, because Marga doesn't know how to read. How to [*expletive*], yes. But how to read, no. Before Marga's vanishing act Nati would read those little booklets with her, but does Your Excellency honestly believe someone like Marga with intellectual disability to the tune of 66 per cent can learn to read in two weeks? And how was Nati supposed to cram any ideas into her head in any case? Nati, who's even more disabled than Marga! Nati, who

328

genuinely thought they were letting her travel unaccompanied to and from her new dance school all the way out in Camp Nou. Marga had pulled her vanishing act so she wasn't around to take the metro to Camp Nou with her, and Nati's behaviour in class had been very good and she hadn't been kicked out or got into too many fights lately, and she'd been picked for the show and everything, so Miss Laia, Miss Susana and Miss Diana wanted to give her a reward: the reward of autonomy, Your Honour. Those three ladies have their heads screwed on just right if you ask me, Your Honour, and they wisely chose not to throw more fuel under the bus, what with the vanishing act and the police coming and going and all the people asking about Marga and rummaging through her things, so they told Nati from now on she could go to rehearsals by herself, but she'd have to be back by eleven at night at the latest, and she could take her bike because they know how much she dislikes the metro, especially in the summer, but she'd have to get one of those flashy-strobey lights and a bell, and she'd have to wear a high-visibility jacket. Her gates would shine like disco balls! You could see them retracting as Miss Laia and Miss Susana and Miss Diana were telling her all this. And what does she do, Your Honour? She goes straight down to the oriental bazaar and buys the flashy-strobey lights, buys the jacket, buys the bell ...

[*The Hon. Judge interrupts the Declarant to remind her that she has already talked about Miss Natividad in her earlier statements, and in fact the Hon. Judge had asked her to talk about Miss Natividad at one point in order to learn more about Miss Margarita's family environment, a request which the Declarant kindly answered with a wealth of detail, for which, incidentally, the Hon. Judge would again like to thank the Declarant, but now it is time to talk more specifically about Miss Margarita because the proceedings for authorisation of sterilisation must conclude shortly.*]

That's exactly what I'm getting at, what I'm saying has everything to do with Marga, Your Excellence, it really does, but it's possible that Your Grace might not have the fullest context of my half-sister Natividad's syndrome and so that could maybe be a reason why you might think the two of them could've been in cahoots, Marga and Nati I mean. Because Gate Control syndrome is like these two sheets in your head, and they cover your whole face from the forehead down to the bottom of your chin, like a Power Ranger, except they're see-through, so everyone can see you from the outside, but what's happening on the inside is you don't listen to reason and you think everything's bad, you think everything's total [*expletive*] and you think everyone's attacking you. It's just like regular depression with persecutory delusions, Your Honour, except instead of just keeping quiet and staying at home like a depressive or a delusive [*sic*], you go around saying I have all the solutions to everything, everybody pay attention to me because I have all the solutions to everything, and you go around saying it to everyone. But the thing is even if she really does have solutions for everything, she, Nati I mean, she doesn't register what's happening on the other side of her gates, and so she didn't register that the reward of autonomy was a trick: she thought she was going to her dance school by herself but actually an aide from the UCID was following her at a distance, also on a bike, a girl who's a super competent professional, Your Honour, a disability aide from the new politics who's very progressive and dresses very alternative and all, and this disability aide, Rosa, she didn't mind waiting around outside the dance school for three hours, and when Nati came out from her little rehearsal, she led Rosa straight to the hovel where Marga was living. Does Your Honour really think that a brick as thick as my sister would be capable of helping Marga disappear without the rest of us figuring it out?

[*The Hon. Judge interrupts the Declarant to thank her for her considerations, which the Hon. Judge has no doubt were extraordinarily useful for the police when they were searching for Miss Margarita, but asks the Declarant to please focus on Miss Margarita's emotional state, given that, she reiterates, these proceedings, which under no circumstances should last longer than a month, have lasted nearly two months, not to mention that it will be August before we know it and the Hon. Judge has to render her decision before the judicial recess.*]

You're absolutely right, Your Honour, me and you have been talking about whether to disable my cousin's [*expletive*] since before she even went missing, like you just said. And now what? Just because Marga got her wires criss-crossed that day, now suddenly Nati isn't getting the love and understanding she needs to live in our supervised flat either? And Marga and Nati have both been taken to live in separate UCIDs, out where they can't even visit their family unit? I understand the need to keep them there a while to administer tests and review their medication and everything, to hit the reset button, so to speak, Your Honour, after the scare of the disappearance and the police and everything, and it's right and good for them to spend a few days at the hospital being tended to by the best professionals, and a few days at the UCID after that. I'm not unreasonable, I understand. But that's just supposed to be a few days, and we're going on a month now. I'm going to be honest with Your Grace, as always: at first, when me and Àngels had the whole flat to ourselves, we were in heaven, just the two of us, I can't even tell you. Àngels with her phone and me with my TV and my nails and my hair and not a harsh word between us. But the few days that Miss Laia and Miss Diana and Miss Susana talked about have stretched into three and a half weeks now, Your Honour, and then on top of that they come by for their inspections and say the flat is dirty. But of course it is, we're two cousins short on the cleaning schedule because one cousin has been taken to the UCID in La Floresta and the other cousin is at the one in Sant Gervasi. Couldn't they have at least put them both at the UCID in Barceloneta, so they could drop by every once in a while? They'll get a lot less love and understanding from their family unit if me and Àngels are on the beach, Nati's up with the snooty-snoots in Sarrià and Marga's out in the middle of [*expletive*] nowhere! The metro doesn't even go out there, Your Honour!

[*The Hon. Judge interrupts the Declarant to inform her that she is up to speed on the difficult times the Declarant and her family have been experiencing in the wake of Miss Margarita's disappearance, but fortunately Miss Margarita has been found and life will slowly return to normal.*]

From your lips to God's ears, Your Excellence, God's and Miss Laia Buedo's and Miss Diana Ximenos's and Miss Susana Gómez's, who keep insisting our personal characteristics make us unfit for the immersion in social life that living in a supervised flat entails. But look at Nati, for example: if it weren't for the supervised flat, she wouldn't have started dancing and reading again. She hadn't danced since the brain injury that moronicised [*sic*] her a month before she finished her PhD, and that was four years ago already. Four whole years without dancing, when she'd been dancing since she was six years old! I still remember the little pink tights and tutu she used to wear, so cute, so tiny! It's only thanks to the supervised flat being right next door to the Barceloneta Civic Centre that she could enrol in classes and start dancing again. And now they've even picked her to star in a show –

[*The Hon. Judge interrupts the Declarant to remind her that she has already talked about Miss Natividad in this and in earlier statements and earnestly implores her to talk about Miss*

Margarita Guirao's health and behaviour, or else the Hon. Judge will be forced to suspend the session.]

Suspend the session? Suspend like end? I know Your Excellency knows I know to cut to the chase, and the chase, in this case, is that there is no reason whatsoever to question the full immersion in social life that Marga, Nati, Àngels and I have experienced thanks to the supervised flat. Our mutual respect and ability to integratiate [*sic*] within the broader community have flourished, along with our personal autonomy and day-to-day self-determination. What do you think Nati took up reading for? I'm talking about Nati again because it's connected to Marga, Your Grace, not because I want to. Because if Nati took up reading again it was thanks to the beneficial interaction she established with her cousin Marga, because Marga, remember, like I told Your Honour, was the one who started bringing her those booklets in the first place, and Nati could read those booklets because they were easier than books from the Easy Read Club that were clearly too hard for her, and that's why whenever Miss Laia gave her a book she'd drop it or throw it or tear it up. She got so much better that the last book they gave us, about a guy who tells his true story of personal achievement where he overcomes his Down's syndrome, and actually he's coming to visit the UCID at the end of summer, but anyway when they gave Nati that book she didn't just not throw it on the ground and not stomp all over it, Your Honour, she actually brought it home to keep reading in the flat. I'm talking about Marga, this is all about Marga, Your Grace, because do you see how a change like that in a zealot like Nati can only be nurtured in an environment of personal motivation and mutual comprehension, like the environment our supervised flat provides? Here, let me give you an example –

[*The Hon. Judge interrupts the Declarant to tell her that she doesn't doubt the benefits of the flat where the Declarant and her family live, that she thinks it's very interesting and even a wonderful model to be followed, but the Hon. Judge also reminds the Declarant that the two of them are in her chambers this morning for the proceedings to finally determine if the Hon. Judge should or should not authorise the sterilisation of Miss Margarita, and she implores the Declarant to please limit her statement to those things that are strictly related to her cousin and her cousin's affective and/or sexual behaviour, since, the Hon. Judge must insist, they have already had several very useful hearings in which the Declarant outlined the context of Miss Margarita's life.*]

But if you think our supervised flat is a model to follow, or, and, and I mean forgive me for trying to tell Your Excellence how to do Your Excellence's job, but if that's what you think, I would think Your Excellence would do something, right?

[*The Hon. Judge asks the Declarant do something why or with regard to what.*]

Because why does it have to happen? I might be 52 per cent disabled but I'm not an idiot, you can't just –

[*The Hon. Judge interrupts the Declarant to inform her that she has always treated the Declarant with the utmost respect and consideration, so much so that she has modified the usual* modus operandi *for this kind of proceeding so that the Declarant can express herself freely and without hindrance, doing away with the stenographer, recording the Declarant's statement with a recorder, then sending the audio off to a professional transcriptionist and summoning the Declarant again two days later so she can read the transcript. In fact, the Hon. Judge has always impressed so much respect and so much consideration upon her relationship with the Declarant that she has done something no judge ever does, which is take more statements than those stipulated by law for this kind of proceeding, in this case*]

*Organic Law 1/2015 on Reforms to the Criminal Code, and
all because the Hon. Judge considers Miss Margarita Guirao
Guirao's physical integrity and sexual self-determination to be
matters of the utmost importance and for whose sake the Hon.
Judge has shelved other, earlier cases in order to prioritise this one.
Because the Hon. Judge thinks that decisions regarding a person's
physical integrity and sexual self-determination should be based
on more than two specialist opinions and one report from the
public prosecutor's office, seeing as the mandatory examination
of the party whose contingent sterilisation is the object of these
proceedings, which is to say Miss Margarita, can't be carried
out because Miss Margarita refuses to make a statement. That,
the Hon. Judge reminds the Declarant, is why the Declarant has
been summoned to make statements four times now, including
today, in the Hon. Judge's chambers: because the best interests
of Margarita Guirao Guirao must prevail in all interventions
that affect her person and property.*]

[*Sobs from the Declarant. The Hon. Judge tells her to calm
down, it's no big deal, does she want to continue with her
statement.*]

I'm sorry, Your Excellency, you've always treated me with
courtesy and respect like I've never been shown before and I
repay you by mouthing off, I'm sorry for offending you, Your
Excellentness, I shouldn't have said I wasn't an idiot, it was
an accident, please forgive me, please –

[*The Hon. Judge interrupts the Declarant to tell her that it's
no big deal and that she can calm down; the Hon. Judge asks
the Declarant if she wants a glass of water and if she wants to
continue.*]

Do you forgive me or do you not forgive me?

[*The Hon. Judge forgives her.*]

It's just been some very hard times for the Lama-Guirao-
Huertas family, Your Eminence, what with my cousin Àngels

and me separated from our beloved Marga and our Nati and dealing with all these admonifications [*sic*] from Miss Laia and Miss Diana and Miss Susana for not telling them Marga was missing the same day she didn't come back to the flat, thank you [*for the glass of water*], the admonifications [*sic*] of being accomplices in her vanishing act, accusing us of putting her in all kinds of unnecessary danger because we didn't tell them that Marga didn't come home with Nati even though Marga was supposed to be there to pick her up from her dance class –

[*The Hon. Judge interrupts the Declarant to ask if she wants more water.*]

Yes please. But the reason we didn't tell them that same day was we trust and respect Marga's autonomy, the same autonomy that Miss Diana, Miss Susana and Miss Laia have been teaching us for the two years we've been going to the self-advocacy group and living in the supervised flat. Isn't it normal for a 37-year-old girl like Marga, who happens to be cute and single, to go out on a Friday night? And isn't it normal for a cute and single girl who goes out on a Friday night to stay out and not come back the next morning, and not come back Saturday night either? Wasn't the whole point for Marga to get a boyfriend? Well, going out and not coming back home because you spent the night at some guy's house is the normalest thing in the world, isn't it, Your Honour? Because before getting a boyfriend you've got to [*expletive*] a little, let him [*expletive*] your [*expletive*] or at least [*expletive*] him once or twice, right? Like a test drive?

How were we supposed to know that Marga, instead of forming an affective and slash or sexual relationship with some guy, was shivering in a hovel with a hole the size of Andalusia in the roof? And how could these disability professionals with whom we share so many moments of our day-to-day lives possibly think that Àngels, Nati and me didn't grasp the significance of Marga's vanishing act? And it's worse than that, they think that we understood it perfectly but that we deliberately hid it from them, even though they're the legitimate representatives of Marga's guardian, the most excellent Generalitat of Catalonia! And that's their reason for kicking us out of the flat, Your Eminence, that's their reason! If they want to kick out Marga and Nati, fine, I get that they might have to leave after the whole traumatic situation with Marga, and I get that they caught Nati there with her, so that'll require plenty of mental, physical and social healing. But there's no justification for them kicking Àngels and I out, especially not me, the only one who's sucked it up and gone to every single [*expletive*] self-advocacy meeting, the only one who hasn't had to see the psychiatrist once since we got to Barcelona, the only one who responded to the vanishing act by answering all the questions the police asked her, the only one who showed the two Mossas d'Esquadra and Miss Diana where Marga kept all her things, the only one who has showed up at Your Honour's chambers and made all the statements Your Honour has ever wanted and more! Nati doesn't respond because of her severe intellectual disability. Àngels doesn't respond because she's a 'stuttering Stanley' and when she gets nervous it takes her half a century to get the words out. I'm the only one who has collaborated with justice and the authorities at all times, Your Eminence. And for all that collaborating with justice, I get what? Nothing? That was what I was talking about when I said the thing about not being an idiot, I was saying your Most Excellent Eminence knows me, you know how I behave, and still no one has spoken up for me during this whole [*expletive*] storm over the flat, and I would hope, I would humbly hope that your Illustrious Eminence would take it upon your Eminent Illustriousness to say something.

337

[*The Hon. Judge tells the Declarant that it was very good of her to do everything in her power to help the police, because when a person goes missing, every little bit of help can be useful or even critical, and it's our civic duty to collaborate with the authorities. It was also very good of her to come and make a statement on every occasion the Hon. Judge summoned her, and the Hon. Judge thanks the Declarant again, saying that without the Declarant's statements she could never have attained a faithful picture of Miss Margarita's real situation with a view to her contingent sterilisation. The Hon. Judge says that the Declarant should be very proud of her exemplary behaviour. The Hon. Judge understands the Declarant has concerns regarding the supervised flat in which she resides, but that issue is outside of the Hon. Judge's jurisdiction and the scope of this proceeding. All the Hon. Judge is able to do is grant or decline authorisation for the involuntary sterilisation of Miss Margarita sought by her guardian who, as the Declarant is perfectly aware, is the Generalitat of Catalonia, as represented by the director of the Declarant's supervised flat, Ms Diana Ximenos. The matter of the supervised flat is handled by the Ministry of Labour, Social Affairs and Family, meaning that it is an administrative proceeding or, in other words, a decision that must be made by the executive branch of the government. What the Declarant and the Hon. Judge are doing right now is not an administrative or executive proceeding, but a judicial proceeding, and the Declarant ought to know that in a democracy we have separation of powers, meaning that matters handled by the judicial branch, which is what happens in the courts, cannot be mixed with matters handled by the executive branch, which is what happens in the ministries. There's also the legislative branch, which passes laws, and that can't mix with the executive or judicial branches either. And that's why the Hon. Judge can't speak favourably or unfavourably about the Declarant with regard to the supervised flat, but the Declarant shouldn't worry, because the Hon. Judge has every confidence that Social Affairs will make the decision that's best for the Declarant and for her whole family.*]

You're saying Your Grace isn't the one in charge of figuring out the supervised flat?

[*The Hon. Judge responds in the affirmative.*]

Yes you are or yes you aren't?

[*The Hon. Judge responds that she is not involved in decisions regarding the flat.*]

So, then, if you're not in charge of deciding to let us stay in the flat, would Your Excellency mind talking to the Excellent Excellency who is? Because if it's one judge saying it to another judge, there wouldn't be any of that branch mixing like Your Grace is talking about, right?

[*The Hon. Judge regrets that she is unable to help the Declarant with that matter and asks her if there is anything she would like to add to her statement, because they need to wrap this up.*]

[*Sobs from the Declarant. The Hon. Judge asks her to calm down and offers her more water, which the Declarant accepts.*]

<u>Guadalupe Pinto</u>
Judge

<u>Patricia Lama</u>
Declarant

<u>Javier López Mansilla</u>
Stenographer/Transcriber

NOVEL
TITLE: MEMOIRS OF MARÍA DELS ÀNGELS
GUIRAO HUERTAS
SUBTITLE: MEMORIES AND MUSINGS
OF A GIRL FROM ARCUELAMORA
(ARCOS DE PUERTOCAMPO, SPAIN)
GENRE: EASY READ
AUTHOR: MARÍA DELS ÀNGELS GUIRAO HUERTAS
CHAPTER 4: PARADOXES IN THE NEW RUCID

I am back, my lovely readers.
Thank you for waiting patiently
for my inspiration to return.

Us writers all know
it's important to put our books away
and leave them in a drawer for a while
so we can look at them later with a fresh perspective.
It's better for the book and better for you.

Fresh perspective means you read what you wrote
and see things you didn't see before
because you were too focused on writing.

Putting your book in a drawer is a metaphor

from the olden days when writers wrote on paper
and used to keep all their pieces of paper in drawers.

Metaphor means comparing something
to something else it's really similar to
so readers understand the first thing better or think it's prettier.

But I'm writing my novel on WhatsApp,
so all I had to do to get a fresh perspective
was not open the María dels Àngels's Novel
WhatsApp group chat this whole time.

It was really hard
because whenever my phone made the WhatsApp noise
I thought it was one of my readers in the group
telling me what they thought about the novel
or asking when I was going to continue the story.

But you have been very respectful readers
who perfectly understand
how drawers and fresh perspectives work
and you haven't pressured me once this whole time.
Thank you.

Now that I have a fresh perspective
I can see maybe I didn't make it clear
how good things were at the old RUCID.
It was really fun to live there
in the middle of a big town like Somorrín
because you got to meet lots of new people
and you and your new friends
could go to the street market every Saturday
and street festivals in the summer

plus discos and church and Holy Week processions
and lots of other cool things.

That was all outside the old RUCID.
But inside the old RUCID it was really fun too
because you got to live with all your new friends
and you could go to each other's rooms
and talk about whatever you wanted,
or play pranks on each other, or play hide and seek,
or dress up in costumes and do skits.
We watched a lot of TV together too
and it was lots of fun because most of us
never saw a TV before in our lives.
We watched the news, and football,
and cartoons, and commercials,
or sometimes we picked films to watch.
We talked about what things we liked and didn't like.
We were thick as thieves.

Sometimes we missed home.
Some people missed home so much they ran away
and the social workers had to call the Guardia Civil.
Or sometimes people started shouting
and hitting the social workers
or pulling their hair
and the social workers had to slap them
and give them a punishment and lock them in their room.
But most of the time it was just fun.

I missed La Agustinilla
and all the cats and dogs in Arcuelamora
but not so much I tried to hurt anyone.

Everything changed when we went to the new RUCID.
The new RUCID was a way bigger, way moderner house.
It was in Somorrín too
but it was at the edge of town and not the centre.

The old RUCID had lots of cool things,
but the new RUCID had way more,
like a pool, a vegetable patch, a greenhouse, a gym,
gardens, arts and crafts rooms, massage rooms,
couches, garages, storage rooms,
enough dining rooms and kitchens
to feed everyone in Arcuelamora
and a fish tank so big
it made the fish tank in the old RUCID look like jack squat.
It took up half a wall and the fish
inside it were so colourful
they made the fish in the river look like jack squat
not because they were bigger
but because they were so beautiful.

With so much big modern stuff
things should have been better at the new RUCID
but they were worse.
It was a paradox.

Paradox means something is back to front
like what's supposed to be white is black.

We couldn't walk around Somorrín any more
because the town centre was far away.
You had to cross a road to get there
and walk along another one

and that made the social workers nervous
so they had to come with us
and we could only go when they wanted to.

For fun they let us swim in the pool
and use all the other new things we had.
We could even go swimming in winter
because the pool was like a convertible car
and you could make it an indoor pool when you wanted
and an outdoor pool when you wanted.

The pool being like a convertible car is another metaphor.

Going swimming in the indoor pool
when it was raining and cold out
and you were warm inside and wearing your bathing suit
was really fun.
Even the residents in wheelchairs
could go swimming in our pool
because we had swimming teachers and lifeguards.

But it was the same as with the TV at the old RUCID
where at first everything you watched was exciting
but only because it was new
and after a while you got bored
because they always played the same stuff
and you knew all the commercials by heart.

The gardens and vegetable patch were better
because the flowers and tomatoes were different every time
but it wasn't fun there either
because you could only go when it was your turn

and you could only plant what the aides wanted to plant
and you couldn't eat the things you grew.
You had to give them to the cooks
so they could cook them.

Sometimes the lettuce would spoil
because you could only go to the vegetable patch or garden
when they let you
and the aides didn't realise
it had to be harvested or watered or needed pesticide.

And they didn't do any self-reflection at all
they just said it was nothing to get upset about
because we were growing lots of other things too.

Self-reflection means saying you made a mistake
and apologising for it.

I got really annoyed about that
because when they made a mistake
they never apologised to you.
But when you made a mistake
you had to apologise
and if you didn't you got punished.

I'm still waiting for Mamen to apologise
for not letting me go to the vegetable patch
when it wasn't my turn
so I could prune the lettuce.
I had been growing lettuce since I was little
and I knew it was important to prune it at the right time
but no one listened to me.

Something else about the new RUCID
was there were more people working there
than at the old RUCID.
There were the social workers from the old RUCID
plus psychologists and nurses and cooks and caregivers
and swimming teachers and lifeguards like I said before
plus physiotherapists and occupational therapists
plus the minibus driver
who drove the people
who came to the RUCID during the day
but slept at home.

Physiotherapist means
person who gives you massages
when your muscles hurt
and makes you do exercises
so they don't hurt any more.

Occupational therapist means
person who makes you do arts and crafts
with poster board and playdough and clay
and makes you plant flowers in flowerpots
and tend to the vegetable garden,
but you don't get to keep what you grow
you have to give it to the cooks.

Having so many people there for the residents
should have been good
but it's another paradox
because it was actually bad.

You couldn't go to other people's rooms at night any more
or stay up late talking to your roommates

even if you whispered.
You couldn't even stay up reading
because at the new RUCID
there were always at least two aides on duty.
You weren't allowed to stay up past bedtime
at the old RUCID either
but there was only one aide there at night
and she was always asleep after bedtime
and sometimes she brought her boyfriend
who was a really good person.

Plus with so many more people working there,
whatever you did they would catch you super fast.

Like for example if I didn't want to eat my boiled cabbage
because I don't like it,
and I wanted to trade with my friend
for a scoop of fried fish,
because fried fish is something I do like,
one of the aides would see us
when we swapped plates
and then she wouldn't take her eyes off us the rest of lunch.

They put me on a diet
and I hated it.
I didn't understand
why they cared so much
about making me eat things
I didn't like.
It's not like I was hurting anybody with my food.
The psychologist said it was
so I could feel better about myself.
The physiotherapist said it was because of my knees.

The nurse said it was so I could be healthier.
Mamen said it was so I could be prettier
and the cooks said it was
because Mamen said so.

I said I didn't mind being fat.
I knew there were lazy fat people
who couldn't even move because their bodies were so heavy
but that wasn't me.
I was fat and strong
like the other fat people in my family
and I'd never had any problems.
I've worked in the fields and climbed cliffs
and done sewing and cleaning and cooking
and danced at the festivals in Arcuelamora
and the other villages near Arcuelamora.
In other words,
I've done all things you have to do to live your life.

But they didn't understand any of that
and they made me go hungry
so what I would do was
I'd use the pocket money they gave me
to buy the things I wanted to eat
like chorizo sandwiches and torrijas.
But this was really hard too because,
like I said,
we hardly ever went to town any more
and there weren't any shops or cafes near the new RUCID,
just farmland,
and it wasn't even my farmland
so I couldn't plant what I wanted

348

or raise the animals I wanted
so I could eat them later.

And they were giving us way less money than before
because now Mamen didn't have to go to BANKOREA
to get the money from Social Security
to pay for our things.
At the old RUCID she used to give us some of the money
to spend on whatever we wanted.

Now the money from our Social Security benefits
went straight to the RUCID
because the RUCID in Somorrín had become
part of a consortium.

Part of a consortium means the government
stopped giving our benefits to BANKOREA
so BANKOREA could give them to us.
With the new RUCID
the government gave our benefits to BANKOREA
and BANKOREA gave them straight to the RUCID.

With the old RUCID
the bank accounts were in the resident's name
but also in the RUCID's name
so Mamen could take out our benefits too.

But with the new RUCID
you never saw the money at all
because Mamen didn't have to go to the bank to take it out
and the social workers didn't have to get receipts
for all the things they bought for the RUCID.

They almost didn't need euros and coins at all any more
because they paid for everything with transfers.

Transfers means the bank
gives your money to another bank
instead of a person
giving money straight to another person.

When I asked Mamen
why she only gave me four euros for the whole weekend
instead of a thousand pesetas like she used to in the old days,
she said because there was nothing left over from my benefit
since RSSM kept it all
to pay for my spot in the RUCID.

RSSM means Regional Social Services Management,
and Regional Social Services Management means the people
in charge of all the RUCIDs and UCIDs
in all of Arcos
and all of Somorrín
and the whole province.

She said I didn't need more money anyway
because the RUCID had everything I could ever want
and if I needed anything else
all I had to do was ask
and they would give it to me.

I needed chorizo sandwiches and torrijas
but I knew perfectly well if I asked
they wouldn't give them to me.

So, since they gave me so little money

and everything was so expensive in euros
all I could buy were gummies and bags of sunflower seeds.
They were less bulky than sandwiches
so I could hide them in my pockets
on the days they took us to town in the minibus.

All that was really bad
but the worst paradox of all
was that the social workers
weren't allowed to hit the residents any more
even if the residents hit the social workers.

They made it against the law.

That should have been good
because the aides,
psychologists, occupational therapists,
caregivers and nurses couldn't hit you any more.
Mamen was the director by then
and even she wasn't allowed to hit you.
But it was actually bad
because instead of hitting you
they would push you away
and make you take the pills
and the pills were even worse than getting slapped.

And if a resident got mad and grabbed a social worker
or another resident by her hair or wherever
and he wouldn't let go
and they couldn't get him off,
like when there's a fight
and they try to pull the guy who's winning
off the other guy,

then the nurse would stick him with a syringe
and he'd fall asleep.
And when he woke up he got punished.

The slaps were really bad
but they were better
because they would slap you
and lock you up for a while
but when the punishment was over
you came out of your room
and that was that, muskrat.

But the pills and the shots
were the worst thing in the world.
They made you dumb
and made you do everything really slow.
They even made you swallow your food slow
or cough slow if you were choking.

That was really dangerous
because if you don't cough when you're choking
you can suffocate and die,
so when they gave residents the pills
they would put everything they ate through a blender.
If boiled cabbage is bad
imagine how disgusting it is after they blend it.

Like I said, I never tried to hurt anyone
even though I wanted to lots of times
so they never had to give me any pills or shots
but I could still see perfectly well what happened
when they gave them to other people.

Even though I thought this was bad
I didn't say anything because I didn't want to get into trouble.
I also didn't say anything
because I'd been with Mamen and the RUCID for ten years
and I was getting used to it.
The social workers liked me and cared about me
and after a few years I got to be one of the few residents
who could go into town alone after lunch to have a coffee.
We had to be back by four
and if you weren't back by then
they wouldn't let you go and get coffee for the next two days.
At first I thought it was a good opportunity
because I could order a sandwich instead of a coffee.
But things kept getting more expensive
even though they were giving me the same amount of money,
and in the end I could only have coffee and a mini pastry,
or coffee with a little splash of cognac,
or coffee with a small glass of anisette,
because a lot of times they would give us those for free
but never whole sandwiches
and I ended up getting skinnier.

But when my cousins Margarita, Patricia and Natividad
were institutionalised at the new RUCID
they started making them take the pills,
because the psychiatrist said
they had aberrant behaviour
and I started getting really upset.

Patricia and Margarita both came
when they turned 19

because when you're 19
you can't stay at the CEMICA school any more.

Natividad came last
after her workplace accident
in her office at the university
when she got Gate Control syndrome
and they put her on permanent disability.

Permanent disability means you used to have a job
but you had an accident when you were working
and it gave you a severe handicap,
so now you can't do your job any more.
But even though you can't do your job
you keep getting almost the same money as before.

I think I started getting so upset
because even though I hadn't seen them very much
since we all left Arcuelamora
my cousins were my own flesh and blood
and I remembered when we were little
and we used to play in the village together.
I also remembered when Natividad
taught me to read books that were actually good
before her Gate Control syndrome.

When they started giving them the pills and shots
I tried to do everything I could
to help them learn the rules at the RUCID
like getting Patri and Nati
to stop shouting and hitting the social workers
and getting Marga to stop touching her private parts
and kissing people

so the social workers
wouldn't make them take the pills any more.

But over the years I realised
the pills were a normal thing.
They gave them to lots of people
and not just when they kissed someone
or hit someone or used impolite language with someone.
Eventually I understood
why they gave you pills for those things,
since of course violence is wrong
and touching yourself in public
puts you at risk of social exclusion.

I could deal with them taking all the fun out of food, fine.
I could deal with them not letting me tend the garden, fine.
I could deal with them not giving me more pocket money
and I could deal with them forcing me to take a shower
every single day
even though I wasn't getting dirty
because they wouldn't let me go to the garden.

But I really couldn't take it
when one day they threatened
to give me the shots too,
even though I'd never kissed anybody
and I'd never hit anybody,
not even myself.

Anarchist Social Centre of Sants, Barcelona
Okupation Working Group
Extraordinary Session, 10 July 2018

Murcia:	I can take the minutes today if that works for folx.
Everyone:	Sure sure sure …
Murcia:	I'm gonna do it Palma's way, that's easier than writing everything like it's a damn book like Jaén does.
Jaén:	Oh come on.
Oviedo:	Don't be bashful Jaén you know you're a writer at heart.
Murcia:	Right so I'm using the recorder and then later I'll transcribe everything we say.
Everyone:	Sure sure sure …
Jaén:	Yeah yeah, once you start typing everything up in a Word document you'll realise it's way more labour intensive than summarising the meeting like I do. To transcribe you have to listen, type a little, stop, go back, type a little, go back … My way, all you have to do is take notes then string them together and you're good to go.
Murcia:	Alright I'll let you know how it goes.
Jaén:	You do you.

Coruña:	Make sure it's clear we always record the minutes with a recorder recorder, not a phone recorder.
Everyone:	Right right right of course …
Coruña:	Not even with a phone in airplane mode or some shit like that.
Everyone:	No what never no …
Jaén:	And nobody's got their phone on them, right?
Everyone:	No no of course not no …
Oviedo:	Alright let's have it Jaén, why the extraordinary session in the middle of July, at eleven in the morning when there's nobody here but us chickens?
Murcia:	Oh Badajoz said she's coming but she'll be late.
Jaén:	I had to call it, even if it's just the four of us. So, Coruña already knows, it's about the girl we helped with her squat.
Oviedo:	Gari?
Murcia:	What happened?
Jaén:	Yesterday afternoon Coruña and me were here cleaning up a little and a pair of mossas showed up.
Murcia:	Oh fuck.
Oviedo:	Shit, what?
Jaén:	Yeah two mossas showed up and started asking about her, they had a picture of her and everything.
Oviedo:	Holy shit.
Jaén:	Yeah imagine me and Coruña when we saw them come in, because it was so hot the door was open.
Coruña:	Yeah so they didn't even have to knock, but they did, they drummed their knuckles on the open door and were all, Can we come in? I lost my shit.

Jaén:	I was like, this is it, they're gonna ID us because after five years they're finally bringing charges, they're gonna evict us. But since they asked for permission to come in I figured we might as well deny it, so we told them no, you can't.
Oviedo:	Of course hahahahaha …
Murcia:	I mean guys I know the heat's a bitch but that's what you get for hanging around with the door open.
Oviedo:	Murcia, dude, every day with the bitch thing. We've talked about this before, using bitch disparagingly is normalised misogyny at its finest. Pick an epithet that's a little less misogynistic, a little less bourgeois, a little less everything.
Murcia:	No no you're right, shit like that slips out when I get worked up. I realise I'm saying it as soon as it's out of my mouth.
Oviedo:	If you realise you're saying it, say so, OK? Correct yourself in the act, yeah? Acknowledge it then and there. I think that'd be really … bitchin'.
Everyone:	Hahahahahahaha …
Oviedo:	But I'm using it with positive connotations!
Coruña:	No we know it's just funny.
Oviedo:	But Murcia's right that shit'll happen when you leave the door open. Back when we had the rented place it was alright, we could leave the door open all year long, but now we've got to be smart about it.
Coruña:	I mean Oviedo it was hot as balls in here, and the courts are closed in August anyway so there's a freeze on new proceedings.
Jaén:	Right but none of that matters since they didn't come to ID us or anything like that.

Coruña: I mean, they did ID us, just not so they could evict us.

Murcia: What for then?

Jaén: So they came by asking about Gari Garay with this laminated photo of her, and get this, they had a thick folder full of zines from the library!

Murcia: From our library?

Jaén: From the zine library!

Coruña: I mean, they could've been from our library or any place else with anarchist zines. They could've been from the social centre in Gràcia, or from Entrebancs, Rosa de Foc, El Lokal, Can Batlló ...

Jaén: You're not seriously telling me they have anarchist zines in Can Batlló?

Coruña: Hahahaha OK no definitely not from Can Batlló, but they could've been from Can Vies.

Jaén: Can Vies has exactly the same zines as us, we bring them their copies.

Murcia: I mean, you could find anarchist zines at La Clandestina in Sagrada Familia, at La Púa in Hospitalet, anywhere really. At the social centres in Besòs, in Manresa, in Viladecans ...

Jaén: Right right but I'm saying these were the latest additions to the library, I remembered shelving them. The latest zines I'd photocopied and started distributing. The María Galindo one on bastardism, the one called Burn Your Phone, the one called Collective Sex, the one about making your own reusable pads, the one about insurrectionalism ... I recognised them all except one that wasn't from here, I'd never seen it before but it caught my eye, it was called Me Too: Let Me Be a Male Like You.

Oviedo:	That's what it was called? Hahahahahahaha …
Murcia:	But how'd it go down? They just showed up and said excuse me gentlemen are these your zines?
Coruña:	Right, so Jaén and me dropped what we were doing and stood in front of them at the door. They'd taken one step inside but that's it. We looked at each other but didn't say anything, twenty thousand things running through our heads but we didn't say anything.
Jaén:	The mossas looked around, took off their caps and put them under their arms like all, we come in peace. They said good afternoon and Coruña goes and says good afternoon back hahahaha-haha … I half expected him to stand to attention hahahahahahaha …
Everyone:	Hahahahahahaha …
Coruña:	Dude I was shitting myself. You weren't?
Jaén:	I mean I was thinking alright, this is it, they're gonna ID us so they can start eviction proceed-ings and that's that, time for Coruña and me to face the music.
Oviedo:	But you said that wasn't it, right?
Jaén:	No. They come up to us and say …
Coruña:	That wasn't it but they did ID us when they left.
Murcia:	But why?
Oviedo:	Wait Jaén you didn't even say hello?
Coruña:	No no this doofus goes up to them like in the movies and goes, Is there a problem, officer?
Everyone:	Hahahahahahaha …
Jaén:	And then they tell us how they're looking for an intellectually disabled woman named Margarita Guirao Guirao because she's gone missing, and they show us her photo and ask if we've seen her.

Can you tell from someone's face when they're trying not to look surprised?

Coruña: I think we did really well, Jaén, we were nonchalant as fuck, like they'd shown us a photo of a total stranger. You didn't even raise your eyebrows.

Jaén: Obviously we said no, we'd never seen that person.

Coruña: That was when they pulled the zines out of a folder and said they'd found them in her stuff and asked if we recognised them.

Murcia: And you said no.

Jaén: I couldn't, they wouldn't have bought it, they were standing in the door with the zine library right there and a fuckton of zines all over the place. I said some of them looked familiar and some of them didn't.

Coruña: That was super smooth, Jaén.

Jaén: I showed them which ones and everything, I was all, I've seen this one, not this one, this one ... hmm let me see ... no not this one ...

Coruña: At first I thought it was another Operation Pandora III and they were confiscating publications, like what happened with *Contra la Democracia*, and that they were following Gari's trail to find the folx who wrote the zines. But nah. The mossas just thought Gari might've got them here and we might've seen her.

Jaén: So we said no again, her face didn't look familiar or anything, and then their expressions changed a little and they told us the missing person had profound mental retardation and psychiatric problems and she needed medication. They said the courts had declared her legally incompetent so it was considered a high-risk disappearance and they were scouring Barcelona for her, because she doesn't know how to take care of herself or understand the scope of her actions, so they said there was no telling what she might do, they were afraid she'd hurt herself.

Oviedo: Paternalistic fascist fucking shitheads.

Coruña: Right?

Jaén: This whole time one of them's talking and the other one's taking notes.

Coruña: Jaén and me were just nodding and nodding and nodding like a pair of bobbleheads so they'd quit asking us questions and get the fuck out.

Jaén: They said everyone at her house was super worried and if we saw her or knew of anyone who'd seen her to please do our civic duty and alert the police. When I heard 'civic duty' I must've made a face, because before that it had seemed like they were getting ready to go and finally quit trying to screw us up the ass, but as soon as ...

Coruña: Jaén, I've gotta call you out just like Oviedo called out Murcia, using homosexual acts as pejorative expressions is a rebuke of everything that strays outside the heterosexual norm.

Jaén: Right no of course, I'm sorry. I ought to know better seeing as I've probably screwed and been screwed up the ass more than the three of you put together! Hahahahahahaha ...

Everyone: Hahahahahaha ...

Oviedo: Ah but that's got nothing to do with it, even when we think our sexuality runs contrary to the heteropatriarchy, we've still got shitheaps of ideological garbage etched in our mind trying to

	undermine us and get us to sabotage our own struggle for sexual liberation.
Jaén:	No of course you're totally right. The mossas weren't screwing us up the ass. Screwing up the ass is something we do to each other and we have a hell of a time doing it.
Oviedo:	Hahahahaha easy there Jaén, nobody's screwing any asses here even if the popular assembly decides it hahahaha …
Everyone:	Hahahahaha …
Jaén:	I mean if we don't even screw each other, we sure as shit aren't letting the mossas anywhere near our asses! They weren't screwing us up the ass, they were harshing our buzz, silencing us, trying to intimidate us. The last thing they said before they left, and I think they said it because they saw how I reacted to the thing about our civic duty, was that concealing or assisting in the disappearance of an incompetent individual was tantamount to kidnapping or concealing the kidnapping of a minor. Those were their exact words.
Coruña:	And then they asked to see our IDs, they claimed so they could add us to their report.
Murcia:	Yeah that's normal, they always ask for your ID after a police interaction.
Coruña:	It might be normal but now they've got us in their sights, for their report but also to eventually evict us, and for whatever the fuck else they want.
Oviedo:	Yeah that goes without saying.
Coruña:	Anyway we show them our IDs and one of them copies our info down, and the other one starts peeking over our shoulders, trying to look around …

Murcia:	But he doesn't come in, right?
Coruña:	No, she doesn't come in, all of this from the door, she's craning her neck to see if she can catch a glimpse of anything juicy, and we're just standing there with our arms crossed, not moving a millimetre. And then they put on their caps like they're getting ready to go and I relax a little, thinking the sooner they're out of here the better. But Jaén couldn't leave it at that, he was on a roll.
Jaén:	Alright come on.
Coruña:	No no listen to this: he goes and asks if he can see the zines again, and of course immediately they pull them out of the folder again, and Jaén examines them like he has some new insight to offer, like something's just dawned on him, and the cops just stand there eagerly waiting for Jaén to do his civic duty hahahahaha ... And then the motherfucker goes and asks if he can keep one of the ones he'd never seen before, the one he really hadn't seen, Let Me Be a Man or whatever.
Jaén:	Me Too: Let Me Be a Male Like You.
Murcia:	For real, you actually said that?
Coruña:	Hahahahaha he said exactly that!
Jaén:	I mean it looked like a really cool zine!
Oviedo:	Jaén you're ... you're too much.
Coruña:	And when the cops were like, And may we ask what you would like it for? Jaén said exactly that, that he just wanted it because it looked like a really cool zine.
Oviedo:	You said that, Jaén? You literally told the cops it looked like a really cool zine?
Murcia:	Or did you want it for something else?

364

Jaén:	I just told them the truth, it really looked like a super well-done zine.
Murcia:	Jesus.
Oviedo:	What'd they say?
Coruña:	Yeah Jaén, tell them what they said!
Jaén:	They said, As I'm sure you'll understand sir, that won't be possible.
Coruña:	And Jaén goes and says of course, he understands perfectly, but we have our own photocopier right inside, and it would only take him a second to make a copy.
Murcia:	Nooooooooo ... And they came inside with you?
Jaén:	Don't worry they said no.
Oviedo:	Their loss, if they'd said yes they could've come in as far as the photocopier and sniffed around a little more.
Coruña:	Shhhhh Oviedo relax, thankfully Barcelona's finest were there to knock some sense into our old pal Jaén here.
Everyone:	Hahahahahahahaha ...
Oviedo:	Right it's all really funny, but the thing with Gari is serious.
Jaén:	Super serious. As soon as the mossas left yesterday we called all the folx at other places with zines to see if the cops had shown up there with questions too.
Coruña:	Don't worry we called from a payphone.
Oviedo:	Ah OK.
Murcia:	What'd they say?
Jaén:	The mossas had talked to all of them too. They couldn't ask any questions at CV because in summer that place clears out just like the schools, but they did at AG and APS, and at RF and LK.

Murcia: Shit.

Coruña: Remember how Gari was living in Barceloneta? They started searching from there, then widened the radius to El Raval and Poble Nou, then outwards to Poble Sec, and finally they got to us here in Sants. Everyone we spoke to described the same pair of mossas: a blonde with a ponytail, fatter and taller than the other one, who had short hair like a boy but with those twisty bangs that get in your eyes, kinda blonde too. Both had dyed hair. The tall one was wearing a lot of make-up and thick foundation, the other one had freckles and blue eyes. The tall one was younger, forty tops, and had a Catalan accent. The one with the freckles had an Andalusia or Extremadura accent and she was a little older, fifty, maybe fifty-five.

Murcia: And they showed up everywhere in uniform?

Coruña: Yeah.

Murcia: OK.

Oviedo: But did you warn Gari?

Jaén: We figured the mossas would be hanging around the neighbourhood for a while, so I waited a couple of hours before going to her house.

Oviedo: I would've thought that would be our first concern, before we started trying to trace the mossas' every step. Our priority should be coordinating an action to help Gari.

Coruña: We needed to know where the mossas were looking to make an informed decision, Oviedo. We weren't doing it to play cops and robbers.

Oviedo: I mean, it kinda seems that way, we've been talking about it for an hour now.

Murcia:	Anyway you went to her house and spoke to her and she said what?
Jaén:	That's one of the things I wanted to talk about. I went to her house and told her they were looking for her all over, they'd reached her neighbourhood, and she should be careful and everything, and I said if she wanted she could spend the night at my house while we looked for a collective solution, but she said no.
Murcia:	That's not so weird, is it?
Oviedo:	A little, I think. I don't know, if you told me the cops were looking for me and you offered me a place to hide, I wouldn't think twice.
Jaén:	The thing is she didn't just say no to that, she said no to any other action too. I told her a bunch of us could all go to her okupa to block the entry like when we stop evictions, or we could help her find a different house to okupy outside Barcelona.
Oviedo:	And she said no to everything?
Jaén:	Yeah. She said she was grateful for our help but she wanted to stay put, because the ten days she'd spent in the house had been happier than the previous twenty years of her life ever since they sent her to one of those centres.
Coruña:	It's brutal what they do to Gari and people like her.
Jaén:	So that's what I said. I spent more than an hour in the house, which is super clean now, by the way, I wish I could make my place look like that, and I kept saying her house is great but now she's in danger not just of getting evicted, but of getting put back in a centre or one of those government-run flats. I said that she was brave

enough to squat a house once, she could do it again somewhere safer …

Murcia: Hold up hold up, Jaén, you said all that?

Jaén: Yeah, why? What's the problem?

Murcia: The problem is it's not true. We can't stop the cops from busting down Gari's door the same way we stop evictions, because like the mossas said, since Gari's considered intellectually handicapped and legally incompetent, any action that helps her remain at large isn't just obstruction of justice, it's a felony the same as kidnapping.

Coruña: But Murcia, if she wants to be in the house of her own free will and she explicitly says so to the police, and we're there at the door and the cops are the ones trying to take her away, how could that be considered kidnapping?

Murcia: Because her own free will doesn't count for shit, Coruña. Being legally incompetent means she doesn't have the authority to make decisions about her own life. Her legal guardian, who I think she said is the Generalitat, makes all the decisions for her. It's just like the mossas said: in the eyes of the law Gari might as well be a minor, and if a minor runs away, even if she's just trying to escape her parents or teachers because they beat the shit out of her, the cops will find her and drag her kicking and screaming straight back into the hands of her abusers. When the courts declare you legally incompetent, you can't even press charges, just like kids can't. All Gari can do is make a scene when they come for her and say she doesn't want to go back because they abuse her at the flat where she lives, and then, if she's lucky, the police will file a complaint. If they feel like going to the trouble. And if they do, while the complaint is being processed, instead of sending her back to her supervised flat, they'll refer her case to emergency social services, who will just send her to another flat run by the Generalitat or another centre, which is exactly what Gari doesn't want.

Jaén: So all the more reason for our action.

Murcia: Yes, but you should all know we're exposing ourselves to kidnapping charges.

Oviedo: At the very least.

Murcia: At the very very least.

Oviedo: I see an issue with something else Jaén said. Even if Gari finds another okupa, she's never going to be safe. I don't know if you all realise this, but for Gari to remain free, she'll have to go into hiding. I mean, this is really serious. If what Murcia says about how they treat disabled people is true, Gari's gonna have no choice but to go underground like a fugitive. Not just like a squatter, but like a terrorist or a drug lord.

Murcia: It sounds dramatic and it sounds like a movie but that's exactly where she's at.

Coruña: Folx come on.

Murcia: No, Coruña, it's true.

Jaén: But I'm saying none of that matters because Gari doesn't want to leave her okupa.

Oviedo: So we'll go and help her, and when the cops show up they'll just find us hanging around like regular squatters, and we'll have Gari hidden somewhere in the house.

Coruña: Yeah but Oviedo, how long could we keep that up? We'd all have to go and live there. And if the

369

	cops get suspicious, they'll show up with a search warrant and it'll be like Murcia said, they'll drag her out and arrest us all on kidnapping charges.
Oviedo:	But look, the defence strategy comes way later. We figure out the defence strategy when things have gone to shit and they've caught us and we know the charges. If we start out by thinking about how they're going to oppress us then we'll never take any action at all, the fear will paralyse us. We've always known our struggle will have consequences, but it's one thing to possess that knowledge and use it to devise better actions that are harder for our oppressors to thwart, and another very different thing to apply the bandage before we've even been cut. It's one thing to stay a step ahead of the enemy and know how they're going to oppress us, because that gives us the advantage, and it's another very different thing to become useless bystanders who just assume they'll be oppressed, which gives the upper hand to the oppressors: the advantage of our inaction, free rein to oppress Gari after she made such a brave getaway. Because hey, maybe our action will be so well executed we won't even get caught. Right? Why can't we allow ourselves to consider the odds of our success, which are substantial?
Murcia:	Yeah you've got a point.
Jaén:	Alright but Gari doesn't want to do anything at all. I already told her about our odds of success and how she's taken a firm step towards freedom and she could take another one, and it'd be a hard step that would involve a lot of sacrifices, but with our support she could get through it.

And I'm telling you guys, she just said she was really grateful for everything we'd done for her and everything we were willing to do, but all she wanted was to be left in peace in her okupa.

Coruña: She doesn't care about getting caught?

Jaén: It's not that she doesn't care, she just doesn't want to think about it. All she wants to think about is chilling out in her house for as long as she's there, without worrying about anything else. That's why she didn't want to come to the meeting either, and I told her we could hold it at her okupa if she didn't want to go outside, and she just said no no no.

Murcia: Shit, I will never understand that girl.

Jaén: I don't know if she's as weird as you think, Murcia. Gari might actually have it all figured out. I think she expects the oppression that's coming her way. It's nothing new for her. She's experienced it over and over in centres for disabled people, from caregivers on the inside and from cops colluding with her caregivers on the outside. She's thirty-seven, and ever since they institutionalised her at eighteen, she's been developing strategies for resistance. That's not what she calls them, but that's the sense I get from what she says. Gari will never chant 'Another eviction, another okupation', but that's really what she's been doing her whole life. They tear her away from one space of freedom and she bides her time until she has the chance to seize another. It's the exact same thing we do.

Coruña: With one critical difference, Jaén, the super critical difference that, unlike us, she's the victim

371

of systemic oppression, imprisoned, in a sense, within four walls controlled by her oppressors.

Oviedo: What do you mean unlike us? Aren't we victims of systemic oppression? We may not be imprisoned within four walls, but we're imprisoned in an entire city, under the absolute subjugation of market totalitarianism, the walking dead putting in ten-hour days as waitresses and interns, choking down exploitation and harassment, stripped of the will to live, the will to fuck, until we forget how to form relationships that are based on anything besides money.

Coruña: Are you seriously comparing your situation as one of seven billion victims of late capitalism to the concrete, systemic oppression that Gari has experienced for the past two decades? For real?

Oviedo: I absolutely am! How could I feel solidarity towards Gari's oppression except by comparing it with my own? Let whoever feels more free than Gari just because they live outside an internment centre throw the first stone.

Coruña: In that case I've got plenty of stones to throw, Oviedo, because you can't gloss over the fact that you, me and all of us at this meeting enjoy certain privileges granted by the system that Gari does not. For starters, we have the privilege of not being legally incompetent and being able to choose where we want to live.

Oviedo: Bullshit, Coruña, bullshit we can choose where we live! How can we when they're driving hundreds of residents out of this city every day by raising the rent so no one can afford it except the fucking tourists? And while they're hiking our rent they're cutting our pay, passing new laws to expedite the eviction process and cracking down on squatters and protesters! So tell me again, Coruña, about all these privileges I have.

Coruña: Fuck, Oviedo, of course that's all true. But don't you think there's some privilege you might have that Gari might not, some privilege you could use to help her? The privilege, for example, of being able to work and choose how to spend your money?

Oviedo: Hahahahahaha ... Coruña, you sound like those geriatric white dudes after Franco died who thought freedom had reached its orgasmic apogee because women were finally allowed to open bank accounts and wear miniskirts.

Murcia: I agree with Coruña. I'm not saying work is a good thing. We can't think of privilege in absolute terms. Our privileges only exist relative to the privileges that others don't have. Any privilege the State or the Market gives you might be crap, it might even be another instrument of subjugation, but you can still use it to help someone who has been denied that same privilege. For example, we're white and European, so the cops give us the privilege of not stopping us on the street based on our appearance just to see if our IDs have expired or if we're undocumented and they're trying to deport us.

Oviedo: I don't know what the fuck you folx are talking about, you literally just said they demanded to see your IDs yesterday for the crime of mopping the floor with the door open. They ID us and put us in jail just for trying to halt an eviction, just for insulting the politicians who live at our expense, just for insulting the yankee imperialist tourist gentrifiers who're driving us out of our homes. They persecute us for everything we do to resist the way of life they've designed for us. Are you seriously trying to tell me sitting at home watching TV is a privilege?

Coruña: I'm trying to tell you you've got a passport that the cops at the airport don't look up and down forty times before deciding whether to let you through or pull you into secondary.

Jaén: Folx let's please come up with a solution for Gari.

Coruña: Or look, Oviedo, here's an even better example. You're a woman, so when you go to a concert or a basketball game or a boxing match, the security guards don't frisk you or look in your bag. Because sometimes there are no female security guards and the male guards don't touch women, and even though they could still do a thorough search of your bag, they just give it a once-over. You can use that privilege the system gives you, which is really a dismissal or a deprecation, a conception of you as non-threatening because you're a woman, and use that pseudo-privilege to your advantage. If the moron in power buys into the same prejudices that he himself creates and thinks you, a woman, could never break the rules to sneak in alcohol or knives, you can take advantage of his stupidity to sneak in alcohol and knives.

Oviedo: Alright now I think we're getting somewhere.

Jaén: Please folx seriously, we're working against the clock if we want Gari to stay free.

Oviedo:	I've already said what I think. Murcia, please make it clear in the minutes that we'll have to continue this conversation about privilege.
Murcia:	Don't worry I'll transcribe everything.
Jaén:	Right so Oviedo could you repeat your opinion?
Oviedo:	I think we should go and be with Gari at her okupa.
Jaén:	I already told you she doesn't want that.
Oviedo:	Let's go and convince her then, give her confidence and reassurance.
Murcia:	I agree, we could at least try.
Jaén:	I'm telling you that's not what she wants. Like literally we even banged one out then kept talking and she just kept saying no.
Coruña:	Wait you hooked up? That's kinda funny.
Jaén:	Kinda funny why?
Coruña:	I don't know, you're usually into dudes and you like barely know each other, right?
Oviedo:	Coruña I don't know what's going on with you today but you're being reactionary as fuck.
Coruña:	What, I can't ask?
Jaén:	We fucked because the body wants what it wants. That's all there is to it. What, you want details?
Oviedo:	Yeeeeeessssssssssssssssssssssss!
Everyone:	Hahahahahahahaha …
Murcia:	Alright alright but off the record so the minutes don't turn into Fifty Shades of Jaén! I don't think I could type that much.
Jaén:	Yeah, see? Transcribing's a bitch. Argh sorry, sorry, calling myself out for the misogynormative language. What do other folx think?
Murcia:	What do we think about you and Gari fucking?

Jaén:	Jesus fucking Christ the second anyone mentions sex around here it's all anyone can talk about, you're like a bunch of Catholic school kids.
Oviedo:	Nobody here's getting much action, Jaén.
Coruña:	If she said she doesn't want to do anything, I think we have to respect that.
Oviedo:	So we do nothing?
Jaén:	Gari made it very clear she didn't want us to do anything. She said: 'Jaén, thank you, for real, but I don't want your help any more. All I want now is to fuck you.'
Murcia:	And she meant it?
Jaén:	Oh she meant it alright. Didn't I just tell you we banged?
Coruña:	Who's the Catholic school kid now.
Oviedo:	That woman's a legend.
Murcia:	Is it possible Gari's intellectual disability really is clouding her judgement? Like, she really might not understand they're coming for her or what an action would look like?
Oviedo:	Sorry?
Murcia:	I mean I don't know, alright? But they say about people with disabilities that lots of them are really preoccupied with sex and nothing else.
Jaén:	Murcia, man, shut your cunt mouth already. Fuck, sorry for the pejorative cunt. Shut your testicles mouth already.
Oviedo:	I can't believe what I'm hearing. Murcia, Coruña, how about you two go and hit up Intereconomía TV and see if they have spots for you on one of their fascist talk shows.
Murcia:	Fucking hell, what did I say that was so horrible?

Coruña:	For real Oviedo, you and Jaén are getting pretty high and mighty. All we're doing is laying out options.
Oviedo:	Do you dudes realise you're talking about Gari like you were her captors? The same captors she's trying to escape! Going on about how retarded people only think about sex, how they don't know what's best for themselves. So we should make her decisions for her, that's what you're saying?
Coruña:	But Oviedo you just said you want to go to her house to convince her.
Oviedo:	Yeah, and there's a big fucking difference between trying to convince her and explaining things to her like she's an idiot.
Coruña:	No, fine, you're right, Murcia went too far plus he made a shit generalisation about people with mental retardation. But if Jaén was over there talking to her for an hour and he explained everything, and if we're serious about not treating her like an idiot who doesn't know what she wants, then we have to take what she says at face value: she doesn't want our help, all she wants is to fuck in peace until the cops come for her. Right? The same as with the informant, she just kept on fucking him, she didn't care if he was a cop, even when she was right in the middle of trying to start an okupa.
Oviedo:	Seriously dudes. I won't just sit here while you speak in the same terms as the normalising power that oppresses us all. 'Mental retardation' is a bullshit concept invented by the Welfare Market-State, alright? 'Mental retards' is just one of the

many categories power uses to delimit one part of the population and justify its repressive measures towards them. We can't keep talking if we aren't all clear on this. And if all she ever thinks about is fucking, what of it? Who the fuck do you think you are to judge how or with who or when Gari has sex? If anything we ought to admire her, shouldn't we? If only any of us had enough cunt to be able to tell some guy, quit dicking around, I just want to fuck!

Jaén: Oviedo if you want you and me can just go over there and ask how she's doing and if she needs anything.

Oviedo: Yeah at least that, at the very least. Will the norms be joining us?

Coruña: Could you chill the fuck out, Oviedo?

Oviedo: Look Coruña I can't with you right now, you're incapable of the least self-reflection.

Coruña: Look who's talking! I can't with either of you.

Oviedo: Murcia are you gonna storm out with Coruña, can your fragile masculinity not take it any more?

Coruña: Fuck, Badajoz, you show up NOW?

Murcia: To be honest I'm not at all happy about the way we're handling this issue.

Oviedo: Alright Jaén it's you and me, let's go and see Gari, clock's ticking on her freedom. You coming too, Badajoz?

Badajoz: I just came from there! Sorry I'm so late, I overslept, it's so hot I couldn't fall asleep until four, plus I stopped by Gari's okupa to check how she was doing, I hadn't seen her since we helped her move the furniture so I figured I ought to stop by and ask if she wanted to come to the meeting

378

too, right? Because she doesn't have a phone or WhatsApp or wifi or anything, right? Sorry I'm so late. Are you wrapping up already?

Jaén: You just came from Gari's house?

Badajoz: Yeah but she wasn't there. It looks like some shit went down, her door was kicked in and police-taped, and I could see broken glass and furniture on the floor from the street. I texted you guys but, duh, you don't have your phones. It looks like they evicted her and we didn't even know. When was the last time you saw her?

Murcia: Turning this off.

The first part of the manipulation was predators devouring their prey. The second was the game of giant chess. The third and final part, which would give the show its provisional name, was the beating. We rehearsed 'The Beating' until it was time to print the posters, when the pyjamaman and his assistant informed us that some participants in the piece didn't like the title and maybe we ought to come up with something everybody would be happy with.

'It makes it sound like we're attacking each other instead of dancing,' said a dancer whose body lists to the right.

'That's exactly what it looks like,' I said, 'that's why it's funny.'

'I don't think it's funny, I came here to do dance, not to do martial arts,' said a fat man who defaults to hip hop whenever he improvises.

'The only one who thinks it's funny is Natividad because she's the star of the show,' said the lopsided dancer.

'I'm the one who takes the beating, yes, and you're one of the ones who administer it. Would you rather be the ones getting beaten?' I asked genuinely, out of my genuine desire for the others to experience the pleasure of taking a beating at the hands of thirteen other dancers.

'I don't want anyone to get beaten up and I don't want to beat anybody up! I hate violence!' said the lister, and I laughed, aiming my cackle at the ceiling.

'I'm a pacifist too, Julia, and no one here is beating anybody up. I hope that much is clear?' said the pyjamaman.

'But that's what it looks like, that's exactly what it looks like. I watch it from the outside and the more they rehearse, the more it looks like someone's being assaulted,' said the Playboy cavalcade float with all the pent-up, smouldering resentment of someone forced to watch from the sidelines.

'I like how it looks like we're beating Nati up, it's like a game we play with the audience,' said one of the new dancers, a slow-paced biped with a firm grip.

'I like it too. Even though it looks like we're beating her up, we're not actually advocating violence, we're criticising it, because at the end of the piece we all finish with a celebration, right? In the finale when we all improvise freely together,' said another of the new bipeds, who dances with the fascist precision of ballet even though she's self-taught and never set foot in a conservatory. The entire debate struck me as so absurd that I had to cover my mouth, but that forced the laughter into my shoulders, which began to shake. Everyone could tell I was laughing, and laughter is just as infectious among my dance classmates as it is among us here in the self-advocacy group, so before long we were all giggling away.

'Did you want to say something, Nati?' Pyjamaman asked me, annoyed. I took a deep breath to quell my laughter and, while the inmates continued giggling and their aide/minder/cops continued shushing them, I said:

'I mean, if you ask me, it's the group improvisation at the end that's violent, not the beating. It's violent because half the dancers are led by the hand across the stage, which is to say they're escorted to a position stipulated by you and your assistant, though that's the least of our worries, seeing as everyone here is taking orders from you all day every day.

What's violent is that their escorts pull them to their positions, release their hands, and tell them to dance, at which point these students dance for a predetermined number of minutes until you give the order for their escorts to again lead them offstage by the hand. The real violence is that you call this "improvisation". The real violence is banishing these dancers to other rooms when we're not rehearsing the grand finale, and the real violence is using that grand finale to obscure this segregation by putting sixty dancers onstage at once and blasting the music.'

'Sixty dancers, Nati?' asked Psykommandant Buedo. 'I thought you said there were twenty-something.'

'That's at the SS, but students at other civic centres around Barcelona rehearse separately with the pyjamaman, and once a week we all rehearse the finale together at the Cineplex. This collective dancing is known as "community dance" or "community-based dance", which is a business model where students pay to perform in a dance company but nobody gets paid except the director, his assistant and the staff at the venue on the day of the performance. The director, his assistant and the staff cash in on ticket sales, too: if their salaries are fully subsidised by public grants or private sponsorships, then they might not charge for seats, but if the company has only secured partial subsidies or partial sponsorships, or if, besides not compensating their dancers with anything other than maybe a plastic cup of sparkling wine on opening night, the director and his assistant also want to turn a profit on the box office, then they charge between six and twelve euros for a seat. Don't get me wrong, they're not making a killing. The director and his assistant are unquestionably middle class. Community dance is one of the many schemes professional dancers and choreographers devised to survive the economic crisis. They couldn't produce big-budget shows like they used to after their audiences and fellowships dried up, and they certainly couldn't maintain their bourgeois lifestyles living off the squalid art circuits, so they monetised their craft by inventing this notion of dance as a social good, dance as a tool to help marginalised populations integrate in society, dance as a public-private service that is either provided free of charge thanks to generous support from public institutions and their allies in the private sector, or funded partially by public grants, partially by private-sector sponsorships and partially by the end-users themselves. I say end-users and not dancers because people who participate in community dance don't enjoy the social status of dancers or dance students, regardless of their artistic abilities. Those of us who participate in community dance are the designated end-users of a public service, no different from swimmers at the municipal pool or passengers on public transport. Meanwhile, the brains behind this froyo shop, the pyjamaman and his assistants, retain their artistic status as directors, choreographers, set designers, lighting designers, graphic designers, musicians and so on. Of all these behind-the-scenes professionals, only the director and his assistant get paid. The rest just do it for the social capital, so they can put the gig on their CVs and get their names in the programme. The performers – the people who go onstage and do the actual dancing – are anonymous. There is such a gaping disparity between the end-users (in the non-artist category) and the professionals (in the artist category) that for the past few years, on the posters and programmes for the Cineplex's community dance shows, the performers appear as 'Residents from the Les Corts, La Mina and La Sagrera Neighbourhoods' or 'Residents from the Les Corts, La Teixonera and Bellvitge Neighbourhoods' or 'Residents from the Les Corts, Trinitat Nova and El Guinardó Neighbourhoods'. They always include Les Corts on the poster because that's where the Cineplex is, and the Cineplex is the froyo-shop mothership because it has massive rehearsal spaces, not to mention it's fully adapted for non-bipedal dancers and it's the headquarters of the Dance Workers Union.'

'What do you think, Ibrahim, seeing as you're also in Natividad's dancing group? Do you think it's bad for people who need help to be assisted to their position onstage? And do you think it's disrespectful to say a person is a resident of their own neighbourhood?' the psykommandant asked from her rehearsed active-listening pose, leaning her upper body forward, twisting the questions like the master manipulator she is.

'Sorry, Ibra,' I jumped in. 'Before you answer I have to respond to Laia: setting aside your absolutely loaded, twisted, decontextualised question, I'll just add that you're right: in community dance, no one finds any of this offensive. All the dancers are perfectly content with their status as end-users, and they buy into the justification that you can't fit sixty names on a poster. The explanation they don't buy – because no one even tries to sell it to them and they would never think it on their own – is that their names' absence from the poster stems from the accumulator logic of democratic capitalism: the more people sign up, the better, regardless of how they dance, even if they're just tugged along like lapdogs, plopped on the stage and goaded into shimmying in the exact spot and time and manner that's been marked out for them, because the goal is not to support students as they learn to dance with greater pleasure (and therefore dance better). In fact, no one is thinking about the students at all. All the community-dancemongers are thinking about is justifying their status, salaries and lily-white consciences through an oppressive regime based on the daydream of universal access to culture. That's how they won the National Dance

Prize of Catalonia in 2012, but of course the award went to the dancemongers, not to the anonymous performers. They gave it to the pyjamaman's dance company, which might be a company in the corporate sense of the word, but it certainly isn't a dance company in the artistic sense of the word, because every year his dancers are just dozens of nameless, interchangeable faces. Pyjamaman Inc. exists only as a legal entity that enables the pyjamaman to receive payments and grants, and to present himself as a professional in the world of dance. It's all a smokescreen. Even their dancemongerly gimmick about bringing together residents from different parts of the city is a lie, because every year it's more or less the same group of end-users, all that changes is the rehearsal spaces. Occasionally some unsuspecting dupes get caught up in it, like me and the other SS dancers did this year, but apart from that, it's always the same people going to rehearse at adult daycare centres in different neighbourhoods across Barcelona.'

'I'm from the daycare centre in El Raval, and proud of it!' said Ibrahim.

'I'm from the one in Sagrada Familia, and proud of it!' A second self-advocate.

'Sagrada Familia's a shithole, it's all tourists!' A third.

'Yeah, well, El Raval is all hookers and junkies!' A fourth.

'Better a methed-up hooker than a drunk Brit on a stag do. El turisme mata els barris!' Ibrahim again. He must have started reading the zine. 'Every Airbnb means another eviction! Tourism is terrorism!'

'Tourists go home! Tourists go home!' another cried.

'Tourists go home! Tourists go home!' everyone chanted, including me.

'Don't say bad words!' The good-looking dudebro, who always uses the most bad words, rejoined the ranks of the military police and sided with the psykommandant in order to retain his masculofascist privileges.

'Thank you, Antonio,' his master Laia stroked his back. 'As self-advocates, I shouldn't have to shout and force you to behave. You ought to maintain order and respect among yourselves, don't you think?'

'Laia, Laia, Laia!' Patricia, with her hand in the air. 'I want to say something about Nati's dancing!'

'Let Patricia speak!' The dudebro, his military-police armband glimmering on the sleeve of his FC Barcelona jersey.

'Thank you, Antonio.' My half-sister, smoothing down her miniskirt. 'I just want to say even though Nati's got all these opinions about her dance group, it seems like she is really perfectly integrated and assimilated with all her classmates, because things aren't always perfect, but she still keeps going to her classes, doesn't she? She keeps showing up to all the rehearsals and she's going to be in the show they're putting on and everything. They even gave her the leading role. Why, you ask? Because my sister has her opinions, don't I know it, but she checks them all at the door for the sake of something as wonderful as dancing, which has been her calling since she was a little girl, right, Nati? Because there might be some annoying stuff she has to deal with, but it's important to take the bitter with the sweet, and I think Nati has a very positive attitude and we all have a lot to learn from her.'

'Great question, Patricia,' Laia said.

'Nati, answer,' ordered the military policeman.

'You won't be giving me a single goddamn order, all right, macho shitbag? You won't so much as look at me.' The military policeman absorbed the riposte and sought authorisation to subdue me from the psykommandant, who lifted her open hand in a hold-your-fire gesture and responded:

'We say please when we ask for things, don't we, Antonio?' He crossed his arms and nodded in a show of complicit submission.

'What was your question, Patri?' I asked.

'Just that dance is a wonderful thing, and you really like it and you're going to be in that show, right?'

'I sure am, and all of you are invited to come see it, except Antonio.'

'But what does that have to do with the furtive fuck you were going to tell me about?' Marga purrs, caressing my hair under the gaping hole in the roof.

'It has to do with today being the first day all the groups from around Barcelona rehearsed together, so it was the first time we all got to see what the other groups were doing. Everyone watched the routines while the pyjamaman and his assistant fitted the different parts together, which meant every group had an audience of between sixty and seventy people, if you count the aide/minder/cops, and I got that feeling you only experience when you have an audience. I've heard people call it getting built up, which means you do everything with more nerve. It's a feeling I haven't had in years, because I haven't had an audience. When all of us from the SS started giving The Beating, I was more excited than usual. I think my other perceptive classmates were excited too, because the scene lasted fifteen minutes, and for at least half that time, the entire group was gripped by this feeling of refocus, alertness and solidarity. It was so powerful, Marga, that even the dancers who treat dance class like a social club or a bingo hall or the rec room at an old folks' home toned down their sanctimoniousness for a few minutes. Even they were overcome by a desperation to push the dance forwards, breathing hard through their mouths, with their eyes unfocused and a look of surrender on their faces.'

387

'All that from beating each other up?' Marga asks me, stretching her caress from my hair to the back of my neck, giving me goosebumps.

'We weren't beating each other up, Marga! That's just what it looked like from the outside. I'm dancing, and the other thirteen dancers are trying to manipulate my body while I move around the stage, so it looks like they're chasing me and I'm trying to get away. And the thing is, Marga, that's exactly what's happening. It is a beating, but with dance movements instead of kicking and punching. Think of it like this. In the earlier manipulations, I had to stay still, so I could only move if the other dancers moved me. But in this variant of the manipulation, the one we're calling The Beating, I can move freely wherever I want, and the others are free to move me as much as they're able. I could be at the north end of the space and two dancers could catch me and send me off to the southern end, and on the way to the southern end, three or four others could intercept me, lift me up towards the ceiling or press me down against the floor. I can let them do this, or, if I want, I can resist. I can make myself stiff as a board so they can't lift me or force me down. And when I get tired of that, I can release the tension in my body and let myself collapse, literally just collapse in the middle of the hall, and if I weren't surrounded by three, four, five or twelve other people, I'd eat shit against the floor. But when I fall, there aren't just twenty-six hands to catch me, but thirteen whole life-saving bodies. Or if I don't feel like resisting the other dancers, I can just surrender, and in those moments, Marga, I fly. During this first rehearsal with an audience, one dancer lifted me by the waist, another by a leg, and another by the arms. Then, another got on all fours, and they put me on top of him like he was a rocking horse. And this time they really did grab me everywhere,

Marga! One tall biped grabbed my throat like he was going to strangle me, it was incredible! He took me firmly by the neck, or not really by the neck but by the jaw, nestling his index finger and thumb into my mandible and picking me straight up.' I grab my throat to demonstrate for Marga, and I grab her throat the same way; she seizes on the opportunity to guide my hand to her breasts. 'A porté like that was only possible because other hands had already launched me into flight, so I was already in motion. Otherwise, he could never have lifted me cold like that, with no momentum, like they do in cartoons. And if he had tried, it would've been painful. I opened my mouth so I wouldn't asphyxiate or grind my teeth or chomp down on my own tongue, and I arched my neck to create a curve along my entire spine. But the best part, Marga, is when you reach these moments of pause or transition where something colossal happens. At one point, I was standing in the centre and the other thirteen had surrounded me in a wide circle. We stared each other down and moved within that formation, a few of us panting from all the action.' Sometimes, like now, my caresses turn into explanatory drawings on Marga's skin, and she squirms because I tickle her by accident. 'Everyone was gauging the right moment to resume the manipulation, and also catching their breath. From the outside, it would've looked like a ring of thirteen people stalking one woman in the centre. That's how it felt from within the dance, too. I was looking for a way to escape, which is to say, a way to enable the dance to continue. I was so in my element and so certain that the pleasure I was feeling was mutual, that I took off my tights, took off my panties, and stood there in just my shirt, gesturing for my thirteen stalkers to come at me, like I was a big man looking for a cockfight, as if I were saying: come and get me if you have cunt enough, what're you waiting for, this is just getting started and we agreed on day one that you had to touch me everywhere.'

'And you all fucked together? How is it possible to have a furtive fuck with thirteen other people?' Marga asks, adjusting her leg on my hip. We're lying on our sides, facing each other.

'Please, Marga, I wish! What happened was, first, the audience started murmuring, shocked by the half-nudity onstage. A few people clapped, and a few other people shushed them, and a few others did that ridiculous whistle dudebros always do when a woman walks by. Some of my stalkers were fazed by the audience's dim-witted reaction and checked out – even though they remained with us physically, they weren't dancing with the same pleasurable degradation as before, they only continued dancing for the sake of the pyjamaman who, to my surprise, instead of turning the music down because he interpreted those few motionlessness seconds as the end of our improvisation, made the excellent decision to turn it up. It was a silly blues piece that suddenly sounded like the music they play in Westerns when there's a gunfight at high noon.' Marga uses the leg on my thigh to pull me towards her. The closeness of our cunts creates a little cave; a warm, moist burrow. 'The other stalkers, the clever ones, the pleasure-seekers, the best dancers, sensing that the circumstances were in our favour, looked at each other with a smirk, almost like they were saying "time to show this girl what's what". Three non-bipeds also took off their pants and underwear and, bare-assed, held their position in the circle. A few more whistles from the audience, but for the most part there was an expectant silence that energised us and helped us take our pleasure more seriously. A non-biped with good mobility in his hands helped another non-biped with limited mobility get his clothes off, and they remained in their positions, dicks hanging loose. The ring of stalkers treated this

390

undressing, which was clumsy, and non-simultaneous, and even ridiculous, like a discrete task of rearmament, which only made them more serious and threatening. At this point, there were three sets of genitalia aiming at my own: two half-flaccid penises, one circumcised and the other with very blond pubes, and one squarish female pubis, her bush thick and shiny like patent leather. Then, the thirteen electric and manual wheelchairs, walkers, crutches, canes, prostheses and canonical arms and legs pounced on me.'

'And you fucked the half-naked ones?' Marga asks in my ear, kissing my neck.

'Only one of them,' I exhale.

'Which one?' She bites my earlobe.

'The one with the circumcised dick, but that was later, not in the middle of the performance. Dancing with my pussy out had turned me on, and I was still horny after rehearsal. I'm guessing the three others who'd stripped down were horny too, but only the circumcised guy was bold enough to fuck me in the accessible toilet,' I sigh, running a hand behind her and squeezing her ass cheek. Now our hips and cunts are bonded like limpets. Our pubic bones rub and sound like sandpaper. 'Dancing bottomless is wild, Marga. Your classmates end up accidentally or deliberately touching your pussy and your ass, and that kind of touching gives rise to new movements, since, for the purposes of dance, those body parts have always been silenced.' Talking about pussies, asses and movement so close to Marga's mouth quickens our nuzzling until it's not nuzzling at all, but one pelvis slamming into the other like a clapper against a church bell. 'But besides that, even without anyone touching you, just the fact that your cunt isn't constrained in your panties makes your vulva dance too. Your inner and outer labia move, they touch each other without you touching them, like you've got a baby rattle between your legs.' Marga's hand presses its way through our clinging abdomens and gently grasps my vulva. I seize on her with my pelvis but Marga forces open enough space to manoeuvre. 'You feel the air in your cunt and, when you sit down, the floor either cools you or warms you, depending on your temperature and the floor's.' I'm having a difficult time getting the words out because it's hard to breathe between gasps, and because all I want is to devour Marga's mouth, throat, nipples. She accepts my kisses but also holds them back because she wants my mouth free so I can continue talking.

'And what were you doing using the disabled toilet, with those two working legs of yours?'

'Peeing quickly before hurrying over here to see you, Marga, because the disabled toilet is on the ground floor and that way I didn't have to go upstairs to the bipedal locker room.' Marga's hand on my pussy started as a claw, but it's transforming into a one-horse open sleigh, sliding down from my pubis to my perineum. It's dramatic when the pads of her fingers pass over (but don't quite penetrate) my vagina.

'And how did this guy fuck you?'

'I was walking out, and he was at the door waiting to come in with his walker, fully dressed by this point, obviously.'

'It was Ibrahim, with the walker.'

'Yeah. I saw his fly bursting over his erection and instantly I felt myself getting wet,' I tell Marga, feeling myself getting wet.

'You felt yourself getting wet?' Marga asks, sliding into my vagina for the first time.

'Wet, I felt myself getting so wet –' I groan, grateful for her penetration – 'I stood there frozen in the disabled toilet's sliding doorway without taking a step forward or back, totally motionless, my heart beating like mad.'

'And then what?' Marga withdraws her fingers to make me anxious for it, to make me eat her up with kisses just so she can hold them off and force me to keep talking with heat on my lips.

'Ibrahim, red like a tomato, released one of his handlebars and touched my shoulder with his hypertoned, muscular right hand. His fingers are so firm and so pliant that they form almost a ninety-degree angle with the back of his hand. He pushed me softly. I stepped back, then the walker came in, then Ibrahim came in. He looked over his shoulder: there were people from the other groups loitering around the Cineplex lobby, but nobody saw us, or if they did, they just thought Ibrahim needed help peeing or showering, because nobody said anything, not then and not when we came out together.'

'And how was it, Nati?' This time Marga gives me a long but measured kiss that restrains my own frantic kisses, administering the arousal in small doses in a way that only intensifies it.

'Ibrahim closed the sliding door, locked it, turned his walker around and sat on the built-in seat. His head was at the height of my waist, and I grabbed his face, which felt like it was on fire. He closed his eyes and sighed like he'd been holding his breath, a sigh that relaxed his back so his forehead ended up on my belly.'

'You're very pretty, Nati,' he said in his strange speech that doesn't require putting his lips together.

'I want to see your cock again,' I told him.

'I want to see your pussy again, too,' he said, and I pulled down my tights and panties. He leaned forward and pressed his nose into my bush, and I leaned forward to grab his erection, which wasn't as hard as I expected. I pulled down his pants – his dick had the medium tension of a fishing rod. I love them like that because you can suck the whole thing at once, and I like to feel them getting hard in my mouth.

'So you sucked him off,' Marga says, lifting my own nipple to my own mouth so I could lick it.

'Yeah, but later. I started out just jacking him off with two fingers around the glans while he slid two of his hypertaut fingers inside me. He penetrated me quick and smooth like an arrow, I was dripping wet. And at the same time, I rubbed my clit and started moaning, and then he started moaning too. He stroked my bare legs with his other hand, which is less toned; with my own other hand, I stroked his hair.' I make eye contact with Marga while I lick my own nipple. 'I asked him to add another finger and he did, but they're so taut he can't hold them together, so his index and middle fingers were penetrating me in a V. That hurt a little, and when I said so he slammed on the brakes and apologised a thousand times.' Marga adds her tongue to my nipple and we lick it together, and we lick each other's tongues. When I pause to talk, Marga treats it as an opportunity to suck and bite, and if I groan, even if it's from pleasure, she shuts me up by biting my mouth.

'It's totally fine, Ibra,' I said. 'Do you want to eat my pussy?' I moved my hips forward so his mouth was at the height of my cunt instead of my pubic bone. He leaned a little further forward, rotated his head and stuck his tongue out of the side of his mouth, which is always open. His tongue is pointy and precise like the tip of a pencil. He pressed it into my vagina and it felt like a little boy's overenthusiastic penis; he pulsed it like a Morse code transmitter on my clit. But we were in an uncomfortable position for both of us, because he had to lean forward and his tongue still couldn't reach very far, and I had to push my hips forward and bend my knees too low. I was stretching my arms behind me to hold the adapted toilet's support rails, but all my weight was still on my legs, and I had to hold them open as wide as Ibrahim's walker, so they were starting to buckle.'

'Let's move to the toilet,' I said, sitting down. He got off his walker and kneeled in front of me. It went better that way, since pleasure wasn't competing with fatigue. Now Ibrahim could penetrate me with his whole tongue and manoeuvre more freely and I could accommodate his V-formation hyper-fingers. I rocked my hips forward and back over the toilet seat, my ass cheeks swinging further back with every thrust. I asked him to put his hyperpinkie in my asshole.'

'I've never done that before,' he said, lifting his drooling mouth from my cunt. I hate it when they stop going down on you to say things. It's such a comedown, you lose all that momentum!

'Does it gross you out?' I asked.

'Noooooo! I'm just nervous.'

'Suck a finger and right in. And please don't stop penetrating me and eating my pussy, I'm really enjoying it.'

'OK.' At this point he had his tongue, his hyperhand and his normal hand all dedicated to my masturbation, plus I had my own hand when I felt like it. With my other hand I was squeezing one of my tits under my T-shirt and bra. I hadn't taken them off.

'Was he good in your ass?' Marga asks me, shifting from biting me to gently pulling my hair in that way that gives you reflexive goosebumps all over your body. I want to devour her and she won't let me. She places my hands exactly where she wants to be touched. I sink an unexpected finger into her curved vagina and she cries out, laughing with the smile of someone who concedes that their adversary has struck a good blow. I penetrate her with an abnormally slow cadence that makes her cry out again, and I continue:

'For his first time he was really gentle, honestly. I didn't feel congested like when they jam up your ass and you feel like you're suffocating. Ibrahim's hypertaut muscles make every-thing easier. And I mean, it was just his pinkie.'

'Do you want my pinkie in your ass?' asks Marga, suddenly solicitous.

'Yes!' I answer, and she pulls herself off my fingers so she can position me on all fours.

'One thing, Nati,' Ibrahim said. Another comedown, but this time I kept masturbating with my backup finger so I didn't lose the crescendo.

'What is it?'

'My knees hurt.'

'OK.' So I helped lift him by the armpits, then stood on the toilet bowl. My pussy was far from his head and the toilet bowl was so narrow I couldn't open my legs much, but at least Ibrahim could grab the support rails so he wouldn't fall. By this point, I figured all that was left was for him to penetrate me with his cock, and that we'd finish with Ibrahim sitting on the toilet seat and me sitting on Ibrahim. That's what I suggested, without letting up with my backup finger, and he said:

'It won't get hard all the way.'

'Really?' Marga asks with her long middle finger (not her pinkie) in my ass. I'm on all threes instead of all fours, because I'm stretching one arm between my legs to reach Marga's pussy, which is pressed firmly against my ass. I can barely stroke her, so she guides my finger like it's a vibrator.

'Really?' I asked Ibra.

'It's been that way my whole life,' he answered.

'Not even if I suck it?'

'Suck it, please.'

'It's just that I'm about to come and I don't want to lose the orgasm. Let me finish then I'll take care of you?'

'OK,' he said, and it occurred to me that Ibrahim wasn't the only one who could use the support rails on the adapted toilet. I fully removed my panties and tights, which had been around my ankles the whole time. I lifted a foot onto each rail and squatted like a frog. At first I had to hold on with both hands, but after a second I released one rail so I could go back to masturbating with my backup finger. I didn't lose balance. I released the other rail to pull Ibrahim's head towards me. The bars were firmly secured, they didn't falter at all.

'Long live accessibility!' I cried, very pleased with myself. Marga pulls her finger out of my ass, lifts my torso so my back is against her chest, grabbing me by the tits. 'I don't know if Ibrahim understood what I said, but he understood that I was gratified. Now my pussy was wide open and he could comfortably navigate with his hyperfingers and his tongue, grabbing one of the rails with his other hand, and I could lean my back against the wall. He moved in and out of me like an elevator, and he kept pressing my clit with his tongue like he was buzzing every flat on the block. I started bobbing up and down with my knees like a leaping frog so that, rather than Ibrahim moving his fingers in and out of me, I was rising and falling on top of them. I came like that, with my orgasmic cry stifled by the enforced discretion, and the shudder that ran through my body almost knocked me off the support rails.'

Marga whispers in my ear how turned on she is and asks if I'm turned on enough to fuck her. I respond:

'Stay there,' I told Ibra. I got out of my frog pose, kissed his mucousy mouth, sat on the toilet and started blowing him. His balls were shaved, and like most hairless dicks, his smelled less like dick and more like fabric softener. Since Ibrahim can't close his mouth all the way, when he tried to suppress his moans, he started coughing and dribbling strands of drool onto the top of my head. This time I was the one responsible for the comedown because I was worried he'd suffocate.

'Ibra, can you breathe?'

'I can, don't worry.'

'OK.' I put his fishing-rod dick back in my mouth and gripped his velvety balls. Someone tried to open the door.

'Occupied!' gargled Ibrahim.

'Hurry it up!' they said on the other side.

'I'm shitting!' he gargled back, and I, without interrupting the blowjob, lifted my hand and gave him the 'perfect' gesture with my fingers.

'What did he say?' someone asked someone on the other side of the door.

'He said he's finishing,' someone responded to someone.

'Well finish quick, bud!' they pressured, and the pressure must have had some effect on Ibrahim because it was only then that his cock blossomed inside my mouth and even brushed against my uvula. Anticipating what was next, I started rubbing my clit like crazy, but now, because of Ibrahim's death rattles, I was the one who felt pressured, and before I could start climbing the crest of my second orgasm, he had deposited a few drops of semen in the back of my throat. I wasn't sure he'd finished coming, so I transferred his dick from my mouth to my hand so I could keep stroking it, and stealthily I asked:

'Yeah?'

'Yeah,' he whispered back. It was easier to understand him whispering because he didn't have to use his vocal cords.

'I'm gonna come again,' I said.

'You want my tongue?'

'But your knees'll hurt.'

'Hurry it up in there, Jesus!' they harassed us again from outside.

'I'm helping him wipe his ass!' I yelled back. Ibrahim held back his laughter and whispered again:

'Are you gonna take long?'

'Please, I could come just thinking about it.'

'All right,' he said, getting on his knees. On his way down, he lapped at my throat with his hypertoned tongue. I intercepted it and put it in my mouth for a second, then settled onto the toilet so he could eat my cunt. He traced the entrance of my vagina with his tongue, gave me a few licks, and that, along with my own sewing-machine finger on my clit, got me there in just a few seconds. Second orgasms are always less intense for me, but they're more precise. The electric current only runs through my legs, but it runs through them like a fucking racecar.

'We should hurry.' And Ibrahim and I hurried to compose ourselves, putting on our clothes. Marga and I are penetrating each other in a sixty-nine formation when we hear a siren pass by, so close I almost have to yell for her to hear me.

'Is the lefto-bumbag waiting for you?' I asked Ibrahim.

'Who?' he asked, wiping his mouth with toilet paper.

'Your Catalan separatist aide who lost her temper at me and tried to use you as an excuse.'

'Ah, Rosa!'

'Yeah, her.'

'No, she only came with me that day because it was her shift. You just go with whoever's working. A different aide brought me today.'

'Of course, the jailers have shifts, not fixed detainees. Prisoners are perfectly interchangeable pieces of merchandise,' I answer, helping him pull up his underwear.

'Prisoners like in prison?'

'The UCIDetention centre, exactly.'

'It's true they don't always let us go out, even if we say please.'

'You don't vote, do you, Ibra?'

'Like in elections?'

'Yeah, or in the referendum on Catalan independence or anything where you put a ballot in a box.'

'No, the court that declared me incompetent said I can't.' I told you, Marga: I could never fuck a Spaniard and I could never fuck a voter.

The sirens sound very close, but I chalk it up to the hole in the roof. I hear four car doors slamming, radios rasping.

'Marga, did you hear that?' I ask, peeking out from behind her butt, as loud as I can so she can hear me over the din of the sirens.

'I farted, did it bother you?' Marga shouts into my cunt, not releasing my ass and still lunging at me with hers, even though I'm no longer penetrating her and my neck is outstretched like an antenna.

'No, Marga! There are cops right outside!' I say, breaking the sixty-nine because my gates have closed and I can't stick my tongue out. 'They're gonna evict you!'

'Don't shout, Nati,' Marga says, lying on the mattress like an odalisque. Naked, I jump off the mattress and into the living room. The front door booms, they're trying to knock it down. I hear them giving each other orders.

'Help me, Marga!' I shout, dragging the table to the front door. 'Help me block the door!' But Marga doesn't move.

'It will be worse if you resist! Release the disabled girls!' a megaphone yells. The battering ram bangs against the door, and the door bangs against the table, and a corner of the table bangs against my hip and I cry out Jesus fucking shit.

'Nativitat, Margarita, sóc la Rosa de la UCID! It's Rosa from the UCID! No us preocupeu, tot sortirà bé! Everything's going to be OK!' another megaphone yells, and in the instant it takes me to realise the person speaking into the megaphone is Ibrahim's lefto-separatist aide/minder/cop, a mosso swings an axe at the boarded-up living-room window. The blade peaks through the wood like in the motherfucking *Shining*.

'Marga!' I shriek. She doesn't answer. I run to the bedroom and she's in the foetal position, facing the wall.

'Release the girls!' the megaphone repeats. Not knowing what the fuck they're talking about or who the fuck they're talking to makes me fucking exasperated, makes me scream until my throat gives out.

'What fucking girls are you talking about, fascists, torturers!'

'If you don't let us in you will face charges of aggravated statutory rape! We know you have engaged in sexual conduct with the disabled girls!' A cop's megaphone.

'Nativitat, tranquila, estem aquí per ajudar-te! We're here to help!' the lefto-separatist's megaphone cries as the first mosso climbs through the window. Naked, I throw the Estrella Damm chair at him, successfully enough that he recedes back through his newly opened hole for a second or two, which is all the time it takes for two other mossos to finish knocking down the door and come in crying freeze, police, don't move, pointing their handguns at me. I throw my bike and they have to duck to the floor; I use the opportunity to throw what's left of the living-room furniture, two more chairs, at two mossos now crawling through the window.

'Hands up!' A string of eight or ten hustle through the hole in the door, drawing semicircles in the air with their guns. I run to the kitchen, grab the sharp knife Marga was using to clean the floor, and when a mosso tries to immobilise me from behind, I jab him in the thigh.

'Come out from there!' another cries.

'Look out, Marga, they're coming for you!' I scramble away, wielding the knife in front of me. I climb on top of the kitchen counter and throw the set of clay tableware at the wounded cop and the two coming to help him. They shield themselves with their hands, but I hit one so hard on the helmet that he falls on his ass.

'Hands up!' they repeat, pointing at me with their guns.

'Can't you say anything else, fascist fucks?'

'Compte! La que té unes comportes a la cara és una d'elles! The one with the gates on her face is one of them!' the lefto-separatist shouts into her megaphone.

'Drop the knife!' they shout from inside a helmet.

'Look who's talking, drop your gun!' I reply from inside my gates.

'Put down the knife and nothing will happen to you!' A fucking laughable attempt at reassurance.

'Lower your weapons!' one helmet tells the other helmets, and it must be the head helmet because all the others obey him.

'How obedient!' I say.

'Drop it and nothing will happen to you! I won't say it again!'

'Yes you will!'

'Drop it and nothing will happen to you!'

'I told you!' Without turning my back to them and without lowering the knife, I walk over the counter towards the back door. One of the robocops gets in the way, blocking my path and raising his baton. I lunge at him knife-first, and, before receiving the baton blow that shatters my gates, cracks my rib and has me doubled over on the floor, I manage to shove my knife into the only centimetre of his arm not covered in riot gear.

NOVEL
TITLE: MEMOIRS OF MARÍA DELS ÀNGELS
GUIRAO HUERTAS
SUBTITLE: MEMORIES AND MUSINGS
OF A GIRL FROM ARCUELAMORA
(ARCOS DE PUERTOCAMPO, SPAIN)
GENRE: EASY READ
AUTHOR: MARÍA DELS ÀNGELS GUIRAO HUERTAS
CHAPTER 5: TOWARDS FREEDOM

The bedroom doors at the new RUCID
were locked during the day
so no one could go in until bedtime.

But one morning one of the social workers
left the key to my cousins Margarita and Patricia's room
in the door.

They locked themselves inside
then climbed out of the window,
sat on the ledge,
and shouted that they would jump
if the social workers didn't let them
out of the RUCID.

They were holding hands
and shouting and crying their eyes out.
Luckily the window wasn't very high up
and if they jumped they wouldn't die
but they would get hurt
and Regional Social Services Management
would blame Mamen
and blame the social workers at the RUCID
and report them
and take away the money
and maybe even put them in jail.

It's true that back then
I was really mad at Mamen
and at lots of the social workers
and I would have been happy if Patri and Marga jumped
and Mamen and the other social workers went to jail.

I was reminded of that day
because I was at a dance show
where non-disabled people
took disabled people by the hand
and two girls sat
with their legs dangling off the edge of the stage
just like Patri and Marga that day
except the dancers weren't shouting or crying
they were just swinging their arms around
like in a sevillana or a jota.
But these girls were holding hands
and when you dance a sevillana or a jota you don't hold hands
so it was more like a sardana.

Sevillana, like you can tell from the name,

means a kind of dance people do in Seville.
Jota means a kind of dance people do in lots of places.
Sardana means the kind of dance people do in Barcelona
even though it's called the sardana and not the barcelonesa.
When you dance a sardana you hold hands,
but you also stand up and like I said
these girls were sitting down.

It was the dance show
my cousin Natividad was going to be in
until she had a very serious crisis with her gates
and had to be institutionalised at the UCID in La Floresta
where they put people with severe intellectual disabilities.

La Floresta is a neighbourhood in Barcelona.
It has lots of flowers
plus trees and feral hogs and even a stream.

Severe intellectual disabilities means
you're the most intellectually disabled
a person can possibly be.
But Natividad gave me a ticket
before her crisis
so I went anyway.
And I had spare tickets because she gave us three,
one for Marga, one for Patri and one for me,
but Marga is in the hospital for her sterilisation,
and Patri is angry because they kicked us out
of the supervised flat,
so I went with two self-advocate friends
because even though Nati wasn't going to be in the show,
Ibrahim was.
Ibrahim is another self-advocate in our group

and we were excited to see him
because he's our friend
and he's a very good person.

End of digression about the dance show
and my cousin Natividad's crisis.

Back to Marga and Patri in the window
at the new RUCID.

Patri and Marga were out there a pretty long time.
All the residents and social workers
came out to the garden to look up at them
and tell them things.

I told them to be careful.
Other people told them they were crazy.
The social workers told them everything was going to be OK,
there was nothing to be anxious about,
and if my cousins just came back inside
the social workers would sit down to listen
to whatever they had to complain about.

My cousin Natividad told them not to give up.
She said don't jump but don't go back inside either
because they were on the right track
to getting out of the RUCID.

Some residents started saying the same thing
and cheering Marga and Patri on
and chanting their names.

What I just wrote wasn't exactly what Nati said

because she's disabled with Gate Control syndrome
and she can't talk like normal.
She uses weird words no one knows.
So instead I wrote what her words actually meant
so everyone reading my novel understands.

The social workers told her to stop talking
but she couldn't stop because of her disability.

And even though the social workers at the RUCID
are supposed to be intellectual disability professionals
they didn't understand about Natividad
because right away
they forced open her gates
and dragged her inside.

The next time I saw her
all the screws on her gates were loose
and she was dumb from the pills.

Patri and Marga didn't jump
but not because they got to leave the RUCID.
They didn't jump because Mamen and the social workers
said lots of things from under the window.
Some of the things they said were true
and some were lies
and some were paradoxes.

Patri and Marga believed it all
and in the end they went back inside
and opened the bedroom door
and Mamen took them to the nurse's office
and the nurse took their blood pressure
and gave them each a shot.

Then they made Marga and Patri sit at a table
with Mamen and the psychologist and me
to have a conversation.

But my cousins could hardly talk at all,
all they could say was yes or no
because of the shots.
It was weird to see Patricia having trouble speaking
because logorrhoea is part of her disability.

Logorrhoea is a condition that makes you talk non-stop.

The only people actually talking
were Mamen and the psychologist.
I didn't talk because I was really nervous
and with my stutter I couldn't finish any of my words.
It was like they gave me a shot too.
The only thing I managed to say
was I thought my cousins
wouldn't be able to talk
because of the shots.
I stuttered a lot, but I said it.

Mamen told me
it's important to solve problems as soon as they arise.
I said we weren't going to solve any problems this way
because my cousins couldn't talk.
I stuttered a lot again,
but I said it.

Mamen and the psychologist said
of course they could talk
because look, they were talking.

'But they're not talking how they talk,'
I said stuttering even more
'because you gave them the shots.'
'They are talking like they talk, Angelita,
they're just more relaxed.
If we didn't give them medicine,
they'd be too anxious to talk at all,'
the psychologist said.
'Then you should give yourselves the shots too
so all four of you can talk the same amount of relaxed,'
I said.

It was really hard to get all these words out
and when I finally finished they looked at me and
they were half laughing and half angry.
And then they said
the sentence that changed my life:
'Maybe we have to
give you a shot too.'

And then I got really quiet
and Mamen and the psychologist kept acting
like all five of us were having a conversation
even though they were the only ones really talking.

For days I was thinking about what they said to me
and finally I decided
I wanted to leave the RUCID,
the same as Marga and Patri,
and I figured if the three of us were leaving
we weren't going to leave Nati behind
so we had to take her too.

I told myself:
'Angelita, you can't behave badly
or they'll put you on the pills too,
or give you the shots,
and then you'll be dumb and sleepy all the time
and you'll never get out of here.
You have to be good
and use your milder intellectual disability
to stay awake and alert to everything.'

That was how my struggle
for autonomy and equal rights began
and how I took my first steps as a self-advocate
because even though back then I didn't know
what any of that was
now I can see equality of opportunity
was always in my blood.

After spending a long time contemplating
all the things going through my head
and all the feelings making me sad
I asked myself:
Can you go wherever you want?
Can anyone tell you not to go there?
Can you go wherever you want with whoever you want?
Do those other people want to go with you?
Where do you want to go?

Contemplating means thinking a lot.
Today it's easy for me to answer those questions,
but back then I had no idea
what free development of personality was
even though it's guaranteed by the Spanish Constitution

and the Universal Declaration of Human Rights
and I didn't know what the right to self-determination
in all aspects of life was
even though it's guaranteed
by the Convention on the Rights
of Persons with Disabilities.

Spanish Constitution is the most important law in Spain.
Universal Declaration of Human Rights
is the most important law in the universe.
Convention on the Rights of Persons with Disabilities
is the most important law for persons with disabilities.

Back then I didn't know how to answer questions
with the force of law
and I just gave the best answer I could.

For example, when I asked myself
if I could go wherever I wanted
I could only answer with the paradox 'yes but no'
even though back then I didn't know what a paradox was.
I just knew something weird was happening.
I could go wherever I wanted because I was over 18
and I wasn't legally incompetent,
but I couldn't go wherever I wanted
because Mamen wouldn't let me
and I did what Mamen said.

The answer to the second question
about anyone stopping me from going where I wanted
was another paradox,
because they could only stop me
if they tied me to the bed or locked me in a room

but I wasn't tied to anything or locked up anywhere
or even dumb from taking the pills.
But Mamen could still stop me
because I never said no to her.

The third question
about going wherever I wanted
with whoever I wanted
was even harder to answer
because one day when I asked my cousins
when they were normal and not dumb from the pills
if they wanted to come with me to live outside the RUCID
they all said yes.
When I asked where we would live
they all said something different.
Marga wanted to go back to Arcuelamora like me
and Patri said she wanted to live in Somorrín,
but in the centre of town and not at the edge
where the RUCID was,
and Nati said she didn't care
as long as we got out of the RUCID.

This was a problem
and I knew we had to agree on something
but before we did I got worried my cousins
might be legally incompetent
because they had a higher level of disability than me
and if they were legally incompetent
they wouldn't be allowed to come with me.

I asked if they ever went to see a judge
or to a courthouse
and they all said no

but I was worried they didn't understand
what I was saying
and I was worried
I wasn't doing a good job explaining it
because back then I didn't understand these things
very well either, I only knew what I knew
from what I heard other people saying.

That is self-reflection.

I was afraid to ask Mamen about it
because she might figure out my plan
and make me take the pills.

I knew it was important for all of us to be together
so we could join forces, since, like I said,
back then I didn't know about the force of law
and I thought force was just about being strong
like how there's strength in numbers.

Then another thing happened
and my life changed forever.
Once a year the RUCID had Family Day
when everyone's families
would come to visit the RUCID
and look at our arts and crafts and watch our shows.
That year Uncle Joaquín and Uncle Jose came
like they did every year
and I had a very important conversation with them.

Remember Uncle Joaquín
was my uncle I went to live with
and remember Uncle Jose
was my cousin Marga's dad.

By then Patri and Nati
were basically orphans
because no one ever knew who Patri's father was
and even though everyone knew
Nati's father was young Gonzalo
he never acknowledged her.
And even though their mother
Aunt Araceli was still alive
she might as well have been dead
because she was in a home
and Patri and Nati hadn't seen her ever since
they were institutionalised at the new RUCID.

I convinced the social workers to take me out of the show
we put on every Family Day.
And my cousins weren't in it in the first place
because they were mad at Mamen.
So I used the time to talk to Uncle Joaquín and Uncle Jose.
They didn't have to go to the show either
because no one in their family was going to be in it.
We walked out of the event room together.

'Do you know if the cousins are incompetent?'
I asked.
'Yeah, same as you,' Uncle Joaquín said.
Uncle Joaquín was mixing up being disabled
and being incompetent.
No one ever understands how they're not the same.
'We're all disabled, Uncle Joaquín.
Being legally incompetent is different.'
Then I turned to Uncle Jose and asked:
'Did you ever take cousin Marga to court?'
'I would never!

Why would I sue my own daughter?'
I explained how you have to take someone to court
to get them declared legally incompetent.
Uncle Jose said he never took Marga to court for any reason.
I thought to myself: 'Perfect!'
Then I asked:
'Do you know if anyone ever took Patri and Nati
to court to declare them incompetent?'
They said they didn't know
but they didn't think so
because word gets around in Arcuelamora
and they would have heard about it.

It was the longest conversation I'd ever had with my uncles.
Since they were in a good mood
and the show had just started
I asked Uncle Joaquín my other question:
'Uncle Joaquín, do I have any other family
besides you and the cousins?'
'Uncle Jose,' he said, looking at Uncle Jose.
That was true.
'And Aunt Araceli.'
That was true too.
'And Aunt Montserrat.'
'Who?' I asked.
'She was at Los Maderos, then
started whoring in La Rambla when it closed,'
Uncle Jose said.
'She's my cousin, and your mom's,
may she rest in peace,' said Uncle Joaquín.
'Aunt Montserrat is dead?' I asked.
'No, Angelita, your mother's dead.'
'So Aunt Montserrat is alive?'

'Far as I know,' said Uncle Jose.
'Where does she live?' I asked.
'Barcelona.'
'Like the football team?'

Back then I didn't know what Barcelona was
but now I understand perfectly
because I live here.

'Do you have her address or phone number?'
'Somewhere probably. I'd have to look,'
said Uncle Joaquín.
'Please, Uncle Joaquín. Look for it and call her.'
'What for? If I can ask,' said Uncle Jose.
'So the cousins and me can take a vacation and visit her.'
'She's probably not whoring any more, too old now,'
said Uncle Jose.
'Angelita, this woman hasn't seen the four of you
since we buried your mother,' said Uncle Joaquín.
'But she's a good person?' I asked.
'Regular I guess
but it's not like the old days.
People don't just take family into their homes any more
especially not four at a time
especially not four retards.'

Then my face changed
but not because my uncle called us retards.
Retards was the word he'd used his whole life
and he didn't know any others
because he was seventy years old
and he'd never left Arcuelamora.

416

My face changed for two reasons,
one bad and one good:
Bad, because Aunt Montserrat
might not let us stay in her house.
Good, because maybe if we told her
we weren't incompetent
and we didn't have any legal guardian in charge of our money
and between the four of us our benefits
were worth almost 2,500 euros a month
maybe she would let us stay in her house after all
because as a prostitute
she would be at risk of social exclusion
and need the money more.

That's what happened with almost everyone
with intellectual disabilities in the Arcos.
They lived with their parents instead of at the RUCID
so their parents could keep the money.

Then Uncle Joaquín asked me something
he had never asked me before:

'You're not happy here?'

It was my chance to ask for help.
Uncle Joaquín was one of the people,
like my mom and Patri and Nati's mom,
who let me go wherever I wanted.
Uncle Jose hadn't let Marga go out as much
but I had to ask now while they were in a good mood.
'Honestly, no, we aren't happy here.
Please tell Miss Mamen the cousins and me

are going to Arcuelamora for a few days for vacation
and then we can figure out what to do.'

I stuttered a lot,
but I said it.

Uncle Joaquín had never asked me to explain myself before
and he didn't ask me to then either.
He just stood there silent.
Uncle Jose was more the kind of person
who wanted explanations
but he didn't ask any more questions that day
and we didn't mention it again for the rest of Family Day.

A month later Uncle Jose and Uncle Joaquín
came back to the RUCID.

It wasn't Family Day
or Open House Day
or any of the days when there are visitors.

They said hello to the social workers
and hello to Mamen
and hello to Patri and Nati and Marga
and came to get me.
We went out to the garden
and they talked to me very quietly.

Uncle Jose said:
'Angelita, if you want us to get you out of here
you have to give us some money.'

I didn't understand.
I looked at Uncle Joaquín and he explained better:

'Angelita, if you leave
they might take away your Social Security
and we won't be able to keep getting money
from the bank account.
So we need you to leave us some money
just in case.'

Back then I didn't really get what was happening.
If we had the same conversation now
I would understand perfectly
that Uncle Joaquín and Uncle Jose
were doing what almost all the families
of residents at the RUCID who weren't incompetent did:
using the credit card you get from the bank
with your name on it
when you have an account
to get money whenever they wanted.
Everyone knows what a credit card is
so I don't have to explain it.
But I should explain how
it's against the law
for someone to use a credit card
with someone else's name on it
and not their own name.

But back then all I could think was
if we paid
we would get to leave
and everything seemed wonderful
and it even seemed normal.

I said yes to everything
and my uncles went to Mamen's office

and when they came out she said to me:
'You must be very happy, Angelita,
you and your cousins will get to spend a few days back home.'

And the next day
when they came to pick us up in their truck
Mamen said:
'You girls sure you'll have enough to wear?'
But she was really calling us vain
because we were taking all our clothes with us.

'Looking this good takes work, Miss Mamen,'
said Patricia
who has always been very vain.
Vain means you care a lot about being pretty.

We all got in Uncle Joaquín's truck
and went straight to BANKOREA.
But instead of the one in Somorrín
we went to a further away BANKOREA
so no one who knew us would see us
and go and tell the RUCID
about how we were taking out money
so we would never have to come back.

The six of us went up to the counter
and my uncles asked me and my cousins for our DNIs.

DNI means Documentation of National Identity,
and Documentation of National Identity
means your identification card
and everyone knows what identification card means
because everyone has one

except immigrants.
Since we didn't know how much money
was in our accounts,
first we had to ask for a balance statement.

Balance statement
means a piece of paper they give you at the bank
saying how much money is in your account.

Today I know exactly what to do at the bank
and I know exactly how to ask for everything
because they showed me how at the self-advocacy group
but back then I had no idea
and my uncles had to ask for everything.

I couldn't even read what it said
on the balance statement
because I was so nervous
and the numbers were jumping around.
Patri couldn't read the numbers because they were so small
and by then her vision was really bad.
Nati knew how to read better than anyone,
but she had started getting nervous like me.
Marga was holding her hand and saying things to her
so her gates wouldn't activate
and make us all even more nervous.

My uncles told the man at the counter
to give them 15,000 euros.
Back then I didn't know if 15,000 euros was a lot or a little.
Now I know 15,000 euros was a whole lot
and it was the money from the damages
for Nati's workplace accident.

I explained workplace accident
in Chapter 3
and you can go back and look.

'How much do you girls want?'
asked Uncle Joaquín.
I had no idea how much to ask for.
I looked at Patri, who was standing next to me,
and she said 100 euros each.

'Better make it 200,'
said Uncle Jose.

They called Nati over to sign a paper
and that was the hardest thing of all.
Marga tried walking with her to the counter
but Nati fought back and pulled her the other way.
Her gates started shutting
and she started shouting the things
her disability makes her say.
The people in the bank stared at us
and when one of the employees at the bank
came out to talk to her
she almost headbutted him with her gates.

I thought it was too bad
they didn't give Nati the pills that day
because with her disability she didn't understand
we were at the bank for her own good
and she needed to sign the paper for her own good
and if she had one of her episodes
she was going to ruin everything not just for herself

but also for the rest of us
who didn't do anything wrong.

Finally we got her to sign it
because I brought her the paper and a pen
and told her this was the last thing she had to do.
If she just signed it
we could leave Somorrín forever
and she would never have to set foot in a bank ever again.
I begged and I was crying
so her gates pulled back a tiny bit
and she finally signed it.

The man behind the window grabbed some stacks of money
like back when Mamen had to go to the bank
before the RUCID became part of a consortium
and they switched to using transfers.

One of those stacks was for us.

'You need to give Aunt Montserrat 4,000 euros
while you stay at her house
and look for a place to live.
We talked to her
and she's going to pick you up at the bus station in Barcelona,'
Uncle Joaquín said.

We left the bank
and got in the truck
and they took us to the bus station in the same village
where no one knew us
so no one would realise Patri, Nati, Marga and me

were starting our new life,
a life where I was starting to understand
you have to do things with the force of law
and not the force of lies.

A life where I was starting to understand
we would have to get Nati and Marga declared incompetent
and maybe Patri too, I wasn't sure,
so no one could take money
out of their bank accounts illegally
except a legal guardian, who would safeguard
the best interests of the incompetent individual.

And so,
on the bus,
with tears of joy in our eyes,
and a chorizo sandwich wrapped in foil,
we left for Barcelona,
land of liberty.

Everything up to here has been my memories
from when I left Arcuelamora
until I got to Barcelona.

But before going to the next chapter,
where I'll talk about my life here,
I want to make something clear:

I'm fully aware
this chapter isn't perfect.

Being fully aware means
you know something perfectly.

I've broken a lot of the rules
from the book 'Easy Read: Practical Guidelines
for Educational Inclusion'
by Óscar García Muñoz
from the Ministry of Education, Culture and Sport.

Ministry of Education, Culture and Sport
is where you go if you're a politician
in charge of primary schools,
high schools, universities,
museums, theatres, cinemas,
libraries and sports centres.

I broke Rule 2 on page 19 where it says:
'Guard against semantic accidents.
Avoid synonyms.
Avoid polysemes.
Avoid lexical complexity.
Avoid metaphors and abstractions.'

Synonyms means when two words are spelled differently
but mean the same thing.
For example, fun and enjoyment
are synonyms.

I already said what polysemes and metaphors are
and gave lots of examples.

Abstractions are things you can't see with your eyes
or with your other senses
but you still feel them,
like violence or hunger or freedom.

Lexical complexity is very hard words.

I also broke the rule on page 80
of the book I already talked about a lot called
'Easy Read: Methods for Composition and Evaluation',
also by Óscar García Muñoz
but this time from the Ministry of Health, Social Services
and Equality.

Ministry of Health, Social Services and Equality
is where you go if you're a politician
in charge of hospitals and services we have in society
so we can all be equals.

The rule says:
'Do not add too many characters.
Use the minimum number required
to drive the main plot.'
It also says:
'Characters should be well defined,
with minimal complexity and simplified traits.'

I broke this rule because I included
all the characters from the RUCID
and from outside the RUCID
who were part of my life story
and I gave them as many traits as I had to
to tell my true life story.

I also broke the rule
on page 71:
'Avoid words that express value judgements.'

I used words like 'good' and 'bad'
and 'better' and 'worse' lots of times.
I also broke one that says:
'Avoid figurative language,
including metaphors and idioms,
which can cause confusion.'
For example, when I said 'thick as thieves'
or 'that was that, muskrat'
or 'there's strength in numbers'
I was breaking the rule
since those are idioms.

I also skipped a rule that's in
both of those books
and also in the other book
I already talked a lot about,
'Guidelines for Easy-to-Read Materials'
by the Section for Library Services
for People with Special Needs.
The rule says to put pictures beside the text
to support the reader.

Section is a part.
Library Services is the library giving you things
or helping you do things.
It has nothing to do with social services.
Be careful with the word services
because it's a polyseme.

People with Special Needs is
a different way to say

people with disabilities or disabled people
or differently abled people or handicapped people
or retards or retarded people.

At first I used WhatsApp emojis because
I thought it would be a good way to follow the rule:
'Use familiar, engaging,
easy-to-comprehend images that are
specific and relevant to the topic.
Images ought to be useful, not attractive:
make them as simple as possible,
keeping detail to a minimum.'
But it's an optional rule
and other good Easy Read writers ignore it
like for example the writer of the adaptation
of 'The Diary of Anne Frank',
which sold lots of books
and was translated into lots of languages.
All it has is a few black and white photos.

I also broke the rule about avoiding digressions
and the rule about putting names of characters in bold text.

I talked about digressions in Chapter 1
and you can go back and look.

And I don't know how to make text bold
on the WhatsApp keyboard.

They say before you can break the rules
first you have to know them.
That's why I just wrote out all the rules I'm skipping,
to show I'm not breaking them by accident

or because I don't know about them.
I know all about them and I'm breaking them anyway.

It's an act of rebellion.

Rebellion is when you break a rule
you don't agree with.

If you skip a rule you don't know about
it's not rebellion
it's just ignorance.

Ignorance is not knowing something.

I'm a rebel writer
because after studying the rules of Easy Read
I've realised a lot of them are bad rules
and a lot of people who aren't ignorant,
like for example the judge who authorised
my cousin Marga's sterilisation,
don't know about Easy Read.
Authorised my cousin Marga's sterilisation means
the judge gives a paper
to her legal guardian the Generalitat of Catalonia
saying she gives the Generalitat of Catalonia permission
to take Marga to the doctor
so the doctor can give her an operation
so she can never ever get pregnant.

Legal guardian is the person in charge
of a disabled person
who besides being disabled
is also incompetent.

Incompetent means a disabled person who can't do anything
without their legal guardian's permission
and their legal guardian is like their parent.

The Generalitat of Catalonia is the government of Catalonia.

I already explained what government is in Chapter 1.
If you don't remember you can go back and look.

If a smart person like the judge
doesn't know what Easy Read is
it's because we need to reform Easy Read.
It has to be attractive and useful for everyone
and not just for the 30 per cent of people
who have reading difficulties
or who have been deprived of the pleasure of reading.
Easy Read has to be universally accessible
to the general population
and to all citizens.

Citizens means everyone:
not just people who live in cities
but also people who live in towns
and even in tiny villages
or alone in the middle of nowhere.

All the novels and laws and contracts
and citations and rulings
and electric and water and gas bills
and statements from the bank
or from the city council
or from any place there are politicians

430

or from any place there are businesses
have to be accessible in Easy Read.

I talked to my support person
from my self-advocacy group
and she said,
being the self-advocate I am,
I'm very good at taking initiative
without getting hung up on the little things
and without indulging outsized expectations.

Taking initiative means having an idea
and trying to make your idea happen.
Without getting hung up means not letting anything
get in your way before you start,
not even yourself.
Indulging outsized expectations means
you have to be realistic and know things
get done little by little.

I looked online and there are lots of people
who have the same initiative as me.
People from Leganés and Ávila and the Basque Country
and Extremadura and Galicia and Oviedo
and of course Catalonia,
which was the first place in Spain
to have Easy Read.

Those are all places in Spain
except for Catalonia
where there's a fight
between people who say it isn't Spain
and people who say it's Spain.

And it's basically the same with Basque Country
where there are also people
who say they aren't part of Spain
and other people who say yes they are part of Spain.

But none of that matters for Easy Read
because Easy Read is about all citizens
from Spain and from other countries
having universal access to their rights,
including their right to information and culture
and to transparency and democracy
and to reliable communication as consumers
and community members and workers,
because if a company communicates
with its customers and its employees in Easy Read
it will earn more money
because its customers will understand its ads better
and because its employees
will understand what their bosses tell them to do better
plus the company will get a good reputation
because citizens will see how it cares
about universal accessibility.

I am a rebel writer and a universal writer
who has taken the initiative
to reform, renew and democratise Easy Read
and I am not afraid to break the rules
come hell or high water
let the chips fall where they may
even if it means I'm an unappreciated writer
and people call me polarising and irreverent.

Unappreciated means no one appreciates you.
Polarising means people either love you or hate you.
Irreverent means like if someone goes into a church
but instead of praying in front of the cross
or a statue of a saint or the Virgin Mary
they sit and read your book.

Reading instead of praying is a metaphor.

Barcelona, 11 September 2017
The day the dancer Maritza
Garrido-Lecca was released after
twenty-five years of captivity
in a Peruvian prison.

Acknowledgements

Thanks to Araceli Pereda, my first contact with the world of intellectual disability; to Sonia Familiar, the first person to tell me about Easy Read and self-advocacy groups; and to R.B.A., who told me what that world was like in the eighties and nineties. I imposed on them as many times as my curiosity and ignorance required, and they always, always, always answered my calls. Thanks for the laughs, for the discussions, for the documents, for the agreements and disagreements.

Thanks to Desirée Cascales Xalma for dancing so passionately with me, making me feel secure in her body and in mine, telling me her life story without leaving out a single detail, and describing the crooked, torturous roadways through Social Security until she found her way out.

Thanks to Lucía Buedo from La Caldera in Les Corts for sending off and receiving editorial material as if her office were a staging post, extra work that isn't her job, but which she has always done while smiling genuine smiles.

Thanks to the dancers and antidancers of Brut Nature 2018 for carousing with me the day they awarded the Herralde Prize even though we hardly knew one another. Experience has shown us over and over again that we have to place our trust in strangers. Thanks, in particular, to Oscar Dasí, artistic director of La Caldera, who not only celebrated with me, but also kept the secret, and who fuses dance and literature in his daily practice.

Thanks to Élise Moreau and to Elisa Keisanen, two of Iniciativa Sexual Femenina's three legs, for placing themselves at the service of this novel's extensive outlandishness, for making that outlandishness their own, and for excusing me from rehearsals whenever my literary pursuits got in the way. Without their understanding I would have caught three pneumonias between September and November.

Thanks to Ella Sher for jumping on flights and phone calls at all hours, for bringing party clothes in her bag and changing in the restroom, and for that care towards me that has never faltered, not even under the pressures of censorship.

And thanks to Guido Micheli Losurdo and Javier López Mansilla, my zinemaking husbands.